REVENGE FOR NOW

BOB HOWARD

This book is dedicated to Chris, so he will always know his grandpa was thinking of him.

ACKNOWLEDGMENTS

If this looks familiar to you, it's because doors keep opening for me as an independent author, so I would like to once again thank the people in the industry who have given us the opportunity to do what we love.

I have seen books by my fellow independent authors adapted for movies and television shows, and acquired for publication by major publishing houses without first requiring they follow the more traditional route of being represented by an agent.

Don't get me wrong, every independent author I know has respect for the traditional route, and there isn't a single one of us who wouldn't like to see our books in the catalog of a major publisher. However, we have been given an opportunity to write our books by taking a different route, and I have to admit it has been more fun than I ever dreamt it would be.

My family also deserves credit for honestly telling me when I make a mistake or need to change something in the stories. I don't always agree, but their input makes me think twice about many things. To my wife, Dawn, and to my kids, Drew and Julie, thank you for your help and support.

Table of Contents

1

Coming Home

Mid-Atlantic Ocean - 2023

The Chief had one goal on his mind, but that didn't mean he wasn't thinking about where he was and what might be ahead while they were still on the water. He felt like there was a trail of unfinished business ahead of him.

After leaving the Isles of Scilly behind, he remembered the Wari. It would mean an extra day at sea, but he had given a lot of thought to what Iris had said to him when they were flying through the thick clouds over the Appalachians. He knew she was right, and even though they had already done plenty to save people from the infection, maybe they could do more. Still, he wasn't entirely comfortable playing the role of judge and jury. That was why he had a long talk with the captain of the HMS Ambush.

Callum Byrne was a bit younger than most skippers of fast-attack submarines, but he had gotten the job through necessity. Just like many other ships, most of the crew of the Ambush was on shore leave when the infection seemed to wash over the countryside and through the towns. The submarine base at Faslane, Scotland was far enough from Glasgow to keep the Ambush from experiencing the hordes of infected, but in an ironic way, their isolation was what caused the infection to go unchecked at the beginning. The reports of flesh-eating people weren't taken as seriously as they were in London, and by the time the Royal Navy understood the full extent of the crisis, it was too late. All three submarines docked at two piers were forced to cast away their lines with skeleton crews onboard.

The Ambush was the first to slip through the narrow gap at Rhu Point and then past the mouth of the River Clyde. As they made the turn near Holy Loch where the United States had maintained a submarine staging area for years, they were met by a flotilla of small boats. Some of the boats carried submarine sailors who were trying to get back to Faslane or sailors stationed at Her Majesty's Naval Base Greenock, but most carried civilians. It was only natural that the Ambush sorted through the refugees and supplemented their crew. There were even a few civilians who volunteered for duty rather than face what was happening on land. After medical examinations were conducted on the deck of the submarine, they closed their hatches and were on their way.

Captain Byrne had been the Weapons Officer until the moment they had pulled away from their berth at Faslane. The orders had come through loud and clear that the boat was to head for open waters immediately. He had informed the base commander that the skipper and his executive officer were only minutes away, but the senior officer had only responded angrily that he would have the next ranking officer take over if his orders weren't carried out in the next sixty seconds. Preparations had begun earlier, and they were only waiting for the Captain and XO, so Lieutenant Byrne had become Captain Byrne in that single minute.

He acknowledged the order and then gave a few of his own. The sparse crew on duty in the Control Room performed their tasks as they were ordered, but they exchanged glances that asked without words if they were supposed to be leaving port under the command of their Weapons Officer. It was Byrne's good luck that a Chief Petty Officer well respected by the crew was on duty when he assumed command. The Chief had the military experience to recognize what was happening, and he had the presence of mind to sound the general alarm. When the klaxon sounded throughout the boat, all crew members not on duty responded by going to their battle stations, and the glances shared in the Control Room became focused on their various displays. Maneuvering orders were given, and the Ambush left its berth faster than any harbor pilot would have appreciated.

That had been the beginning of the longest deployment of any nuclear submarine, and Captain Byrne had settled into the job. With no clearly defined mission, they had patrolled the southern coast of the United Kingdom near the English Channel while the other two submarines had gone north. Over the years they had brief contact with a few surface ships, but the closest thing to real orders had been encrypted messages to simply protect their country from invasion. That was clear enough to the crew of the Ambush, but the arrival of the Americans had been a welcome distraction.

When the Chief had approached him and described a particularly brutal group of degenerates who occupied a derelict tanker named Wari, he could have said it wasn't his responsibility, but he knew the apocalypse would never truly end if they didn't eliminate the people who had capitalized on the misery of others. He wished he could aid the Chief with his quest in America, but a submarine wouldn't be much help where they were going. At least he could help with the Wari. Besides, he felt like his crew had displayed a sense of purpose since meeting the Americans, and morale was high. Another act of justice might be just what they needed.

It didn't take long for the HMS Ambush to find its target, but Captain Byrne didn't rush in for the kill. At periscope depth, the silent submarine circled the rusty tanker, and he surveyed the spectacle from a distance. The Chief stood across from him waiting for his reaction. Unlike the old submarine days when the man at the periscope was the only one to see the outside world, the view through the scope was being fed to a monitor where everyone present could see what had made the Captain speechless.

The pirates on the Wari had been busy. There were almost a dozen small sailboats and four luxury yachts tied up at the makeshift dock. Damage to the boats was evidence that not all of them had surrendered without a fight, but there was little doubt that the crews and passengers of those boats were now either dead or occupying space in the cages high above the deck of the tanker. Even as they watched, a fishing boat was leaving the dock and trolling live bait behind it, but the biggest surprise was the scene that was playing out on the far side of the tanker. The pirates were rapidly closing in on a new victim.

Captain Byrne ordered his crew to make flank speed on a course that would intercept the pirates as he turned toward the Chief.

"Sometimes justice should be delivered face to face," he said.

The Chief didn't need to ask him what they were doing, and he had a new appreciation for Byrne as the submarine surged to a position that would place them in the direct path of the pirates.

"This is going to be good," said the Chief.

"Surface the boat," ordered Captain Byrne, and since they were already shallow, the sail broached the surface in seconds.

The massive bulk of the Ambush appeared in front of the pirates so suddenly that they were forced to throw their craft into a hard turn to port. The combination of their turn and the swells created by the water displaced by the submarine caused a wave to wash across both boats, but it was like a bug hitting the windshield of a car. The small boat was dragged into the strong current that ran alongside the submarine, and its hull was ripped apart.

Captain Byrne ordered, "All stop. Prepare to recover survivors."

"Captain?" asked the Chief.

Before the Chief could ask why they were going to rescue the pirates, Captain Byrne cut him off and gave the rest of his orders to the senior Chief Petty Officer.

"Open the small arms locker and issue rifles to six men designated for disciplinary action. I shall pronounce the sentence myself."

Iris had quietly come into the Control Room and watched without saying anything, but as the Chief Petty Officer announced over the interior communications system for specific sailors to report for duty at the small arms locker, she got out of the way by moving further inside and closer to her husband.

"What are they doing?" she asked.

"They're doing it the right way," he answered. "He's giving them the dignity of a firing squad. He'll be able to live with executing them by first explaining why they're being shot. It's more than they deserve, but it's a token of civilized behavior. Then he's going to sink the Wari."

Being a man of the sea, Chief Barnes was granted permission to be topside for the proceedings. They were brief and to the point. The four men who were dragged from the water resembled wet rats, and at first, they were jabbering in gratitude almost nonstop. When they were positioned shoulder to shoulder across the deck and realized they were facing six armed sailors who were formally arranged in two rows of three, their smiles faded.

Captain Byrne stood behind them and made a simple proclamation that piracy was punishable by death, and he only wished there was a more appropriate form of punishment at his disposal...something that would allow them more opportunity to think about what was going to happen to them.

The front row of sailors dropped to a knee, and all six rifles were aimed at the wet pirates. Two of them opened their mouths to speak, but the one-word command from Captain Byrne interrupted them. The rifle shots were perfectly delivered with one single sound. Two of the four executed pirates fell to the center of the deck, but the two on the port and starboard sides slid over the side into the ocean.

As if it was a duty they performed every day, the sailors formed a single line and returned to the open hatch, leaving the bodies where they fell. Captain Byrne didn't need to say it, but as he passed the Chief he said, "Let's finish this business."

The appearance of the submarine had caused concern on the deck of the Wari, but the concern turned to panic when the firing squad disposed of four of their people. Some knew what was about to happen and hurried to escape their fate. A fight broke out at the rope ladders on the stern, and the first few to climb over the railing made the long fall to the dock below. Some were smart enough to know they wouldn't be able to fight the crowd without getting tossed over the side, so they jumped wherever it was clear below. As soon as they hit the water, they swam to the boats.

HMS Ambush slid beneath the surface. Unseen by the pirates on the Wari, the submarine moved to a position directly behind the big ship. Instead of establishing a firing solution to hit the tanker broadside, Captain Byrne gave orders to target the staging area at the stern. It was a simple task for the warship, and it would guarantee that no one would escape with one of the smaller boats.

Below the surface, Captain Byrne decided to break with protocol one more time.

"Attention all hands, this is the captain. All crew not on a duty station proceed to Control."

As the warship moved into position and established periscope depth, the Control Room was packed with excited faces, all eyes on the monitor that displayed the image of the Wari. The order was given, and a torpedo was sent on its way toward the dock where the sailboats and luxury yachts were moored. The explosion was spectacular, and the fireball that rose upward practically erased the name of the ship. It also expanded outward and ignited the sailboats and yachts as if they were nothing more than dried leaves.

When the initial blast cleared enough for everyone to see the stern of the Wari, they could see that it would sink slowly, but it would definitely sink. Water rushed into the gaping hole to fill the dark compartments behind the place where the dock had been.

******

Kathy found the Chief sitting in a booth in the crew's mess. A half-eaten meal was on a tray pushed to one side. He was so immersed in what he was reading that he didn't even notice she had eased into the seat across from him. She waited patiently for him to turn a page before she spoke.

"You know the Captain said we should be back tomorrow. Have you decided where you want him to drop us off?"

"I guess I should talk to him," he said without taking his eyes off the book between his elbows.

"What've you got your nose buried in now? Whatever it is, it must be interesting."

"One of the officers loaned me this. He has a pretty good library about the US. This is a history of the area around Atlanta, and I'm stumped about something. The population was immense at the time of the outbreak, and we both know the worst places to be were the big cities. People were trapped in their homes, their businesses, their jobs, their schools, and places like sports stadiums. Can you imagine what it was like at that airport?"

Kathy nodded in agreement as she considered how lucky they were to be near the coast at the start. As a former police officer, she didn't have to think hard to know the first responders in Atlanta were pulled in every direction until their resources were stretched beyond their breaking point.

"So, what are you saying?" she asked, "We already know how bad it was. Is there something that's making you have second thoughts about us going there?"

"We have to go there, but if I'm right, we won't find what we're looking for when we get there. I think our friends got too close to someone else who was just passing through. We already know how hard it is to sustain any sort of large presence near big cities. What if the home base they use is somewhere else?"

"I don't know," said Kathy. "I guess we won't know until we get there."

"That's my point," said the Chief. "We could spend weeks searching a large portion of northern Georgia and not find anything except the infected. We might even lose more people in the process."

"Are you having second thoughts about getting even? Now that the AC-130 is gone, we won't have the tactical advantage we planned on."

The Chief got a half-grin that was more from the thought of sweet revenge than from humor.

"Not having second thoughts, but giving more thought to how we can get the plane back and then rain a little hell on someone's head."

Kathy sat back in her seat and studied her friend closely. There was something about him that said he had worked out some of the details.

"Am I detecting the telltale signs of Plan A?"

The Chief grinned again, but this time it was because he was at least a little amused.

"Maybe," he said, "if we get a bit lucky. Then again, we've generally gotten lucky more often than a lot of people. This time we'll be searching for luck while we search for the people who attacked the soldiers."

The Chief laid the book in front of Kathy, and she saw that the page had a map of northern Georgia. She didn't see anything that caught her eye, and before she could say so, he flipped to a page toward the end of the book. It was a map of the southeast, and the Chief put his finger on Kentucky.

"Ever been to Fort Knox?" he asked.

"No, I don't think they do tours, so I never had a reason to go there."

The Chief traced a line with his finger between Georgia and Kentucky.

"If I wanted to gather an army around me and take over what's left of the eastern half of the country, I think I would want to have my headquarters here. There are plenty of bases in Georgia, but those would be sources to plunder for supplies. Fort Knox would be my safe place because I would be able to watch my own back."

Kathy frowned as she listened to the Chief. At first, it was because she was considering what he suspected, but then it was because she remembered something Doctor Bus had said about the locations of other shelters.

"Wasn't Fort Knox on the list of shelter locations Bus gave you?"

"Yes, it was, but he said he didn't know if they had ever finished that one. He said the place was so secretive to start with that Titus Rush wouldn't talk about it. Bus tried to get it out of him once, but all Titus would say was that he had a deal with the government, and he

7

wasn't going to mess it up over one shelter."

The Chief picked up a laptop from the seat next to him and flipped it open. The warship had maintained an extensive digital library to keep the crew entertained as well as informed. There were strict policies in place to prevent viruses from getting into the LAN, such as no personal flash drives allowed and virus detection software working at all times, but the crew valued their network because it was a reminder of what had been lost. They treated it as a connection with the past.

"I found some good material in the reference section of the ship's library. Here's a picture that was taken from the outside of Fort Knox. The only picture from the inside is so generic that it could've been taken anywhere and just labeled as inside."

The inside picture was of a man sitting in a sparsely furnished office behind a very nondescript desk. Judging by the suit and the man's hairstyle, the photo was taken around 1956. The outside picture was dated 2010, but the only differences between it and an earlier picture taken in 1970 were the clarity and the addition of taller towers at the four corners of the main structure. There was no information about when the towers were added, but they made a lot more sense than the short structures that used to sit at the corners. The outside pictures appeared to have been taken from the same distance and location.

The Chief had that excited tone in his voice that showed up when his mind was working overtime. He talked just a bit faster, but the tone gave away the fact that he was putting together the pieces of a plan. He hadn't said enough for Kathy to know what it was, but it was at least obvious that they would be on a road trip to one of the most heavily fortified vaults in the world.

"Check this out," said the Chief. "This place was so secret that only one President has ever been there. It had its own police force, and it was located on an Army base. It's surrounded by minefields and fences, but there's nothing in the references about upgrades that would've been installed as technology advanced. I wouldn't be surprised if laser beams were used to set intruders on fire."

"I'm about two steps behind you, Chief. If it's that hard to get into, what good would it be to us or to the bad guys? The only people it was likely to be useful to were the staff members who were inside when the infection hit."

Kathy trailed off as she asked the last part of her question. If the place was that well fortified, then there were two likely scenarios that played out at Fort Knox. They either shut the place down and kept the virus out, much like the way the LAN was controlled in the submarine, or someone breached protocol for a family member or coworker, and the infection had gotten inside.

The Chief was already weighing the two likely outcomes just as Hampton came into the galley. He slid into the bench next to Kathy.

"Hey folks, what did I miss?"

Hampton was in a jovial mood, which fit with his overall outlook on life, particularly given their recent success getting Henry home to his family. Still, there was a piece of pessimism that he had expressed for a long time, and it was a good fit in the conversation the Chief had been having with Kathy.

"Kathy and I were just talking about you. Well, not directly about you, but a philosophy you've expressed repeatedly since the day we first met. Your arrival just now was good timing."

"You've got my attention," said Hampton, "and judging by that picture you have up on that laptop screen, my guess is that you guys have been talking about whether or not the infection got inside Fort Knox. My answer to that question is of course it did. Sooner or later it gets inside everywhere."

Kathy said, "It's never gotten inside Mud Island or Green Cavern."

"But it got inside Fort Sumter, Ambassadors Island, and Maybank's oil rig. Look how many holes we plugged inside the UK shelter. If we hadn't been invited to help secure the place, how long before it would've been breached?"

"You're right," said the Chief. "The question is whether it got in at the start, or did it get in later."

"Later," said Hampton. "Fort Knox undoubtedly had a protocol in place that locked it down as soon as there was evidence that the world was going to hell. How many times before this started did you hear someone say that something was locked down tighter than Fort Knox?"

"Good point," said Kathy. "So, what happened next?"

"That's easy," he answered. "They tried to help someone, guard's families showed up, or they ran out of essentials. They went out for supplies, maybe rescued a family, and brought the infection back with them. Why are we talking about this anyway?"

"The Chief and I think there's another shelter under the main building."

That brought a smile to Hampton's face, but this time it was total amusement.

"Who would be crazy enough to try to break into that place even now? If the infection got inside, then that's just another layer of security. If it did or didn't get inside, then the guards that were watching the gold before are still watching it today. They're a little slower, but they're a touch more deadly. Besides, gold is worthless now."

The Chief answered, "Tell that to people like the sheriff in Huntsville. There was no shortage of people like him before the infection. I promise you there's someone out there who would consider themselves to be rich if they managed to reach the gold inside Fort Knox."

"I'll give you all that gold for a few cases of 9mm ammunition," said Kathy, "but I know you aren't thinking about getting inside for the gold, and how does this fit with the people in Atlanta?"

"I was going to ask the same thing," said Hampton.

The Chief took in a deep breath before he began. He had been mulling over a plan for Atlanta since the day that Sparks left them stranded. A land assault on a superior force had never been what he wanted to do, but the loss of the plane left them few options.

"I don't think we're going to find those people in Atlanta. I think they were only there to find the things they needed to get into Fort Knox."

"Like what?" asked Kathy.

"Well, the AC-130 for one thing. If you want to clear the minefield and take out the guard towers at the four corners, one pylon pass around the building would do it. You know, like the one we did at Ambassadors Island."

Hampton shook his head, "You'd only need to do that if the place was still guarded. If the infection got inside, you should be able to walk right up to the front door. They didn't bury mines in the road, did they?"

"Okay," said the Chief. "Let's go on the assumption the infection got inside. How many people are we talking about? I'm going to guess they had at least thirty guards on duty with three shifts. If every guard made it to the facility when things went bad, that would mean nearly one hundred people. Add to that the number of family members, friends, neighbors, and stragglers, and there could be four to five hundred infected inside. This book says they employed about seventeen hundred people, the high-end number of people inside could be up to five or six thousand."

Hampton let out a low whistle. "Maybe someone plans to just open the doors and let everyone out. The plane could safely eliminate them."

Kathy said, "If that's their plan, they should think of something new. The place isn't like a coliseum jammed with people. The inside is likely to be a twisted maze of corridors constructed with the intention of making it difficult for people to find their way around."

"That's what I'm counting on," said the Chief.

That one comment stopped his companions from saying another word. They had known him long enough to recognize when he already had something in mind, but he also liked to make a dramatic pause when he knew he had his audience on a hook.

Kathy said, "Spit it out, Chief. We know you've already made a plan. What is it?"

Instead of answering, the Chief pulled his immense body sideways and stood up from the booth. Few people fully appreciated his size until he stood up, so his simple action drew the attention of sailors sitting in the other booths. The top of his head was almost to the ceiling…or overhead as they called it on a submarine.

"You're not going to tell us?" asked Kathy.

"Right now it's just a thought," he said, "but if the timing is on our side, what if we can get there before them? What if we could be inside waiting and pull off an ambush the way they did to our guys?"

Hampton was still skeptical and asked, "What makes you so sure they'll even show up there?"

"I've had hunches before, and they haven't all been good, but this time there's something that makes me very sure. I don't know if it was something that I heard or something I read. I just know that my gut is telling me Atlanta isn't where we'll find these people. Fort Knox seems to be logical."

Kathy nodded, "I agree, and maybe it's worth checking just on the off chance we would find another shelter there. I still have one minor problem, though. Breaking into the most secure vault in the world is hard enough, but if it's also occupied by the infected, it might be impossible."

Iris walked into the galley, and although the crew was fairly used to female shipmates, she still drew a fair amount of admiring glances. Her tall, slender body was accented by her silver hair. Long and straight, she could have passed for a tall elven queen in a fantasy movie.

"There you are," she said to the Chief. "The Captain would like a word with you about where we want to get dropped off."

"Good," he answered. "I hope Captain Byrne wouldn't mind a detour."

"You don't want to go to Charleston or Mud Island?" asked Iris.

Kathy answered for him.

"That busy little mind of his has a plan, but he hasn't told us the details yet. He wants to go to Kentucky now."

Sometimes stating the obvious was fun, so Iris said, "Oh, I'm sure Captain Byrne can get us there in a nuclear submarine."

That earned a grin from the Chief, and his smiles were so infectious that the others had to join in with their own.

"Cute," he said, "but I have somewhere less landlocked in mind. When we traveled down the coast to circle Florida and get to the Gulf of Mexico, we gave the Beaufort, South Carolina area a wide berth for a good reason. We didn't know how the military would react if we dropped by, and we were in a bit of a hurry. I think we should finally visit the place and see if they left any Ospreys sitting around."

"Ospreys?" asked Kathy.

"You most likely saw one and didn't give it much thought before the infection," said Hampton. "They flew up and down the coast between Marine bases like Camp Lejeune and Parris Island. They can do vertical takeoff and landing, so you don't need a runway."

The Chief nodded, "I always wanted to fly one of those things. If we can get lucky one more time, we can make good time getting to Kentucky."

"Any chance we could check on the other shelters on the way?" asked Kathy.

"Time might be important, but we should be able to at least make radio contact," he answered.

"That's why I asked. We were gone longer than expected, and I've been a bit worried about those people attacking Green Cavern with the AC-130. Sparks knows where the shelter is, and by now his friends have had plenty of time to do something."

As if on cue, a sailor stuck his head in the door of the galley and asked, "Anyone know a lady named Gentry Campbell? We've got a radio contact from Huntsville, and she says she's trying to reach you guys."

* * *

12

******

The news wasn't good, but it could have been worse. Gentry was both surprised and relieved that she was able to contact her friends, but they were evasive about their exact location. The radioman she had spoken with had an English accent, but he hadn't given her much information to work with. Wherever her friends were, it had to be somewhere safe because she could hear music in the background. Neil Young was singing Heart of Gold.

Based on recent events, she understood that open communications might be heard by the wrong people. She told them Green Cavern had been attacked by the AC-130, and that it had leveled the village above the shelter. Gentry described the destruction as complete. The good news was that the network of people above ground in the neighboring mountains had radioed Green Cavern in time for an evacuation. Green Cavern was locked down tight, and even though the plane had fired directly at the blast doors that covered the windows on the side of the mountain, it had been unable to penetrate the shelter.

She could tell by his silence that the Chief felt the anger return as he listened to her report. Even though they hadn't lost any innocent lives, someone was trying to stop them from saving a small part of civilization. Whoever it was, he considered them to be short-sighted parasites, and he needed to exterminate them. Sparks was at the top of his list. The town had flourished as a safe haven for people on the road who had heard from other survivors that there was still a place to go where they didn't have to fear for the lives of their children.

The Chief asked Gentry to relay a message to Green Cavern that was both natural and puzzling at the same time. They weren't coming back to Guntersville yet because they were going to resolve the problem. The puzzling part was when the Chief mentioned how much he missed her fried chicken. She didn't recall ever cooking anything for him. Then he said something about the next time they would see each other. They would make time for a walk down a country backroad for the fun of it just like her parents did.

It took her about an hour to put the pieces of the puzzle together. If it had been a computer problem, a math equation, or anything related to outer space, Gentry would have solved it in a few minutes. After she understood, she had to appreciate the Chief's knowledge of obscure music. He had pieced together lyrics from songs that her parents might have known, but if anyone had been listening, they would have just

13

heard a normal conversation between two friends.

Glen Campbell wrote a song about fried chicken with the Green River Boys. She thought that was a little too coincidental to be simply conversation. Glen Campbell was a big favorite of her parents, and Green River was close to the same as Green Cavern. The part about fried chicken didn't fit with Kentucky in her mind until she remembered that Bobbie Gentry had a line in a song that said something about walking down a Kentucky backroad just because she wanted to.

"So, the Chief wants me to meet him in Kentucky, and he wants it to be on a backroad. That makes sense, but that could be anywhere," she thought.

Gentry liked to take notes, and she had a page of them from the call. As she read them over for the third time, she realized she was humming the song she had heard in the background, and she knew that hadn't been an accident. Two song references and a song.

"Fried chicken and Glenn Campbell, Bobbie Gentry walking on backroads in Kentucky, and Neil Young," she thought. "Fried chicken, backroads, and gold. Does he want me to go to Fort Knox?"

2

1969

"No one will approve this. The history books aren't going to be rewritten to include a chapter about how preppers got access to one of the most secure facilities in America."

The Colonel said it as if it was his final word, and it wasn't open for discussion.

Titus said, "The history books hardly have more than a page about the place anyway. Why would putting a shelter under Fort Knox have to be advertised in history books? Besides, the deal was that we could pick any location we wanted except in the capitol."

That wasn't true, but the Colonel didn't need to know that.

Titus Rush wasn't just convincing when he wanted something, he always made sure he had an ace in the hole, and right now that winning card was the contract that had already been signed by the Secretary of Defense on the President's behalf. For good measure, he laid a copy of it in front of Colonel Thomas. The Colonel saw it next to his elbow, but he hadn't touched it yet. Fort Knox was his responsibility, and he didn't like handing over any part of it to a hippy.

Titus said, "I can call the President and tell him we're stopping construction on his shelter in Ohio. When he asks why I'll just tell him someone broke the contract. May I use your phone?"

The Colonel put his hand over his phone when Titus reached for it.

There wasn't a trace of humor on the Colonel's face, but Titus grinned anyway. He was willing to stroke the Colonel's ego with a compromise, but it wasn't going to be one he would have to make.

"If I agree with this, I want it in writing that it will be classified. I don't want anyone to know that the nation's gold supply was exposed to a bunch of government contractors and some doomsday club."

"We're not exactly running ads or selling seats, Colonel, so classifying it will not be a problem. In return, one member of our organization will become a permanent resident, and a small contingent of politicians will be on a list of people who will come to Fort Knox in the event of a national emergency. Look at it this way. If you wanted to build a shelter that was totally secure, where would you put it?"

The off-handed compliment caused a slight change in the Colonel's expression. He would be the last person to say it wasn't a smart place to build a shelter. After all, Fort Knox was already the most secure shelter in the world for America's gold.

"I would also want to be heavily involved with the construction," said the Colonel.

"You can oversee the construction but not supervise it."

"You want me to just watch? What if I don't agree with something?"

"Like what? The shelter won't even be located anywhere near the vault. We'll just be taking advantage of the security you already provide. Look at it this way, this will be the best-protected shelter in our entire network. I'll bet the government would even consider using your facility to protect national treasures during an emergency."

Titus stressed the word "your" to stroke his ego a bit more, and it was also a subtle way of letting the Colonel feel like he was still the owner of the whole thing. Frankly, he didn't plan to let the Colonel inside the shelter after it was done, but he would cross that bridge when he came to it.

A heavy sigh was the Colonel's indication that he gave up. He most likely knew it would end this way when Titus Rush showed up at the front gate of the military base where the US Gold Bullion Depository was located. They didn't get many people who dropped by unannounced, and when he wouldn't go away after he was denied entry, the Colonel had gotten a call from the Secretary of Defense. The message had been clearly worded, and the guards at the gate were instructed to make no further comments to the man about his hair when they arranged to escort him to the Colonel.

Titus handed over a letter of introduction that had the letterhead of

16

the White House and a copy of the contract. It explained that an ultra-secure shelter was going to be built under the Depository. Private contractors would arrive within a few days who were connected to the Army Corp of Engineers to do secret projects, and the Colonel was to provide anything they needed. He would have to follow orders, but only after he would have the last word.

"If I see something I don't like, I'll put a stop to the whole thing and throw you and your people out the front gate."

His last word was accompanied by a finger pointed at his face, but Titus was used to feathers being ruffled by the project. The National Park Service wasn't choked up about the idea of building a shelter under Fort Sumter, and the mayor of Columbus, Ohio wanted a personal guarantee that he would be allowed to go to the shelter if there was an emergency. That was actually approved, but he would have been surprised to find out his job as mayor didn't come with any other perks. Titus would be surprised if Colonel Thomas welcomed him with open arms.

"Thank you, Colonel. The first shipment of materials will arrive today along with a busload of contractors. Work will begin in the morning at sunrise, so I would appreciate it if you could expedite their gate access."

"Today? Are you expecting a national emergency this week?"

"Yes, I am. It could happen any day," said Titus. "I just hope we can get the project done in time. Oh, and by the way…the official name of this project is not the Fort Knox Shelter. It's the Redoubt."

The Colonel had to admit he had never seen a group of people attack a project more efficiently. The trucks carrying construction equipment only came in at night, and he never saw contractors except for when they came or went from the base. His early concerns about the Redoubt were gone long before construction was done. It wasn't finished in a week, but by the time they informed him that it was done, for some odd reason, he felt the same urgency Titus Rush had at the start. He didn't know what was coming, but something had rubbed off on him. Whatever it was, he was glad he would have a place to go.

Time went by without the Colonel seeing the end of the world arrive. He was eventually promoted and transferred to the Pentagon. Before his departure, he passed along the information about the Redoubt to his successor who immediately wanted a tour of the facility. When his request was denied, he decided he didn't need permission and went to the entrance on his own. The "permanent resident" inside wouldn't open the door despite his threats, and he found no one knew how to open the door from the outside. As a matter of fact, there was no keypad or combination dial that he could see, and his demands to open the door were met with silence.

Over the years that followed, the Colonel's complaints to the Pentagon were at first rejected, but then they were completely ignored. When his time at Fort Knox came and went, he was transferred to a new command, but he didn't even bother to tell his replacement about the Redoubt.

Barrett Singletary was the original member of the survival club who asked for his shelter to be built under the Depository at Fort Knox. He died two weeks later in a car wreck, and Andrew Fleming asked if he could change his original choice from Staten Island to Fort Knox. Since he was the first to ask, his request was approved by Titus.

He arrived with the contractors as if he was there to work, and base security quickly detected a discrepancy in the logs at the front gate. They notified the Colonel who filed a complaint with the Pentagon, but before the Pentagon even answered with a response that said there must have been a mistake in his own command, front gate security notified him that somehow the logs had changed. Andrew Fleming had come and gone on a regular basis. The Colonel never noticed, nor really cared, that Andrew Fleming checked out at the gate one day but never came back.

No one arrived at Fort Knox to inspect the Redoubt when construction was completed, and Colonel Thomas had wondered why, but unknown to him, his promotion and transfer were timed to take away his natural curiosity. He only hoped there was another shelter near the Pentagon for him because he had become as paranoid as the old hippy. As for his successor, Colonel Thomas assumed he had been added to the list of lucky people who had a place to go when the emergency came to pass. After many years and new base commanders, it was no surprise that no one was aware that there was an unoccupied shelter under Fort Knox. They just knew there was a secret vault that couldn't be opened. It was a typical, bureaucratic operation despite the efficient construction.

2016

Congressman Stephen Marks had arrived in Washington with a

natural talent for his job. Relatively young but well-liked by both sides of the aisle, he received coveted committee assignments that gave him access to sensitive information. He reminded people of John F. Kennedy with his full head of hair and ready smile, but most of all everyone knew he was smart.

One of the pet projects he found interesting was a shadowy initiative that had cost more than some of the most expensive military hardware. As a matter of fact, when he compared it to nuclear submarines and modern aircraft carriers, the costs were similar. It wasn't that he suspected misuse of funds. On the contrary, he knew from his own experience in the military that there were some highly secret but expensive programs. Research and development wasn't exactly something that could be open to the press, and the military had gotten better at hiding the costs than those days when toilet seats cost seven hundred dollars.

He got his first clue to the existence of the Redoubt under Fort Knox while on a visit to a secretive Air Force base in Nevada where he thought he might find something related to that program. His military background and easy-going approach to people tended to get others to be too comfortable around him. That also meant they talked more than they should have.

The clue came as he was being escorted into a large hangar at a remote end of the base. He had expected the hangar to be the hiding place of an experimental aircraft, possibly even one of the planes that had been seen by civilians and reported as a UFO. He was surprised to find that the door he entered led to a well-furnished lobby with a security desk. It was so cool and comfortable inside that Congressman Marks stepped backward instead of forward. He had to see the building from the outside again.

"Is something wrong, Sir?" asked Captain Wayne, the man who had been his escort.

The side of the hangar was a faded white with streaks of rust at the seams of the metal. The faded paint was caused by the harsh sun that baked the windowless building, but since it seldom rained, the rust seemed out of place. Even more out of place was the cool interior.

The Captain anticipated both reactions because he had seen them before.

"If you're wondering about the rust, it's caused by washing the walls. We get some heavy winds that coat the hangar with dirt. When they wash it off, the water causes the rust, and that serves the purpose of making people think there's nothing important in this hangar. You were also surprised by the lobby, right?"

"Yes, I thought this was…you know…an airplane hangar."

"That's the rumor we prefer, Congressman. Everyone has always thought there's either a flying saucer or an experimental airplane inside. This is a research facility, but not that kind. If the public finds out it's not a hangar, it won't be long before the conspiracy theorists come to the conclusion that we're dissecting aliens here. Let's go inside so I can show you."

Two armed guards greeted them at the security desk. Behind them was a large, circular vault door with a brushed nickel surface. The surface shone as if it was polished daily.

"That's got to be the biggest vault door ever made," said the Congressman.

Having shared a level of comfort seldom allowed by a Congressman, Captain Wayne replied, "The only one bigger is the one in the basement of Fort Knox, or so I've been told."

Congressman Marks had already been to Fort Knox on his tour of secret military installations, and there were two things wrong with the Captain's remark. The vault at Fort Knox was smaller if his memory was correct, and it wasn't in the basement. As a matter of fact, when he went to Fort Knox, he wasn't taken to the basement. He also wondered how this Air Force officer had picked up information from a grapevine that didn't exist. He made a mental note to run that answer down later.

The rest of the tour was filled with surprises because the hangar turned out to be a biological research facility. When the Captain said it was a research facility, he had neglected to add that it made Fort Dietrich look like a high school chemistry class, but the logo for USAMRIID was prominently displayed on equipment and arm patches. The work they did was called research, but Marks knew they were the tip of the spear when it came to biological warfare.

"What exactly are they working on here?" asked the Congressman.

The Captain hesitated but said, "I guess you're cleared to know what this is, but I don't want to get into trouble if I say too much."

Marks gave him a steady glare that didn't need any words.

"It's the Venezuela Project, Congressman. You know, I'm just the administrator here, so I don't really get briefed on all of the details myself, but I've heard some things."

"Like what?"

The Captain was uneasy talking about it, and Marks saw that when he spoke he lowered his head a bit and moved his mouth like a ventriloquist. It was almost like he was afraid that someone was going to read his lips. It made it harder to understand him, but he could hear him well enough to follow what he said.

"From what I've been told, the CIA wanted to test something…in Venezuela, but they couldn't just put it in the water or spray it in the air."

"Wait a minute…you mean they tested a biological weapon in Venezuela? How and when did they do it?"

As a Congressman, Marks knew the relationship with the government in the South American country was always balanced on a razor's edge. If not for the oil they produced, the country would be of little strategic value, but in recent years they had been courted by countries like Russia and China. They were geographically close enough to the United States for the CIA to pull off something like a biological weapon test but far enough away to claim innocence.

After a short pause, the Captain asked Marks, "Did you hear anything on the news about a weird infection that causes people to get a bad fever and then bite people?"

Marks had recently heard about similar infections in different states and a few foreign countries, but things like new strains of viruses were popping up all the time, so he hadn't made the connections. They were calling it a zombie virus on the news, so he just brushed it off as sensationalist.

"Well," continued the Captain, "some of the things on the news sound like what we did in Venezuela. You see those glass tanks in there?"

He pointed at the back wall of the lab, and Congressman Marks took a step closer to the window. There was a row of aquariums on the far side of the room, and he saw some form of crustacean move along the bottom of one. When he focused on a spot, he realized there were dozens of them.

"They infected crabs and dropped them in the rivers of Venezuela near the border of Guyana. They figured local fishermen would catch them and sell them to seafood markets in Caracas."

The Congressman hid his emotions well. He hadn't gotten as far as he had by wearing them on his sleeve. Despite the horrors of what he had just heard, he acted as if it was just one more government secret. His close proximity to that horror was what bothered him the most.

Inside the labs were some of the most lethal pathogens known to man, and Marks felt a touch uneasy knowing there was only reinforced glass separating him from certain death. Especially since the windows appeared to be quite old. Watching the technicians work while wearing their heavy biohazard protective suits made him wonder if they weren't as nervous as he felt, but he understood clearly why the nature of this particular hangar in the middle of nowhere was such a guarded secret.

Marks absently scratched at a welt on the back of his hand. At first, he thought he was just getting a case of hives because he was nervous about being so close to whatever it was inside that lab. It was the same reaction people get if they find out someone sitting next to them has something in their hair. Suddenly, their scalp starts itching too. The problem was that he wasn't imagining the small spider he saw disappear up his sleeve. He slapped the spot and saw the dead body fall to the floor with its legs curled inward.

"You need an exterminator in here, Captain."

Captain Wayne stepped on the dead spider as if he needed to help.

"I'm sorry, Sir. They get in through there, and it's been a problem for a long time. The labs aren't completely isolated from the rest of the complex."

He gestured toward the access door at the end of the hall so Marks could see for himself, but Marks was getting an uncomfortable feeling about the integrity of the lab. He had just killed a spider on one side of the glass, but he could clearly see a spider web inside the isolation room window.

The lab was connected to the other buildings by a tunnel that also housed the massive power plant for the building. It needed redundant systems to control the temperature and airflow inside the labs. The extent of the project was far greater than what it appeared to be on the surface, and no matter how hard he would try, Marks couldn't get his mind off of what the Captain had told him.

He went through the motions of inspecting the rest of the facility while wondering if there was a way to get the Captain to tell him about something else without being obvious. He began to see where he could drive a wedge into the Captain's weak military discipline when he complimented the officer for his level-headed and cool demeanor while in the presence of the dangerous pathogens. Captain Wayne turned out to be susceptible to praise.

"Doesn't it make you nervous when you think about what's on the other side of that glass window? It makes me feel a bit weak in the knees being this close to a bug that I can't see, yet it would kill me if it got out of that room."

"All part of a day's work," said Wayne. He appeared to hold his chin a little higher as he beamed outwardly.

"You seem to be well-educated about secret military initiatives. I could use someone with your level of expertise as an advisor."

The thought of reassignment away from the remote Nevada hangar was mouth-watering to the Captain, and Marks was dangling it in front of him like a piece of prime rib.

"Ask me anything, Congressman. I've been briefed about several projects and learned even more on my own."

Once again, Marks saw that there were some security concerns to address, but that was nothing new. Even in the military, there were always people who needed to feather their own nest by proving they knew more than everyone else. He could plug those leaks on another day, but for now, he wanted to exploit one of them. It wasn't what the Captain expected.

"I've always wondered why there's a vault in the basement of the Gold Depository at Fort Knox when everyone knows the gold is stored in a vault on the main floor. Maybe you can explain it to me."

The Captain laughed. "I thought you were going to ask me more about the other thing. Frankly, that was making me a little uncomfortable."

"Forget about it. Let's talk about something else. Tell me about the rumors of a second vault at Fort Knox."

"That just shows you how far rumors can go," said the Captain. "I heard they quickly built a second vault after the attacks on the Twin Towers and moved the Constitution and the Declaration of Independence into that vault because they worried some of our national landmarks were going to be hit next."

"Why didn't they just put them in the same vault with the gold?"

The Captain didn't have an answer to that question, but that didn't stop him from giving an answer.

"The temperature and humidity, of course. Gold can be stored in all kinds of conditions without being damaged, but the documents had to get special treatment."

Marks doubted he would want the Captain to be briefed on anything bigger than the project he already worked on. He could picture the man getting caught up in a "honey trap" with an attractive foreign agent. A few drinks and a promise of romance would have him flipped on the first try.

The Congressman managed to shake himself loose from the Captain and ended the tour with a vague comment that he would be in touch to discuss his transfer. Wayne insisted on giving him his private phone number, but Marks had no plan to do anything with it except turn it over to the investigative branch that would begin monitoring the officer's personal communications. He wondered how many people he had told about the contents of the remote hangar.

Before his plane took off from Nellis Air Force Base, Marks sent a request to make a detour to Godman Army Airfield at Fort Knox. There were some protests from a few of the officers who were in the chain of command for such a request, but he assured them his visit was in their best interests. They weren't sure what a young Congressman could do to influence their best interests, but his popularity in Congress had already given him the right kind of reputation. When he was pressed for more details about his request, he simply said he was reviewing the possibility of increasing funding to the Gold Depository but needed to review existing infrastructure to determine how much funding would be needed. That particular "white lie" was at least half true because he had already decided they could use some upgrades at the Depository.

It was late in the evening when his plane touched down at Fort Knox, so he checked into temporary quarters reserved for visiting officers and government officials then made sure the Colonel in charge of the facility knew he would visit the building in the morning. He arrived at the Depository shortly after breakfast and found the Colonel waiting anxiously for him.

Colonel Morrison had already gotten wind of the good news that Marks was there to assess additional funding requirements, so he greeted the Congressman with open arms. He excitedly told Marks the facility was at his disposal. Marks got straight to the point and told the Colonel he wanted to inspect the second vault in the basement. He was surprised to see it knock the smile from the Colonel's face.

The excuses began with, "What vault?" They progressed to, "Oh, that vault. That's just an abandoned fallout shelter."

"Well, it might be useful for the purpose of expansion. I'd like to take a tour of it while I'm here," said Marks.

"That could be a problem, Congressman."

The Colonel hadn't regained his previous ebullient demeanor yet, and if anything, was deflating by the second.

"You see, no one really knows how to get inside the thing. There's almost no written history about it, and what little bit of history I have just calls it a special project in case of an emergency."

"Why was it abandoned?"

The Colonel shrugged his shoulders. It wasn't a customary response for him or Congressman Marks.

"Did they call the project something? Did it have a name?" he asked.

The Colonel nodded, "They called it the Redoubt."

It only took ten minutes to reach the basement, and as soon as they arrived, Marks saw why the Air Force Captain had commented on the size of the door. It was at least twice the size of the one at the research lab in Nevada. He let out a low whistle.

"Colonel Morrison, I know projects get abandoned for lots of reasons, and this may be just another example of government waste, but from time to time you find the Holy Grail of secret projects. I don't know about you, but I'd like to find out what's behind that door."

"Good luck with that. No one has figured out how to open the door, and experts who've come in promising they can open anything have left here scratching their heads."

******

Marks had two advantages that the experts didn't have. He had access to archived paper trails that showed him there was a project that began in 1969 that was named Redoubt, and he was in a serious relationship with Jackie Benedict, a truly gifted engineering student at MIT. All he had to do was give her minimal information about his problem, and she gave him a good starting point.

Marks asked her how she would open a vault door that had been installed in 1969 if there was no clear or obvious method for unlocking it. She thought for less than a minute before suggesting that the first order of business would be to discover what technologies were available in 1969 that could be connected to a locking mechanism. He was constantly amazed at how she made things sound easier than they were because he still didn't know where to start other than by talking with locksmiths. She found his solution to be humorous and said she would get back to him within a day with a list.

Jackie didn't need a whole day to get back to Marks because the solution to opening the door came down to one explanation. He answered her call on the first ring because he knew she wouldn't be calling back so soon if it was bad news.

"Ultrasonics?" asked Marks.

"Don't tell me you don't know what that is," she said teasingly.

"Well, as a matter of fact, I do. What's that mean for me, though? Someone has a remote control that opens the door?"

"I'm impressed," she said. "Most people don't know that remotes ever used anything except infrared."

"I paid attention in some of my classes in college."

Jackie had a pretty laugh to go along with her brains and good looks. She had often joked about how he would sleep during class but still do well on exams. He told her it was his superpower, and she had asked why he only had one. That had been a passing joke before they even started dating, but it had endured throughout their relationship.

"You must've picked it up subconsciously," she said. "So where did you find a remote-controlled vault door that was made in 1969? What's inside it, or is that what you're trying to find out?"

"I can't tell you," he answered, "but if the remote is ultrasonic, doesn't that mean all I have to do is get a remote that has programmable ultrasonic frequencies and try every one of them until I find the right one?"

"That depends on how much time you have. A typical remote can be programmed using a four-digit number, and that would give you ten thousand combinations. Unless the original remote was never used to program the lock."

That got his attention. He said, "I read somewhere that there are about twenty common combinations, but the factory settings were usually all ones or all zeros. I need to go, but I'll get back to you in a bit."

"So, you aren't going to tell me where you are or what you're trying to open?"

"Maybe later after I have a chance to find out if it's a state secret."

When Marks put his finger over the button to end the call, he paused for only a split second before putting the phone back to his ear.

"Still there?" he asked. "I just thought of something. I need a universal remote, and I'll bet you made one for show-and-tell in the third grade, didn't you."

"Ummm...I think it was the first grade. Wherever you are, if you're near a military base, there must be someone who can make you one."

After saying goodbye for a second time, Marks rushed to Colonel Morrison's office and asked him to bring in his best electronics specialist. Morrison made a call and asked for Sergeant Finley to report to his office on the double. He must've been in the building because he practically materialized a few minutes later. The Colonel introduced Marks to the middle-aged but very fit man who was obviously a career Army NCO. The Sergeant's eyebrows went up when the Colonel said he was a Congressman.

Marks simply said, "It's a pleasure to meet you, Sergeant. Colonel Morrison says you're the best man he's got on the base in electronics, so I'll get right to the point. I need an old-fashioned ultrasonic remote. I need to be able to reprogram it fast to go through all possible four-digit codes until it sends out the right signal."

"The right signal for what, Sir?" asked Finley.

Congressman Marks could hardly keep him in the dark, so he explained it to him, but he reminded him first that it was a highly classified issue.

"You'll need a transmitter and receiver combination, Congressman. If the correct code is sent, the mechanism receiving it will most likely send back an acknowledgment. If the transmitter sends another code too soon, it may interrupt the cycle. I can make you one with an indicator that will flash a red light for a wrong code and a green light for a correct code. I can program it to stop sending codes if you get a green light."

Colonel Morrison was right when he said the Sergeant was good because he had a working device ready in less than two hours. It was hardly more than a wooden box with the components stapled to the wood, but Sergeant Finley was sure it would work...that is if the vault door would respond to an ultrasonic signal.

They carried the box to the basement along with three folding chairs and set up a table across from the vault door. Finley pressed the unlabeled start button. The red light flashed, and after it flashed a second time, Finley said, "It's working. The second flash meant it had rejected a second code. There's a built-in sequencer that changes the code by one digit, so this thing will go through every code until it finds the right one."

"How long will it take to go through every possible code?" asked Marks. "It looks like about four seconds per number."

He did the math in his head and answered at the same time as Sergeant Finley, "A little over eleven hours if it's the last number."

The Sergeant shook his head, "Odds are it's somewhere in between, Sir. If we reach the last number, you're trying to open a lock that isn't ultrasonic to four digits. It could be a twelve-digit code for all we know."

"We're talking about 1969, Sergeant. I'm inclined to believe it will be a number in between. By the way, does this contraption of yours keep track of the numbers as it tries them?"

Sergeant Finley fixed his eyes on Marks with a totally blank expression, and Marks knew the Sergeant wanted to say it was a stupid question, but he wasn't going to insult a Congressman.

"I'll take that as a yes," said Marks.

The three men were all standing when Finley turned the remote on, but after a few minutes of watching the light flash red, it became obvious that they could be there for a while, so they unfolded the chairs and got as comfortable as they could.

"I should've brought a deck of cards," said the Colonel.

Sergeant Finley reached into a pocket and pulled out a familiar red and white box. He opened one end and shook out the stack of smooth cards.

"This isn't my first rodeo, Sir. Every time we test an idea, the test phase is an exercise in hurry up and wait."

Marks added, "Ah, the motto of every military man in the world."

"You're ex-military, Sir?"

Marks was in the middle of answering as he slid cards from the table into his hands when he realized the green light was on. They all saw it at the same moment, and it would be fair to say they were collectively holding their breath. If someone would ask them why they were frozen in place, the answer was obvious. The green light meant something had responded to an ultrasonic code, and unless someone had an old-fashioned Zenith television set nearby that had turned on or changed channels, the door had to be the receiver.

"Anyone hear that?" asked Colonel Morrison.

Marks had moved his eyes from the green light to the door, so he was sure the faint sound of movement was coming from inside the shiny metal surface. He could almost picture gears turning, rods extending and retracting, and large pins moving into or out of smooth cylinders. Nothing moved on the outside, but the sound of the lock withdrawing the four huge pins from the frame of the vault was loud enough to make all three men jump.

The forgotten cards were placed on the table as all three of them rose slowly from their seats. Just as they had all held their breath in anticipation, they couldn't have explained why they had to approach the door with caution. There was a musty odor near the door. It was the smell of something old. It brought back memories of long-closed basements, attics, and even crypts.

3

Charlie & Sue

Beaufort, South Carolina - 2023

The Ambush slipped silently through the coastal waters as it approached South Carolina. The Gulf Stream was smooth and glassy, and Captain Byrne watched through his periscope as a pod of dolphins ran ahead of the warship.

"Contacts?" he asked his sonar operators.

"Nothing to report, Sir. Nothing on sonar or the towed array."

The Ambush had deployed an array of listening devices along what was essentially a long cord. It was called a wire, but the heavy cable had to be able to withstand strong currents while giving them the ability to watch for another submarine behind them.

"Bring us to the surface slowly," he ordered. "If there's anyone out there, I would prefer they get a good look at us and know we're friendly. We don't have anyone following us, but that doesn't mean they aren't out there. Retract the towed array as you surface."

The Chief watched from a corner out of the way and understood the logic. The only likely observer out there in the water would be one of the ultra-silent American fast attack submarines, and if there was one watching their approach, they would recognize the hull design and engine noise of the British submarine.

As the submarine surfaced, the Captain and the Chief went up through the sail to get a good view of the coast through binoculars.

The Chief wasn't surprised to find Kathy had followed them.

"You guys can't have all the fun," she said. "Oh, wow that air smells nice."

They each had a set of binoculars so they didn't have to share, but before they put them to their eyes, they each took a moment to breathe in the fresh morning air. It was a nice change from the recirculated, artificial atmosphere of the oxygen scrubbers inside the boat.

The moment passed, and they got down to the business of locating the best place to enter the coast near the air base. All three aimed their binoculars toward land after first making a sweep of the ocean behind them. The water was smooth, and the clear sky gave them a good view. The sun would have reflected off of anything on the surface. Not seeing anything, they turned to the low coast ahead.

To the inexperienced eye, the coast would appear just as it had in the days before the apocalypse, but the Chief and Kathy both were familiar with this particular coast, and they saw the differences. Captain Byrne knew the coast of the United Kingdom, but this was his first time seeing South Carolina.

"Our ancestors thought this coast was an island at first," he said. "From this distance, it appears so flat."

"It's called the Lowcountry for a good reason," said Kathy. "There's only a marginal elevation toward the middle of the state, so they called that the Midlands. Swamps extended so far inland that it was easy to create lakes but harder to make roads."

"It's changed a lot," said the Chief. He pointed at a spot about fifteen degrees to starboard.

Kathy saw what he meant immediately, but Captain Byrne didn't know what it had been like before. He waited for them to fill him in.

The Chief said, "That used to be an inlet where we could have gotten close and then used a zodiac to cruise right up to the Marine airbase. I see a sandbar across the entrance now."

"It's low tide," said Kathy. "Good time to go crabbing."

They had already told Captain Byrne about the blue crabs along the coast of South Carolina, and they weren't alone with that particular problem. Fresh seafood had been a staple on the menu of the entire world at one time, but crabs were bottom feeders that weren't particular about what they ate, and the infected people that walked into the ocean had been an increased food source for crabs. The result was a population explosion that had made crabs as common as big mosquitos, but as the number of infected decreased, the crabs had become much more aggressive, and the survivors of the apocalypse had to be ready for crab attacks at any time of day.

They were still too far away to see the movement, but there was no doubt in their minds that the blue crabs were there, either in the shallow water or in pools among the trees. Anyone walking through those trees during the day could avoid the crabs if they were wearing thick boots, but while they were watching where they put their feet, it was too easy to walk face-first into a spider web. Although the spider population had self-corrected, there were enough of them to make a walk in the woods miserable.

Captain Byrne asked, "Am I correct that alligators are indigenous to this area?"

"He's a mindreader," said Kathy.

The Chief said, "If our ancestors had arrived here under the present-day conditions without any knowledge of the local wildlife, they would've been disappointed. They would've left and never come back. We've seen alligators attacked by crabs, and we've seen both alligators and crabs chase people. Forget about the infected for just a moment and consider how it would feel to wake up with a dozen or so of those crabs crawling around on you."

"Not to mention alligators closer to twenty feet long and crabs the size of cats," said Kathy.

Captain Byrne regarded both of them in an attempt to solve whether or not they were just having fun with him. His judgment told him they weren't, and he decided there would be no need for him to go ashore even though he had considered it.

Word came from the control room that the boat was in shallow water, and the Officer of the Deck had ordered that they stop their forward motion. Kathy nudged the Chief and nodded with her head toward one inlet a few degrees north of the original target, and he saw what she had spotted immediately.

A mud-streaked white bow with the name *Charlie Sue* painted on it, slowly coasted into open water, and they saw that it was a shrimp boat that had been modified from bow to stern with a safety net. Spikes stuck out from all sides at intervals of four feet. They were angled slightly upward, and a net was strung around the entire boat. Even from a distance, they could see crabs hanging from the net.

Captain Byrne saw their attention was drawn to something and adjusted his position too.

"What is that?" he asked.

"A survivor," said the Chief. "He modified his boat to keep the crabs from climbing into it. Crabs might be aggressive, but they aren't smart enough to climb over his nets."

They watched the boat exit the narrow inlet and turn to starboard as it picked up speed. It didn't take a genius to see that it was coming straight toward them, and as it got closer, they could see the elderly couple in the small wheelhouse. Both had gray hair, but he had a full gray beard to match. They were waving at the submarine excitedly.

"I think we found our ride up the inlet to the airbase," said the Chief.

The old boat was almost broadside to the submarine when they learned the full extent of the crab defense system. The net turned out to be made of chicken wire, and with the flip of a switch, there was a sizzling and crackling sound as crabs that hung from the net were electrocuted. Smoke arose from those that were too stubborn to let go, and a few fell to the water leaving their pincers behind.

Captain Byrne ordered a deck crew to come topside to receive passengers, but it was a well-rehearsed response. Everyone had to be careful to keep the infection from getting aboard. As a precaution, the deck crew was told to wear high rubber boots in case crabs climbed the hull. It turned out to be a good decision because the first blue crabs were already roaming around near the stern where they could virtually walk aboard. The deck crew brought brooms and rubber gloves for good measure, and some took crab duty while the rest brought the elderly pair aboard.

Sue and Charlie Sloan didn't object to the medical exam they received as soon as they crossed from their boat to the deck of the sub. Like most ships that could still be put to sea, the Ambush had female crew members, and one of them was a nurse. The Sloans said they hadn't been treated by a doctor since the infection began, and they would be grateful for any medication they had for high blood pressure. To their surprise, the exams showed they were not in need of any prescriptions, and the nurse explained it was likely because they were getting more exercise and eating no fast food over the last seven years.

When they were cleared by the medical crew, the elderly couple was brought in through a hatch on the deck, and the boat was buttoned shut leaving the crabs to explore for openings. Charlie Sloan warned them that the crabs would eventually climb the sail, so Captain Byrne reassured him they would use the periscope to check the hull before they went outside again.

The first order of business was to do what neighbors do. The couple was escorted to the living quarters in "officers country" and allowed to shower. Afterward, they were given clean clothes and then taken to a dining room where they were fed the best meal they had enjoyed in years.

"I feel like we're in a hotel," said Charlie, "and your cook is better than the roadkill Sue ever made."

Sue didn't miss a beat and added, "That's because he wouldn't know roadkill from Chicken Marsala. If the man will eat anything, why should I bother to dress it up?"

"We don't eat seafood anymore though," said the old man as he shoveled in food between the thick beard and mustache. "Crabs aren't particular about what they eat, but I am."

The Chief had been amused by the couple, but he was also impressed. The fact that they were even alive this long after the infection started was a testament to their ingenuity.

"I like your crab repellant system," he said. "Did you realize the threat from crabs at the beginning, or was it something you discovered?"

"Discovered," said Sue. "We suspected that all the dead people in the water wasn't a good thing, but the first time we saw one of them infected people walking along the beach with a few dozen crabs hanging off of it, we kind of lost our appetite for crab dip and she-crab soup."

"Then there were those people who were eating the crabs anyway," said Charlie. "They said if people get hungry enough, they'll eat each other, and if they can do that, eating crab meat doesn't sound so bad."

"What happened to them?" asked the Chief.

"We didn't hang around to find out," answered Charlie. "We had the shrimp boat, so we did some work on it to keep those creatures from getting to us. If you drop anchor in one spot for too long, they try to get to you while you're sleeping."

Iris walked into the officer's galley and slipped into a chair next to the Chief. Her silver hair was the same color as Sue's and Charlie's, but it was long and straight. Charlie forgot about his food for a moment.

"Sue, why don't you wear your hair like that?"

"Why aren't you big and handsome like the Chief?"

Iris deftly redirected the conversation before it went further downhill.

"Hi, I'm Iris. I hope my husband hasn't come on too heavy with his request to use your boat to go inland."

Charlie hadn't resumed eating yet, or he would probably have spit his food out onto the table.

"What in the world would you want to do that for?" he asked. "If the crabs aren't bad enough for you, there's plenty of dead people stumbling around out in the trees. The spiders and snakes drop off the branches where the trees grow out over the water."

The Chief wasn't going to let Charlie change his mind. While a zodiac might get them to the beach, it wouldn't be good protection from the crabs.

"Am I correct that your boat has a shallow draft?" he asked.

"Almost a flat bottom," said Charlie. "You didn't answer my question."

The Chief knew that he wasn't going to be able to give the man half of the story, so he decided to lay all his cards on the table.

"We need to get to the Marine airbase to get one of their planes, and frankly, I didn't know how we were going to do it until your boat appeared. After seeing how many crabs were hanging on your nets, I could see that we weren't going to have a choice. We would be forced to go back to Charleston or south to Savannah and then travel by land."

Charlie paused with a fork of food halfway to his mouth and said, "You must be new here. The only way to get to the airbase would be in a boat like mine."

The Chief knew when to speak and when to shut up. He shut up and just waited for Charlie to realize what he had said.

******

On the following morning, the crew of the Ambush managed to evade the crabs roaming around the deck of the submarine long enough to force their retreat. Fire extinguishers proved to be a potent deterrent, and since the only other options were fire and bullets, they were much safer for the crew to use. After removing the pests, they inspected the wire mesh that surrounded the shrimp boat to see if they could improve Charlie's handiwork.

They found that the crabs had concentrated their efforts on weak spots. That was disturbing because the behavior was a sign of intelligence that went beyond the normal habits of crabs. The crew also found that the electric current had caused the wire mesh to overheat in the places where the crabs had hung onto the wire long enough to cook. That accounted for at least half of the weak spots, and they estimated that the wire wouldn't last six more months if too much electricity was used.

The solution to the problem was to remove the wire completely and replace it with smooth plastic panels that were cannibalized from various bulkheads throughout the sub. The seams were closed by screwing aluminum strips over them, and they provided the strength to support the panels. By placing them at a thirty-degree angle, the crabs wouldn't be able to climb into the boat.

Charlie inspected the finished project and said, "I suppose the least I could do to repay you is to give you a ride. Sue and I would have woken up to a boat full of crabs one day if not for you guys."

The entire Mud Island family was gathered on the missile deck of the sub and had even assisted with the retrofit of the safety net. They had all found things to interest them and to keep them busy on the voyage across the Atlantic, but it was obvious that they had only been attempting to occupy their minds to pass the time. Now that they were close to land, they were eager to get moving. There was a collective concern for the head start Sparks had gotten, and Iris was worried that he would target Ambassadors Island after Green Cavern. They were also worried about the Chief because he appeared to be carrying the weight of the world on his shoulders. It wasn't just revenge he was after. It was a need to remove a threat to what was left of humanity. They didn't know how to stop the infection. They only knew how to fight it. The threat of a power-hungry opportunist was something that could be stopped.

Captain Byrne joined the Chief where he stood in the sail and watched as supplies were loaded into the small shrimp boat.

"I suspect you'll be leaving as soon as preparations are finished. I'll miss you and your people. Are you sure you won't join us and help fight for humanity at sea? You know that history dictates control of the oceans is necessary for control of the lands."

"I'll have to pass on the offer, Captain. We still have work to do here. Besides, sooner or later you're going to hook up with our Navy, and we still have that unresolved issue of Captain Miller. I don't think they'll change their minds about him just because he was right."

"It was worth a try," he answered. "We're sending along supplies, but I imagine your people won't need them. The Sloans can keep them, that is unless they join up with you."

The Chief smiled at the suggestion, but he knew they were two of the rare people who would prefer to fend for themselves. They were independent and had shown enough resiliency to survive long after the infection had begun.

"If they say they want to come with us, we'll gladly bring them in, but I wouldn't hold my breath."

The Chief regarded Captain Byrne long enough for the Captain to see it.

"You want to ask me something, Chief?"

"As a matter of fact, Captain, you asked if we would like to join you, and you asked if we're going to take the Sloans with us. What about you? Any chance you would consider being more than a visitor?"

Now it was the young Captain's turn to smile. "Touché, Chief. We all have our own calling. Yours is here, and mine is England. I suppose the Ambush will pass this way again. Maybe after we get ahead of the infected."

"We owe you some favors. You know we'll repay you someday."

Hampton caught the Chief's attention and held up both thumbs to let him know everything was ready. Captain Byrne climbed down through the sail and out onto the deck with him so he could shake hands and exchange hugs. The bond between the Royal Navy crew and the Mud Island family would be important to the future survival of people, but just as importantly, they had grown close as friends.

They all climbed onto the boat, and while it seemed a bit crowded, they had the benefit of being able to spread out to all parts of the newly installed railings where they could be sure their idea had worked. As they cast off the lines that held them close to the massive, black hull of the submarine, they saw that the water was teeming with blue crabs that were trying to climb the side of the shrimp boat. Some of the larger crabs made it as far as the plastic panels, but from there they couldn't find anything to grip. One by one they dropped back into the water.

Charlie Sloan turned the boat away from the Ambush and lined up the bow with the inlet where they had first seen the boat appear. The sun was still at their backs, so they knew it wasn't even noon yet, but it was going to be a warm day, and they would be sweating soon if there wasn't at least a breeze between the trees that crowded the banks on both sides. A glance back at the Ambush was just in time for them to see the tall sail of the submarine disappear as it glided under the surface.

"If you aren't wearing a hat yet, I'd recommend it," yelled Sue from the cover of the wheelhouse. "One spider in your hair, and you'll be begging me to shave your head for you."

She didn't have to say it twice, and as the boat slipped under the canopy of trees, everyone was scanning the trees for webs. The shade felt good, but they had been right about the lack of a breeze and the mosquitos. They passed around the bug spray that Sue handed them and fanned themselves with anything they could find that worked.

The Chief leaned over a chart that was spread out on a table by the wheelhouse. It predated the infection outbreak, but Charlie had scrawled notes on it to show the depth all the way to the airbase. His only concern was the added weight of nine people plus their supplies. The chart showed a few shallow places where they might scrape the bottom, and getting out to push wasn't an option.

Cassandra joined him at the table and asked, "Worried about how deep we're drafting?"

"Yeah, we have a couple of places that get shallow."

"Maybe I can help. I'll go out on the bow and give you some soundings."

Cassandra got a heavy wrench from a toolbox and a durable line that wasn't thick but was strong enough to tow a car. She tied it to the wrench and then climbed out as far as she could on the bow where she had plenty of room to swing it around her head before throwing it. The wrench flew out almost to the full extent of the line, and she reeled it in as the boat got closer to where it had landed. When they were almost on top of it, Cassandra pulled it from the water and estimated the amount of line that had been below the surface.

"At least ten feet to spare," she called out as she wound up for another throw.

The Chief put his finger on the chart where he guessed they were located, and the note said twelve to fourteen feet. That worried him until he remembered that high tide was arriving with them. The water should get a little deeper if they didn't outrun the tide.

"Hey, Charlie," he called into the wheelhouse. "Slow your pace a bit so the tide catches up with us. It might be too shallow for our weight up ahead."

Charlie acknowledged his suggestion and cut the throttle back, but the timing was bad. Cassandra was just beginning to lean as far out as she could when the reduced forward motion caused the bow to drop lower. In that split second, it was like she had been riding on top of a race car that came to a stop, and she kept going.

It wasn't like her to yell for help in a combat situation, but this was different. There were too many things in the water waiting for something living to eat, and she let out a scream that everyone could hear. Then there was the sound she made when she hit the water. The crabs were on her fast.

Sim was the first to reach the bow with Tom and Hampton right behind him. Tom had to grab Sim by the back of his shirt because he was getting ready to jump. Hampton saw the line looped around a deck cleat and grabbed for it just as fast as Tom had grabbed Sim. When he pulled the line hard, he knew he had done the right thing, because he felt the weight on the other end. Despite the searing pain of pincers, Cassandra held tightly to the rope.

"Give me a hand," yelled Hampton. "I've got her."

Sim was wrestling to free himself from Tom, but Kathy and Colleen had arrived. Colleen helped Hampton to brace himself while Kathy added her own strength to pull on the line. Cassandra appeared at the outer edge of the plastic panel that was bending slightly under her weight. Tom freed himself from Sim and used his long arms to reach out and grab her by the back of her collar. Sim understood what he needed and held Tom's other arm while putting his feet against the side rail. With one strong pull, they dragged Cassandra onto the deck as they slapped at the crabs. The crabs angrily waved their pincers in the air, but at least they let go of Cassandra.

It was a group effort to stomp on all of the crabs while they helped Cassandra past the wheelhouse. As soon as they had her on the deck, they pulled away her clothes to get at the deep cuts. All of them had enough experience with first aid to know that Cassandra was likely to be okay if she was treated immediately. It wasn't like being bitten by the infected dead, but the wounds could make her sick enough to wish she was dead.

"This is going to hurt," yelled Kathy, only inches away from Cassandra's wide eyes.

They poured alcohol over all of her wounds. Her entire body arched from the pain, but she held back the scream she desperately wanted to let loose. Antibiotic cream was spread liberally over her exposed skin before gauze bandages were wrapped over holes as big as bullet wounds. Duct tape was stretched over a couple of places where the crabs had torn the skin as they were pulled away.

Everyone worked quickly, and as soon as they had every bleeding spot covered, Kathy shoved two pills into Cassandra's mouth.

"Antibiotics," she said. "I'm giving you a load-up dose because there's no telling what kinds of bacteria are on those crabs or in the water. We're going to take the bandages off in an hour, clean you up again, and put fresh ones on. Here, take a swallow of this."

Kathy handed her a bottle of bourbon that Charlie was saving for the right occasion. It burned going down, but she preferred it over the multitude of cuts.

Cassandra nodded her head, but she was afraid to speak because it would reveal just how much pain she was in. A minute later, her eyelids drooped, and her head slowly lowered to one side.

"What's happening?" yelled Sim. "Cassandra! Wake up, don't you leave me!"

Kathy put her face in front of Sim's and said, "She's fine. I lied about the pills. One of them was a heavy-duty painkiller. Mixed with the alcohol and adrenaline crash, it knocked her out. I knew she wouldn't willingly take it, but it'll make it easier for us to clean her wounds again once the bleeding has slowed down."

During the entire scramble on the bow, the Chief had been helpless and could only watch. He had started to go forward, but Charlie had jumped out of the wheelhouse and blocked his path. It would have been too much weight forward, and if the boat was too close to the bottom, they could all be thrown over the bow. He could remember a time when they had traveled through the creeks along the coast and not worried about anything except the current, but everything had changed.

It took two hours for them to navigate the narrow and shallow creeks until they came to an opening in the trees. Sunlight burst onto them, and they could see the big warning wall that marked the end of the runway at the airbase. Along the way, they held their breath as the boat had scraped the bottom twice, and they were afraid the screws would bog down in the mud, but each time the shrimp boat lurched forward. By then, Kathy had gently removed the bloody bandages, cleaned the wounds, and even put in a few stitches. Cassandra was going to feel like she had fallen into a dumpster full of broken glass.

There was still no way to know if the cuts were going to be the same as bites from the infected, but there was no doubt that the crabs caused nasty infections. Maybe it was because the same pincers that sliced through her skin had at some point in time been attached to the infected, or maybe it was because they were simply dirty. They would never know for sure, but they were ready for the fever when it hit. By the time they had coasted as far up the creek as they could go, it was raging.

Charlie pulled the Chief aside and said as nicely as he could, "The tide is as high as it's gonna get. When it drops we're not gonna be able to make it back to deep water in time."

"What you're saying is that we have to get you turned around and headed back out now."

Charlie didn't want to force the issue, but he nodded his head slightly. It was Sue who stepped in and made the final decision for them.

"She shouldn't be moved yet. A fever like that can take her heart or her brain at any moment if she's forced to move. Let's just raise the mosquito nets and light some citronella pots. It might be muggy and crowded, but you can give up one more day to keep from losing one of your people."

The Chief considered Cassandra to be one of the two people he wanted at his side in a fight, whether it was against the infected or a living adversary, but even more importantly, he thought of all of their group as family, and he would always weigh his decisions based on their welfare first.

"I'll go with your recommendation, Sue. I know you need to get back to safe water, and we need to get home, but Cassandra comes first. I have another idea, though. You guys get comfortable here. I'll take Hampton and Kathy with me while we still have some daylight left. After it gets dark, we won't be able to get close to the boat without winding up like Cassandra, so if we don't make it back in time, we'll find shelter somewhere. Our short-range radios should be able to keep us in touch."

Getting from the boat to the bank wasn't as easy as it used to be. Tall grass lined both sides of the creek, and the swaying of the grass wasn't just caused by the breeze that blew from the open area where the runway was. There were constant splashes around the boat from crabs falling into the water after failed attempts to climb aboard. After discussing the risks, they decided against setting fire to the grass because the infected were attracted to fire like moths to a flame. The best thing they could think of was to use the fire extinguishers again, but they hated the idea of leaving the boat without a way to put out fires. That could be a nightmare on a boat even if it was on a shallow creek.

Hampton finally came up with an idea that could be used to get them off the boat and even back on when they returned. The outriggers on the shrimp boat weren't as long as on the bigger trawlers, but they could be retracted or extended far enough to the sides of the boat to literally drop people past the tall grass. They had been retracted while the boat traveled under the trees, but out in the open, they could be extended to their full length and then be rotated to the best spot.

Since it was his idea, Hampton lobbied for the right to go first. With a backpack and a few weapons strapped across his back, he climbed the starboard side outrigger while it was retracted. Charlie gave instructions to the Chief and Tom, and they extended the long spire away from the boat. Hampton surveyed the ground below and signaled them to stop when he was over a clear spot. They lowered the outrigger as far as they could, and Hampton dropped out of sight. Colleen didn't like not being able to tell if he was okay, or if he had been immediately covered by hungry crabs, so she climbed the ladder to the top of the wheelhouse.

Hampton was busy stomping on a crab, but he raised his hand in a gesture to tell them the others should follow him. Colleen relayed the gesture, and Kathy skillfully climbed onto the almost level outrigger. With good balance and speed, she practically ran along the pole until she reached the end. She easily grabbed the end with both hands and swung like a gymnast to the ground.

The Chief grumbled, "That's going to be a hard act to follow," as he adjusted the weight of the gear on his back and climbed onto the outrigger.

His SEAL training had been a long time ago, but it turned out to be like riding a bicycle for him. They all had to wonder if the curve of the outrigger under his weight would be a problem, and Charlie must have guessed that was what they were thinking because he reassured the others as the Chief passed the halfway point.

"It'll hold. It can haul in a load of shrimp that weighs more than him, so it'll hold."

"That would be a lot of shrimp," said Iris.

A crackle on her hand-held radio let her know the Chief was calling in.

"We're on a clear spot that stays open all the way to the tarmac. We'll check in if we find what we're here for. We can already see we have company near the hangars, so don't call us unless you have to. You might give away our position. We'll keep you posted, over."

4

Redoubt

Fort Knox - 2016

Sergeant Finley used both hands to grip the edge of the vault door. When he pulled they could see by the muscles in his back that it was heavy. The hinges didn't make a sound in protest, but they were tight from the years of sitting in one place. The gap grew wider at the open side, but all they could see was darkness beyond the rim of the door.

The Colonel and Congressman Marks stayed well back from the door and waited, but the musty odor came out to meet them. No one expected the darkness beyond to hold an unspeakable monster or booby traps like the ones in a long-lost tomb, but each of them felt their own lack of preparation for the moment when the door opened. For Marks, it was a flashback of the facility in Nevada. One glass wall separated him from an invisible death. In the darkness, there was no glass wall that he could see, and it felt like the invisible death had followed him to Kentucky.

"Close it," said Colonel Morrison. "That's an order, Sergeant."

He probably didn't need to tell Finley it was an order because he was closing it as soon as the Colonel said to.

"Wait a minute," said Marks. "What if it locks again? We could be passing up on a chance to find out what's inside."

"The Sergeant can get it to open again. I should have been smarter," said the Colonel. "Part of me didn't think we would accomplish this much or I would have taken some precautions. We need to get portable lighting down here and send in a team of munitions experts first. We can go in after they clear it."

"They use white mice in labs, Colonel. Are we sending people in first because they're expendable?"

The Colonel visibly bristled at the remark, and Marks regretted saying it. It popped out because his nerves got the best of him.

The Colonel said, "White mice aren't trained experts, Congressman. The people we'll send in know their jobs."

Marks offered as much apology as the Colonel would accept, and even though there was never a question of authority, he added that he had no illusions about who was in charge. When he admitted that he had become apprehensive about the darkness inside the door, the Colonel realized the Congressman hadn't thought it through either.

"Apology accepted, Congressman. It won't take long to assemble a team, so let's get to work."

In less than an hour, everything was in place for the second opening of the door. This time the team that pulled the door open wore an array of lights and weapons. They didn't smell the musty air because they were completely enclosed by hazmat suits that appeared to be streamlined for combat. Colonel Morrison explained to Marks that they had been specially made for the defense of Fort Knox. If a biological or chemical attack was launched against them in an attempt to steal the gold, this unit was prepared to respond.

The powerful lights that illuminated the entry helped to calm their nerves. They couldn't see much from a safe distance, but there was nothing like a light switch to change a room from sinister to ordinary. One of the men came out almost immediately and approached the Colonel. He held up a smartphone for them to see, and they saw it was a picture of a wall-mounted floor plan. The extent of it was not what they expected.

The man's voice was distorted by his mask, but they could understand him well enough when he said the main power would be restored in a few minutes, and preliminary analysis of the air was that it was safe to breathe. There were no indications that the facility, whatever it was intended for, was hazardous. Even though there had been nothing to worry about, they were glad they had taken precautions.

A few minutes later, overhead lights inside the vault came on, and the entry team reported power was restored. One by one they filed out of the door and gave their report that they had inspected a couple of floors and found nothing that caused concern, but they joked about some of the "Best used by" dates on the boxes of food. One of them suggested they should get rid of everything except the Twinkies.

"Can we go in?" asked Marks.

The Colonel gestured with an open hand toward the door to let him know he could go first. The Colonel and Sergeant Finley followed. What they found was a sterile hallway that had a red arrow on the floor. The floor plan on the wall had a similar arrow marking the spot where they had entered. The legend on the side of the map was color-coded to indicate what was in specific rooms, and the list next to it was extensive.

One floor was labeled as an armory, and one was labeled as quarters. There were several kitchens, a laundromat, a hospital, and a theater. Sports and exercise centers were scattered throughout the facility, and their excitement about exploring the unknown was growing.

"I want to see the whole thing," said Marks, "but I have to admit, I don't know that I feel up to it. I think I've been having an adrenaline rush since Finley opened the door."

That was the first time Colonel Morrison noticed the dark patches under the Congressman's eyes. Maybe it was the change from the lights inside the Redoubt, but Marks didn't look well.

"It's going to take at least a day for the security teams to do more than a casual sweep of every floor," said Colonel Morrison. "I want to be sure they didn't miss anything. Why don't you go back to your quarters and get some rest?"

"That might be a good idea," said Marks, "but I think I'm just going to sit down here for a bit before going back. I need to savor the moment." He tried to laugh, but for some reason, the effort made him dizzy, and he felt bile rise in the back of his throat.

Colonel Morrison saw the way the Congressman's eyes rolled back in his head, and he knew he was going to faint. He reacted fast enough to keep him from falling and managed to get him over to a row of waiting-room-style chairs. Marks collapsed backward, and when his chin came up with his face pointed toward the ceiling, Morrison saw that he was wet with perspiration. If it was a fever, it had come on quickly.

"Stay here, Congressman. I'm getting you a medic."

The inspection team had already gone down to lower floors, and his instinct was to catch up with them and have them go for help, but the way Marks was starting to groan made him feel like it was far more serious than he thought at first, so he went on his own. Morrison glanced back as he went through the vault door and saw that Marks had rolled onto his side and vomited on the floor. He knew he had better hurry.

It felt like he was running in slow motion, but Morrison took the stairs two at a time until he reached the main floor. The Depository security guards saw him burst through the door to the basement stairwell and knew something was wrong. Their hands automatically went to the grips of their holstered weapons, but then they understood what he was shouting. One of them picked up a phone while the other ran to meet the Colonel, obviously thinking he was the one who needed medical treatment.

It didn't take long to sort out what was needed, but the nearest medical personnel were fifteen minutes away. The guard put the phone back in its cradle and told the Colonel they were on their way.

"Send them straight down when they get here."

Colonel Morrison was worried about the young Congressman, but in the back of his mind, he was also thinking about how he was going to explain this sudden turn of events. The visit by Marks had been unscheduled, and questions always arose about anything that didn't survive the smell test. It smelled like a bigger problem than what it appeared to be on the surface.

When he arrived back at the vault and went through the door, Morrison realized two things in one moment. The Congressman wasn't where he had left him, and his thoughts about the situation not smelling good were a little too close to home. There was a rancid odor in the waiting area that made him gag and cover his own mouth. The floor by the chairs where Marks had vomited was his first thought, but then he saw there was more further down the hallway, and there was no mistaking the blood for something the Congressman ate for breakfast.

The security officer who had called in for a medical team appeared behind him, and he visibly recoiled at the stench.

"Wow, what is that, Sir?"

"Congressman Marks is gone. I left him over there on that bench, and I was only gone long enough to come to see you. He couldn't have gotten by me because there's no other way out of here."

The guard pointed to the spot further down the hall where the second splash of vomit spread across the floor.

"He must've gone that way, Sir."

Colonel Morrison regarded the man with a stare that asked the question, "Do you really think so?"

A fork in the hallway was just past the mess on the floor, and Morrison gestured for the man to go ahead of him. As they reached the turn, they could see wet footprints that went down the left fork, so they followed the trail. A set of elevator doors were on one side of the hall, and a stairwell door was on the opposite wall. The buttons on the elevator doors were lit up and indicated they only went down, but nothing happened when Morrison pressed the button. They listened for the sounds of elevator motors and cables, but there was no indication the cars were rising to their floor. Above the doors, there were two rows of numbers that went from one to twenty-four. Both rows had the number six illuminated.

The guard asked, "Why does it only go down?"

For a second time, Colonel Morrison wondered about the deductive reasoning abilities of the guard. He spotted a handprint on the stairwell door and went in that direction without answering the man's question.

"He can't be moving too fast. Come with me. Maybe we can catch up with him before he hurts himself."

The door had a standard push bar on it, and Morrison hit it harder than necessary. As he burst through to the landing and went straight to the rail, somewhere below he heard footsteps. They stopped, so he did too. He listened for more sound, and he heard the unmistakable click of a door latch as it closed.

"Congressman Marks," he yelled.

No answer came back from below. His stomach felt like it had a knot in it because there was going to be no way to tell which door it had been that Congressman Marks went through. The way sound carried in the stairwell, it could have been the floor below his or any of them in between. He assumed it was Marks, but it occurred to him he may have heard the inspection team in transition to another floor.

"This is bad," he said over his shoulder to the guard. "How many people are on duty upstairs?"

"At least twenty-five guards per quadrant, so that's over a hundred, Sir."

"Go back to the main desk. Tell them I said to lock down the facility to everyone except the medical team. Then have the quadrants send at least ten people each. I want you to personally organize each group into search teams. Order each team to take a different floor so we have four floors being searched at a time. Tell the medical team to find me. I'm going to guess that Marks made it to the fifth floor, so I'll start there."

"What's wrong with the Congressman, Sir?"

"I don't have a clue, but this is really an emergency, so get going."

The guard left in a hurry, and Colonel Morrison hurried down to the fifth floor. On the way, his eyes scanned the railings and the floor in the hope that he would see a clue about where Marks might have gone. He checked each door handle as he went by, feeling like he might miss something, but at the same time thinking he had guessed right to go down to the fifth floor.

He chose the fifth floor for three reasons. First, his gut told him that the sounds he had heard came from that far away. Second, he would rather pass him than waste time searching floors above him, and third, he could count on the search teams to find him if he was wrong. What he didn't count on was what he found when he went through the door to the fifth floor.

The map on the wall opposite the door was more than what he expected. If each of the floors was like this one, they would need more than ten people per search team. The corridor where he stood went to his left and right. In each direction, the corridor ended at a central hub. The map showed there were five wings sticking out from each hub like the spokes on a wheel. The place was immense, and it could take days to search every room.

Morrison chose to go left for no particular reason other than the fact that he felt like it was urgent to find Marks as soon as possible, and he had to make a guess quickly. He hoped he guessed right about sending the medical team to the fifth floor, and he wished he had thought to bring a radio with him. He remembered his cell phone and pulled it out...no signal.

The lights were on everywhere, and he reached the central hub in less than three minutes. He was surprised again by the size of the room. It resembled the food court of a mall. Small restaurants surrounded the entire room, and tables were spread out in between. At regular intervals, the wings were spaced between the restaurants and disappeared in the distance. Nothing was out of place until he noticed one chair was on its side near the entrance of a wing. He would have felt better if he had heard a sound, but it was so quiet he could hear his own breathing. The chair was the only thing different, so it was a better place to start than at a random wing. If it turned out to be wrong, at least he would know where he started.

If he thought it was quiet in the food court, that had been nothing compared to the silence in the wing. The unexpected discovery was that each of the rooms stood open, and none of them had their lights on. He didn't relish the idea of going into them and searching for the light switches.

He stood in the doorway of the first room and let his eyes adjust to the gloom. Everything was just vague shapes, but nothing appeared to move. Of course, his imagination found everything that gave even the slightest appearance of being a man standing upright, and if he stared at things long enough, he wasn't so sure that they weren't getting closer.

Panic hit him like a fist, and despite his military training, he shakily searched the dark wall with his right hand. If the light switch was on the other side of the door, he felt like he would be too late. It was where it was supposed to be, and he pushed the switch upward.

The overhead lights flickered but turned on, and he was bathed in bright light. The shapes he had seen as people were so far from realistic that he was amazed by how his mind had stretched the truth. It was a supply room of some kind, and he imagined if he had time to open any of the crates, he would find the food that was served in the closest fast food restaurant. He didn't know how many people were supposed to live in this redoubt or for how long, but he hadn't expected a room bigger than the food court. Shelves ran in row after row as far as he could see, and each was stacked with crates. The black stenciling was typical military style with US Army on top, but beneath the top line, it was clear that the contents were prepackaged supplies that were intended to last for years.

Colonel Morrison realized he had become so fascinated by the quantities of supplies that he had stopped searching for the Congressman. He thought to himself that the contents of the redoubt could be cataloged and updated now that they had access to it, but the first order of business had to be the well-being of Congressman Marks. He wanted badly to go down each row of shelves to see what else was there, but he chose to just pass the ends of the rows one at a time. Each row was so long that he couldn't guess the distance, but they were well-lit, and the only way he could miss someone would be if they were around the corner at the very end.

He left the light on as he went from the first room to the one across the hall, and he found the light switch was less difficult to locate now that he knew where the other one had been. He had his face turned toward the switch when he pushed it up, so he only saw the movement out of the corner of his left eye. When his head snapped up, it was too late. Morrison's fight-or-flight instincts didn't even have a chance to choose one or the other, so he froze. Congressman Marks fell on him so completely that Morrison felt like the man was embracing him in a hug. Then came the searing pain.

Marks had his arms wrapped around Morrison's head so far that his face was almost to the back of his neck, and his mouth was stretched open so wide that his teeth pierced both of the big neck muscles at the same time. Morrison felt like he was watching it happen to someone else…a classic sign that he was already going into shock from the pain. Marks was pulling his head backward in an attempt to remove the flesh, but his teeth had reached the cervical bones, and pulling simply caused Morrison's body to buck reflexively.

When they fell together to the floor, Marks still had his teeth embedded in Morrison's neck. Morrison was face down, but the last thing he saw before he died was the procession of slow-walking people going by. Some were wearing bloody Hazmat suits. He didn't recognize Sergeant Finley, and it wouldn't have mattered if he did. A few minutes later he would follow behind them.

******

The search teams spread out through the first four floors, and the six-person medical team went straight to the fifth floor, just as Colonel Morrison had instructed. While the search teams marveled at the endless rooms filled with doomsday supplies, the medical team saw wounded soldiers who needed help. Their arrival on the fifth floor caused chaos in the food court, and the infected dead collided with each other and fell to the tile floor. It was no wonder that the medical team ran straight toward them, unwrapping bandage packs even as they ran. No one was there to save them when they screamed for help.

By the time the search team from the third floor finished their search, there were fourteen of the infected dead on the fifth floor. Team Three exited into the stairwell expecting to find the other search teams already going to another floor, but it would have been against orders for them to do anything except go to their next assigned floor. They were all told to skip the fifth floor because Colonel Morrison and the medical team would be there ahead of them, and if they had already located the Congressman or if that floor had been empty, they would come out and go down another floor even if a search team had gotten there first.

The guard who Morrison had personally assigned the responsibility of organizing the search felt proud of the way he had recruited teams and assigned floors. Team One was on the first floor at the start, so they were told to go to the sixth floor next. Team Two was on the second floor, so they were assigned to move to the seventh floor. Team Three had finished the third floor already, so they counted off doors as they went all the way to the eighth floor. Team Four would go to the ninth floor when they got done with the fourth floor, but they were way behind schedule because they were too caught up in the supplies they had found. It was packed full of Vietnam-era weapons.

All of the other teams were well into the searches of their second assigned floors when team four finally broke free of the armory. Some of them had even taken advantage of the immense inventory of weapons and slipped handguns into their belts. They didn't think anyone would miss a few.

Their boots were echoing loudly on the stairs as they descended to the ninth floor, and the sound drew the attention of the infected dead as they went by. The last three people in Team Four heard someone pounding on the stairwell door of the fifth floor and called to the others. Before anyone could reverse direction and come back up the stairs, one of them opened the door. A wounded man fell into his arms, followed by several more. Amid the screams of pain were orders shouted by the team leader, but gradually they were all screams of pain as every team member fell under the teeth of their attackers or slipped in the blood that was sprayed over every inch of the landing outside the door.

When it was over, there were no more screams. The only sounds were the unreal noises made as the infected fed on the warm flesh of the victims that still moved. When they stopped moving and the flesh cooled, the infected lost interest and crowded against each other. It was inevitable that they would push each other until they tumbled down the steps, and the steady progression to the next floor began. The landing outside the door of the sixth floor was already crowded with the infected when Team One burst through on their way to another floor. Over two dozen bloodied and mangled bodies fought with each other to reach the new arrivals.

It was a natural reaction for living people to put their hands out in defense, but to the infected dead, it was like offering them food. They reacted to the exposed "finger food" predictably, and new screams were added to the chaos in the open doorway. The melee spilled over into the exposed entry of the sixth floor, and a few soldiers in the back fired shots over the heads of their friends in front. Because they aimed high, the attackers were shot in the face at point-blank range, and they fell away quickly. Wounded soldiers were pulled backward by friends, and at least six of the members of Team One escaped behind a closed door. Three of the six frantically squeezed at the painful stubs that used to be their hands, the memory of seeing their fingers bitten off still fresh in their minds. They continued to scream as their buddies did everything they could to give them first aid and hold them down. They shouted encouragement, and yelled, "Look at me! Stay with me!"

Outside the door, two of their friends were still alive and buried under a tangle of bodies. They had gone down under the press of attackers but hadn't been bitten because of the headshots fired from behind them. They made eye contact long enough for one of them to say, "Play dead! Don't move no matter what!" They both shut their eyes to narrow slits and used every ounce of willpower to stay still as two of their friends were eaten on top of them.

The gunshots had echoed down the stairwell and were heard by the remaining teams. Teams Two and Three burst through their doors in a frantic search for the source of the gunfire, and this time their extended hands were all gripping semiautomatic handguns. The bloody battle they found in progress on the landing above theirs was coming to a rapid conclusion, and the only thing they knew for sure was that bloodied mouths turned toward them and then moved in their direction. They shot at anything that moved, but because they were trained to pull the trigger twice and aim center mass, they only succeeded at punching back the infected. They were shocked to see their targets get back to their feet, and they almost reflexively shot again at center mass. Bullets ripped holes in chests, but the infected didn't stay down.

When the first volley was fired, the two members of Team One who were playing dead pushed bodies from on top of themselves and tried to reach their rescuers. Both were punched backward by two bullets along with the infected. Ironically, it only served to confuse the team that was shooting because they saw the two men go down and stay down, while others got right back up. If Teams Two and Three had stayed alive long enough, they would have seen the two men convulse on the floor and then stand up to join the others attacking them, but the attackers didn't just charge toward them. They fell forward without feeling the pain of the bullets that only served only to slow their progress. The last two teams were overwhelmed by the weight of bloodied bodies and snapping teeth until none remained alive.

The only uninjured survivors were the three men who had dragged their fingerless comrades back into the sixth floor. They knew they had to get them out of there for medical help, and the stairs were not an option. When they searched their floor, they found the elevator doors were open, and someone had pressed the red POWER button inside each of them. The only logical thing to do was get their friends to the elevators and unlock them. Once they were all inside one car, one of the uninjured men pressed the green RESUME POWER button, and then pressed the button labeled LOBBY. The car noisily rose to the top level inside the vault, and the three men drew on every bit of their remaining strength to get their friends to the safety of the Depository's main floor.

When they arrived at the corridor down the hall from the main security desk, there was no easy explanation they could give for the carnage below their feet. Everyone talked at once while an officer attempted to restore order. Medical kits were retrieved from lockers, and the hurriedly applied bandages were replaced. The men and women who gave first aid to the three pale and listless men were appalled by the injuries. Three men who had gone to the newly opened vault in the basement with thirty fingers and thumbs had returned with only six of them intact.

The officer in charge managed to shout his question over the confusion, but he didn't comprehend the answer.

"What happened? Did their hands get caught in some kind of machinery?"

"They were bitten by people from the other teams, Sir. We don't know what happened to them, but they were like mad dogs... attacking with their teeth. They pulled four of our team through the door before we could shut it."

The officer knew that over fifty people were down there, but since he had not been invited to go along, he had no idea of the layout. When the survivors told him they pulled four men out before they could shut the door, he didn't even have a clue about what door. The only thing he could logically do was assemble a rescue party and send the three injured men to the hospital.

Within minutes the three men were on stretchers and being transported to the base hospital. Within another fifteen minutes, the officer was leading a team of twenty men down the stairs to the vault. When they reached the room outside the big door, there were several more injured soldiers, but they were missing more than a few fingers. As a matter of fact, they shouldn't have been standing. With everyone entering the small room so quickly, it was too crowded to avoid their teeth, and in the melee that followed, the press of bodies forced the vault door shut. No one heard it lock, but lacking a way to know for sure, they just hoped it did.

A few of the soldiers tried to go back the way they had come. The officer in charge had his sidearm out, and he pulled the trigger out of reflex when teeth pierced his arm. The remaining soldiers took that as permission to fire, and the result was a close-quarters massacre.

******

Less than three hours later, the base hospital was being evacuated along with over a dozen bite victims, and nine injured soldiers who had gone back to the basement were receiving medical care near the main door of the Depository. By the end of the day when the sun set on the Gold Depository at Fort Knox, only a handful of living people of the nearly four hundred who had been inside the building that morning were hiding under desks or in closets. Most were wandering from room to room searching for people to bite...people they had worked with for years. Some were barricaded in restrooms with no windows and had no way of communicating with the outside. Cell phones were prohibited for most of them by Depository policy, and were not allowed to even be brought into the building even if they were turned off, so they couldn't call for help. They also had no way of knowing that help wouldn't be coming because things were almost as bad outside. Things would soon be worse outside.

******

Just over sixteen hundred miles from Fort Knox, Kentucky at the secret biological research hangar in Nevada, Captain Wayne wondered if he had caught the flu or something from Congressman Marks. He had gone home after the Congressman left, showered, and put on fresh clothes before making the one-hundred-mile drive to Las Vegas. He felt like celebrating the possibility of transfer from the god-forsaken isolated base. Even though he felt a bit nauseated he wanted to have some fun.

Wayne checked into a casino hotel and dropped his belongings off at the room, then he went to the main floor. When his cell phone received the call to tell him that a contagious disease had escaped from the room in the hangar that he had shown the Congressman, he didn't answer because he had left it on his bed in his room.

When it became apparent to the guests around him at the casino that he was either ill or had too much to drink, security had been summoned to speak with him. They had dealt with plenty of customers like him, but none could recall ever needing stitches because a customer had bitten their hands. They carried him outside and unceremoniously tossed him onto the sidewalk where they expected him to stay while they waited for the police.

He didn't feel like staying and managed to disappear into the crowd of tourists. The two security guards filed a police report and provided a description of Wayne, but they didn't know yet that he was a guest of the casino hotel. More important to them was the fact that the bite wounds on their hands hurt badly and were oozing blood despite continually rewrapping them with new bandages. The officer volunteered to give them a ride to the hospital, but their supervisor said they could leave at the end of their shift. A few minutes later they didn't care what their supervisor said because neither of them felt well enough to even stand up. They caught up with the police officer before he had time to finish writing his report and told him they needed to go to the Emergency Room fast.

5

Marine Airbase

Beaufort, South Carolina - 2023

It was never easy for Iris to get settled in when her husband went off on one of his adventures. Deep down inside she knew that he was always going to be the one to go, but if she made a list of what could go wrong and what could go right, one column was always longer than the other. In the "positive" column there was finding an Osprey or helicopter that could still fly. She knew the Chief wanted an Osprey because they could fly faster, and farther, carry twenty-four people, and they were armed. They needed those things to be able to have a chance against the AC-130. They would be outgunned, but because the Osprey could takeoff and land vertically, they could use it more strategically than Sparks could use the fixed-wing plane. It would also help them to find and rescue other survivors.

Iris checked on Cassandra in the small cabin below the wheelhouse and found her still feverish, but at least her temperature hadn't gotten higher. She gently changed some of the bandages on the more serious wounds and was relieved to see there were no red streaks running away from the punctures. She remembered when a crab had grabbed her by her thumb once when she had gotten careless. The sharp pincers had gone through her thumbnail on top and the flesh on the bottom and had only stopped when it had reached the solid bone. She didn't have a frame of reference for another injury that hurt worse because so far she couldn't think of anything that compared. Getting shot or stabbed probably hurt worse, but she couldn't imagine the pain Cassandra would be feeling if she was awake and not feverish.

After she finished administering to Cassandra, Iris found Charlie and Sue aft by the hatch that went down into the engines. Sue was mostly just keeping him company, but she was also in charge of handing him the right tools. Charlie said he worked on the engine whenever he could because they needed it more than anything else. Today was just an inspection and testing of some components to keep them occupied. They didn't need to forage for drinking water or food because the skipper of the Ambush had been so generous, and with the modifications to the trawler that kept the crabs from being a constant nuisance, they didn't need to waste time knocking the crabs from the wires. They also didn't need to dodge the occasional creatures that had managed to get past the old wires into the boat. That was particularly a nuisance at night, but it was nice not to spend so much time keeping one eye on their surroundings.

Iris sat down cross-legged in front of the old couple. She thought Charlie would fit right in on the cast of an old Western television show. She could see him pulling a stubborn pack mule by the harness and complaining every step of the way, but it was good-natured complaining. Sue would also fit into the same cast, but she would be wearing an apron and flitting around a hot kitchen. If she was complaining it was because she was juggling supper and the children. What Iris couldn't see them cast in would be a zombie apocalypse movie. They might be able to cope with primitive needs, but this new world didn't allow for mistakes. She realized she had never gotten around to talking with them about how they had survived even though she knew they had talked about it with the Chief and some of the others.

"I'm sorry I haven't gotten to know you better," she said. "I think we've all had our minds on what comes next."

"If Charlie did half the things your husband does, I wouldn't have time to do anything but worry," said Sue. "Maybe we could spend a little time together while we wait for him to get back. It might help you keep your mind off whatever he's doing."

"I was hoping you would say that," said Iris. "I'm really curious about how you two have managed by yourselves so long?"

There was a noticeable pause and Sue seemed to be concerned for Charlie. One woman to another, Iris read the way Sue's eyes moved to

Charlie as she held her breath. There was history they avoided talking about.

"I'm sorry, I didn't mean to pry," said Iris, hoping they would just forgive her for dredging up a bad memory, but they stopped her before she could gracefully escape.

"It's not your fault," said Sue. "I've been trying to get Charlie to accept that there's nothing he could have done about it, and being around you people has helped him realize I'm right. I mean, your group has been through so much that we should consider ourselves lucky."

"We didn't know how to survive at first," said Charlie. He didn't even look up from the engine when he spoke. His mind was focused on a memory somewhere in the past. "We got this boat as a hobby we could enjoy with our grandkids. Our son-in-law wanted us to get a pontoon boat or some kind of family boat we could use on lakes, and the children would have been with us when this all started if we hadn't gotten into a fight about it."

Sue said, "Charlie was going to take the children out to the Gulf Stream and let them watch the dolphins run at the bow. Our son-in-law said it was too dangerous and wouldn't let them go. They got into an argument over the phone, so we went out by ourselves. Charlie tried to have a good time, but it wasn't the same. We were about twenty miles from shore on our way back when we saw other boats. People were shooting at each other, and not just at other boats. We saw people getting shot in the head and then dumped overboard."

"I should have made him listen," said Charlie. "They would be alive today."

Talking about it somehow made Charlie seem even older and smaller. His shoulders slumped like he didn't have bones to hold them upright.

"You never spoke with them again?" asked Iris.

Charlie lifted his head, and Iris saw the red-rimmed eyes that had puddles of tears ready to spill over the lids.

"It would've been better if we hadn't," he said.

Sue interrupted because she knew how Charlie would get talking about it. It would reopen the wounds.

"There's a dock for trawlers at a marina a few miles from here. We had to take a chance and try to find them, so we went there. Louise was our only daughter, and we couldn't just abandon them. It took three days before we were able to get near the marina, but when we did, they were there waiting for us. They saw us coming, and we waved at each other. It was our daughter and our two granddaughters. Then Larry came up behind them, and there was something wrong with him. He…". Sue couldn't finish the sentence, but Charlie said all that was necessary.

"I know now why he did it, but I'll still never be able to forgive him. If he had let them go with us that day and just stayed at home by himself, our daughter and the kids would be alive."

"How terrible," said Iris. She had seen her share of death, but there was nothing she could think of that compared.

Sue reached over and rubbed Charlie's shoulder, and he reached up and put his hand over hers. He was finally able to go on and gave Iris a weak smile.

"We learned so much about staying alive in those few minutes. There's not a moment that goes by that I don't think about keeping my wife safe, and I owe it to what we saw that day."

Sue said, "Charlie was a different man from that moment on. I don't think he spoke more than ten words over the next week, but before the Internet went down he was downloading and reading everything he could about survival. I'll bet he could build a boat if he had to, and he'd find a way to make clothes or grow food on the boat if we run out of supplies."

"You stayed near here the whole time?" asked Iris.

Sue answered, "We talked about moving up or down the coast a few times, but I guess you could say we got lucky too often staying right here."

Charlie huffed at her comment, "Lucky? God has a plan for you," he said to his wife, "or he wouldn't keep dumping things in our laps."

They both shared a private laugh, and Iris saw the tears had turned to a fond twinkle in their eyes.

"Like what?" she asked.

"Like the barge," said Charlie. He was clearly past the painful moments in the beginning and was much more animated. "We came across a barge that was just drifting south along with the Gulf Stream. We had good, calm weather, and we were able to tie up with it. It had fuel, food, and even weapons on it. We don't have a clue where it came from, but we stayed with it until we saw bad weather on the horizon. It probably sank after we got done taking as much stuff from it as we could."

"Then there was the distress call we got from another boat," said

Sue. "We knew there were plenty of pirates along the coast. They would call out for help and then steal from the people who would come to help them. There was something different about this one, though, and we decided to see if we could get close without getting caught. It seemed safe, so we took a chance. It turned out to be a larger boat than ours, but no one on the boat knew how to fix an engine. Charlie was all they needed, and in return, they gave us things we needed."

Charlie said, "It seems like every time we need something, someone comes along just when we need it most and takes care of us. Like you guys showing up in a submarine. People working together because they want to and not because they have to."

"What about that time we got a warning over the radio to stay at sea?" asked Sue.

"Oh, I had forgotten about that," said Charlie. "We knew we had to find places where we could just come inland like when a storm would be bigger than we wanted to weather, so we were about to do that when we got a radio warning from someone we didn't know. They said something had happened to the spider population, and small boats were practically getting swallowed by webs if they got too close to trees along the coast. We listened to the warning, and it was a good thing we did."

Sue finished for him, "We saw a boat the same size as ours, and it looked like a big cocoon. It was wrapped in spider webs so well that we didn't know it was a boat at first. We only got close enough to use binoculars, but we could see people hanging in the webs along with birds and small animals. We were lucky we had enough supplies to stay at sea that time."

"Luck had nothing to do with it," said Charlie. "I'm married to someone who has a guardian angel."

Sue added, "My guardian angel is on loan to the Chief, Hampton, and Kathy at the moment, so you better take care of us all for a bit, old man."

Iris took that as her cue to leave the old couple in peace.

"I need to go check on Sim," she said. "He's really worried about Cassandra."

******

There was no doubt that there were plenty of Ospreys to choose from, but it wasn't going to be as simple as picking one and getting it ready to fly. The trio was in the tall grass that lined the runway and even managed to grow up through cracks in the asphalt. A row of Ospreys sat in a neat line, wing to wing, a few hundred yards away, but between them and the planes were hundreds of infected dead.

"How can there be so many of them after so much time?" asked Kathy. "Some of them hardly have any wounds."

"You know what that means," said the Chief.

Hampton stated the obvious for them all, "They were survivors who made it this long and just ran out of time."

"It's not fair," said Kathy. "If we had gotten here a few days ago, maybe we would be joining up with them right now instead of watching them stumble around out there."

"Got any ideas?" asked Hampton.

The Chief said, "If we go for the planes, we might get to one of them, but then we'll be trapped inside it just like everyone else we've seen at airports. If we go for the buildings, we've got to hope there are none inside and that the building can be secured."

Hampton said, "I was wondering if we could draw them away by setting the grass on fire, but it would have to be close enough to get their attention but far enough away that we wouldn't have to worry about the fire spreading all the way to the planes."

"Too much can go wrong," said Kathy. "Whoever sets the fire might get spotted by the infected and won't be able to get back."

"We need a vehicle," said the Chief.

Hampton scanned the entire area with his binoculars, and it was obvious that there was no shortage of vehicles.

"Unless I miss my guess, those are vehicles," he said. He had picked up the habit of stating the obvious while also delivering a touch of humor. The Chief had rubbed off on him, and no matter how hard he tried, he couldn't stop himself. It usually set him up to be the Chief's straight-man.

"You've learned a lot in the last few years," said the Chief.

Kathy rolled her eyes. "Don't even expect me to say anything just so you two can add me to the list of people you've set up for your warped sense of humor."

The Chief had his binoculars to his eyes, but he was grinning from ear to ear. Hampton noticed he was studying something near the buildings and not near the planes or the wide variety of small and large vehicles. He could practically hear the Chief saying he had a plan before he said it.

"What does every military base have no matter what branch it is?" asked the Chief.

"I always like the food," said Hampton. "I don't know why people complain about the food. I love it."

"Weapons?" asked Kathy. "We can always use more if that's what you mean, but right now we have what we need."

"A motor pool," said the Chief. "All of those vehicles had to be serviced in-house. The military didn't send their vehicles to Jiffy Lube for a thirty-two-point check or Goodyear for new tires. See the buildings with garage doors? One of them is a motor pool."

"Not to be negative," said Kathy, "but if there's a vehicle in there, it was most likely in need of service."

"I'm counting on it," said the Chief. "If there's something in there that was just getting an oil change when everything went south, it might still be up on a lift. If it's on a lift, there hasn't been any weight sitting on the tires, so they might need air, but they won't be in bad shape. It'll probably have a dead battery, but we'll cross that bridge when we come to it."

Hampton asked, "Why don't we check? If that's all we need, we can grab a few batteries and take them back to the boat. We can charge them up and bring them back."

"We can go one better," said the Chief. "Let's see if we can get one of those portable generators back to the boat. We can charge batteries, and we can also use it to jump-start a plane."

Moving through the tall grass as far from the main part of the base as possible, they circled until they were closer to the buildings. The planes were no longer visible to them, but at least that was where most of the infected were. Now all they had to do was get inside the motor pool without attracting attention.

The Chief knew there were always places that were almost neglected on military bases. If anyone went to those places, it was either out of curiosity or because they were lost. The oldest building was where the Chief wanted to go first. If it was one of those rarely used spaces, at least it wouldn't be occupied, and it was only a short distance from the building with the garage doors. One thing that he felt supported his suspicions about the old building was that the grass was tall right up to the door.

All three of them made it to the building without being seen, and they lined up against the wall by the door. When everyone nodded that they were ready, the Chief gently rapped on the door near the ground. He hoped the tall grass would keep the sound from carrying to the infected that wandered around by the main buildings.

They listened for any indication that the knock would be answered, but after a minute of silence, the Chief rapped again. This time he waited only half as long because a moan came from somewhere nearby, and it wasn't where the other infected were. It came from the grass where they had crawled only minutes before. The Chief turned the handle on the door and it protested with a rusty creak. The moan was louder this time, so there was no choice. They all went through the door into darkness, ready to face whatever was there.

Once the door closed behind them the darkness was so complete that they kept low to the floor with their shoulders pressed together.

"Knives," whispered the Chief.

Not knowing if they even had room to move, they all made the same choice and laid their rifles on the unseen ground in front of them. Elbows collided as they all reached for knives that were sheathed on their legs.

"Lights coming on," he said next, but it was only so they would know he was about to light a chem-stick.

They heard the click as he snapped it and tossed it across the floor. Blue light bathed the room, and they saw they were inside a storage area that was very small. At most, it was twelve by twelve feet along each wall, and it had crates stacked along the walls on the left and right sides. A small window was in the wall opposite the door, but thankfully it wasn't too small for them to fit through if they needed an escape route. Judging by the moaning they could hear coming from the other side of the door, they would have to take advantage of it. Something bumped against the door behind them, and mere seconds later there were several bumps. They didn't need a window on the door to know that more infected were joining the first one.

Kathy moved to the window and scraped at the glass. There was a thick layer of dirt on both sides of it, but she was able to see well enough to tell that the ruckus being caused by the infected at the door was helping to draw the rest away from the motor pool.

"How many infected were between the planes and the motor pool?" she asked.

"At least fifty," said the Chief.

Hampton pulled out a small flashlight and was examining the hinges of the door. He moved the beam from the door to the seams of the sheet metal walls.

"I hate to be the bearer of bad news, but this place won't last long when fifty of them start pounding on it."

"You don't think the door will hold up?" asked Kathy.

Hampton answered more emphatically, "I wasn't talking about the door. The whole storehouse will collapse."

"Nothing useful in here," said Kathy. She had moved from the window to the stacks of crates. "I think this was just a paint locker."

The Chief agreed, "The military stored paint, hydraulic oil, and a few other chemicals away from heat and power sources to prevent fires. So, we're not staying, but we have to time it right when we go. I have an idea that might work better than anything else given how few choices we have. Let's get that window ready to open as soon as possible. We can't break it out, or the noise might draw some away from the front. As soon as it seems like most of them are around by the door, go through the window and head for the motor pool. When we get inside, find me a bottle, a rag, and some gas."

"What are we going to blow up?" asked Kathy.

"This storehouse should burn for a long time without exploding. I'll get back here and toss it through the window. Notice how dry it feels in here? One Molotov cocktail should be enough to get it to start burning. After that, it should act like a bug zapper."

Hampton added, "And while it burns, we can try to get a vehicle running."

"Exactly. Let's do this."

The metal around the window protested as Kathy pried at one side and the Chief slid the edge of his knife into the gap on the right side. They hadn't made much progress when Hampton held up a familiar can with a long spout on it.

"Lubricating oil," he said. "If we don't get that window open soon, we aren't going to need it."

Judging by the pounding against the door and the walls on one side, the majority of the infected dead had arrived. Above the sound of the dull thumping, there was another sound, and as many times as they had heard it, it wasn't a sound they could get used to. It was the frenzied moaning the infected did when they had a victim cornered. If you could say the infected dead were capable of getting excited, then this would be the way they showed it. They didn't just moan and groan. They groaned faster, louder, and higher when they were closing in for the kill.

Hampton poured oil across the top of the window sill so the oil ran down the gaps on both sides. When the last of the rust broke loose, the window slid upward with hardly a sound, and Kathy didn't waste any time diving through it head first. She moved quickly to the side so Hampton wouldn't have to worry about landing on her, and Hampton did the same thing. When the Chief landed between them, they knew things hadn't gone as they had hoped.

To their left was a wide alley between the paint locker and the main building, and for the moment, it was clear. They couldn't say the same thing about the open area to their right. In the past, it had been the parking lot between the motor pool building and the hangars where the Ospreys were given routine maintenance. Now, it had more of a resemblance to the hordes they had seen on the interstate highways.

"Where'd they all come from?" asked the Chief.

It wasn't that he really needed an answer, but there were far more of them than they had seen when they were watching from the grass.

"I think I know," said Hampton. "Unless I miss my guess, that guy running the other way just let them out of the hangars."

They all saw the man in the green shirt because he was the only one going in the other direction. Previously closed hangar doors were now wide open, and the infected were moving toward the trio that had just dropped out of the window. They most likely had already been going toward the sounds made by the throng that was beating on the aluminum building, but the appearance of Kathy, Hampton, and the Chief was much more tempting than the noise. The crowd of infected veered their way, and for a second time, they heard that excited groan.

They had no choice but to go left, but that meant moving away from the planes and going behind the motor pool. There were no guarantees there would be a back door. If there was one, there was no guarantee that the motor pool was any less populated than the hangars had been.

They didn't need to say anything to each other as they pulled their blades out again. This time, though, they drew machetes from the straps across their backs. The building they had just come from was on their left, and it wasn't even half as long as the big motor pool on their right, so they found themselves in the open again much sooner than they would have liked.

Kathy was the first one to swing, but the others were only a split second behind her. Hampton had been right about the paint locker getting pushed over. The small storage building fell under the weight of the infected pushing against it just as the three survivors were out from behind it. The infected fell forward with it, and if it had been burning their plan would have worked well. The collapse and the surge from the infected pushing the others caused several to fall toward Kathy. Her machete went straight from one to another while the Chief and Hampton took care of a pair. Even before the infected hit the ground, Kathy changed directions and ran from the fight, knowing there were far too many for them to clear a path.

The Chief and Hampton were right behind her. Kathy had her machete raised before she even went around the corner of the big motor pool, and it began its downward arc with a ferocious swing. From their angle, the Chief and Hampton couldn't see what she was fighting, but they could see that she did everything she could to stop her swing in time.

The infected didn't put their hands in the air to shield themselves from attack, and they also didn't yell. The man in the green shirt did both.

"Whoa! Hey, I'm sorry!" he yelled from behind his arms. "I didn't mean to let them out!"

The Chief caught just enough of what the man yelled to understand why they were in a bad predicament, but there wasn't time to learn more. They were totally flanked on the left and from behind, and if they didn't keep moving, they would be cornered in seconds. The Chief reached out with a big hand and grabbed him by the back of his collar and dragged him along with them.

The man was much shorter than the Chief had thought when he saw him running away from the hangars. He was also younger, and he realized he was dragging a boy who couldn't have been older than fourteen. He released his grip but herded the boy in front of him, making him run along the backside of the building shielded by Kathy on his left.

The boy must have understood his options had narrowed because he pointed up ahead and yelled again.

"That door is unlocked, and it holds better than that shed."

Kathy sprinted ahead and pulled the door open. There wasn't time to sweep the whole building, so she switched to her Smith & Wesson as she went inside. The Chief and the kid pushed in behind her, and it wasn't until that moment that he realized Hampton wasn't with them. One quick glance back the way they had come was all he needed to see that Hampton was trying to buy them some time.

He was about thirty yards away, and the Chief saw he was about to be surrounded if he didn't move soon. The problem was that there was only a narrow corridor that had opened through the swarm of infected that surged toward him, and it was away from the motor pool. The Chief pushed the kid toward Kathy and turned back to the horde to try to create another path for Hampton. He pulled his own fifteen-round Smith & Wesson and took careful aim.

It seemed like the Chief never missed a shot, and before releasing the magazine and sliding in a second one, there was a pile of bodies between him and Hampton...but it didn't help. Hampton knew he had to take that one escape route while he could.

Hampton yelled over the heads of the infected for the Chief to get inside, and he would meet up with them when he could. He sprinted past outstretched arms and used his machete only to clear away what he had to before disappearing into the tall grass. If the Chief was right, Hampton was headed for the main part of the Marine base. He knew Hampton could take care of himself, but judging by the number of infected still in the immediate area, he was worried about his friend. There wasn't anything he could do about it yet, so he ducked back inside with Kathy. He glared at the kid.

The kid reminded him of the boys they had rescued from the Coast Guard Station years ago. It seemed like forever ago, and that made the Chief wonder how the boy had survived. He couldn't have been more than seven years old before the infection outbreak.

"Where's Hampton?" asked Kathy. The fear in her voice made it shake.

"He's okay for now. He made it to the tall grass between here and the main base. He was buying us time and got cut off. At least he knows where we are, and he can concentrate on getting back to us knowing we're fine until he gets here."

"I can get to him."

The Chief shook his head. "No, you can't, and he wouldn't want you to try."

The Chief focused his attention on the kid again, and the boy took a step to his right to keep Kathy between himself and the Chief.

"I'm not going to hurt you. What did you mean back there when you said you didn't let the infected out on purpose?"

Kathy gently ushered the boy around in front of her, and he bent his head back to be able to make eye contact with the Chief.

The boy answered in a low voice, "They got out of the cage somehow."

It was hard for the Chief and Kathy to hide their surprise, but they managed not to show it. They kept straight faces and waited as if they expected him to say more.

"The hangar is divided into sections with steel cages separating them. I've been trapping them inside, and then I get them all into one section. When I have a section empty, I lead new ones in there. It's been working great but getting kind of crowded. Something caused the hangar doors to open, but I don't know what."

"You sure you didn't open them?" asked the Chief. He made sure it sounded accusatory so he could judge the reaction. The kid's defensive expression gave him what he needed to know.

"You're the first outside people I've seen alive in a long time, mister. Why would I do anything to you? I'm happy to see real people. Is the other guy gonna be okay?"

The Chief studied the kid and his bushy black hair, and for a second time, he wondered how the kid had survived so long without adults to teach him how to stay alive. He was handsome and was practicing good hygiene, unlike most survivors. Short and lean, his shirt and pants appeared to have been laundered recently.

"He's probably somewhere safe by now, and there's a strong chance he's thinned the crowd for us."

******

Hampton couldn't remember the last time he had to run so far to get away from the infected that were pursuing him. He didn't really consider it pursuit because they were so slow, but to get away from one, he had to run past another. That one would join in on the chase, and it wasn't long before he would pass another. Hampton knew that when he found a place to hole up, it wasn't going to be a secret to the infected.

An overgrown street in front of some barracks gave him the opportunity to slow his entourage of followers even more. There was a fuel truck parked on four flat tires in the middle of the street, and he stopped next to it long enough for the infected to close the gap within a few yards. He dropped down to his knees just as they reached for him and crawled under the truck. When he reached the other side, he popped up and sprinted as hard as he could toward the base chapel.

6

Contagion

Nevada - 2016

The Las Vegas police department didn't know what to make of the calls answered by the emergency operators, but they were similar, so it didn't take long for them to get a warning out to all officers and EMS crews. They were told to avoid being bitten, and at first, they thought they were dealing with one crazy person who had left a casino before they arrived. An hour later they got a call about two security guards from a casino biting people at the emergency room, and the crazy person they were already searching for had assaulted at least a dozen people within a few blocks of the casino. All of the assault victims had been bitten.

The two security guards had been given stitches for bite wounds on their own hands, but they had become gravely ill right before the eyes of the nurses and doctors. Their conditions declined quickly, and they both went into cardiac arrest moments apart. They were pronounced dead, and the police were called due to the suspicious nature of their cases. While the nurse was on the phone with the police department, one of the casino security guards stumbled out of the examination room where he had died and attacked a doctor who was updating his notes about the dead men. Before the doctor could pull away, the second security guard emerged from his room, but he stumbled in the other direction and went through the swinging doors into the lobby.

The chaos that followed was mostly because bite victims were streaming from the doors of the Emergency Room, while some of the unluckier victims were being dragged to the floor and partially eaten by their attackers. By the time the police arrived, they were at a point where orders were given to shoot anyone who wouldn't stay back when told to. The result was unbitten people being shot as they sought help because they ran toward the blue lights. The hospital parking lot effectively became ground zero for facilitating the spread of a contagion that had never been seen before. Despite it becoming the worst place to be, hundreds of people who didn't know better were going toward the hospital from all directions.

It took less than three hours for the first one thousand people to become infected. In less than four hours, there were five thousand dead or dying people in Las Vegas. By sunrise, the airport was closed to incoming flights, but outgoing planes carrying hundreds of people already bitten by the infected were flying their passengers back to their cities across the country. All they wanted to do was get home. Police were no longer responding to 911 calls, and those people who were not yet infected were hiding in the casinos, diners, stores, and homes. A city with over six hundred thousand people plus tourists took one night to fall. The infection had begun.

Fort Knox - 2016

The morning shift didn't arrive at the Gold Depository to relieve the night shift because the base had been placed on alert. Hundreds of civilians were storming the front gates hoping to enter the base to reach safety, and the guards weren't prepared to deal with this unique situation. If it had been one car, the people would have been detained until the local authorities arrived, but there were so many cars within minutes that the guards weren't sure what to do, and they couldn't even roll the metal gates into place. The civilians swarmed past the guard station while the soldiers frantically called for support and requested new orders.

The officer on duty in charge of base security kept a cool head and told the armed soldiers not to shoot civilians because something was obviously wrong outside the base. As policy dictated, he called the Depository to inform them that they would need to stay on duty while a serious issue was resolved, but he got no answer on the security lines. He decided to send a courier to deliver the message in person, but he never knew if the message was delivered or not, and the civilian situation was so out of control that he didn't really care what they did at the Depository. He had too much to deal with at the gates, and the courier never returned to tell him if the night shift got the message.

Less than an hour earlier, two civilian flights from Las Vegas had arrived at the airport. One of them was a scheduled flight, while the second flight was diverted from its original destination of Richmond, Virginia. It was forced to land in Kentucky because so many passengers were sick, and the crew called for ambulances to meet them. When the passengers from both planes disembarked, most of them went to the nearest hospital, while some of them went home. Both groups spread the infection quickly, and the hospital was overrun faster than the one in Las Vegas because more than two people had walked in at the same time with bite wounds.

When the injured civilians arrived at the Army base and were allowed inside, the base medical personnel took over and treated their wounds, but as the first ones unexplainably died from minor injuries, it was too late to stop what had gone too far. The officer in charge had already contacted the base commander, and the gates were forced shut against a steady stream of new arrivals. By noon there were occasional gunshots as soldiers fought back, but the sound was gradually replaced by the combined moans and groans of everyone inside the closed gates. One by one, survivors were found and eliminated.

Fort Knox - 2023

The gates stayed closed, and over the years the grass and bushes were untended and grew to a height where few people would have recognized what had been there before. The thousands of infected dead that had roamed the streets inside the Army base had mostly wasted away and rotted into piles of bones and clothes, but the lure of the gold inside Fort Knox never lost its shine. Because people would always think gold would make them rich, the living and dead populations inside the fence never stayed at zero.

Every year there were survivors who weren't there for the gold. Those were the ones who knew what a fence could mean. They thought they could take permanent refuge inside the secure confines of Fort Knox, and some of them could have made it work, but sooner or later the temptation would be too much. It just wouldn't let them ignore the fact that there was so much gold nearby.

Most of the would-be billionaires gave up at the doors of the Depository not long before they died. As much as they wanted the gold, they were hampered by their lack of knowledge about the complex locks that blocked their entry to the main doors. When they ventured away in defeat, they would circle the outside of the building in search of another entry. The lucky treasure hunters were the ones who made it back to the front, but there were seldom any that got lucky. Some found landmines buried in the tall grass. Others found the infected dead that hadn't withered away. One population decreased, and the other increased in a never-ending cycle.

When an armored caravan rolled up to the gates, the vehicle in the lead was a bulldozer liberated from the Army Corp of Engineers in Georgia. The driver could have gone straight into the heavy chain link fence and flattened it to the ground, but this was an organized force, and the leader had given strict orders not to damage the gate. He had already used other military installations effectively by not damaging the protective barriers, and his plan was going according to schedule. Fort Knox was his ultimate destination, and he had told the driver of the bulldozer he would make him drive through the minefield if he damaged the gate. The driver wasn't the brightest man in his army, but he was good at following exact orders. He had also seen what Brother Silas had done to the last bulldozer driver.

The man had deliberately gone off the road to run over a "crawler" that probably hadn't gone ten feet in the last week. The bulldozer had tipped over when the shoulder of the road collapsed under the weight, and it had taken a day to pull it free. Brother Silas had been furious, and as a reminder to everyone that he would not tolerate such stupidity, he had the driver strapped on his back to the middle of the bulldozer treads.

Everyone thought he was just going to scare the man by driving forward and then stopping with the man just a few feet from being crushed under the tread, but Brother Silas was in the driver's seat, and he loudly ordered everyone to watch as he continued forward. At times he was as loud as the screams from the man strapped to the tread, but when the man reached the front and his back arched with the curve of the metal tread, the screams were louder and higher in pitch. Then Brother Silas was only shouting over the sound of the engine. He kept driving until the body came over the back of the tread, and he stopped where everyone could easily see what remained of the man.

"This is what happens when you get stupid," he yelled. "So what're you going to do?" he asked the crowd.

With one voice they answered, "Follow orders, Brother Silas."

"And?" he yelled impatiently.

"Don't get stupid," they added.

The new driver had accepted the job with a clear mission in his mind...don't drive off the road, follow orders, and don't get stupid. As he stopped in front of the gate, he let the engine idle. Every time he shut it off and then restarted it, he thought about the last driver. He pictured himself strapped to the tread if it failed to restart.

The sound of an Army Humvee coming to the front of the column was his signal that Brother Silas was arriving, and he sat up a little straighter. The vehicle stopped next to him, and he kept his eyes forward as a short man with a gray crew cut practically bounced from the passenger door to the overgrown front gate. The driver of the Humvee stayed where he was, but a pair of armed bodyguards covered Brother Silas on both sides. The bulldozer driver had a fleeting thought that he could be free again if the bulldozer was fast enough for him to run over the three men, but he knew he would be dead long before he reached them, and Brother Silas would watch with amusement.

After a short assessment of the locks and chains on the gate, a second vehicle rolled up behind the Humvee, and a group of men unloaded some big cylinders and dragged a cutting torch from the back. It took less than five minutes before the gates swung open wide enough, and a signal was given to drive forward. Brother Silas climbed onto the bulldozer and rode inside as if he had conquered the impenetrable Depository, and if anyone doubted his true intentions, they became even more obvious when he directed the driver to make all of the turns that led straight to the front gate of the building that held the vault.

The caravan followed other orders and had fallen in behind the driver of the Humvee. Thirty-two vehicles rolled inside and took up strategic positions that formed a perimeter around the area that would be their main camp. Sentries were posted while a small army of men and women went about duties that had been theirs since joining the Brothers and Sisters of the Apocalypse. They erected the tent that would be used by Brother Silas first, then moved on to the other tents. The cooks prepared the evening meal, but no one would eat until

Brother Silas had been served.

******

Lynchburg, Virginia 2016

The ministry at the Church of the Holy Chalice was struggling, but not so much that the minister and deacons could ignore the overzealous fervor of one of its members. They needed more people to join their crusade, but the reason for their dwindling membership was the behavior of Marvin Corn. The short, abrupt man had actually confronted fellow worshipers after the collection plate was passed. He felt like they could be more generous and felt free to tell them so. He even followed them to their cars pointing out that they could make it up next Sunday. They didn't bother to come back.

When Marvin didn't attend the following week, the ministry gratefully accepted that they could live without his meager donations if it meant they wouldn't have to deal with him. Then they got a telephone call from a larger, more affluent ministry expressing their outrage about a member of their ministry attending their service and attempting to recruit its members. The minister apologized and promised they would deal with him. The larger church said they would take action if he came back.

Marvin didn't take it well when he was turned away at the door, and the deacons got to see his real personality. Somewhere in the middle of his many threats, he told them that the "minions of hell would devour them" for what they did to him. If not for the Deputy Sheriff who was asked to be there in anticipation of his outburst, it would have been worse, but it was bad enough for him to find himself in handcuffs. He ranted on the ride to the county jail, while being booked, while in the holding cell, and as he paid his bail. It took everything he had in his savings account, and he swore a curse on everyone.

It was good fortune that it was a Sunday, and Marvin couldn't go to work as a clerk at a local hardware store. Even though they were open, they were always glad to give him Sunday off. Since he wasn't scheduled to work until Tuesday, he decided to go to a campground in the mountains and get away from people. Not that he would be that far from the other campers. One of his favorite ways to pass the time was to wander into the woods to locations that gave him good views of other campsites.

Deep in the woods north of Roanoke, Marvin got comfortable with his binoculars to his eyes. From his preferred spot, he could see three campsites, and even when the other campers weren't doing anything special, it gave him a feeling he couldn't explain. It was like he had power over them because they didn't know they were being watched. Today he felt lucky because all three campsites were occupied. It was late in the afternoon, and he chewed beef jerky while the campers made their evening meals. It didn't matter to him that one site was occupied by men, one with mostly women, and one with an equal number. He saw them all as beneath him because they were camping instead of going to church, and also because they didn't know they were being watched. That made them vulnerable.

Something was happening in the largest group. It looked like they were fighting, and several of the men were restraining someone. He couldn't tell if it was a man or a woman.

"What is that?" he said out loud.

Even from a distance, he could see the red arterial spray from a smaller group in the same campsite. It appeared to him that the people around that person were scrambling with strips of white material.

"Bandages?"

The larger group of men had turned over the person on the ground and were holding him with his face down. He thought it was more likely a man because they were being so rough. Then they were tying his hands behind his back and his feet together.

"This is some serious entertainment," he said.

They left the tied-up man squirming on the ground, and he was able to see that he had been correct about the gender. He was surprised to see there was also a strip of cloth tied around his head and across his mouth.

"They gagged him?"

The group of men holding him down had gone to the other group and surrounded the person on the ground, but he saw that two of the women appeared to be helping to wrap bandages on the man. Even though they were a long way from him, he thought he could hear someone screaming. It took a few minutes for him to realize it was coming from one of the other campsites.

Marvin focused his binoculars on that site and was just in time to see a man strike someone over the head with a piece of firewood. A woman was on the ground nearby, and she was covered in blood.

Judging by her twisted torso, he wasn't sure she was alive.

"What in the world is happening out here?"

In all of his years indulging this particular desire to observe without being seen, he had never had a front-row seat to anything more than minor indiscretions. They fueled his fantasies, but they never made him feel so invigorated. He turned toward the third campsite and saw that the campers were hurriedly loading their tents and gear into the back of a small SUV. They stopped every few seconds and faced in the direction of the campsite where the man was tied up, probably because that was where most of the yells and screams were coming from.

Marvin switched back to that camp, and he was shocked to see the men were tying up a second person, and he was fairly sure it was the woman who had only moments before been shooting blood from an artery. She was fighting with the men, but it seemed like she was more interested in biting them than she was in getting free. She twisted around under their weight and pushed her face against the upper thigh of one man. Even though he was wearing heavy denim jeans, she pulled away a mouthful of red flesh. He fell back grabbing at the wound, and the woman tried to follow him. The other men grabbed her by both feet and dragged her backward on her stomach, but as soon as they stopped dragging, she turned over and went after them. One of the men delivered a well-aimed kick to her chin, and she went down in a heap. Even from a distance, he could tell the kick had broken her neck. The man had done it just like a field goal kicker in a football game.

Marvin didn't recall ever seeing someone die like that even in a movie, so he wondered why the woman's mouth was still opening and closing. The rest of her body was still, but the mouth still snapped at the air. A few feet away, a woman wrapped a long, white strip of cloth around the leg of the man in jeans, but the man with his hands and feet tied together had somehow managed to stand upright. The field goal kicker charged toward him and delivered a well-aimed kick to the man's groin, and he sat down backward.

Watching the kick was more painful to Marvin than it was to the man who got kicked, and he winced from the memory of a similar kick he had gotten from a guy in high school. He heard the engine of a car and saw that the campers who had packed their gear were making their getaway. Almost at the same moment, a second engine grew louder as Park Rangers arrived at both of the other campsites. He couldn't recall ever seeing a Ranger carrying a gun, but these came prepared. They pulled their guns as soon as they got out of their Jeeps, and they held them out in front of their bodies as if they didn't know who to aim at.

As Marvin melted back into the dense forest and disappeared, he felt a sense of rebirth. He was exhilarated by the carnage, and he wasn't sure why. Something made him feel like things were about to change, but he hadn't quite figured out what it was. He went back to his own campsite and packed up to leave. If he hurried, maybe he could make it to the afternoon services at church. He wanted to be ready, so his modified AR-15 was on the seat next to him. Marvin was going to show them that he didn't need their hypocritical church anymore.

Whatever misfortune might have visited the church that day, it wasn't at the hands of Marvin Corn. He had hardly gone a mile when a woman walked out of the woods into the road a few hundred yards away. He slowed to a stop and saw that she was missing her left hand, and she walked with one shoulder lower than the other. Her hair was long and stringy, and besides the blood, she was covered in dirt. She turned around and walked toward his car like she was totally unaware that she was blocking the road.

His first thought was she had been attacked by a bear, but there was something about her missing hand. It wasn't bleeding. He had no real or practical understanding of first aid, but he knew that when you stopped bleeding from a major wound, it meant you were out of blood, and that meant you wouldn't be walking around in the road.

He locked his door and raised the window all the way, then watched with curiosity as the woman approached his car. She walked right up to the window and pressed her face against the glass. Marvin leaned close enough to kiss her if the glass hadn't been there, and he laughed as she worked her mouth across from his. He could hear the wet growling noise she made, and he knew she would have given a really new meaning to the slang expression, "eating face," if he opened the window. That's what they had called making out in his high school, not that he ever got to find out why.

Marvin reached over and slipped the car into drive. He only took his foot off the brake long enough to roll forward a couple of feet, and he was amused by the way it made the woman's face slide across his window until her mouth hit the door frame. She didn't seem to notice, and as soon as she got her balance, she resumed trying to reach him through the glass. He playfully drummed his fingers against the inside of the glass and watched with glee as she snapped at them. He took his foot off the brake three more times until he got bored with the game. The last time he put the car in park and waited until she had her face firmly against the glass, then he violently pushed open the door.

He got out and pulled his AR-15 rifle with him. The woman was on her back on the pavement, and he could see that he had knocked out her front teeth. He stood over her and watched as she made an attempt to push herself up using her missing left hand. Marvin aimed the rifle just by raising it with one hand. He pulled the trigger and sent a short burst of bullets into her upper torso. He was astonished to see how devastating the bullets were at such a short range and how they threw her back onto the pavement hard enough to make her head bounce. He was even more astonished to see her sit back up. She kept making that growling sound, but she went back to her efforts to stand. That was when he learned a valuable lesson. He raised the rifle slightly higher and sent the second burst into her head. She was thrown backward again, but this time she stopped moving.

All Marvin could say was, "Huh." It wasn't a question. It was more like an exclamation of understanding. "I'll have to remember that."

The sound of a car approaching at high speed made him turn around, and he saw the small SUV he had seen at the campsites. It was coming at him fast, and he had nowhere to go except over the hood of his own car. He had seen it done a hundred times in movies, but he never thought it would hurt so much. Even though he landed on the shoulder of the road, he felt a sharp piece of gravel stab him in the hip.

He was furious at the driver of the SUV and fired his rifle wildly in its direction as it sped away. He watched with amazement as it swerved from side to side and left the road. It didn't stop until it slammed into a tree. He wasn't sure why he cared because it was the driver's own fault, but he jogged to where the car sat with its front end spewing radiator steam and coolant into the air. Besides the hissing, the only sound was the ticking of hot metal. Both passengers were buried in airbags that were slowly deflating, but as the bags lost the air that had cushioned the impact, the man and woman both remained slumped forward.

The glass was gone from all of the windows, and Marvin wondered how he could have shot them out with that short burst. He figured he might have hit the rear window, but the impact must've blown out the rest. He checked the back of the driver's seat and saw that two of the bullets had gone through the seat and hit the driver, but the seat belt and airbag hadn't saved the lady in the passenger seat. Just as he came to that conclusion, she raised her head and peered at him with glazed eyes.

The driver also began to stir, but when he lifted his head from the steering wheel, his eyes were different. They were milky white like he had thick cataracts. A growl escaped from his throat, and he leaned as far as he could toward Marvin. His teeth began that snapping motion the woman had done at his own car window, and Marvin took a step backward. The woman continued to stare at him as if she wanted to ask him something, but all that came out of her mouth was perhaps half of a word. It was barely past her lips when the driver turned toward her. It was as if he didn't know she was there until that moment, and he reached for her with a feral groan.

Marvin was fascinated, and he realized the man was like the woman lying back by his car, but the passenger was still alive and screaming hysterically. The man, whoever he had been to her, was no longer alive. Marvin was sure of that. The bullets had killed him, and the impact had been a secondary insult that had only knocked the lady unconscious. He watched as the man grabbed the lady by the arm and pulled it to his mouth. He sank his teeth into her soft flesh and pulled. Marvin blocked out the screams, and for a second time in one day, he got to feel that same power he felt when he watched other campers through his binoculars. He felt powerful. He had never seen someone eat another person before, and although he had no urge to try it himself, it didn't revolt him the way he thought it should.

He raised his rifle toward the open window, but he paused before pulling the trigger.

"Naw, I might need the bullets later."

Marvin walked back to his car and drove past the SUV without even glancing at it as he went by.

******

Marvin Corn never made it back to Lynchburg. The roads were all blocked by police cars with blue lights he could see from miles away. As soon as he saw them he felt like they were there for him. Somehow the lady in the car must have called and given the police his description. He wished he had wasted the bullets. He didn't think it would be safe to go back the way he had come, so he took a state road

80

deeper into the mountains. He knew he had to be quick about it before they blocked all of the roads.

As the sun went down and darkness descended on the mountains, he lost himself in the wilderness. He decided to leave the car on a hunting trail and get as far from there as he could on foot. With his camping gear and supplies, he could last as long as he needed to, and he managed to get his car so far from the state road that he would be long gone before the authorities found it.

That was the beginning of the new Marvin Corn because things didn't go as he expected. He expected to run into Park Rangers or campers, but there were new inhabitants of the woods. There were more people like the woman in the road and the driver of the SUV. They were slow, they fell down easily, and it wasn't hard to get away from them on a steep hill. If they made it up the hill, he just gave them a shove and watched to see how far they would roll.

He also decided it was time to change his name and go by his middle name, Silas. He couldn't settle on a last name he liked, so he had several ready to use if he had to give one. His first disciple made a last name unnecessary when he called him Brother Silas.

7

Caleb

Beaufort Marine Air Base - 2023

"Colleen will go searching for Hampton herself if we go back without him," said Kathy.

The Chief shook his head, "Well, I guess we won't go back without him, but I'm not worried about him anyway. He's survived on his own before. I'll bet he's holed up somewhere, and he'll find us when the sun comes up. In the meantime, we have some business to take care of."

The Chief turned toward the boy and studied him. He was maybe five and a half feet tall and one hundred pounds soaking wet. His black hair went in every direction, and he felt like the boy could be related to Jean. The thought of Ed's wife, who he knew from his time working on a cruise ship, made him remember that time was against them. He had hoped they hadn't stayed gone so long that Sparks had gotten back with his people and they had gone after the shelter inside Green Cavern. He had faith that no one could breach the shelter, but he was angry that the plane had been used to attack the village on top of the mountain. Since it had, it was fortunate that casualties had been avoided.

"What's your name?"

The boy was amazed by the Chief's size, but he wasn't afraid of him. If he was right about the big man, he would be a lot safer now that he was around. In a world where his father wasn't around long enough to have an influence on him, the boy was drawn to the Chief's kind face. As for the blonde woman, just like any teenager, he felt like he could look at her all day.

"Caleb, sir," he answered.

"No last name?" asked the Chief.

"Caleb Wilson, sir."

"I guess you know that was just the first question," said the Chief. "You couldn't have been more than seven years old when things fell apart. How is it that you're still running around out here by yourself?"

"My dad was a Marine pilot, and I lived with my mom here on the base. My dad was away on a mission or something when people started doing things."

Caleb paused as he remembered the first time he saw it happen. It was literally half his life ago, and his eyes seemed unfocused as he thought back to what it was like to be in the second grade and to see his teacher being pinned to the floor by the principal. At first, the children thought the principal was trying to hurt her, but then they saw the blood on her mouth and the way she snapped her teeth at him. He remembered hiding in a closet with some other kids until they thought it was safe to come out. They didn't know that it would never be safe to come out.

"There were lots of us at first. The Marines shot the sick people, and sometimes the sick people were Marines. There were too many of them, and the Marines put me and my friends inside a Cougar. They put food and water inside with us and told us not to come out through the back door until it was safe. There was a bigger kid with us, and they gave him a gun."

"What's a Cougar?" asked Kathy.

Caleb pointed toward the far end of the building where brown tarps covered something big.

"It's under there," he said. "I keep it covered just in case those people ever get in here. If they don't see me, I can shoot them from the top hatch."

"Does the engine start?" asked the Chief, then to Kathy he added, "A Cougar is a personnel carrier. It's called an MRAP for short...Mine-Resistant Ambush Protected. They're real beasts."

Caleb shook his head.

"Battery died years ago."

The Chief knew there would be a long list of bad memories across seven years, and he didn't want the boy to relive them all, but he had to ask.

"You're the last one?" he said in a gentle voice.

Caleb nodded. The question caused his eyes to unfocus again, obviously because he was remembering the deaths of his friends.

"I saw some of them out there today," he said. "I couldn't shoot them when I had the chance."

Kathy's forehead furrowed as she tried to remember the faces of the infected dead outside. They all looked the same now, but she didn't remember seeing any children in the crowd. It dawned on her what that must have meant.

"Your friends died recently?" she asked.

He nodded, clearly disturbed by the memory.

"One of them was my girlfriend. You, uh…" he trailed off.

Kathy was horrified. "I didn't kill her, did I?"

Caleb was quick to correct her.

"She was already dead when you did it. I'm glad it happened. It wasn't easy seeing her out there like that."

Kathy knew he meant it just by the way he reassured her, and after everything she had seen over the years, she knew better than to think his girlfriend was better off walking around in that crowd of infected dead, but it was still hard to know she had taken the final step to end her existence.

"It just happened not long ago?" asked the Chief. He put every bit of softness he could in his voice. For a big man, he could give so much comfort just by speaking gently.

"Her name was Marcy. I told her to let me go for supplies, but she said it was her turn, and she wasn't going to ask for special treatment just because she was a girl. She said we were Marine kids, and that meant we were tough."

Caleb dragged a sleeve across his eyes and sniffed once. Then he put his shoulders back and shrugged away the memories. Kathy and the Chief both thought it was sad to see a kid have to do that. It was sad enough to see an adult do it, but this kid was shouldering a lot of pain.

The Chief reached out and put a big hand on the boy's shoulder.

"We're getting out of here, and you're going with us to a safe place where there are lots of kids your age."

Caleb brightened, but he asked two questions, both with a heavy dose of skepticism.

"There's a place like that? How are we getting out of here?"

"There are several places like that," said the Chief. "We're with a group of people who have shelters...safe places that can't be penetrated by the sick people. By the way, we call them infected dead. We're pretty sure it's an infection that spreads by fluids in the bite from one of the dead ones that came back."

Caleb surprised them by responding sarcastically, "You figured that out by yourselves? They can get in anywhere sooner or later."

Both Kathy and the Chief were a bit stunned at first, but even though they weren't parents, they were smart enough to know their mistake was in the way they sounded. This kid had survived for seven years without an adult around, and they were talking to him as if he was a kid. They were acting like he didn't have to worry because the adults were there now, and he had seen the adults all fail at the one thing he wanted most, and that was to stay alive.

"Sorry, kid," said Kathy. "We won't talk down to you. We just want to bring you up to speed about things you might not know. We've seen a lot, but you've been stuck here on this base."

The Chief decided to temper the sarcasm just a bit though. Caleb was still a kid, and he needed to recognize that one thing hadn't changed. Adults were still in charge.

"If we tell you something you already know, it's okay to say you already know it. We can save our breath, but do me a favor and don't try to make us feel stupid for saying it."

Caleb weighed being disciplined against being apologized to and came to a quick conclusion.

"Sorry...I'm sorry. I just haven't been around grown-ups in a long time. There was a guy who came here about four or five years ago. He started giving orders right away as if we needed him or something. He's out there somewhere, and it didn't take long for him to get that way."

"Do you think you need us?" asked Kathy.

"I did okay when my friends were still alive," said Caleb, "but I'm not going to last long by myself. I'd be really glad to go with you."

"Well," said the Chief, "We'd be happy to take you along, but that's a mess out there, and we need transportation and a way to work on an aircraft without getting killed. We'll take any ideas you have to offer since you know this place."

"Can you charge a battery from a solar panel?"

"You have a solar panel that works?" asked Kathy.

"The Cougar does."

The smile on the Chief's face was all they needed to see to know that a solar panel on the Cougar was good news. He handed his rifle to Caleb as he headed for the vehicle under the tarps. Caleb's smile was almost as big as the Chief's.

Over his shoulder, the Chief said, "There's only one reason the Cougar would be carrying a solar panel. They have a generator in it, and they were using it to jump-start the planes. When they would do maintenance on the planes, they'd have the engine on external power. Now we just have to get it to work."

He undid the straps that held the tarps to the Cougar and slid them off into a big pile. It was clear to Kathy that the Chief felt like he had found a gold mine. The Cougar wasn't pretty, but it was the beast the Chief wanted it to be. It was twenty-one tons of hardened steel that stood tall enough for them to be safe from the infected. A machine gun was mounted behind protective shielding on top, and they saw the possibilities open up in front of them. Even if they couldn't get a plane in the air, this could get them where they needed to go.

"What's the range on this thing?" asked Kathy.

The Chief said, "As I recall, three hundred and fifty miles even when it's fully loaded with people and gear. More than enough for our trip, and it would take an anti-tank weapon to stop it."

Caleb was still studying the M4 the Chief handed him, but he had his ears on the conversation.

"Is that something you're worried about?" he asked. "I mean, those infected things out there don't have enough sense to get out of the way of something like a Cougar, let alone shoot at it with an anti-tank weapon."

"Yeah, I get your point, kid. Problem is that there are a few people who have been happy about the way things turned out."

Caleb tilted his head to one side and said, "I think they were like that before the infection. This just gave them a chance to be themselves."

"That's what I meant," said the Chief. "Good people will always be good deep down inside, but bad people take any opportunity they can get to show how bad they can be."

"They've come here before," said Caleb. "People searching for supplies, for guns, for a place to be safe...they all wind up out there in that crowd. There was one guy who tried to make us do everything for him, but we put him outside."

Kathy and the Chief both noticed how easily Caleb said what they had done, and it was sad that a fourteen-year-old had reconciled execution as a means to his own survival. They had talked about what had to be done to the people who attacked Captain Miller's soldiers, and about how they were the good guys, but there was still a part of them that didn't like being the judge and jury. There wasn't much doubt that Caleb would consider it necessary to remove the threat of further attacks if it meant protecting their people.

"We'll cross that bridge if and when we come to it," said the Chief. "In the meantime, let's have a look at this beautiful beast."

He easily climbed the side of the sand-colored vehicle and settled into the cage surrounding the machine gun. Then he dropped down inside through the open hatch. Caleb was about to do the same when Kathy stopped him.

"Give him a minute. If you knew the Chief as well as I do, you would know this is like a Christmas and birthday present rolled into one. He needs a moment to explore."

The Chief's head appeared at the back door almost a full fifteen minutes later.

"Are you two coming?"

Caleb said, "I never open the back door because those infected things might be inside the building."

"Get in here fast then, and we can button her back up."

He gave them both a hand and then pulled the door shut behind them. They could see he was as excited and wanted to share it with them.

"This thing not only has a solar panel, but it also has a massive generator. It puts out more than enough power for us to work on a plane, but check this out. It's connected to the auxiliary systems of the Cougar. That means air conditioning. I want a plane, but if we can't get one in the air, this thing will get us where we want to go."

Kathy asked, "How do we get the solar panel into place so we can charge this baby?"

"Already thought of that."

The Chief didn't feel like wasting time, and he wanted the panel in place as soon as the sun came up. He grabbed the case that held the collapsible solar panel and pulled a long charging cable out of a gear locker. When he climbed back through the upper hatch he did a quick mental inventory of the motor pool and saw what he needed hanging in a coil from a wall. He retrieved the rope and was back on top of the Cougar in a matter of minutes. From there he was able to throw the rope over the steel rafters above him. Before making the climb up the rope, he secured the solar panel to the straps on his backpack and hooked the charging cable to his belt.

"Hey, kid. Does this place have any weak spots?"

Caleb pointed at the doors at the front of the building.

"If they opened on the other building, they could open here," he said.

"So it would be a good idea for you to cover up the beast again."

Caleb nodded, and with Kathy's help, they dragged the heavy tarps back over the Cougar. The Chief went up the rope without making a sound and caught a grip on the steel beams below the door. It didn't take him long to find a spot in the metal roof that had been patched by a sheet of aluminum. He remembered from his Navy days that metal buildings were usually repaired with more metal, and roofs were patched from the inside whenever possible. That was a good way to keep people from unscrewing a patch from the outside.

The patch he found was held in place by eight screws and some kind of rubber sealant. The screws were rusted into place, but that meant they would break when he twisted them as hard as he could. He heard the familiar snapping sound as they broke one by one. He cut the rubber sealant with his knife and then pushed against the opening just hard enough to move it. The metal patch protested, but it wasn't loud enough to draw the attention of anything in the dark streets outside the building.

The Chief poked his head through the opening. There was no moon, and the air was humid. He remembered from previous visits to Parris Island Marine Recruit Training Center that the air always seemed heavy and wet. This time he could also smell the infected dead, and he knew they were down there even if he couldn't see them.

As quietly as he could, the Chief eased the solar panel onto the roof. It wasn't flat, but the slope of the roof was gentle enough that he didn't have to worry about anything sliding toward the edge. He unfolded the solar panel and aimed it to the east to catch the sun as it rose, but he wouldn't have to reposition it until well after noon when the sun moved toward the west. He connected the charging cable and then let himself drop back down through the hole in the roof.

When the Chief got back down to the Cougar, he found that Kathy was out foraging around the motor pool. She was going through hand tools and occasionally stuffing them in her backpack. She had seen him descend from the rafters and knew he would come straight to her to see what she had found.

"Did you check in with the boat while you were up there?" she asked.

"No, I wanted to, but it's pretty busy out there in the street. I think that a lot of them went after Hampton, but there were plenty that followed us. The sound would carry too well tonight. How about you? Any reception inside all this metal?"

"Enough for me to tell them we're spending the night," said Kathy.

"Colleen coming out here on a rescue mission?" he asked only half joking.

"I didn't tell her about getting separated from Hampton. Wasn't much sense in telling her anything she couldn't do anything about."

The Chief nodded. "We'll find him tomorrow once we have a charge on the battery in the Cougar. In the meantime just listen for him to key his radio so we know he's okay. Find anything useful?"

"Charlie can use a resupply of his hand tools, so I've cherry-picked my way through the good stuff. Some of it was still wrapped in plastic and never used, so no rust on them. Those gauges on the welding rig show the tanks are still full, but from what I can see on the MRAP, it won't need much to get it going. I don't think we'll need to do any welding. No power for the instrument panel yet, so I checked the fuel the old-fashioned way. It's over three-quarters full of diesel, and those big drums over there are full too. We can top off the tank with a hand pump. I've got Caleb over there using a plumber's snake to stir up the gas tank."

"A plumber's snake? I'm impressed. I was just about to suggest we find a way to stir it up in case it settled. A blocked fuel filter is all we need."

"I found spare filters in a parts cabinet. If you know where they're located on the chassis, it might be a good idea to change them before we start it," she said.

The Chief was just about to agree when both of their handheld radios clicked three times. They knew that it was Hampton, and three clicks meant not to respond. It was likely that he was cornered somewhere safe, or he would have just gone ahead and told them he needed help.

Kathy noticed something about the Chief as he foraged through the tool chests with her.

"You're worried about something," she said. "I can always tell."

He nodded. "We're taking too long. If we had a wide-open amount of time to work on an Osprey, I would say no problem. Let's get one in the air, and go find those guys who think it's okay to kill fellow survivors. On the other hand, we have an MRAP that's been protected from the elements, and it actually has tires that haven't dry rotted."

"I hadn't thought of that," said Kathy. "Wouldn't that mean someone brought it here sometime in the last seven years? Is there something Caleb isn't telling us?"

"In fairness to him," said the Chief, "we didn't ask."

"So, what are you saying about the plane?"

The Chief let out a heavy sigh. "The chances of getting one in the air are good, but the chances of keeping it in the air are bad. Imagine how many rubber parts there are on planes besides the tires. The MRAP won't fall out of the sky if something quits working, and I keep telling myself the clock is ticking."

"Then let's just go with the best option. After we get the battery charged and get it running, let's go get Hampton and ride out of here instead of wasting a day on a plane that may or may not fly."

They spent another hour finding useful gear and tools around the motor pool before settling in for the rest of the night. It would take a few hours of sunlight before they could begin putting a charge on the battery, so the Chief decided to get some rest and then change the fuel filters in the morning.

There was plenty of room for them inside the Cougar because it was designed to carry eight fully equipped soldiers and two crew members. It was by far the safest place to be on land, and even if the infected got inside the building, they wouldn't know people were inside the vehicle. It also gave them the time to get a few more mysteries solved with Caleb's help.

The way Caleb described life over the last seven years, it resembled a controlled retreat. At first, there were a handful of adults that fought a losing fight on the main part of the base where there was dependent housing, a commissary, a church, and a base hospital. As time passed by, it took its toll. The adults took greater and greater risks, and they didn't always pay off. Then there was a long stretch of time where it seemed to get quiet, but something caused the infected dead to become agitated. They migrated away from the part of the base where the planes were, and it seemed like something was calling them to come north.

The Chief and Kathy both knew it had to be the big "zombie whistle" on the Cooper River Bridge, but they didn't tell Caleb. They wanted to hear more of his story. He went on to describe how it was peaceful because so many of the infected walked right into the coastal waterways and inlets. Some were dragged away by big alligators, some were so covered in blue crabs that they couldn't walk, and once they fell down more crabs would get them. The crabs would leave when there was nothing left, and that didn't take long because the crabs were getting bigger.

"The worst time was when the spiders showed up. We had to just about burn the place down to get them to stay away from us."

"You burned diesel on the floor, and the place turned into a big smoker?" asked the Chief.

Caleb nodded. "We didn't know what else to do, but that's when we killed the battery in the Cougar. We couldn't get the engine to start, but we had to use the air conditioning because of the smoke. After the AC quit, we stayed inside for two whole days."

"How have you survived this long without more food?" asked Kathy. She was worried he might have been eating crab meat.

"Up until last week I was able to get canned food from the main base. There was the commissary warehouse and the chow hall. There's still a lot of it, but I couldn't get to it anymore. I don't know where they all came from, but new infected things keep showing up."

"I know where they're coming from," said the Chief. "There are still survivors out there who have picked the grocery stores clean. They know there's a chance that there was a big supply of food on the base, and they try to get it…unsuccessfully."

Kathy added, "Then there's the possibility of getting weapons and ammunition. Going onto a military base is like it was at the beginning when too many people went to hospitals. The things we need most are also at the places where you'll most likely find the infected dead."

Caleb said, "You said there are safe places. Are we going to one of them?"

It had crossed the Chief's mind that Caleb added a new dimension to their plans. Plan A was to get a plane and then try to rendezvous with Gentry Campbell. Plan B was to use the Cougar instead of the plane. Either way, they still had a teenager to take with them on the road to a confrontation that wasn't going to be pretty. He could leave Caleb with Charlie and Sue, but he wasn't sure how they had survived so long. He hoped they would live to see the end of the madness that had eaten their world, literally and figuratively, but he didn't think the end of it was coming any time soon.

91

* * *

******

Hampton was beginning to wonder if the infected had mutated like the crabs, except their special super-talent had become a heightened sense of smell. No matter where he hid, they found him, and he was forced to move again. He wasn't sure but they also seemed to be able to climb a set of stairs faster than before.

The church felt like a logical place to go because it had several entrances and exits, had a wide field of vision where he needed it the most, and had high places where he could retreat to if needed. He knew he was wrong as soon as he was inside. The wide field of vision revealed at least a dozen of the infected trapped inside. When he immediately went to the stairs that led to the choir loft, he found that some of them had gone up there already. Faced with the infected on the stairs behind him and in the choir loft ahead of him, he was forced to go forward.

Hampton grabbed the closest infected dead by the front of its shirt just below the chin. Circling hard, he wound up like an athlete about to do a shot-put throw and tossed the ragged infected three-quarters of the way down the stairs. He almost launched the disgusting creature over the heads of the first ones on the stairs, but its flailing arms and legs made contact and took them all down.

He had just a moment to admire his aim before the next one got close.

"Ohhhhh! The Romanian judge gave me a perfect ten-point zero for that one."

The second one didn't get as much distance, but it rolled to the bottom of the stairs and took out two new arrivals. Hampton got into a steady rhythm of grabbing, whirling, and throwing until they were all at the bottom of the stairs, but when he checked his surroundings for obstacles he could toss in their path, he saw nothing. His only choice was to go down the stairs on the opposite side of the loft. At least the infected had all followed him to the side he came up, so he had a clear path to a side door.

A quick glance behind him was when he found that the infected were making faster than normal progress on the stairs. Four were already halfway to him, so he needed to decide fast. He took the steps two at a time, hesitated when he reached the door, then said a silent prayer that the other side of the door was safe. It wasn't.

Hampton's first impulse was to ease the door open to see if it was clear, but the years of humid weather made the door creak noisily from its rusty hinges. He might as well have just yelled at them.

There was no doubt that he didn't have time to choose a direction, so he went to the right. His instincts told him to stay along the wall of the church and try to outflank the crowd around him. He couldn't do that if he went straight because they would be able to close in on him from all sides. He ran straight at the infected near the building and threw his left shoulder into the chest of the nearest one. It flew to the side right where he wanted it to go, and it clipped the legs out from under three more. Sometimes you took the time to end their miserable existence, and sometimes you had to settle for just knocking them down.

When he turned the corner at the back of the church, there was a clear path to a building that appeared to be an administration building, and Hampton knew it wouldn't be his first choice for hiding places. Offices meant a lot of dead ends. Cubicles were only useful for putting distance between him and pursuers because he could hop over them. They would follow him into the first cubicle and then try to figure out how to get to him as he would exit on the other side, but that wasn't a long-term solution. He needed a place where he could hide for the night.

There was also the possibility that he would go over a cubicle wall and land right on top of an infected that was just trying to find a way to reach him. Once again, he felt like he had too few options, and he ran for the nearest door of the office building. As soon as it shut behind him, Hampton put his back against the door and just listened. The smell was exactly what he expected. There was no shortage of death and decay inside buildings even after seven years. People just like him got trapped inside and became one of the things they all wanted to hide from.

The building was quiet. In the darkness, he could just make out the stairs that went up on the left. In front of him was another door, but for some reason, he felt like the ground floor was a bad choice. Maybe it was because he felt like the infected could just walk right into the ground floor. What nagged at him was the fact that he knew he was thinking like every other cornered prey. Go higher, climb something, trees were safer than the ground…they were all death trap instincts.

An infected bumped against the other side of the door where his back was, and it startled him into motion. He went for the stairs, but he had something in mind. Instead of entering the door at the next landing, he kept going.

"If I need to go higher, I'll go higher," he said out loud between breaths.

At the top of the stairs was a ladder that went up one wall, and it didn't need a sign on it for him to know it went to the roof. He imagined that it was heavily used during the first days of the infection, and just like other rooftops he had seen since it began, there would be plenty of evidence left behind.

Hampton chose the ladder for several reasons, one of which was the ability to see what was happening outside the building. Another reason was that there were sounds coming from below that told him there were infected dead following him up the stairs.

"How did they know I went up the stairs instead of through the door? You guys might be better with stairs than you were before," he said, "but let's see you climb a ladder. On second thought, let's see you *try* to climb a ladder."

He slung his rifle and gear across his back and climbed the metal rungs, and just like before when he left the church, he eased the hatch upward. It creaked more than he would have liked, but in the dark stillness of the roof, he knew that there would be a response that he could hear if there were any infected on the roof. One good thing about rooftops was that the infected tended to fall over the edge without much encouragement.

Hampton waited and didn't hear an answer to the sound of the hatch opening, so he pushed himself onto the rooftop. He stayed low to the rough surface and moved forward on his belly. He froze, hardly breathing as he watched the dark outline of two men moving near a tent about thirty yards away. They were in the far corner at the opposite end of the building. There was just enough light coming from inside the tent for him to tell there was a third person inside. He wanted to close the trap door behind him, but he couldn't risk it. The only way they could have missed the sound of it opening before was because they were talking.

He reached around to where his radio was clipped to his belt and depressed the key three times to signal he was okay, then he switched off the radio. It wouldn't be a good time to get a call from Kathy or the Chief at the moment.

8

Fort Knox

Kentucky - 2023

Brother Silas kept to himself as much as possible. It was important to be seen, but he preferred to have people see him more as an enigma... more than he was. He wasn't tall in real life, so he wanted to be taller *than* life. While his personal quarters were being prepared, he sat inside his Humvee and enjoyed a cold beer and a sandwich. Thanks to the occasional survivors they encountered on the road, he had never gone hungry or thirsty since that day when he had gone camping. His disciples made sure he got the best of whatever people had to offer, whether they offered or not.

His disciples, also known as the Brotherhood, only numbered twelve among the one hundred or so people who followed him. He had strictly commanded that there would only be twelve, and the only way they could add a member was if one of them died. When that happened, the selection process for a replacement involved acts of dedication to him. The bigger the show of dedication, the higher a disciple would rise in the Brotherhood. Right now, the number one member of the Brotherhood was Sparks. His triumphant, although late, return with the AC-130 had earned him the top spot. The number two spot was occupied by Bernard Ancrum, the man who had been the first disciple and the man who had anointed Marvin Corn by naming him Brother Silas.

Brother Bernard was working night and day to regain his status as the number one member of the Brotherhood, but unless he found a better plane and learned how to fly it, he was stuck with more mundane offerings.

He was short and stocky with an impressive beard to go with a curly mass of hair on top of his head. His muscular arms and chest were enough to make people avoid getting into a fight with him. It was his idea to raid the military base outside Atlanta, and it was his idea to go to Fort Knox to collect the gold. The thought of billions of dollars in gold was symbolic, but he had convinced Brother Silas that gold would still be what separated the rich from the poor once the infected dead were all gone. He intended to be among the former.

At the moment, Brother Bernard was at the gates of the Depository. If he was going to get his number one status back, he had to find a way to get inside the building. He had circled the outside of the enclosure surrounding the Depository, and he had seen some interesting things. The grass was shoulder-deep between the fence and the main building, and he was sure there would be a few infected dead crawling around, but in some places, the grass appeared to be shorter than others, and he wondered why.

Using a truck to gain enough height to see the grass from above, Brother Bernard saw that the grass was shorter because it was growing in pits, and the discovery of a rusted old sign that had fallen from the fence years ago filled in the rest of the story. The sign warned that the other side of the fence was heavily mined. The pits were either created by infected dead or by living people who wanted to get rich. Either way, he got it. Stay off the grass.

The ropes hanging from the guard towers were an interesting discovery. The very existence of the ropes said something about the front door. He considered the possibility that someone had used the ropes to get out of the towers, but the reason had to be because the front doors were impenetrable. It was easier to believe someone couldn't in than out. The problem with that idea was whether or not the person had been successful. If they went in through the guard towers, he had to wonder if they got the gold. Brother Bernard decided he had to check the front doors, and if they were locked he would use the ropes.

Bernard was waiting for Brother Silas when his leader climbed out of his Humvee. The Sanctuary, as they were taught to call it, was completely assembled, and Bernard knew the ritual well. Brother Silas would exit the vehicle and walk directly through the entrance that was being held open by one of the workmen. If it took more than three steps for him to reach the inside, he would have the man's head. Brother Bernard would follow a few steps behind and wait for Brother Silas to ask for his report.

The fourth step carried Silas into the entrance, and he nodded his approval as he passed the laborer. Bernard saw the relief written on the man's face as he fell into step behind Silas. He knew that the man was probably long gone before the flap of the tent fell completely shut.

The interior was already furnished with a living room set and a large table where Brother Silas could hold his meetings with the Brotherhood. His bedroom was behind a curtain toward the back of the tent. Brother Silas extended a hand in the direction of a sofa, and Bernard went to it without a word. The sofa was actually a place of honor because no one was allowed to sit in the presence of Brother Silas unless he said to do so.

Silas got right to the point and asked, "What did you learn of my gold?"

"On your command, Brother Silas, I didn't enter the actual compound. I surveyed the grounds from outside the fence and saw some interesting details to report."

"Proceed."

Bernard described what he found, and he offered the conclusion that the front door would probably be locked. Someone had climbed the towers using ropes, but they either failed to get into the Depository, or they got in but never came out.

The last part of the conclusion piqued Brother Silas' curiosity.

"How did you assemble the facts to justify that observation, Brother Bernard?"

Bernard had anticipated the question and had wanted to delay having to answer it until he was allowed to enter the compound and inspect the door, but he wasn't sure how to avoid it. If he had told Brother Silas he thought someone had beaten them to the gold, his position in the Brotherhood might have been in jeopardy, so he had to bring him news that sounded good. He attempted to convey confidence when he answered.

"The front gates were locked, Brother. If someone left with the gold, they would have left them open. I mean, why bother to close and lock them?"

The truth was that Brother Bernard had found the gates unlocked, but since he was ordered not to enter the compound, it would be tough to deliver good news. He had added a lock to the fence to solidify his thinking, and he could see that Brother Silas was pleased.

"Take a team into the compound and verify that the front door hasn't been breached. Take that one man with you who bragged about being able to open any lock. If he can't open the door, find out if he can climb a rope."

When Brother Silas said to take a team, Bernard was relieved. Standing outside the fence, the Depository seemed haunted. He hadn't expected to see lights anywhere, and he didn't doubt it had seen its share of deaths in the previous seven years, but there was something else about the place. It almost felt like it was welcoming them to try for the gold so it could eat them.

It took an hour to gather the team together. He found ten men who he felt good to have at his back, and they walked in a loose group to the Depository. Everyone was heavily armed with an assortment of rifles, handguns, and knives. Machetes were tucked into belts, but as they approached the gate with the sun setting at their backs, the team felt what Brother Bernard had earlier. The rifles were slung, and the machetes were drawn. He sent a man forward with bolt cutters to remove the lock, but just like the others, he kept his eyes on the dark building.

"Why can't we do this in the morning?" asked one of the men.

Bernard didn't even bother to turn around. He just kept his eyes on the building that seemed to be waiting for them, and said, "Go tell Brother Silas you decided he could wait until tomorrow. Tell him that you're afraid of the dark."

"Does that place have any windows?" someone else asked.

No one answered the question because they could see for themselves that there were none, but someone said, "What difference does the time of day make? Everyone got flashlights?"

There was a general grumbling of assent as the men dug flashlights from various pockets. Fortunately for them, they had found a large supply of batteries at the Army base in Georgia. Batteries had become more and more scarce as they were used or expired on storeroom shelves, but some worked better than others. The problem was that none of them lasted very long, and they were likely to lose their charge at the worst times.

"Everyone listen up," said Bernard. "Stay on the road. The grass is mined. Dead guys have stepped on a few, but if you're not standing in a hole, you're standing close to a mine. There might also be a few dead guys crawling around out there, and even if you don't get bit on an ankle, you might get blown up when a dead guy crawls over a mine a few feet from you."

There was more grumbling, but Bernard couldn't tell who it was in the failing light. If he could identify the person, he would have them go first. Everyone could see that he was trying to figure out who was complaining, so he couldn't even find someone who would make eye contact with him. The truth was that Bernard was stalling, and everyone was going to catch on if he didn't get on with it. He turned back to the road and started walking, and everyone became so quiet that they could hear the sounds of their feet.

It was over four hundred feet from the gate to the door, and the grumbling started again when someone's flashlight quit working. There was a slapping sound as the man tried to get it to come back on. He banged it against his other hand and cursed at it.

"Someone give me a couple of batteries," he said to everyone around him. He held out his hand, but everyone just walked around him. After everyone was past him, he slid spare batteries into the flashlight. He had only taken the opportunity to be at the back of the group when they opened the main door.

The building felt like it was dead, but it also felt like it was waiting for them. That feeling of dread grew as they got closer. Bernard walked up the short flight of steps at the entrance and reached for the handle. As much as he wanted it to be unlocked, he was more afraid that it might be. He wasn't sure if it was good news or bad news when it didn't budge. He could see where crowbars had been inserted at various places around the frame, but the reason he didn't bring one was that only short-sighted people would think they could open the front door of the gold Depository with a crowbar. He was sure that security didn't begin at the vault.

"You, what was your name again?" he pointed at one of the men. He apparently didn't want to be singled out because he hopefully checked behind himself to see if Brother Bernard was pointing at someone else.

"Ipolito, Brother Bernard," he stuttered. "I'm from Jersey, Sir."

Bernard knew the man was nervous, and he had to think for a moment about what he had said to him, mentally reviewing in his own mind if he actually asked the man where he was from.

"That's nice, Ipolito. Be sure to write home when you get the chance, but for now, I just want you to take three men and go around the left side of the building. Stay close to the walls so you don't blow yourselves up. If you find any ropes going up to the towers, see if you can climb them. Send one of the others back around to here to let me know."

Bernard felt like he did a good job keeping the sarcasm out of his voice, but he couldn't keep himself from shaking his head and mumbling, "Jersey...whatever."

"You," he said to another man. Even though he knew him, he said, "I don't need to know your name or where you come from. Just pick three men and go the other way. The last two of you stay here with me."

"If we find ropes, should we climb them?" asked the man.

"No, I want you to lasso a zombie and bring it back here," said Bernard with as much sarcasm in his voice as he could muster. "Yes, I want you to climb them, dummy."

As the two teams departed, Bernard was pinching the bridge of his nose because he was getting a headache between his eyes. He had been taking blood pressure medicine when the zombie apocalypse began, and he was fairly certain he would have a heart attack or a stroke if he didn't find a bottle of pills before one of these morons asked the wrong dumb question. He noticed that the two guys left with him were both smiling.

"What?" he asked.

"I've got ten bucks that says he lassos a zombie and drags it back here," said one of them with a grin.

Brother Bernard didn't like the man because he was always scratching at his forearms like a tweaker who hadn't gotten his hands on any meth for a long time. The truth was, Bernard had wondered if the man wasn't managing to cook it without getting caught.

"If he does, shoot him," answered Bernard. "The guy holding the rope, not the zombie."

The tweaker thought that was really funny and had fits of laughter for several minutes.

The other guy, a skinny guy with bent, wire-framed glasses, had kept quiet and considered himself lucky that he wasn't sent with either team, but he didn't think he was going to be so lucky that all he would do was hang around and wait for the other teams to break in or report back. Bernard focused his attention on the man.

"Didn't I hear you say you could open any door, pick any lock, or break into any security system?"

Everyone called him Specs because he was constantly adjusting his glasses as if they were bothering his nose.

"With the right tools, I can."

"Well, do I have to ask if we have the right tools?"

The man was having a hard time standing still, and he shifted his weight repeatedly from one foot to the other.

"I think we need explosives, Brother Bernard, but that wouldn't be for just this door. I've never seen a place like this that didn't have a back door, and it's going to be a tough nut to crack too."

Bernard didn't know which comment dumbfounded him more, the one about lassoing a zombie or this one.

"By the back door, I take you don't mean around on the other side of the building." It was more of a statement than a question.

"My guess would be a tunnel. It would have to be a long one, and if I know government workers, it's somewhere near transportation."

"Why?" asked Bernard.

"To bring in or take out gold without the need for more security."

Brother Bernard felt like he had underestimated the man.

"So you think the entrance is somewhere over near the landing strip on the Army base."

The man shook his head and said, "No, they built Fort Knox back when trains were the big thing. I doubt that they dug a tunnel to the airstrip later. They most likely laid some railroad tracks from the train depot to the tunnel. All we have to do is follow the railroad tracks to find it."

Bernard wished he hadn't wasted his time at the front door and considered sending each man to retrieve the teams, but he decided he would at least give them a chance to get inside first.

******

The team that went to the left nervously hugged the wall until they finally came to a guard tower. The grass had grown tall all the way to the building, and there was no shortage of mosquitoes. Added to the bugs and the humidity was the smell of something decaying nearby. They didn't talk because decaying didn't necessarily mean the same thing it used to. It used to mean the smell was coming from something that wasn't moving anymore. The smell seemed to be getting stronger, and they worried it was coming toward them instead of the other way around.

Ipolito panned his light back and forth on the wall as they got closer to the guard tower. He yelped in surprise when he walked into the rope that dangled in front of him. He jumped backward and swung his machete at it as he fell into the guys behind him. The man behind him had to duck to keep from getting hit because he swung so hard.

"Hey, watch out where you swing that thing, man. What're you killing there anyway? It's a rope. Isn't that what we're looking for?"

For several minutes they argued about who should climb the rope and who should go back to Brother Bernard. The argument was settled when they heard a groan from somewhere out in the tall grass. Ipolito slipped his machete into his belt and jumped to get a grip higher up the rope. Instead of just climbing the rope, he found he could walk on the wall as he pulled the rope with his arms.

The man in the back took the initiative and said to the other two, "I'm going back to report in."

Before they could protest, he was on his way. To pass him, they would have to cross the grass, and neither wanted to get blown up, so they frantically searched for more ropes. Neither of them wanted to be the last man on the ground.

Another rope hung against the wall instead of out in the open air, and they both lunged for it at the same time. After a brief struggle, one of them got a good grip and pulled himself upward. The loser of the fight grabbed the bottom of the rope and tried to shake his former comrade into slipping, but the higher the man went, the less effect it had on him. Not to be beaten, he got a firm grip on the rope and ran away from the building. He made it ten feet before he ran out of rope and ran out of luck.

The blast from the mine shattered the night, and Brother Bernard suspected it was Ipolito. What he didn't know was that Ipolito was just climbing into the guard tower when it happened. The man who stepped on the mine wasn't dead yet, and his screams carried far enough for Bernard to understand that he wouldn't be alive much longer.

The other man who had climbed several yards up the second rope found himself suspended in the air as the unfortunate man at the bottom ran away from the building. When the explosion ripped through the night, the man on the rope felt weightless for a split second before he rocketed toward the solid wall. He hit hard and fell with a wet thud into the grass. In his attempt to stop himself from hitting the wall too hard, he hit feet-first and managed to propel himself further from the wall than he would have liked.

He felt around in the darkness for his dropped flashlight, and when his hand closed around it, he immediately clicked it on. He found himself face to face with the upper half of the man who had stepped on the mine. The man who had run back to report their progress reached Brother Bernard just as the explosion happened, and he was just about to tell him Ipolito was climbing when they heard new screaming. They had all heard that kind of screaming before.

The man with the flashlight found his own feet and pushed the growling half-man away from him. He ran in a straight line through the grass toward the road. A second ear-splitting explosion was close enough to Bernard that a piece of the man landed between him and the two men who had stayed behind at the front door.

"Now I know why Brother Silas told me to bring ten men with me. What part of stay off of the grass didn't you understand?" he yelled in the direction of the explosion.

Ipolito couldn't see everything that happened outside because he had been busy crawling through a broken window, and he was watching out for jagged edges. He cut his right hand when the first explosion happened, and he was wrapping a piece of cloth around the cut when the second blast disturbed the quiet. He aimed his light at the glass for a second time because something bothered him about it. He had assumed the ropes had been used by people to break into the tower, but he could see that the window had been broken out from the inside. One end of the rope was securely tied to the handle of an open door. When he played his light past the door, the darkness beyond was so complete that it just seemed to absorb the light.

"You can do this, Lou," he said to himself in a low whisper. Hearing his own voice in the darkness was enough to convince him that he couldn't do it. His voice shook as if he was standing barefoot in six inches of ice water.

He wasn't a big man, but he had made up for his small size with quick thinking and a bit of speed. He had good upper body strength and could sprint faster than most people when he had to. He was also brave enough to keep himself valuable to the group. He hadn't been with this group long, but they had survived seven years, and judging by the size of the group they would survive seven more.

He made a mental decision not to speak out loud again. If there was something in that darkness, he didn't want to advertise his location. It was bad enough that he was shining a flashlight ahead of himself, but the sound of his voice carried further even if he kept it low.

Three steps were all it took to get from the observation room of the tower to the door, and he didn't know if he was sweating from the climb or if it was hot inside the building. The room he was standing in was almost three hundred and sixty degrees of glass. The door was the only thing that touched a solid wall. He saw that the glass was gone on the other side as well, and a second rope was tied to the window frame. Whoever it was that had gone out that way didn't know how weak window frames were, but for some reason, he suspected it was done in a hurry.

Ipolito stumbled against something on the floor. It was high enough to bruise his shin. He aimed his light at it and saw that it was a rolled-up chain ladder, and a metal tag on the single strand of wire looped through it said it was for emergency exits during fires. He pushed at it with his toe, and it didn't move, so he gripped it with his free hand and tried to lift it. It was obviously intended for use by two people strong enough to lift it over the edge of the window sill. Someone had given up on the ladder in a hurry and left it there.

There wasn't anything else to see in the tower, so he decided it was time to do as he was told. For a moment he considered climbing back down and telling Brother Bernard the door inside the tower had been locked, but that was too easily disproven. He checked the lock on the door anyway and found it could be locked from his side but not the other side.

"That makes sense," he thought, "and Brother Bernard might even suspect that."

He took one cautious step through the doorway and turned from side to side to check his surroundings. He saw immediately why his flashlight beam was absorbed by the darkness. He stood on a metal catwalk that went left, right, and straight, and the light wasn't strong enough to show what was at the end in any direction. He aimed it at his feet and saw that the metal wasn't solid. It was a grill or grate pattern, and he could see below him to the next floor. Shadows moved under him, and he almost screamed. He aimed directly at the spot where he saw the shadow, and he saw that the shadow only moved because his flashlight had gone to another target.

Ipolito put the back of his cloth-wrapped hand against his forehead and wiped away the sweat that was about to run into his eyes. His thick black hair and good hairline made people jealous, but right now it was soaked with salty sweat and his scalp itched like something was crawling on it. He had to decide which way to go first, and he ruled out straight because he preferred having a wall on at least one side of him. As far as he could see, the catwalk in the middle disappeared between railings on each side, but there were no walls. Just to be sure, he took four steps outward and turned from side to side. The beam of light disappeared in the distance just like the railings. He turned around and saw the door he had come in through. The walls on both sides of the door were ink-black, but they were still there.

He had an inspiration and dug one hand down into a deep pocket. He carried a few coins in his pocket, not because money was worth anything, but because he liked the way it reminded him of better times. He could part with some of them if it meant he would have a better idea of his surroundings. He dropped one over the railing on his right and counted. He heard it make contact with another metal surface after counting to five.

"Twenty to thirty feet," he said.

Despite his earlier decision to stay quiet, he wanted to see if he could judge how far his voice carried. Judging by the hollow sound, he was at the edge of a wide-open area. He took a nickel from his pocket and flipped it straight down the middle of the catwalk. He kept his beam of light on it as best as he could, but it disappeared quickly. His aim was good, though, and he heard it bounce on the metal a couple of times before it careened over the side. He waited and heard it hit below.

Just as he lowered the beam of his flashlight in hopes of spotting where the coin had gone, the light dimmed and winked out. He pressed the on/off button several times and then slapped the flashlight in the palm of his good hand. It was done working, and he didn't have any spare batteries.

"Great."

Ipolito backtracked to the door. He put one hand on the wall and kept it there as he walked slowly away to the right of where he had originally come in. This was not his favorite place to be, because his scalp had that crawling feeling again. It was pitch black only an inch away, warm and moist air, and totally silent except for his breathing. Sweat poured down his face, and the crawling feeling reached his spine below the base of his neck. The wall felt smooth until his hand touched something that had an almost velvety feel.

It reminded him of a game he had played at a party once. Put your hand in a box and identify what you felt inside. It was amazing what the mind would conjure up when you couldn't see what you were touching. He had gently probed at a hardboiled egg that had the shell removed. It was smooth, a bit spongy, and he had only been told not to squeeze it. For some reason, he pictured himself holding an eyeball instead of an egg, and ever since then, he had wondered why he had thought of that first. He had never been able to eat a hardboiled egg again.

Now, his hand felt the velvet surface of the wall, and he mentally saw a blue velvet dress just like in the song by Bobby Vinton. He almost laughed. He hadn't heard that song in years. His mother had liked it, and she had talked about how she saw Bobby Vinton in concert in New Jersey once. What bothered him the most about the velvet surface was his lack of any other reference.

"Why doesn't it feel like anything else to me? Come on...give me a second choice," he said.

It seemed like once his mind saw what it thought it felt, it refused to replace it with a second choice.

He brought up his other hand and felt next to his right hand, and it seemed like the velvet broke away from the wall and landed in his hands. He stepped away and hefted it from one hand to the other. It still felt soft and velvety, but it was heavier than velvet should be... and moist. He hadn't noticed the moisture until it broke away from the wall. Now his hands were wet, and that crawling feeling was more than just crawling...it stung a little. It had been at the base of his neck, and now it was down to his lower back, and it was pushing against his shirt where it had gotten damp with sweat.

Ipolito dropped the velvet, or whatever it was, and ran back the way he had come, trailing one hand on the wall so he wouldn't miss the door. Totally blind to what was in front of him, he ran straight past the door, even when his hand felt nothing under it, and he collided with something taller than him. He was moving so fast that both he and his invisible collision victim embraced each other and fell to the steel floor. He tried to scream, but his body went through a paralysis that he couldn't seem to overcome.

9

Beaufort Marine Air Base - 2023

Colleen was packing a bag and already had a semiautomatic pistol strapped to her side in a holster. Tom stood behind her watching and waiting for the opportunity to tell her she wasn't going after Hampton. For backup, he had Sim and Iris. They were crowded into the small area at the cabin door to make her understand they would stop her physically if they had to. She didn't know they were there until she turned around.

"What's this all about?" she said.

"As if you don't know," said Tom. "You know what our orders are. The Chief said to stay here until they get back, and under no circumstances should we come after them."

Colleen took a deep breath and stared down at their feet before she answered.

"That's my husband out there."

"And my wife," said Tom.

"Then you should be strapping up your gear, and so should you, Iris. That's your husband out there too."

Colleen stabbed a finger at each of them as her fiery Irish personality broke through. It wasn't exactly a temper. It was more like a controlled explosion to bring down a building quickly. This was one time when Tom was glad he brought backup.

Colleen took a step closer, and she knew she wouldn't be a match for the former professional baseball player. Tom was the only member of the group that even came close to the Chief's height, and he had at least a foot on Colleen, but he didn't want it to come to a wrestling match. If it did, the only way he could see it ending was with Colleen tied up, and he would much rather talk her down.

"We haven't heard from them in hours," she argued. This time she aimed her finger more at Iris trying to get her on her side.

Iris had known the Chief for years before they married, and she had known early in their relationship that worry would be one of those useless emotions. The one where she worried about where he was, what he was doing, and if he was okay. She was worried about him now, but not enough to do what he said not to. He had made it clear that they weren't to come after them if they were overdue, mainly because they didn't know for sure how long it would take for them to get a plane. He had also said a rescue party stood a poor chance of succeeding if they didn't know what they were getting into.

"I understand better than you know," said Iris, "but if you go out there on a rescue mission with no useful intel, you're the one who's going to need to be rescued. We'll hear from them, or we won't. Either way, we have our orders, and I think Hampton would want us to keep you from going after them alone."

Colleen wasn't the kind of woman to cry, but the frustration she felt was bringing her closer to it than any time they could recall. It wasn't just the fact that Hampton, Kathy, and the Chief were overdue. It was a long wait on the boat. It was hot, the mosquitoes were relentless, and they could hear the crabs scraping against the hull, searching for something they could climb. Colleen didn't think she could stand the wait any longer.

It was silent at the right moment. In the enclosed cabin they all heard the triple click on their radios at the same moment. They all knew it meant someone was okay, but they didn't know who sent the signal. Most of all they knew three clicks meant not to answer. Colleen put her pack on the bed and reached for the zipper, but Tom stopped her.

"Don't unpack yet. Let's all get our gear ready. It'll save time if we get the signal to send help."

Colleen gave Tom a hug.

******

* * *

Hampton wondered how the three men had stayed alive for so long. They didn't have anyone on watch, they didn't patrol their perimeter, and they weren't quiet. They had even done the unthinkable and all gone inside the tent at the same time. Hampton crawled closer until he could hear them better. They were talking about something that had gone wrong. One of them sounded defensive.

"There's no way I did that on purpose. I don't care what you think."

"We don't know anything about them, and they might have been our ticket out of here."

"I agree, now they'll shoot us if they get the chance."

They each took a turn at having their say, but the last two comments were both aimed at the first guy. Whatever he had done, the other two weren't happy about it. Hampton listened as the conversation turned into something like a broken record. The first one kept defending himself, and the other two kept blaming him. The more he heard, the more he disliked the whining, and he finally couldn't resist putting a stop to it.

"If you guys don't stop moaning and crying, I'll give you something to cry about."

There was silence on the rooftop, but Hampton could see all three silhouettes inside the tent. They were staying very still with the exception of one arm that was slowly moving toward the lantern. The inside of the tent went dark, and Hampton heard the sound of the zipper on the flap to the left.

"Oh, really?" he said. "Is that supposed to keep me from knowing where you are? If I wanted to I could just spray the tent with bullets, unless that thing is made of Kevlar or something."

One of the three men inside spoke up and said something that made Hampton feel like he was watching a really bad movie.

"We don't want any trouble, mister."

Hampton shook his head from side to side and said, "Well, now that I'm reassured, I guess I'll be on my way."

He waited a minute to see if they would answer but decided to move the situation along.

"In case you guys are wondering if I left, the first thing you're going to do is turn the lamp back on. I don't care which one of you comes out first, but after the lamp comes on, I'll count to ten. If one of you doesn't have his hands outside the tent where I can see them before I reach ten, I'll start shooting."

There was only a brief pause before the lamp came on, and he heard the whisper of the zipper traveling around the flap again. The first pair of hands appeared before he reached three.

"That's good. Put your hands behind your head and stay on your knees," said Hampton. "Now for contestant number two, and if a hand comes out with anything in it, I'll put a bullet in contestant number one."

Hampton knew that they wouldn't be able to see him at all after having their night vision wrecked by the lantern. He could see the first guy's face well enough to tell that he was searching the darkness to figure out where the voice was coming from.

The second guy didn't have to be told what to do. He saw how his friend was kneeling and just put himself next to him with his hands laced behind his head. The third man hesitated, but just as Hampton was about to encourage him to cooperate, his hands appeared. Hampton waited until the third guy had joined his friends before he spoke again. He used their night blindness to move to a position that was almost behind them, and he used the third man for cover knowing the first two might glance his way. Their backs became rigid when he spoke.

"You're going to have to forgive my manners, but before I introduce myself, we have to do a little housekeeping. Have any of you been bitten?"

All three mumbled their answers in different ways, but judging by the relief in their voices, he believed them. One thing Hampton had learned over the years was that people who were bitten knew what would happen if they answered wrong, and there was always a touch of fear in their voices.

"Starting with contestant number one, reach down and grab the bottom of your shirt and pull it over your head without taking it off. Okay, now contestant number two. Contestant number three, you know what to do."

They were wearing tee shirts, so it was like they each had a sack over their heads. Hampton moved toward them quickly and checked them for weapons and injuries. They were clean, and for a second time, he wondered how they had stayed alive for so long. He backed away from them and sat down cross-legged. He laid his rifle across his lap, but he pulled out his pistol and kept it in his hand as he talked.

"Okay, turn around and sit like me. You can put your hands down."

He was about a dozen feet from them, so he knew he could drop all of them before they could reach him, but judging by the caution they took turning around, there wasn't any chance of it coming to that. They were clearly afraid and would do whatever he said to do. Having spent time around the brothers from Boston, Hampton was used to the way they functioned as a group. He had a feeling these three weren't brothers, but the reason they were still alive might be because they had each other.

"Let's hear it, guys. What's your story?"

"Mister, we didn't mean to let all of those dead people out of that building. We were just trying to find a place to hide. We saw you...we saw some people and didn't know if they were safe."

It was the third one to come out of the tent who spoke up, and from the sound of his voice, he was the one defending himself from the other two. Both of them turned toward him as if they were going to renew their verbal assault. All Hampton had to do was clear his throat and motion with his pistol, and they stopped.

"Let's cover that in a moment," said Hampton. "Let's start with you since you were the first one to come out," he gestured with the gun again, "and tell me who you are and where you're from."

"Um...I'm Darren Blanchet, and I'm from New Orleans."

"Introduce me to your friends," said Hampton.

Darren motioned with his thumb to his right and said, "This is Brett Gillan, and that's Grady Durant. Brett's from Charleston and Grady is from Savannah."

With prompting from Hampton, he was able to learn that all three of the men had traveled away from their homes with no particular destination in mind. They were all just trying to stay alive, and they were driven by circumstances to this location. The circumstances were all too familiar to Hampton. One day you don't see any of the infected, and the next day you can't seem to turn around without running into another one. Sometimes you feel like they're herding you. And sometimes you feel like something is herding them.

All of them were in their thirties and had worked steady jobs. Brett wasn't married, but he had a girlfriend and lots of family in Charleston. He had seen them all die, so he wasn't trying to get home to rescue someone. He had run into Darren and Grady when he realized he was outside the Marine base, and the other side of the fence might mean safety. Brett had worked as a mechanic at a car dealership, so he had been able to fix a few vehicles when he had to. He said he had lived in an abandoned camper for a long time, but he was forced to move on when some drunk bikers decided they liked it enough to take it from him. He said he never went back that way, but judging by the noise those guys made with their bikes, he doubted they lasted very long.

Grady's story was pretty much the same except that he had a wife and two children. His haunted expression told Hampton that he wasn't going to get the same happy ending as Henry Tisdal. There would be no reunion, no hugs, and no tears of joy. He had made it home too late when it started, and Hampton stopped him before he got too far. There was no need to make him relive it. He had been at work when everything started, and like everyone else, he fought to get home and then fought to leave. He was a grocery store manager, and he hated himself for wasting time trying to keep people from ransacking the shelves instead of going home, but then he hated himself more for trying to stop people from doing what he would have done if he hadn't worked there. Either way, he had never really stopped hating himself, and Hampton knew survivor's guilt when he saw it.

Darren's story was almost the worst one to hear. He was with his family at the beach not far from New Orleans when people started screaming. Everyone thought a guy had been attacked by a shark or something, so they were trying to help him. That was almost the same story everywhere, but his wife was an off-duty paramedic, and she was one of the people helping the man. He watched her put her ear to the man's face to hear his breathing. Then he saw the man rip off the side of her face with his teeth. He watched, and their three young children watched. It seemed like only minutes later that the EMS crew that responded was treating her, and she was biting them.

He pulled his children in the only direction he could, and that was toward the water. There were too many people attacking each other on the boardwalk, and the beach access walkways were jammed with people running in both directions. Once he was in the water, he thought people in a boat would help, and he handed his children to them first. When he tried to board the boat, someone hit him over the head with something heavy.

He never even saw it coming. All he knew was that he must have been unconscious for at least a few minutes, and he should have drowned. The current carried him onto a small sandbar that curved away from the end of some rocks. If he hadn't washed up there, he would have most likely ended up in the marshes as alligator food because he had a nasty cut on his scalp. The cove on the other side of the rocks was deep enough to keep anyone from getting to him, but he could see what was happening up on the beach, and he didn't want to go there.

Darren watched in a disconnected sort of way until he remembered he had his children with him. He flailed around on the sand searching the water in all directions. There were countless numbers of boats. Some were moving at high speed zigzagging between the other boats, some were on fire, and some were upside down. The ones that were still afloat but not moving were all overcrowded, and he couldn't tell them apart. He didn't know if his children were on one of them or not, but he saw his wife on the beach.

She was wandering toward a group of people who were giving first aid to someone on a stretcher. One of the people broke away from the group and calmly walked toward her. He saw it was a police officer, and he had his pistol out. As he walked toward her, he raised it to shoulder level and shot her in the face. Darren passed out for a second time.

When Darren regained consciousness, it was because of the searing pain on his right thigh where a blue crab had latched onto the skin with a big pincer. He was surprised that he could stand up at all, but the cut from the pincer stung even more because of the salt water. The crab fell off his leg leaving the pincer behind. He pried the ends apart and threw it away with disgust, then he fell down again. This time his forward momentum made him land in the water on the other side of the rocks. Despite the chaos on the beach, his splashing around in the water drew the attention of several people. They walked the same way his wife had walked toward the police officer, and their jaws all appeared to be working on something tough to chew.

One by one they walked into the water in his direction, and Darren waited for them. He was amazed to see their bodies slowly getting shorter and shorter as they walked into deeper water, and they eventually were completely submerged. A few moments later, he was shocked to see the heads reappear closer to him. There was no current inside the small cove, and they had walked to him as if it didn't matter that they were under several feet of water deeper than their heads.

Hampton chose that moment to interrupt because Darren stared at his hands and didn't go on.

"They don't breathe. We found some in freshwater lakes in Alabama that had been nibbled on by fish for years. Parts were missing, but those with teeth were still dangerous. How did you get away from them?"

Darren didn't seem to have heard the question, but he answered just as Hampton asked him again.

"Some people in a boat," said Darren. "I couldn't believe it after what had happened when I lifted my kids into the first boat. These people just coasted up next to me, and one of them held his hand out to me. I grabbed it, and he pulled me aboard."

Hampton knew the answer without asking, so he didn't want to ask if Darren ever saw his children again.

"Darren, I can see that you still feel guilty, but you didn't abandon your wife or your children. No one could have done anything for your wife, and you did what any parent would have done for their children. You didn't know that the people who took them aboard weren't offering you the same deal. For all you know, they made it to somewhere safe."

"Really? Do you think I haven't said that to myself a few times over the years? If it was true, then shouldn't I be out there trying to find them?"

Hampton knew there was nothing else he could say. Darren had a seven-year head start on Hampton when it came to guilty feelings about his children, and there wasn't anything new about the way he felt. Every living person had lost someone, and every living person felt like they could have done something differently to keep their loved ones alive.

Darren ran his hand across the top of his head. His hair, or what was left of it, was cut short, and judging by the way he studied his hand, he was surprised that his palm was wet.

"Anybody besides me getting rained on?" he asked.

Brett's sandy blonde hair was thick, so he hadn't noticed there was a coating forming on his head. When Darren asked his question, the other men all saw the same thing. Hampton held out his hand with his palm facing upward and watched as fluffy, white flakes settled on it.

Grady pulled a ball cap from his back pocket and put it on his head. He had cut his hair short because of the heat along the Georgia coast. He was used to it, and he was used to rain popping up out of nowhere. This was different, though.

"Is there a fire somewhere? Are those ashes?" asked Grady.

Hampton shook his head and said, "It's wet, I mean has it ever snowed here?"

"Yes, it has in the winter," said Grady, "but unless I've really lost track of time, I think it's summer."

"It's June...I think," said Brett.

Hampton sniffed at the big flakes that settled on his hand and then touched it with the tip of his tongue.

"Doesn't taste like ash."

Darren said, "I read that a snowflake falls sometimes for hours before it reaches the ground. That's why some flakes are so big. I don't know if that's true, but if it is, these snowflakes have been falling for at least a day."

Against the night sky, the snowfall appeared to blanket everything behind it. Every bit of light from the rooftop seemed to reflect back at them. Hampton clicked on a flashlight and aimed it upward. As suddenly as it had started, it was hard to believe it had already increased as much as it had. Hampton had seen snow a few times in South Carolina. It wasn't unheard of, but Grady was right. It wasn't supposed to be doing this in June. He decided he had to risk breaking radio silence.

He held up his radio and gave three short clicks on the send button followed by a pause and then three more short clicks. It was their signal that meant it was safe for them to receive a communication, and it was reserved for times when the sender hoped it was safe on the other end of the line. It was also agreed that the signal was only to be initiated by the team in the field, and if the rest of the crew on the boat heard the signal they would answer the same way but wait for the field team to report.

The answer came back almost immediately, and Hampton could imagine Colleen had been sitting with a radio in her lap waiting to hear from them. He wanted to call her first, but he had to think of Kathy and the Chief. A second set of clicks came through, and it had to be them. He depressed the key to speak this time.

Without introduction, he asked, "Do you have eyes on the outside?"

"Negative," was all the Chief said back. Until he knew more, he wasn't going to say more than what was necessary.

"Can you get eyes outside?" Hampton really wanted the Chief to see this for himself.

"Give me three minutes."

Even though Hampton couldn't see where the Chief and Kathy had found shelter, he knew him well enough to know he wouldn't let himself get cornered twice in one day. The paint storage building was their best option at the time, but at least it had a window on the back of it. What he couldn't see was the Chief making his way onto the roof where he had placed the solar panel. It didn't take long for him to get back to Hampton.

"Why is it snowing?"

Despite the stress of the day and their circumstance, Hampton had to be amused by the terse question.

"I was hoping you could tell me," he answered. "That is snow, right? It's not some kind of wet ash?"

"What month is this?" asked the Chief.

"Got a guy here who says he thinks it's June."

"I thought so. That's snow. What guy?"

"I made some friends. I'm okay for tonight with them. Do you mind if I check in with the rest of the crew?"

The Chief answered, "We have a friend too, and we're good until sunrise plus about four. Check in for us too."

Hampton understood that the Chief was telling him he needed time for something, and there would be time to find out what. He signed off and then switched to a frequency monitored by the boat. Colleen answered immediately, and they both felt like normal people talking on a phone for a few brief moments as they reassured each other that they were both safe. He told her he had been separated from the others, but everyone was secure for the night. He asked her to let Iris and Tom know that the Chief and Kathy were working on something, but he wasn't sure what it was.

"It's snowing really hard over here," said Colleen. "We're covered in a blanket of it already. What's happening?"

Colleen stopped short of saying the boat was covered in a blanket of snow in case someone was listening.

"I don't have a clue, but I can't say it's bothering me all that much. The temperature has dropped like a rock. On second thought, I was so caught up with the snow that I didn't realize how cold it was getting. I need to get some shelter set up."

Grady heard what Hampton said and gestured toward the tent. It wasn't large, but it would do for one night. With four men inside it, there would at least be more warmth. On second thought, Hampton mentally kicked himself for being like them for a moment. He signed off from Colleen even though he wanted to feel normal for just a bit longer.

"Guys, when I saw you camped up here, I couldn't believe you don't even post a watch. I'll take the first two hours and then wake up

Darren. Darren, you can wake up Brett after two hours. Grady, you're up after Brett. Keep the light out inside the tent, and when it's your turn, don't stay in one spot for the whole two hours. Check the hatch that leads to the roof every fifteen minutes. It's noisy, so don't touch it. Any questions?"

Hampton took out the only extra clothing he had crammed into his backpack. It was only a thin pullover, but it at least had long sleeves. He found his own ball cap and pulled it over his head. His hair was already wet, but at least he wouldn't lose any heat through the top of his head. His shirt was getting damp fast, and he knew that two hours would never feel longer than the next two.

The three men ducked into the cover of the tent, and Hampton watched as the flap zipped shut before he briefly covered his eyes and let them adjust to the darkness. When he was ready, he eased quietly across the roof to the access hatch and just listened. There was noise coming from somewhere below, but it was the random banging around that only the infected would do in the middle of the night. If they ever became capable of climbing a ladder, he didn't think this would be the night.

Hampton noticed that the snow was coming down even heavier, but it was melting against the rooftop. The surface had been too hot during the day, and it would take time for it to cool enough for the snow to accumulate. He told himself to remember to warn Darren that the melting snow might freeze before it accumulates, so he should watch out for ice, and he should pass the warning on to Brett. By the time Grady would get up, the roof was probably going to be like an ice skating rink. He checked his watch so he would know when two hours would be up and made his first full sweep of the area around the building.

There was very little light in the streets below, and the snowfall was so heavy that Hampton could barely see the ground. He would occasionally see the movement of an infected dead, but it was like watching shadows. He was never really sure if his eyes were seeing what he thought they were seeing. The swirling flakes made everything appear to be moving.

At the beginning of his second hour, Hampton could tell the snow was beginning to stick without melting. The streets around the building reflected tiny bits of light back at him just enough for him to see nothing was moving. The blanket of snow that was falling still caused moving shadows, but bulges on the streets were the places where the infected had stopped long enough to get buried. It was covering them so fast that they were freezing.

"Join the club," said Hampton. He had his hands under his armpits and kept moving just to stay warm. Besides warning each other about the ice, he needed to pass along that anyone who got too cold should come inside for at least a few minutes to get warm.

Hampton made another pass near the access hatch and listened again. This time there was no sound of movement, but there was a new sound that he was slow to notice. It was the howling made by the wind as it passed through one opening and went out through another. He had been so focused on the cold and the snow that he hadn't noticed the wind had picked up. He could see it buffeting the side of the tent and guessed they were at least twenty-knot gusts. He decided it wouldn't break Darren's, Brett's, or Grady's hearts if he told them to stay warm instead of taking their turn on watch. It was time to get himself warm before the cold killed him.

When he squeezed through the flap of the tent, Darren just assumed it was his turn. He groggily forced himself into a sitting position and walked on his knees to get past Hampton.

"Go back to sleep, Darren. It's too cold out there."

Despite being so cold that his teeth were knocking together, Hampton was fascinated as Darren stopped right where he was. Still on his knees, he went back to sleep before he reached the floor. Hampton gently pushed him to one side where Darren fell over and then curled into a ball.

The inside of the tent was only a few degrees warmer than it was outside, but being out of the wind was almost as good as being in front of a roaring fire. Hampton was glad that Colleen and the others could be warm on the boat, and wherever the Chief and Kathy were, he hoped they had it better than him and his three new friends.

10

Team Two

Kentucky - 2023

Team two had done a little better than team one. Cory Wilkes was the team leader, and as he liked to think, a notch above Brother Bernard or Brother Sparks even though he didn't carry the title of Brother like them. Before the infected dead came along he was the poster child for bullies. He was barely out of high school and was on his way to establishing a sizable rap sheet of misdemeanors. He hadn't crossed the line into a felony yet, but it would have happened if not for the interruption.

Now he was leading his team around toward the guard tower on the southern side of the Depository at Fort Knox, and he felt that same self-importance he had seen in Brother Silas when he said they were going to take possession of the gold. He was still bristling at the smart comments Brother Bernard made when he asked what they should do if they found ropes. He had at least considered throwing a lasso around a zombie and sending it back with one of his guys, but he got over it when they heard the explosions from the north side. As funny as he might have thought it would be, Brother Bernard wasn't going to be in the mood for it.

Two ropes hung from above right where they hoped they would be, and Wilkes singled out one of his three men to go make a report. The man left without a word, practically hugging the wall for safety.

It should have been a simple mission for him to accomplish. All he had to do was make it back to the main entrance and tell Brother Bernard that the group led by Cory Wilkes had found ropes at the guard tower and was about to climb them. He hadn't considered the possibility that the explosions on the north side of the building would cause activity to begin in the tall grass.

He was halfway back when a pair of the infected materialized in front of him. They were close to the wall, so they would see him if he continued on the only safe path he could follow. They hadn't noticed him yet, so he took a step backward in the direction of the south tower. He considered his options and could only think of two. He couldn't get past them, and he didn't think he could kill both of them, so he could either go back and climb one of the ropes, or he could circle the entire building. In his mind, he pictured how big the building was, and he still felt like it was a better idea than facing Wilkes. He took a few more steps backward, but he kept his eyes on the two infected dead. When he was far enough away, he turned around and ran.

The man kept going when he passed the ropes. For only a brief moment he considered shaking one to get the attention of the men who had climbed them, but he knew what Wilkes would say. He wouldn't hear the part about two zombies blocking his path. He would only see a scared man who hadn't followed orders. There was hardly a hitch in his step as the decision was made, and he began the long trip around the building.

As soon as the man had left to report to Brother Bernard, Wilkes singled out a second man and told him to wait on the ground until he and the last team member reached the top, and then he made his climb. He made it look easier than it was, and he enjoyed hearing the other team member straining at his own rope. He went head-first through a shattered window and rolled into a standing position, ready to defend himself if necessary.

It was pitch black in the room, but he didn't want to waste his flashlight batteries so soon. The second guy struggled over the frame of the window and made considerably more noise than Wilkes. If they needed the element of surprise on their side, they were out of luck.

"I don't suppose I could get you to be quieter, could I?" whispered Wilkes.

The man said he was sorry, but he said it in a normal voice, and Wilkes was fairly sure that the man was smirking even though the darkness would prevent him from being able to tell for sure.

The rope used by Wilkes had become tight as soon as he had released it, so he knew the third climber would be at the window soon. He went over and met the man as he arrived and gave him a hand so he could get him to be quiet. Even if Wilkes helped someone, it was for his own good. Otherwise, he would have let the man flounder the way the other one had. They were both expendable in his mind, so if they drew unwanted attention to themselves, he didn't really care as long as he wasn't part of it.

"Listen up, you two. From here on out, if you make any noise at all, I'm putting you in front. Got it?"

Neither of them said anything, and he took that as their acceptance of the warning. It was almost pitch black inside the guard tower, and there weren't any clues about what to do next, so he whispered that they should follow him. He would use his flashlight for a few seconds at a time, and he told them to take in as much of their surroundings as they could before he turned it off. If they saw something important, let him know, but don't wake up the whole neighborhood. This time he heard their low acknowledgments. Neither of them wanted to be in front.

Wilkes clicked his flashlight on for a moment, and the beam shone directly into the eyes of one of the men. He had thought it was aimed at the side of the room where the door should be, and the sudden brightness made the man cry out defensively. Wilkes clicked it off again, but the damage was already done. The man was seeing big white spots in front of his face, and he moved away from Wilkes as if he thought Wilkes would turn it on again. He collided with an old rolling chair and noisily crashed to the floor.

All three of them stayed exactly where they were and listened. The sound of the man falling and the chair being knocked across the room echoed back at them, but long after the echo stopped, there was something else. There was something moving inside the building.

Wilkes had a mental image of what was most likely lurking in the darkness. The infected had probably sat or stood dormant until something gave them a reason to move. Still, he wasn't sure if he was really hearing it, or if it was just his imagination filling in the blanks. All sound seemed to be swallowed by the darkness, and it was silent again.

He turned on the flashlight for a second time, but this time he intended to shine it on the man who had fallen over the chair. The man shielded his eyes against the glare and avoided being blinded again.

"Are you crazy or stupid?" asked Wilkes. "What's your name? I need to know so I can write it on your tombstone."

It was a classic line Wilkes used all the way through high school, and he just kept pulling it out when he had a new victim in his sights. As always, he hoped his victim would take the bait and answer so he could use his next well-worn tactic. He stared at the man as if he was waiting for something. The man had seen his act before, so he didn't answer. He knew if he told Wilkes his name, the bully would interrupt and say he didn't really care what his name was.

The rusty hinges on the door that led out of the guard tower hadn't moved in a long time. The moisture in the humid Kentucky air had worked on the metal until the creases of the hinges were caked with a brown and red crust. It flaked away as the door was pushed from the other side. The sound was like fingernails on a chalkboard.

Wilkes could have done what most people would have done. He could have aimed the beam of his flashlight at the door so they would all know what threat had come into the room. He was wired for self-preservation, though. He clicked the switch and turned off the light. At the same time, he backed away from the doorway, putting the man on the floor between himself and whatever it was that was pushing on the door.

In the scuffle that followed, all three men knew by the smell what had walked into the guard tower. The man on the floor was smarter than Wilkes had thought. He pulled the rolling chair closer and then pushed it toward the spot where he had last seen the door. It caught the infected dead squarely on both knees. The sinew that held the bones together snapped audibly, and the infected fell forward onto the chair.

Even though they couldn't see more than the shadows caused by the chaos, all three men assumed the door was clear for a moment, and they did their best to go in that direction. They arrived at the door at precisely the same moment, and the collision was like bowling pins getting hit by a perfectly thrown ball. The fourth bowling pin in this case was an infected dead that had been attracted to the racket inside the guard tower. Human voices had not been heard inside the building in a long time, and it was like someone rang a dinner bell. The collision in the doorway was a guarantee that the dinner bell was heard from as far away as possible.

The infected dead that blocked the exit was knocked backward, but the three men made a pile in the doorway. They wrestled to get out of the pile, each one sure that they were about to be bitten by the infected. When Wilkes broke free, he pushed himself back into the room. With his weight gone from the others, the man who had fallen over the chair went blindly in the same direction as the infected. He never saw the waist-high railing outside the room, and it did nothing to slow him down. He flipped over it with spectacular style and spun away into the black interior of the building. The third man had the sense to reach out with his hands before he moved. His left hand found the door frame, and he pulled himself away from the opening to the left without getting off the floor.

Most bullies aren't nearly as brave as they want others to think they are, and Wilkes was no different. He could see shadows better from where he was because a small amount of light had filtered through the windows behind him. He searched the darkness around the door for shapes he could recognize, but he couldn't locate two of them. He knew there should be three, but he could only find one moving shadow, and it was crab-walking to the left along the wall. Wilkes moved to the right and got down behind a console where guards had sat and monitored security systems long ago.

Few things could fuel the imagination more than a fear of the dark, and in the mind of Cory Wilkes, it was like gasoline being poured on a fire. A scraping sound made his skin crawl, and there was a smell in the air he could only describe as wet.

It reminded him of a cold night last year when he was burning everything he could find to stay warm. He was holed up in an old farmhouse that had lost part of its roof. Newspapers from long ago were stacked high along one wall, and the dry bundles burned hot. The wet bundles burned, but they made smoke billow from the fireplace that made his eyes burn. It hadn't occurred to him that rat urine was what had yellowed the newspapers and not the rain. To make matters worse, when the pile of newspapers collapsed toward him, the spiders that inhabited the abandoned rat nests inside ran in every direction.

Remembering the smell of ammonia and the way it made his eyes burn, caused Wilkes to be convinced that the wet smell inside the guard tower could only be from rat urine, and if there were rats, there were likely to be spiders. That made his scalp itch, and he wasn't able to fight back the urge to turn on his flashlight.

The glow from behind the console reflected off the walls and ceiling more than Wilkes would have tolerated if it had been someone else, but it revealed how accurate his fears had been. He had crawled into something so green and spongey that it was crushed under his hands and knees. It was as lush as a putting green, but it practically disintegrated under his weight. He lifted a handful of the fragile substance to his face for a closer look and saw that it was moving.

Wilkes felt his throat tighten as his chest tried but failed to release the scream he desperately wanted to make. The movement inside the substance that resembled thick moss was a dense mass of spidery legs and bodies. He drove himself forward from the floor and went head-first through the broken window he had entered minutes before. His hands somehow found the rope that was literally his lifeline to safety, and he descended fast enough to wear the skin from his palms and fingers.

It was almost the same pitch blackness outside as it was inside the guard tower because clouds blocked out the little bit of light that had been there before. Wilkes didn't forget the explosions earlier that meant someone had strayed too far from the building, and he didn't charge blindly back to the front door. He stayed close to the wall, trailing a bloodied right hand on the rough surface of the building. He didn't feel the roughness, nor was he aware of the amount of skin that rubbed free from his palm and fingers. His only bit of luck was that the two infected dead that had caused his messenger to retreat were somewhere out in the tall grass testing their own blind luck with the landmines.

By the time he rounded the corner to stand in front of Brother Bernard, white pieces of bone with chunks of flesh dangling between them were all that was left of his hand, but he didn't seem to be aware of it. Even as he stood there in front of Bernard and the other two men, the chunks of flesh were getting smaller.

"Dude, what happened to your hand?" asked the tweaker.

Wilkes held up his hand and gazed at it through glassy eyes.

"Something's wrong with it," he said.

"You think so?" said Bernard.

Specs leaned closer to Wilkes and shone his flashlight on the hand.

"There's something on it. That green moss is moving. Wait a minute, that's not moss, Wilkes. That's a mess of little spiders, but I've never seen spiders do that before. Look how fast they're moving."

"Is there something wrong with you, Specs? The man has bugs eating his hand, and you act like you're watching the Discovery Channel."

Specs didn't get the 'not so subtle hint' and said, "Spiders aren't really bugs. They're more like crabs."

"You think I want a science lesson right now? If you don't shut up, guess what they're eating next."

Specs might have missed a hint, but the threat was something he heard loud and clear. He backed away from Wilkes, but he kept his distance from Bernard too.

"What happened?" asked Brother Bernard.

Wilkes kept his damaged hand in front of him and held it higher as if it answered Bernard's question.

"This."

"I can see that."

Bernard was torn between wanting to be patient with someone who was undoubtedly in shock and beating him over the head for a straight answer. Wilkes didn't elaborate, so Bernard asked again in a calm but measured tone of voice.

"Can you tell us what happened to your hand? Did you get inside the tower? You were supposed to send back someone to report your progress."

Wilkes heard every part of the question, but he was fading with each passing second. None of the men had noticed that Wilkes wasn't bleeding out as his wrist was being consumed by the green-bodied spiders that were swarming beyond his hand to his forearm. He was in shock because his blood was being eaten as fast as his flesh, and the bloated green bodies that were eating him weren't diminishing in number even as they fell off under their own weight.

"We climbed the rope. There's something in there. This happened."

Brother Bernard resisted the temptation to grab Wilkes and shake the answers out of him. He would have slapped him for answers, but at the moment he didn't want to touch him.

"What happened to the other men with you?"

Wilkes seemed to let that question register with whatever was left of his mind, and his head turned in the direction of the south tower. His eyes searched for something, presumably the other men, but if he intended to answer, it only came out as an unintelligible syllable followed by a trail of blood-tinted saliva.

Bernard, Specs, and the tweaker all backed away from Wilkes. Bernard backed all the way up the steps to the front door, but then he realized whatever happened to Wilkes, it most likely happened inside. He took one look at the building over his left shoulder before moving quickly to a spot that put Specs roughly between himself and Wilkes.

Specs felt like Bernard was going to push him closer to Wilkes, so he circled to his right to get further from both of them. The tweaker wasn't about to go toward the building, and he felt safer by Specs, so he met up with him several feet behind Wilkes. By the time the two of them were in the same spot, the tweaker was scratching his arms raw, and Specs had picked up the habit too. Watching the tiny spiders crawl around on Wilkes made him feel like they were between every hair on his own scalp.

Wilkes didn't turn with them, and his eyes were still locked on something in the distance. It was doubtful that he was able to see ten feet in front of his face because the damage happening to his right arm was happening at a much more grand scale inside his body. The crab-like creatures had traveled with lightning quickness to reach his brain, and there was already a crusty green and red discharge coming from the corners of his eyes. It ran from one nostril and pooled on his upper lip. Thick and sticky, it didn't drip and fall over. It just collected until it trailed across his partially open mouth to his chin.

Bernard was still to the side, so he saw the color of Wilkes' skin change even in the darkness. Wilkes became so pale that his skin appeared to be transparent. Then it took on a green shade as every drop of blood was consumed, followed by the appearance of the tiny creatures working their way through the pores of his skin. It was amazing that he was still standing.

Just as that thought crossed Bernard's mind, Wilkes' knees shook and then buckled. He fell to the ground in a crumpled heap as if there were no bones in his body. The three men around him kept their distance, but they were too fascinated to take their eyes off him.

Specs said, "I think we need to do something."

"Like what?" barked Bernard. "You wanna give him mouth to mouth, be my guest."

"I was thinking more along the lines of shooting him in the head."

Bernard obviously hadn't considered what would happen because he stopped talking with his mouth open ready to deliver his next comment. He leaned around to see the face of the dead man and saw no sign of life or Wilkes returning as an infected.

"He wasn't bitten, was he?" he asked Specs.

"When did that become a requirement?" answered the tweaker.

That earned him an angry stare from Bernard who was already thinking about what he was going to tell Brother Silas. He was less worried about Wilkes being dead than he was about being able to explain what killed him. Most of all he was afraid Silas would tell him to climb the ropes to find out.

The body twitched, and the three men scrutinizing it from a safe distance all took another long step away from it. When Wilkes had dropped to the pavement, it was as if he had collapsed into himself. The pile of his body was stacked in a small space only a couple of feet high. When it twitched, the left leg unfolded from under the pile like it was being inflated. Once it was straightened out, there was a brief pause before the right leg appeared. It was pointed upward at an angle, but it lowered to the pavement as it became fully exposed. Wilkes was slumped forward, but he was in a sitting position. As his back and neck straightened, his chin lifted from his chest. His face was blank and gave no hint of intelligence.

The reddish-green discharge from his mouth and eyes was definitely more green, and there was a lump of green inside each ear. The thing Wilkes had become rolled onto its left side and pushed upward using an arm that was bent in an unnatural direction. There was an audible crack as a bone broke in the arm, but he continued to push.

The roll to one side caused the creature to be on its knees facing Specs and the tweaker. Another step backward felt like it was enough for them to be safe, but both of them were ready to run. When Wilkes got his legs under him and he pushed himself to a full standing position, that was enough for the two men. They didn't hesitate another second as they bolted for the main gate. Brother Bernard was left standing off to the side, unsure of what to do.

If he hadn't acted when he did, Bernard would have been cornered between the tall grass and the infected dead Wilkes had become. One thing Bernard knew for sure was that he didn't want the thing to even touch him. Those tiny green spiders weren't easy to see in the darkness, but Bernard figured if he was close enough to see them, he was closer than he should be. Getting them on his skin wasn't going to happen.

Brother Bernard pulled his semiautomatic pistol from the holster on his hip and fired two shots at close range. The first bullet hit Wilkes in the forehead, and the second bullet was on time to hit Wilkes above the left ear as his head spun away from him. The body went down in a heap for a second time, but unlike the hundreds of infected dead he had shot over the years, the body twitched for several minutes.

Specs and the tweaker were already out the front gate by the time the body quit twitching, and Brother Bernard was trying to decide what to do next. He didn't think he had much choice. He had sent four men to the north tower and four to the south tower. Seven men were unaccounted for, and if he excluded the idiots who had stepped on mines, he was still missing several with no idea what happened to them.

******

On the eastern side of the Depository, Michael Demmings, the man who had been circling the building, was questioning his own decision. It had been so long since anyone had been on that side of the secure area that the grass was as tall as him and grew closer to the building. At about the halfway point, the narrow path along the wall came to an end. He was faced with walking blindly into the grass or going back.

He stood still and listened for any sign of danger, and he took some small comfort in the sound of crickets. If the crickets were quiet, it would mean they had gone silent for their own safety. While he watched and listened, there was just enough light for him to see that the irregular shape of the building meant he was only a few yards from the guard tower on the eastern side of the Gold Depository. He wondered if it was his imagination that there was a dark line against the sky that might be a rope.

It wouldn't be his first choice to climb into the building, but he had a long way to go if he stayed on the ground, and without the path along the wall, he would face the risk of running straight into any infected dead that were near the building. He decided to go for the rope.

Parting the grass with both hands, he took a few cautious steps closer to the tower. The crickets stopped making their music close to the building, and he stopped moving to be sure he was the cause. After a few seconds, they resumed chirping, and he was reassured that he could reach the ropes safely.

After all of the times in the last seven years when Michael had been faced with the possibility of making a fatal error, he didn't recall ever being more afraid. It was hot, humid, and dark, and he was alone. It was the perfect recipe for dying, and he wondered how he could have become so stupid to get himself into this predicament. He knew the answer was that he had hooked up with the wrong crowd.

Wilkes was a fool, and he was still amused by Bernard telling him to lasso a zombie. Brother Bernard was a bigger fool who just lived for the chance to make Brother Silas happy, and he knew what Silas was. Silas was a power-hungry little tyrant who should be hung before he got any more of them killed.

A few more carefully placed steps brought him to the rope. The crickets were going quiet again, but he couldn't see movement in the grass that would mean an infected dead was coming his way. He reached up and got a grip. He didn't notice how sweaty his hands were until he squeezed the rope and tested how well it was attached somewhere above. Demmings saw a fleeting image of himself watching the sunrise from a place on the ground where he lay with a broken back after falling from the tower. He forced the image from his mind and pulled himself up the rope.

After getting his feet off the ground, he put both firmly against the wall. One tentative step upward with his right leg and one hard pull with his arms, and it seemed to him that he could actually do it. It was an exhilarating feeling to be above the grass again. At least it was at first.

There was a tug at the material on the inside of his left pants leg. His mind didn't process the extra weight on his leg as a problem, just that something was wrong. He didn't even look down to see what caused it. He just lifted his leg with more effort. Then he felt the tug become a pull, and then the pull was a grip that encircled his entire leg like a vise. It was at that moment when it finally came together in his mind what was happening, and he had seen it happen to other people enough times to know what he could expect to happen next. That didn't make the searing pain easier to endure.

Michael couldn't even see the infected dead that had his leg in an embrace as it buried its face into the heavy denim just above the ankle. It crossed his mind in a detached way that it was amazing how hard the emaciated creatures could bite. He tried not to scream, but he had never felt more pain in his life. He had to let it out.

The scream that escaped from his mouth echoed into the darkness. As he exhaled every bit of air he had inside him, he let go of the rope and landed with his full weight on the shoulders of the infected. The results were spectacular. The infected dead felt no pain, so getting them to let go once their teeth were sunk into a victim was almost impossible. It was totally unexpected when the pressure of the teeth stopped, but when he saw why, he wasn't going to question his good luck. Its lower jaw was missing from its face.

That wasn't the most incredible thing Michael saw because it was only a small part of the damage done to the infected dead crushed by his weight. In the trampled grass, he saw that it really was possible to break someone in half. The lower half of the creature was on his left side facing away from him. The upper half lay on its back to his right facing upward. It appeared to be trying to bite the air with its missing jaw. A gurgling sound came from the exposed airway at the back of its throat.

Michael realized that everything under his body was stretched between the two halves of the infected dead. He pushed himself up with disgust from the middle of the sticky mess and wiped his hands furiously against his pants. He also realized staying around to see what might have heard the commotion wasn't the best choice. Michael retreated to the wall and continued his journey toward the north tower. He limped, but he was alive.

11

Cold

Beaufort Marine Air Base - 2023

The sun was up, but it was hidden behind a solid wall of gray clouds. Light filtered through and reflected off a white blanket of snow that covered everything, and it was still falling. The temperature had dropped well below freezing, and the infected dead were mostly immobile. Those that were still moving were on the ground only making feeble attempts to lift arms weighed down by ice. Their usual groaning was muted as if it took more effort to make noise.

"It's going to take longer for the solar panel to collect enough light to charge the battery," said the Chief.

They were warm inside the MRAP, and when they discovered how cold it was outside, they had to convince themselves that they hadn't lost track of time. It was hard enough to accept this much snow in South Carolina without trying to figure out how it was happening in the summer. It should be around one hundred degrees outside, but it was closer to thirty.

The Chief cautiously pulled open a door and found himself staring at a snow drift over three feet deep. Even though it was overcast, he had to shield his eyes from the light reflecting from the white surface.

"Do you suppose Hampton found a place to stay warm?" asked Kathy.

"He was an outdoorsman before the apocalypse," said the Chief.

131

"He's probably got a roaring fire going somewhere. When he checked in last night he said he was safe with other people, so I imagine they had shelter."

"That's exactly what we could use right now. I'm going to see if I can use one of the empty oil barrels. Maybe I can rig up a smokestack for it so we don't suffocate while we stay warm."

"Speaking of smoke," said the Chief, "I don't see it, but I smell it. If it's not Hampton, I'll be surprised, but I'm going to find out before you send up a smoke signal too."

"Makes sense," said Kathy. "I think we need to check in with the boat and ask them if they can still get radio contact with the Ambush."

"I feel like I should know this, but what do we need with the British Navy right now?"

Kathy said, "You know why. You just have your mind on other things. The Ambush has long-range communications. They may have some idea about why it's snowing in June."

"And I thought I was the brains for this operation," said the Chief.

Kathy said something about being both the beauty and the brains, but the Chief knew it was coming and managed to get away from her before she could finish. She shook her blond hair and even flipped it when he walked away. He noticed, but he kept going to keep her from winning their little sparring match. She mentally filed the tactic away and was determined to use it on him the next time.

Caleb watched the exchange, and since he hadn't really grown up around adults, he wasn't sure if they liked each other or were just playing.

"Is he mad at you?" he asked Kathy.

She laughed and said, "No, he just likes to plan everything. It's part of his training as a Navy SEAL. Do you know about SEALs?"

"Yeah, we knew some who were Marines first. They were bad dudes."

"The Chief can be a bad dude when he has to be."

Kathy thought for a moment about some of the times she had seen the Chief be his most ferocious self and opened her mouth to tell Caleb about what he did to the man who had buried Iris, but she stopped herself. She decided it was enough for Caleb to know the Chief had a reputation, but he didn't need to hear the details.

While the Chief took care of changing the fuel filters on the Cougar, Kathy got her radio and hailed the rest of the group. It only took a minute to get the crew on the shrimp boat to answer. They were apparently waiting with the information they had already gotten from the Captain of the Ambush. Kathy was stunned by their explanation of the reason for the snow, and she had to sit down to hear it all.

Tom was the one to give her the report, and he felt helpless. It was inevitable, and there was no way to stop it. The only thing they could do was adapt to a world that was changing again.

"Nuclear winter?" said Kathy. "But how?"

"Captain Byrne said they had detected large changes in thermal layers of the ocean, and that the surface temperature was much lower than anything he had ever seen at their location."

Submarines routinely used thermal layers as shields against detection. The change in water temperature occurred in layers that they could duck below to hide from other ships that might be tracking them, but those layers were usually below warmer surface layers.

Tom continued, "Byrne says they were reading surface temperatures they would expect at the North Pole, and that they contacted Gentry Campbell to see if she could get access to any weather satellites that would help explain what's happening, and why is it happening now. She found something we've been expecting ever since the nuclear power plant in South Carolina leaked radiation."

"How bad is it?" asked Kathy.

"Satellite imagery isn't great because of the cloud cover, but apparently it wasn't something that started yesterday. It's been building up for the last seven years. We were naive to think all of the reactors were shut down in time before the reactor operators were overcome. Byrne said there were somewhere between four and five hundred reactors in operation at the time, and he's surprised we didn't see the effects sooner."

"Where?"

"China," said Tom. "Gentry told him the cloud cover was really dense over a few of the most rural of their reactors, but heat signatures pretty clearly showed the operators of those reactors didn't have time to pull the rods and shut down. The heat blooms caused the weather we're seeing now, but it's been going on in Asia for years already. They had forty-seven reactors in operation when the infection began, and at least three have been heating the atmosphere."

"What about the spread of radiation?" asked Kathy.

"Good question," said Tom. "It's always going to be based on which way the wind blows, but so far it appears to be limited to the areas surrounding those reactors. Of course, we don't have anyone monitoring it that we know of. We can tell what it's doing to the weather, though."

"Wait a minute," said Kathy. "Huntsville is about six hundred miles northwest of here. Is it snowing there?"

"Gentry said it's coming down hard. They've sealed off the shelters and are getting buried as we speak. She expressed concern about not being able to run an errand for the Chief."

Tom and Kathy both knew that someone could be listening to their radio call, so they didn't say what the errand was, but it was hard enough to get from Huntsville to Fort Knox without snow. Kathy told Tom she would break the news to the Chief, and maybe they could figure out a way for her to help that didn't involve her traveling to meet them there.

Kathy and Tom signed off, and she saw that the Chief had gone up through the hole in the roof again. It was going to be difficult to get enough charge through the solar panel without direct sunlight, but they were going to be forced to remove the snow from the panel every thirty minutes.

Kathy enlisted Caleb's help, and together they rolled a big steel drum over to a door. It wasn't hard to find enough sheet metal to make a stovepipe, and after some creative cutting and fitting, they had a stove they could feed from the side. They cut a hole in the wall for the pipe and then set about the task of finding things they could burn.

The Chief arrived just as they were fitting the stovepipe to the wall, so Kathy was able to give him the news as they broke wooden pallets into firewood. Nothing seemed to faze the Chief enough to make him show any emotion, but Kathy could see the set of his jaw tightening.

"More delays," he said in a low voice that was more of a grumble than a statement. "Go ahead and light your fire because it's so overcast out there that no one will be able to tell where the smoke is coming from. I couldn't spot the source of the smoke I smelled."

"We've faced worse things than this," said Kathy. "Imagine what it would be like if we were on foot traveling to Kentucky or even Atlanta. Snow like this would've forced us to dig in and wait until it let up, or even worse until we got hungry."

"Speaking of food, we didn't bring much with us. We need to find Hampton and get back to the boat, but I don't know how long it's going to take to charge the battery in the MRAP."

The Chief had barely finished the last part of what he was saying when there was a rapping sound at the door. There was a pattern to it that they had used many times over the years, so they knew it was either Hampton or someone from the boat, but on the off chance it was someone who got lucky and mimicked the knock, Kathy and the Chief both drew weapons and took up defensive positions to the sides of the door.

Kathy rapped a different pattern on the metal wall. This one was their request for confirmation, and it also meant the unknown person outside could speak if they wanted to.

"It's me," said Hampton. "I have friendlies with me."

The Chief holstered his gun as he unlatched the door. When he pulled it open, they saw Hampton and a trio of men gathered in a small clearing they had made in the snow. They were all stamping their cold feet and were hunched over against the wind.

"Get in here," said Kathy.

Hampton came inside first and was talking through teeth that were knocking together.

"I didn't really need to knock on the door. It's so cold out there that my teeth banging against each other was enough. Does anyone have any ideas about what's going on?"

"You haven't checked in with the boat?" asked the Chief.

"Last night right after I talked with you," said Hampton. "They didn't know anything."

"They do now," said Kathy. "They managed to make contact with the Ambush, and it wasn't good news. Some reactors in China popped, and they're apparently causing nuclear winter."

Hampton didn't speak immediately. He was letting it sink in. The three men behind him all seemed to be staying behind him, waiting for someone to say they could speak.

He finally said, "Does that ever go away? I mean, once nuclear winter starts, does it ever stop?"

One of the men behind him said, "Depends on how big the source was and if it's continuing to fuel the problem."

"Are you a scientist of some kind?" asked Kathy.

Brett Gillan stepped forward and said, "No, Ma'am. I've just read a lot of theories about it. Since it's never happened before, there isn't complete agreement about what it would take to reach climate disruption. You know, all of the above-ground tests combined with the bombs dropped on Hiroshima and Nagasaki didn't cause nuclear winter."

Kathy stared at him without giving away any emotion, and it made him feel like getting behind Hampton again for protection.

She asked, "Do any of those theories include warnings about calling a woman Ma'am?"

Gillan shrunk even further behind Hampton.

Hampton had seen Kathy do that stare often enough, but it never got old to him.

"She's just yanking your chain, Brett. I should've introduced you guys first."

Hampton took care of the introductions, and Kathy lightened up so they would know she was just kidding around. The fact that he was a Charleston native was enough explanation for her. It seemed like all women were called Ma'am in Charleston before the infection showed up.

Kathy said, "Go ahead and finish what you were saying. It sounded interesting even if it's just a theory."

"Well, like I was saying, one theory says the climate changes will be directly proportional to the size and duration of the event. The snow we're getting right now is probably being caused by something that began a long time ago, like shortly after the infection began. The real question is whether or not the reactors that popped are still feeding this phenomenon."

"If they're still fueling it," said Kathy, "we can expect this to keep going."

"Correct, but the effects are cumulative. They add onto each other."

The Chief said, "You mean the bad weather will cause more bad weather, and if the reactors are still fueling the nuclear winter, it won't just get worse, it'll go on longer?"

"Right," said Gillan, "but that's just one possibility. There are a lot more people who think a nuclear winter will trigger an ice age that just has to run its course."

Kathy stopped him again, "But if those people are right, what happens if the reactors keep fueling it?"

"Well, I guess that would mean temperatures would keep dropping until the whole planet freezes over. On the bright side, all the zombies would freeze."

No one bothered to tell Gillan they weren't zombies because they were too focused on how he would be able to see a bright side in any scenario that included a nuclear winter that never ended.

The Chief asked, "Do any theories include us not freezing too?"

Gillan saw that his audience was waiting. The kid, the woman, the big guy, Hampton, and his two friends were all giving him their undivided attention, and it dawned on him that he hadn't given them anything except the worst-case scenarios.

"There's one theory that says nothing will happen."

"You call this nothing?" said Kathy.

"Well," he stammered, "it could be a one-and-done type thing. This could end today, or it could end in a week or so."

The Chief didn't say anything else. He simply turned and walked away. A slight hand motion told Kathy she should follow.

"What's up, Chief?"

"He's right about one thing. The infected will freeze, and even though it hasn't occurred to him, this will most likely be a setback for blue crabs and spiders. If it lasts long enough but not too long, it would be a good thing."

"I've seen that look before. You've got a plan bouncing around inside that big head of yours."

"I do, but it's going to require a bit of luck. I don't think we have what it takes to get an Osprey in the air, but we need sunshine to get the solar panel to provide enough power to start the MRAP."

Brett Gillan walked right past the Chief and Kathy as if they weren't there.

"Oh, man...that's an MRAP. That thing's a beast, and the company that made them knew what they were doing. They were in business for over a hundred years, and they knew they had to make something that was hard to break but easy to fix. When they designed it, they started with making the body strong enough to withstand explosive devices, but when they got to the engine, they went back to basics."

The Chief knew his voice sounded abrupt, but he couldn't believe he had just told Kathy his plan needed a bit of luck, and he was getting a dose of it almost immediately.

"How did they get back to basics?"

"Well, for starters...no pun intended, the ignition system is a weak link on any piece of equipment that requires an engine. I heard you say something about getting an Osprey in the air, and I hate to tell you, that ain't gonna happen. Too many complex systems. The MRAP is another story. The starter on the MRAP has a redundant system that operates like the engine on an airplane when you turn the propellor manually."

The Chief couldn't believe his ears.

"You mean a magneto? Are you a mechanic or something? Did I

miss the propellor on that thing?"

"I worked on cars and small trucks, but I know these things too. When they got them ready to ship overseas from the Charleston harbor, I made a little extra money on the side loading them. I remember when they got one or two that had dead batteries, they used a hand crank to build up enough juice to get them started. The battery would charge up by running."

"Show me."

Gillan was more than happy to be useful, and the Chief followed him to the back door of the MRAP. He climbed inside and easily released four small knobs that held down a section of the deck plating. Once he set the sheet of steel floor aside, he pointed for the Chief to see what was inside the reinforced compartment.

There was a metal wrench that was shaped like the lug wrench for removing tires, but the end of this one was an exact fit with a tight hole in the middle of a drum-shaped device. Gillan grabbed the wrench and attached it to the drum.

"Want to see if it still works?" he asked.

"By all means. I'll get in the driver's seat to give it some gas."

The Chief gave him a thumbs-up signal when he was ready, and Brett Gillan put his weight behind the metal wrench. The device hadn't been turned in years, so it stubbornly resisted. Hampton had followed behind them when they had walked toward the MRAP, and when he saw what they were doing, he knew exactly why because he had seen similar systems on small airplanes. He climbed in with Gillan and got his hands around the wrench with him. Together they got it to budge.

When the engine turned over, it didn't catch at first, but when it did, it roared into life. Kathy was standing outside the driver's side door, and the Chief saw she was slowly shaking her head from side to side.

The truck let out a monstrous backfire, but he still heard her ask in a loud voice, "How's that for a little bit of luck?"

"We need to let it run for a few minutes," yelled Gillan, "and if you haven't done it already, someone should stir the fuel."

"Already done, and I changed the fuel filters just before you guys got here."

While the Chief climbed up to the roof to retrieve the solar panel, Hampton and Brett Gillan went over the MRAP making sure it was ready to roll. They checked every detail. Kathy took Caleb and the other two new arrivals with her to all of the tool benches and supply cabinets. They gathered up anything that they could use, but they also kept the shrimp boat in mind. Charlie would appreciate the odds and ends they collected for him.

In just over thirty minutes, the Chief let out a whistle and pointed at the makeshift stove. Everyone gathered around it to get a little warmth and to hear what he had to say.

"I'll make this quick. It won't take long to get back to the boat, but I don't know how the ground is holding up under all that snow. It wouldn't be much fun if we got that heavy piece of machinery stuck in the mud. There isn't a tow truck big enough to pull it out...at least not around here."

"So, we're not all going to enjoy the ride?" asked Kathy.

The Chief nodded.

"Hampton, I want you behind the wheel with Caleb riding shotgun up top."

Caleb's excitement was obvious.

"I get to shoot the zombies?"

"Not a chance," said the Chief. "I don't want you to touch the gun. You could shoot one of us by accident. I want you to just watch for movement. Let us know if you see anything we should know about. The rest of us will be out front and in the back. Four of us will walk in two pairs ahead of the vehicle to be sure the ground is solid. Any questions?"

"We aren't really dressed for this," said Kathy. "It was summer when we got here. As a matter of fact, everyone on the shrimp boat is probably crammed into the pilothouse. That's where the best heater is."

"I knew I was forgetting something," said the Chief.

Caleb hesitantly raised his hand. Being the only kid around adults who had been surviving out in the wild, he felt a little useless until this moment.

"I know where the pilots kept flight suits. The next building over from here closer to the planes has a ready room. Problem is that it's been full of dead people for a long time. We never needed anything from there, so we just kept it closed."

"Kid, you're a lifesaver," said the Chief.

Since he never really had a father figure in his life, or at least he hadn't during the years it mattered most, Caleb was drawn to the Chief, and the effect of the big man's praise was obvious to all of them. Kathy especially liked seeing it. She had seen how the Chief was around kids. They brought out something in his personality that she guessed was part of his own upbringing. She had never gotten him to talk about his own father, but she figured he was either passing along the good parenting he had gotten, or he was trying hard not to be like his father. She hoped that one day she would find out.

Kathy asked, "When you say it's full of dead people, how many would you guess there are?"

"Ummm...I don't know, maybe twenty or thirty?" Caleb was unsure, so his answer came out as a question.

The Chief turned to the three men who had come back with Hampton.

"Any of you ever been inside that building?"

They all shook their heads to indicate they hadn't.

"Well, if it was a ready room, then there would have been an area up front for the pilots who were already in their flight suits. That would be the place with the door facing the planes. The next space would be the bunk room and maybe a locker room next to it. The locker room should be our target."

Hampton said, "Maybe we could do this the easy way for once."

When Hampton laid out his plan, the Chief and Kathy were both in favor of doing it his way. Caleb and the three newcomers went to the back of the MRAP and climbed inside. Kathy closed the door and made sure they locked it while the Chief got ready to back the huge vehicle out through the door. Hampton waited at the corner of the door ready to pull the chain that would roll the door upward.

None of them expected the dead to be waiting for them to come out because the temperature had been below freezing for so many hours, but that didn't mean none had frozen against the outside of the door. Until they opened it, they wouldn't know if there was a threat. Kathy joined Hampton to be sure he was able to pull the door all the way up once he started.

The MRAP Cougar had been idling since they started the engine, and it was running smoothly when the Chief gave Hampton the signal. Kathy crouched with her pistol pointed at the gap that appeared along the bottom of the door as Hampton raised it higher. The first thing she saw was a wall of snow where the wind had caused it to drift against the building, but that changed when it was only three feet from the floor.

Heads and other body parts that were frozen to the metal door were jerked upward. Where the snow was loose, the infected were pulled into standing positions. They stood as if they had been sculpted from the ice. Four of them were facing inward in a pose that suggested they were just waiting for the chance to come inside. They must have been leaning against the door with their arms in front of their bodies when they became too frozen to move, and the door had raised their arms. One was pointing straight at Kathy and even had the index finger extended.

There was never a time when Kathy felt like the infected dead were lucky, but if she had ever become infected, she would consider herself lucky to die quickly. As she watched the door go upward, there was a brief moment when she considered one of them to be less lucky than the others. It stood in the center of the opening with its right arm pointing straight up. Its left arm was gone, but it hadn't gone far. It hung from the bottom of the door and swung gently as it rose even higher.

"That one's having a bad day," said Hampton, "and it's about to get worse."

The huge personnel carrier rolled backward as soon as the door was high enough, and the infected dead that was pointing upward at its detached arm disappeared along with the others. Judging by the way the rear end of the vehicle rose slightly and then dropped downward, there must have been a crowd directly outside the door. The cracking sound of frozen bodies being crushed was similar to the sound the Cougar would create if it was driven onto a frozen lake.

As the front of the big vehicle passed Kathy and Hampton, the Chief called down to close the door when he was clear because they might have to come back to the motor pool again. They waved at him and followed in the places where the wheels crushed the snow. She and Hampton both inspected the tire tracks that were now a combination of crushed ice and bodies. It was hard to avoid stepping on any of the red spots, but sharp bones poked upward in places, and they knew stepping on one was as bad as getting bitten if it punctured the skin.

The Chief cut the wheel hard to the right and lined up with the road outside. Hampton brought the door back down, and they carefully climbed onto the hood in front of the Chief. From there they easily climbed over the cab of the truck to the shielded gun turret.

Kathy climbed into the gunner's seat first and let out a sound of disgust.

Hampton was right behind her, and he saw her recoil from something.

"What is it?"

"Oh, man. That's gross," she answered. "That arm that went up with the door must've gotten caught in the turret shield as it went by. It's in my seat."

Hampton reached out with the tip of his knife and jabbed the arm. He lifted it out of the seat and tossed it over the side. The Chief saw it go by from inside the cab of the MRAP and couldn't keep himself from laughing. He didn't know how the arm got up there, so he couldn't wait to hear the explanation...if they had one.

It was a short drive from the motor pool to the building where the pilots waited for orders to fly. Operations had been scaled back in the years before the infection, and many of the missions flown out of the Marine airbase were either training or rescue missions. A few were drug interdiction flights in support of the Coast Guard, but almost everything except the rescue missions were scheduled. If a rescue mission came in, they had flights in the air within minutes.

The easy way that Hampton suggested to the Chief was also simple. There was no need to risk lives if all they had to do was get the infected dead to come outside. The Chief drove right up to the door of the building and put the front bumper of the MRAP only a couple of feet away. Hampton climbed down across the hood and pulled the door open without so much as a glance backward. The door only came open far enough to stop against the bumper, and since he pulled the door open and stayed behind it, the infected inside couldn't get to him.

It worked perfectly up to that point with one exception...nothing came out the door. Hampton peered around the door and then signaled to the Chief that he was going in.

To Kathy he said, "It was simple on paper, but I guess they need encouragement."

The room was dark, and someone had papered the windows. He assumed they had done it to prevent detection from the outside, but it also kept light from penetrating the dangerous rooms.

"I guess we have to go in," said Hampton.

Kathy climbed down from the hood and peered into the darkness.

"I thought this was going to be easy," she said.

"They were supposed to be drawn to the sound of the MRAP," he answered. "I guess they found something better to do. Don't tell Colleen I did this."

Before Kathy could stop him, Hampton went through the door, but the Chief saw what he was about to do and turned on the headlights of the personnel carrier. The way the headlights lit up the room was like the difference between night and day, and Hampton immediately saw that going inside was a mistake. The only reason the infected hadn't streamed through the open door was the cold. There wasn't any heat in the building, and several had fallen in a frozen heap between two pool tables. The rest were on the other side of the pile and had already been attempting to climb over them when Hampton appeared.

To Hampton's left was a hallway that led back to the bunk room and showers, but if he went that way, he would be trapped at that end of the building. He also doubted those rooms would be empty. He saw movement in the darkness where the headlights didn't reach, and his suspicions were confirmed by growling that grew louder by the second.

Hampton wanted to go back out the way he had gone in, but too many infected came from the hallway and blocked his path. Kathy was still outside the door, and her first reaction was to follow Hampton, but the sudden appearance of the infected made her pause, and that split second of indecision was costly. Hampton was cut off. Some of the infected came out through the door toward her, and she had to back away. The rest of them followed Hampton.

With hands grabbing at his back, Hampton could only move toward the center of the overcrowded ready room. There were far too many of them to shoot, and stopping to take aim would only mean the ones behind him would have time to reach him. There was only one thing he could think of to do, and he had no idea if it was a good or bad idea, but he knew he had to buy time for the Chief and Kathy to get inside the building.

Hampton got down on the floor and crawled under the pool table. The infected dead behind him saw where he went, and they followed, but they weren't nearly as agile as a living man. They labored against atrophied muscles and took longer to reach the floor, so he had a head start.

The infected on the other side of the table didn't have the intelligence needed to make the connection between his disappearance and the space under the table. Hampton didn't know what was behind that group, but he hoped it was another pool table. If it was, he would keep going under it. It wasn't. It was the back of a sofa.

Hampton crawled as fast as he could through the legs of the crowd. A couple of times he felt them fall across his legs, but each time he jerked free and kept going. He understood that every second was one more chance for him to feel that wrenching pain that he knew their teeth would cause. Why the one set of muscles in their emaciated bodies that worked well had to be their jaw muscles, he didn't know, but he had seen their power enough to know it wasn't worth stopping to think about it.

He had been on the road fighting the infected for seven years, and even when he and Colleen had fought side by side on the interstate highway through Charlotte, he hadn't really been afraid. On that day he had felt some level of control even as they lost the battle, but that was because he had an avenue of retreat. Inside this small, dark building, he was retreating but didn't know if he was going from bad to worse. This time Hampton actually felt afraid, and it was a helpless feeling.

Something pinned his legs together and held them to the floor, and the only thing that went through his mind was, "This is it."

He tried to turn over and kick at the weight on his legs, but he could only manage to get his hips high enough to reach his machete. Somehow he got the blade free, and he swung blindly over his body. There was a sound when the blade hit something, but it was too dark to know what. The weight on top of him increased, and he knew by instinct that he had caused an infected dead to fall onto him. He hoped it was because he had ended its miserable existence.

A second, harder swing produced the same sound, but he didn't know if he had hit the same infected dead or a different one. He pulled back his arm for a third swing, but the blade was embedded in something solid, and the handle of the machete slipped from his fingers.

An infected fell hard on Hampton's back, knocking the air from his lungs, but the bite he expected to follow didn't happen. It felt like he was under a stampede as feet stepped on him and bodies fell. Some of the infected stepped on his back but then fell over the sofa that had blocked his path. Then he felt himself sliding backward.

Above Hampton, a heavy table went hurling from the spot where it had sat for years and took with it over a dozen of the infected. There was just enough light for him to see it go over the sofa, but everything was happening so fast that he didn't even consider the possibility that someone had actually lifted it and pushed it through the growling creatures.

Kathy grabbed his ankles and pulled, or the table might have hit him too. She was afraid that she had the wrong ankles at first, but his legs were the only ones with pants that were intact. He slid free from under the pile of bodies that had been knocked over by the table, and somehow his hand connected with the hilt of his machete. He came to a standing position and found himself between the Chief and Kathy. The three of them were free to cut a path through the dead.

When they were done, the room was silent. Kathy pulled the covering from a window so they could see, and she studied the way the big table that had flipped over and crushed the infected under its weight.

"Just how Hampton planned it...nice and simple."

12

Toxic

Kentucky - 2023

When Michael Demmings came out of the tall grass onto the road behind Brother Bernard, he almost got shot. Drenched in sweat and with strings of body tissue hanging from his shirt, his appearance was so much like that of an infected dead that it wasn't totally unexpected that Bernard didn't recognize him as alive. The thing that saved him was Bernard knew that the infected didn't smile, and even in the darkness he could see that this creature was smiling from ear to ear. What he had to smile about was a mystery when Bernard considered the sorry state of his clothes.

"Brother Bernard...I made it back."

"You went that way, Demmings. How come you're showing up over there? You didn't go all the way around, did you?"

Demmings took several steps closer to Bernard, and Bernard took a few steps backward. Demmings hesitated when he saw the other man's cautious behavior and held up one hand as if he would stop him. That only made Bernard take a few more steps away.

"I had to go that way." He gestured toward the place where he had emerged from the left side of the building. "I couldn't come back the same way. I circled the whole building and almost got caught by one of those infected things, but I killed it."

"Uh, huh. Where's everybody else? There were four of you who went that way." He gestured to the right. "And if you went all the way around the building, I don't suppose you ran into anybody from the other team."

Demmings shook his head and took a few more steps toward Bernard. This time Bernard didn't give any ground, and he could see Demmings a little more clearly. The man had obviously been involved in some kind of contact with the infected dead because his clothes were bloody, and he smelled like a cadaver that had been sitting out in the sun for a couple of days. He was also limping.

Bernard held up a hand with the palm facing Demmings.

"Start at the beginning, and don't leave anything out."

There was a cold tone in his voice that might have had the chilling effect he intended except for the fact that Demmings chose that moment to realize Brother Bernard was alone. Not only was he alone, but there was also a body on the ground that was only recognizable by the clothes.

"Is that Wilkes?" he asked.

"Don't pay any attention to that, Demmings. Answer my question."

Demmings persisted.

"What happened to him? His arm is gone."

Bernard pulled his pistol and aimed it at Demmings.

"Don't make me ask you again. What happened out there, and why are you limping?"

"Wilkes sent me back to report that there were ropes hanging from the tower. I was blocked by the infected and had to go the long way around. When I reached the east tower, there were more ropes. I tried to climb one just like you said, but I slipped and fell. I landed wrong and twisted my ankle."

Demmings wasn't about to tell him that he had been pulled from the rope by an infected dead, and he certainly wasn't going to mention the fact that the infected had his mouth wrapped around his ankle. He knew that Bernard would treat it as a death sentence and would shoot him in the head even if it didn't break the skin.

"You didn't try to climb the rope again? Why not?"

"It was already slippery," Demmings said defensively, "and my ankle hurt too much after I fell. I didn't think I was going to make it back at all." By the time he finished, he was whining.

"How do you explain all that other stuff?" Bernard waved the hand holding the gun like it was a pointer. "You've got blood all over you."

Demmings made a show out of faking his surprise at just how much gore he had gotten on his clothes when he fell on top of the infected. He turned left and right as if he was examining himself, but he was careful not to show Bernard his back. He knew it had to be even worse than the front of his shirt and pants because it still felt wet on his skin.

"Oh, this happened on the way past the north tower. I heard the explosions over there, but it was way too dark for me to see where they were. I fell over someone's body when I passed that tower. There wasn't enough left of him to get back up, but he was a mess."

Demmings turned his attention back to the thing that had been Wilkes. He wasn't sure, but more of his arm was gone than before, and his other hand was missing fingers. He could have sworn they were all there before. There was also a green smear on his exposed left forearm that was new.

Bernard saw what Demmings was looking at and decided it was time to do the same thing that Specs and the tweaker had already done.

"Let's go, Demmings. Brother Silas is going to have a fit, but he's waiting to find out if we got inside the building. If he talks to those idiots Specs and Tweaker before I do, he'll shoot all of us. There's no telling what they'll say."

Demmings gave the remains of Wilkes plenty of room as he went by, but he was also curious about why his fingers were getting smaller. It was too dark to see anything useful, so he picked up his pace to catch up with Bernard. His ankle felt like it was on fire, and for a moment he considered going to see the medics, but the last thing he wanted to do was give someone else a reason to suspect how he really hurt himself. Once he pulled even with Brother Bernard he did his best not to limp at all.

It took almost a half hour to walk all the way from the Depository, but they finally approached the guard outside the big tent and told him Brother Silas was waiting for their report. Demmings was hoping that Bernard would tell him to go to his quarters, and he could handle Brother Silas, but he wasn't going to get what he hoped for. Bernard needed a witness, and he didn't know where the other idiots had gone.

The guard ducked inside to announce their arrival, and judging by how quickly he returned, Silas was anxiously waiting for some good news. Bernard knew it wasn't going to be what Brother Silas wanted to hear, and for the first time since he had joined the Brotherhood, he considered the possibility that he might get shot. The guard eyed Demmings and his bloody clothes and guessed it was going to be an interesting meeting.

He sniffed at Demmings and said, "You smell like you've been rolling in rotten meat. You sure you want to go in there like that?"

Demmings would have been grateful if Bernard thought twice about making him go in with him, but Bernard said, "How would you like to be assigned to go to the Depository with me the next time? Wanna guess how many didn't come back?"

The guard held the flap of the tent aside for them and avoided eye contact with Bernard as they went by. He did glance at Demmings again, though. He noticed that aside from the stench, the man was sweating heavily. Before he let the flap close behind them, he saw that the back of Demmings' clothes was worse than the front.

Brother Silas sprang from the back of the tent to greet them, but the smile that stretched across his face disappeared quickly. To him, it was as if someone had thrown a dead animal on his bed while he was sleeping. The smell that emanated from Demmings was so bad that it seemed to arrive before him.

They weren't inside for a full minute before the guard heard Brother Silas yelling, and Demmings popped back through the flap again. Demmings turned in a circle outside the entrance as if he wasn't sure whether or not he should leave.

"Stand over there," said the guard. He pointed at a spot at least ten yards away.

There was a bench in front of a small building, and Demmings headed for that with the obvious intention of getting off of his sore ankle, but the guard angrily yelled and pointed again.

"I don't need to be downwind from you! I said to stand over there."

Demmings limped to the spot where he was told to go, but from what he could hear through the thin walls of the tent, he preferred the way things had worked out.

Brother Silas was livid, and he wasn't holding anything back. The first item he wanted to be explained was why Brother Bernard would bring Demmings inside the place where he would be sleeping later.

"Why did you drag that sack of rotten meat into my home?" he screamed. "What were you thinking? Was there something important he could tell me that you don't already know?"

Brother Bernard searched frantically for the right answer, but the best he could come up with was, "I thought I might need a witness, Brother Silas."

"A witness?"

Silas hit a shrill note that sounded unnatural, even coming from him. His small size was something of a puzzle to his followers. Almost any of them, even the women, were bigger than him, but there was something in his personality that made people follow him instead of the other way around.

"You thought I wouldn't believe you, so you dragged a walking carcass in here? Why wouldn't I believe you?"

Silas had both hands on his hips and practically stood on tiptoes to get in Brother Bernard's face. Bernard knew better than to step backward because Silas would get even worse if he fell forward.

"I'm sorry, Brother Silas, but only three of the people that went with me made it back."

"Where's Wilkes? Did he make it?"

Bernard knew that he was always just a breath away from being replaced by Wilkes, and even though it would make life easier for him now that Wilkes was dead, it might have been better for him if Wilkes had survived.

"Demmings said Wilkes climbed into one of the towers. The next time I saw Wilkes, he was alive, but something was eating him."

"He was being eaten by an infected dead, but he was still alive? Wait a minute, you said *something* was eating him. Now I know why you needed a witness. You don't even know what you saw."

Brother Silas didn't realize just how accurate he was. He was attempting to be sarcastic, but he hit the nail on the head. At first, Bernard thought that was a good thing because if anyone ever thought he was always right, it was Brother Silas. Except for this time, saying he was right was likely to get him killed because he knew Silas was just being sarcastic to belittle him. He made a quick decision to get the answer out as fast as he could. The last thing he wanted was for Silas to feel like he was having to drag it out of him.

"I sent two teams in by having them climb ropes that hung down from the towers. Wilkes came back missing an arm, and he was covered with tiny, green spiders that were eating him. They looked like big lumps of moss on his body. I had to shoot him."

Brother Silas was scary when he got mad, but Bernard was more afraid of the stone-cold stare that he gave him when he finished his sentence. There was something missing from his eyes, and Bernard was fairly sure it was the absence of a soul. He knew better than to speak or break eye contact with his leader because Silas was searching his own eyes for signs that he wasn't telling the truth.

Silas said in a slow, measured tone, "Are you telling me I'm going to have to burn the place down to get to the gold?"

Bernard was pretty sure the Depository was fireproof, but he was sure it would be the last thing he ever said if it slipped past his lips. He was just about to suggest that they try to locate pesticides when the guard pulled back the flap over the door of the tent. He couldn't believe the good timing of the interruption.

"Brother Silas, I thought you'd like to know that it's snowing out here."

******

Demmings had drawn an angry stare from the guard after relocating downwind from him. Despite the stare, he sat cross-legged on the ground. Less than five minutes later, there was snow accumulating on his knees. There was no camaraderie between him and the guard, but there was a common bond in the way their eyes met each other. Both men wanted to know if the other was seeing the same thing. When Demmings raised a hand as if to let the snow land on his palm, the guard didn't hesitate. Demmings didn't either and jumped to his feet. He knew better than to be sitting on the ground if Brother Silas came outside.

The guard spoke to the inside of the tent and then stepped aside holding the flap open. Silas burst through with his head aimed upward, and Bernard followed a few seconds behind. There was confusion written on the leader's face, but his steely-eyed glare was ordering the snow to stop. The fact that it didn't stop only served to intensify the anger that always seemed to be just below the surface.

"What is this?" demanded Silas.

All three men stayed quiet, each hoping the question was aimed at someone else. Demmings and the guard could defer to the chain of command, but Bernard couldn't, and when he saw the other two were artfully avoiding Silas by directing their attention toward the sky, he knew someone had to answer. He desperately searched for the best thing to say because he also knew that stating the obvious was a good way to die.

"We should get you back inside, Brother Silas. Whatever it is, it could be toxic."

That comment galvanized the group of men, including Demmings, to get back inside the tent, and Silas considered it to be the smartest thing Bernard could have said, but he was still angry. His guard was supposed to be in charge of his well-being, but he had led him outside into unknown danger.

Demmings had done his part without even knowing he was doing it. He had already dipped the tip of his tongue into the powdery flakes that had collected on his palm.

Silas had seen the simple taste test and pointed a finger at him. "I need to know the moment you feel sick."

The assumption wasn't that the snow was safe even if it was falling in June. Brother Silas assumed Bernard was right to be cautious, and that Demmings would be affected by ingesting it. He would be their guinea pig for the time being. The problem was that Demmings wasn't feeling so great before he tasted it.

Bernard asked Demmings, "What'd it taste like?"

"Uh, it was kind of bitter, and it was gritty."

"What's that mean?" said Silas in an accusatory tone. It sounded like he had never tasted snow before, but they all knew they had done so as children.

Demmings said, "It didn't seem to melt the way it should, and there's a kind of film on my tongue. I can't get the taste out of my mouth."

That simple statement would only prove to confuse the already unusual situation later because Demmings was feeling weak. He wanted to ask first before sitting down because he was in the presence of their leader, but the shaking in his knees was more than enough reason for him to skip the formal request for permission. They all saw him stagger to his left as he attempted to remain upright, and he fell more than sat heavily into a canvas chair.

"Are you sick already?" asked Brother Silas. There was a hint of concern in his voice, but as sick as he felt, Demmings didn't mistake it for worry about him.

"I'm going to throw up."

Demmings leaned forward and clutched at his stomach with one hand while covering his mouth with the other. Brother Bernard tried his best to get a bucket in front of Demmings before he let loose inside the tent, and he almost made it…but not quite. The end result was that he missed the bucket and drenched Bernard.

To Michael Demmings the pain in his stomach was the most agonizing cramp of his muscles he had ever felt. Like everyone else, he had felt his share of knots in his calves and his hamstrings. It was always something he could rub and stretch to make it go away. He absently considered the possibility this was a cumulative combination of every cramp he had ever had in his life, and it was all happening at one time in his lower gut. If someone had handed him a knife at that moment, he would have cut open his own abdomen in an attempt to let out the pain.

Brother Silas was revolted at first, and then something inside him clicked just like the day he stood by the wrecked car...the day his life as Marvin Corn ended, and the day he became the person who would become known as Brother Silas. He became an observer. Something new was happening, and he wanted to see what it was. He needed to see it.

He moved closer to Michael Demmings and leaned over to better see his face. He saw that the man was as pale as a ghost, and there was a trail of bile and blood stretching down in a long strand from his mouth to the floor. Bernard stepped back, still holding the bucket, and he surveyed the foul-smelling slime that coated his own arms and clothing. He stepped further away because Brother Silas had eased between him and Demmings. Bernard wasn't sure, but at the moment he preferred the raging Silas over the observant Silas. There was something odd about his face that conveyed questions without speaking.

The guard pulled out a pistol and got ready to shoot Demmings if he made a move toward Brother Silas. To him, there was no doubt that Demmings was turning right before their eyes, but it seemed like he was turning without dying first. That was a new development to him, but he was convinced it was because Demmings had tasted the snow.

That reminded him. They would have to deal with the snow when they were done with the spectacle of Demmings turning right before their eyes, and he took a few steps toward the flap of the tent.

Demmings chose that moment to fall forward, and he clawed the air wildly to keep from falling on his face. His hand managed to catch the front of Brother Silas' shirt, pulling him with him to the floor. Since Bernard was behind him, he could only grab Silas from behind. It was something he was hesitant to do even under the circumstances because Silas had a rule that no one was to ever touch him. The rule carried a penalty worse than death, or so he had been warned.

The few steps toward the entrance of the tent had cost the guard the precious seconds he could have used to get between Demmings and Brother Silas, but his gun was already in his hand. He raised it and fired in one motion, and the bullet caught Demmings between his temple and forehead. It made him spin away, and he lost his grip on Brother Silas. Silas almost landed on the dead man's back, but the risk taken by Bernard to touch their leader was early enough to pull him away. He fell backward with Bernard, and for a moment Silas felt gratitude. The most harm he had suffered was some blood splatter on his shirt.

In the next minute, there was mayhem at the entrance of the tent because three more of Brother Silas' bodyguards arrived after hearing the gunshot. There was confusion because of the mess they saw when they entered, but they had also been forced to run to the tent in a blizzard. Bernard and the guard had helped Silas to a chair where he sat as if he was in a wide-eyed trance. There was a small smile on his face.

Bernard grabbed each of the new arrivals and pulled them inside. He was careful not to touch the snow that had collected on their clothing, and he was relieved to see they had draped blankets over their heads and shoulders since none of them had coats. He shouted instructions at them to not get any of the snow in their mouths. They didn't know why, but they were happy to listen.

Brother Silas came out of his trance with an announcement.

"We're being tested again, but if we're being tested, so is the rest of the world. The snow is toxic. We've already seen that it can kill quickly."

He pointed at the new arrivals and said, "Cover your mouths and noses and go warn the others not to taste the snow. Tell them it killed Demmings in seconds, and he turned before he died. It must be that the snow carries the infection."

They didn't relish the idea of going back outside into the toxic snow, but they knew what would happen if they didn't do as they were told. They draped the blankets more over their faces than they had before and left without a word.

"Get him out of here, and find someone to clean up the mess."

Bernard would be glad to get himself into a bath as soon as possible. He and the guard carried the body outside and unceremoniously disposed of it in an old dumpster, he told the guard to go back to see that Brother Silas was comfortable while he would find someone to clean his tent.

Bernard found Specs and the tweaker in the middle of the most crowded tent. They were the center of attention for almost everyone inside as they described what had happened to Wilkes. It wasn't going to be easy to get another group to go with him to the Depository, and now they had the snow to worry about.

He took the floor from Specs and the tweaker just as someone was shouting at the pair that they were either liars or juiced up on something the tweaker had cooked.

"They're not lying," he yelled.

Everyone parted to make a path for Brother Bernard. Specs and the tweaker saw that the path led directly to them, and the tweaker scratched furiously at his arms. A few people subconsciously did the same thing as a reaction to the description the pair had provided about the green moss that was tiny spiders. Bernard walked through the path and extended an index finger toward them.

"You two come with me. Everyone listen up. If you haven't already heard, it's snowing something fierce outside."

He meant to give everyone a warning about the snow, but his comment got the same reaction as if he had shouted fire in a crowded theater. People close to the entrance were practically crawling over each other to be the first to confirm what he had just announced. Apparently, the guards who had been dispatched to warn everyone hadn't gotten to this overcrowded place yet.

"Stop!"

He yelled the order and punctuated it with one shot from his semiautomatic pistol. Even though he shot straight upward, everyone between him and the entrance hit the floor.

"You idiots! I wasn't done yet! You can't go outside!"

Bernard was so mad that everyone stayed on the floor, and the people closest to the entrance of the tent eased backward. He had lowered his gun with it loosely aimed at the entrance.

"The snow is poisonous if you get it inside your body. Everyone with a hat and something to use for a mask needs to help find stuff in the old buildings for us to wear. It's getting cold out there, so we need coats, blankets, hats, and anything else that's useful. Specs, Tweaker… get some buckets and soapy water."

After a considerable amount of grumbling, followed by an equal amount of cursing and threats from Brother Bernard, the crowd thinned as they bundled up as best they could before going scavenging. A thin-haired man with stooped shoulders approached Bernard cautiously.

"I found gas masks in one building. I brought one back."

He extended his hand to Bernard and showed him the bulky piece of gear.

Bernard happily took it from him but then paused as he was about to pull the rubber straps to place it on his own head. He surveyed the man and made a mental guess that he hadn't had a bath in months.

"You didn't wear it already, did you?"

Even though he didn't have a clue why it mattered if he had tried it on or not, and even though he had worn it for a few minutes, the man shook his head vigorously.

"No sir, I just brought it back with me figuring I could trade it for something."

Bernard still had the mask poised above his head, but he had fixed his steely eyes on the greasy face of the man in the hopes of reading whether or not he was telling the truth. He couldn't tell if the man was bluffing, and in truth, he wanted the mask badly enough to just take his word for it. He pulled it on the rest of the way and adjusted the straps.

His voice sounded hollow inside the mask, but the man understood what he said.

"Find yourself a hat and a mask then show me where you got this gear from."

******

The camp was active for the remainder of the night as people went about the business of finding ways not to ingest the toxic snow while they located warmer clothing. If Brother Silas had been outside, he would have questioned how they had arrived at the hasty conclusion that the snow was toxic because Demmings wasn't the only one who tasted it before the warning had been given. Also, the bite on his leg had gone undetected because of that conclusion. Normally, Silas would have had the body stripped and checked for bites. The result was that a large number of people were living with unspoken fear as they waited to get sick.

It was sunrise before enough warm clothing and protective gear was distributed throughout the camp. Old oil drums had been rolled into tents that had been reconstructed to allow for smoke to drift upward, and there was finally heat. Even though the old paperwork records and furniture smelled as they burned, everyone huddled closer to the warmth. The small army that followed the Brothers wasn't ready for winter weather.

Bernard had a massive headache and had only gotten thirty minutes of sleep, but he wasn't surprised when he got a message with instructions from Brother Silas to go back to the Depository. He had hoped for a reprieve or at least a better idea about how to penetrate the building. Then he remembered his discussion with Specs. He told the messenger to inform Brother Silas that he hoped to have good news for him in a few hours, even though he was just stalling. It had already occurred to him that he had another alternative. If he couldn't find another way into the Depository, he would find a way to disappear rather than be shot by Brother Silas.

Specs got his message and showed up at Bernard's tent. He was tempted to ignore the summons and claim he had never been told Bernard needed him, but part of him felt like Brother Bernard would see through the lie.

"You wanted to see me?" he was hoping for an errand rather than another assignment to go back to the Depository.

"Yeah, we're going hunting for railroad tracks today. If we get going early, maybe we can avoid being seen by the rest of the camp."

Specs hesitated. "Why would that matter?"

Bernard Ancrum had never been really successful before the zombie apocalypse, but he hadn't been stupid. He had survived in menial jobs by keeping his head down and knowing when to keep his mouth shut. Ironically, his stoic appearance and cautionary approach to employment had made him appear to be thoughtful and introspective, and those were characteristics that got him promoted no matter how hard he tried to be inconspicuous. The same thing had kept him close to the top of the Brotherhood, so Specs was surprised by the answer to his question.

"Because I don't plan to come back if we don't get inside today. If we don't find a back door, we ain't coming back. If we find a back door and can't open it, we ain't coming back."

He didn't give Specs the chance to answer. He pulled the gas mask over his face and pushed past him. He only stopped long enough to survey the strange landscape outside his tent. The snow was deep and was piled in large sloping mounds against tents. It covered everything in a lumpy blanket, and it was still falling. The sky was a deep gray compared to the white blanket that came to his knees.

Specs had a blanket wrapped around his head that covered most of his face, and he fell in behind Brother Bernard. He did his best to step where Bernard did because his shoes weren't made to keep out the freezing cold moisture.

"We're not coming back?"

Bernard whirled around and snarled angrily, "Keep your voice down. If you want to come back with bad news, it's up to you. You can even have my old job. Now, where do you think we would find those railroad tracks?"

13

Changes

Any sailor would tell you that a fire on a ship was what they feared the most, and it wasn't any different aboard the *Charlie Sue*. A day ago there would have been no need to think differently, but as the temperature dropped and the snow accumulated on the deck, it became obvious that they could either build a fire for heat or waste precious fuel to run the engines and warm the cabins. The wheelhouse was kept warm because it had to be manned at all times, but it had an electric heater that was powered by a small generator. At first, they all gathered in the wheelhouse, but it didn't take long for them to realize that was only a temporary solution. There were too many of them for it to be comfortable.

The shrimp boat had several large fuel drums at the stern, and one was nearly empty. They topped off the fuel tanks of the boat and then pried the top off the drum. Captain Miller said he had a little experience with metal engineering, and he showed them how to make a free-standing stove that wasn't likely to burn a hole through the deck. He used everything he could find in Charlie's scrap metal supplies to get it up on a set of legs, and he cut holes for vents near the bottom.

While Captain Miller built the stove, the rest of them stretched tarps into place above the center of the main deck. The end result was a giant tent with sloping sides. Their hope was that the warm air inside would rise and make the snow slide off the tarp before it could accumulate and freeze.

The last thing they needed was something to burn, and it was going to be hard to find anything dry in the trees around the tidal creek where they were moored. Tom had done a lot of camping when he was a kid, and he suggested they could bring as much wet wood into the tent as they could and use the stove to get it dry. He hated to break it to Charlie and Sue, but the cabin doors below would make enough firewood to get the process started.

The idea of burning any part of his boat was almost sacrilegious to Charlie, but no one would have expected them to even need firewood yesterday. If they had known, they would have collected it while it was dry. He gave in only because he knew there was no other way to get warm.

It took over two hours for them to gather the wood, but by the time they got back, there was warmth inside the canopy they had made. Sue had used a variety of metal deck tools to construct a rack where the wood could be dried. What worried them the most was that they would need to keep the wood supply replenished to stay ahead of the cold.

They huddled around the stove, and Sue passed out cups of coffee. Everyone nursed their cups to get the feeling back in their fingers before they sipped at the hot liquid.

Cassandra appeared at the door to their crude tent wrapped in a blanket and asked, "What am I missing?"

They were all surprised to see her, and Iris rushed over to help her.

"You shouldn't be out of bed."

"I feel fine, but why is it so cold?"

Iris guided her to a seat near the stove, and Colleen handed her a cup of coffee. Iris put her hand on Cassandra's forehead and nodded her approval.

"Fever's gone. I'll bet the cold helped that to break, but after you cooled off, you probably just about went into shock from the cold."

"I thought I still had a fever," said Cassandra. "So, how long was I out? The last thing I remember about the weather was that one thin layer of clothes felt like too much. Wasn't it June?"

"It still is," said Sim.

He couldn't resist giving her a hug even though her cuts were still sore. She winced, but she was grateful for the attention and hugged him back as best as she could. He gave her a quick update on what they had learned about the snow, and she had the same question that was on all of their minds. They all wanted to know if the snow would end, but none of them knew any more about nuclear winter than the rest of them did.

"We can't keep this up," said Tom. "We're going to be forced to forage further and further from the boat, and after we leave, what are you going to do?"

He pointed to Charlie and then to Sue.

"There's ice forming on the tidal creek," said Charlie. "If I wanted to live near the ice, I would've already left for one of the poles a long time ago."

Sim was bundled up in everything he could find to wear, and his teeth were still banging into each other when he tried to speak.

"Salt water freezes at just over twenty-eight degrees. I didn't think the temperature was that high."

"Thermometer says it's close to that," said Tom. "For some reason, I think it's going to get worse. Maybe we should get the sub back on the radio and ask them to come back for us."

Charlie was shaking his head even before Tom finished what he was saying.

"By the time they get here, we won't be able to take the boat back out of the creek, and I don't think they can get anybody to us without risking their own lives. We couldn't ask them to do that."

Iris said, "It's settled as far as I'm concerned. I was planning to ask you to come with us even before this change of circumstances. You two have done well on your own, but trust me when I say that you would be able to live out your lives with a fair amount of comfort in one of our shelters."

A deep rumble seemed to vibrate the deck under their feet. They turned to each other with questioning eyes, each asking the others if they heard or felt the same thing. As it grew in volume, understanding dawned on them. Something that had to be big was getting closer. Colleen's radio clicked to life, and Hampton's voice came through the speaker.

"Good morning, everyone. Anyone care to get in out of the cold?"

"We hear you, Hampton. You sound way too cheerful considering this weather. We also hear something else…what is that?"

"Wait until you see this. How soon can everyone be ready to roll out of here?"

"That depends on how soon you want. You said something about getting out of the cold. We got a stove working out on the deck, but we're so low on firewood that we'll be burning the boat in a couple of hours."

That comment drew a sour glare from Charlie, but he knew the boat wasn't going to do them any good if they froze to death. Sue gave him a pat on the shoulder just to let him know she understood.

The rumbling of the big engine in the MRAP was coming through the radio, but it also seemed to vibrate the deck under their feet. They crowded together as a group at the entrance to their makeshift tent, and even though they were letting the heat escape, the spectacular bulk of the vehicle was worth seeing. The top of it was visible before they saw the heads of their own people appear above the tall grass on the banks. The Marine aviator jumps suits they had acquired made them resemble an assault force on the move.

Kathy was in the lead, and she raised her hand to wave. She stopped in mid-motion and jumped to one side. They could see Hampton run up to her, and they both were interested in something hidden in the grass. They skirted around it and continued toward the boat. The MRAP changed course slightly to avoid the same spot.

They were almost close enough to shout, but they saw Hampton raise his hand to his mouth, and his voice came through the little speaker on Colleen's radio.

"Frozen alligator with a frozen infected dead in its mouth. Frozen crabs also hanging onto it."

The Chief didn't want to test the ground too close to the inlet where the Charlie Sue was anchored, so he put the vehicle in park but left the engine idling. More heads appeared behind Hampton and Kathy, and they saw the size of their group had grown again. Everyone was armed with automatic rifles and dressed in jumpsuits.

Iris called out to them, "I hope you brought enough of those outfits for all of us. It's cold over here."

Kathy gave her a thumbs up and they all saw a kid throw her a bundle that was still sealed in plastic. Kathy pushed back the tall grass and got close enough to the bank to toss it onto the deck of the boat. Behind Kathy, the kid was tossing more packages to newcomers who formed a line to Kathy. One by one the packages were tossed over and passed out. Everyone on the boat tore at the plastic on the new uniforms and pulled them on over their thin layers of clothes. With the snow covering everything, it was almost like Christmas when the jumpsuits were followed by boots. They caught them and then passed them around matching up the sizes with the right people.

"Don't put on the boots yet," yelled Hampton cheerfully. "Here come the socks. There's enough for everyone to keep two dry sets in their backpack."

"I never thought I'd feel warm again," said Sim as he pulled socks over the pair he had on.

The Chief appeared at the edge of the bank with a long metal ladder. With the crabs and other creatures frozen, it would be much easier to go on and off the boat. He extended the ladder out to the boat like a gangplank and crossed over.

"It supported me, so everyone else can make it, but it's going to get slippery as ice builds up on it. Let's get everyone across as soon as we can."

"We're leaving now?" asked Captain Miller. "We all packed bug-out packs. What else do we need?"

"All the fuel we can carry," answered the Chief. "Everyone grab anything you think is important and carry it up to the MRAP. We have plenty of room for everyone, but there aren't enough seats to go around, so stack gear down the middle that can be stepped on. If we can't fit something in, we can leave it at the loading spot."

It took longer than they wanted to load everything, but the Chief always wanted things done faster than they could be done. The fuel drums were strapped to the outside of the Cougar because they had no other choice. The Chief didn't think they would actually be driving the vehicle into combat or have to worry about mines or improvised explosive devices. The fuel drums would be a bad idea in a firefight, but they weren't going to assume that more fuel would be easy to find on the road. Depending upon road conditions, they would need at least two full tanks of fuel for the trip.

The gear was divided into two piles. The first pile was anything that could be strapped to the top of the vehicle. The rest was stuffed into the passenger compartment where it was going to be a snug fit for so many people. On the plus side, that meant there wouldn't be any complaints about being too warm.

This particular model of personnel carrier was designed to carry two crew members and eight passengers. The Chief was the logical choice to be the driver because he would take up too much space in the back, and Tom was in the front seat with him. His long legs needed the room to unfold. By the time they got done squeezing everyone else into the passenger compartment, they were making jokes about circus clown cars.

In the end, they decided to free up a little more room by having one person ride in the machine gun turret. It would be cold, but no one complained about the idea. Cassandra argued for the right to be the first one behind the M240 machine gun. The reason she gave that won her the seat was that the cold made her cuts feel better. No one could argue with that. She bundled up with all the spare clothing she could find and settled in behind the metal shield that surrounded the turret. A pair of goggles retrieved from the pilot ready-room with the jumpsuits made her look like she was going to fly out of the Marine air station.

The twenty-six-ton vehicle rolled easily away from the inlet where the shrimp boat was anchored. Everyone saw the wistful look Charlie gave the boat that had been his and Sue's home for over seven years. Despite the hard times, it had served them well.

Kathy leaned in closer to him and said, "I know you feel like that boat saved your lives, but remember that it was the tool, and you were the person wielding the tool."

That earned Kathy a grateful smile.

"It's time to use some new tools. Maybe someone else will find her and she can be the tool that saves them."

******

The snow had covered everything with a blanket that rested undisturbed on the roads, and the only way the Chief could tell he was actually driving on a road was by navigating between signs and landmarks. It made their progress much slower than they would have liked. It also meant they would run into obstacles on the road that he would rather have avoided.

Large flakes were still swirling in the gray light in front of them, and he had to strain to see anything useful as a guide to where the road was straight or where it turned. Tom did his best to call out when he detected signs that something blocked their path, but his best wasn't enough help in the first few miles. The Cougar repeatedly slammed into cars that had been abandoned years ago.

It was particularly hair-raising when they came to the first of many bridges they would have to cross. The passengers tried not to think about why the gray sky appeared to be on all sides of them and the angle of the ascent was so steep. Cassandra could see better than she wanted to from her perch in the turret. From her view, the Cougar appeared to have lifted off from the road, and it really was flying like a plane. She knew that wasn't possible, and she also knew it would be a really bad thing to do.

When they crested the bridge and the angle of descent increased, their momentum made them almost feel weightless, and the Chief knew that they would probably crash if he used the brakes. As the seconds ticked by, the passengers felt the tension in their own legs as they mentally applied brakes in the passenger compartment. No one talked as they waited for the inevitable collision they were sure would come at any moment.

When the road leveled out and the steady drone of the engine continued without the impact they expected, everyone exhaled with relief.

"Only six hundred or so miles of that," said Kathy.

As soon as she said it, she regretted it. The Cougar was slowing to a stop, and everyone could hear the Chief telling Tom something about not having a choice. As soon as he put the vehicle in park, he turned around in his seat.

"Maybe we'll have better luck when we reach the interstate, but I'm afraid there's no way around some of these old pile-ups. The snow is hiding some of it, and the shoulders are sloped. I might be able to push through it, but I need people outside telling me when to push and when not to."

One thing everyone in the group had in common was their ability to accept situations rather than complain about them. The four newcomers watched with wide eyes as everyone piled out the back of the MRAP into the tracks made by the big personnel carrier. Cassandra stayed in the turret where she could be the most useful. She felt better, but she still had to move carefully so she wouldn't pull open any of her cuts.

Navigating the highway on foot was almost as treacherous as driving blindly into the snow with the MRAP. It could withstand the explosion of a mine, but it could also get stuck in a tangle of rusted metal. The difference was that it wouldn't feel the pain of a misstep. Climbing over the cars, it was hard to tell where it was safe to put their feet. Ice under the blanket of snow caused more than one slip and fall, and with each fall the entire group reacted with concern, worried that there would be a serious injury.

Captain Miller let out a loud whistle and waved for everyone to come back to the front of the Cougar. When the last person made it back, the Chief climbed down from the front seat to join them.

Over the rumble of the idling vehicle, Captain Miller told the Chief that it would be better to clear the wreckage from the road. He suggested that they attach a tow line to the cars one at a time and pull them out of the pile. Once they made some progress through the middle, maybe they would be able to force their way through the rest of it.

It took almost two hours to move enough cars out of the way for the MRAP to bulldoze a path the rest of the way.

As they settled themselves into the small but warm passenger compartment, Kathy said, "All we need now is a tornado to make this day feel complete."

"A tornado?" asked Caleb.

Hampton said, "Seems like a long time ago, but I guess it's just that it was warmer."

"I know what you mean," said Colleen. "Was that two years ago?"

She directed her question at no one in particular, but she explained to Caleb that they had been traveling a highway in the northern part of Alabama when they had come across a big pile-up like the one they had just cleared. The only difference was that it was much better weather until they got hit by a tornado.

"The strangest part of that was when we found out the Chief had a set of teeth stuck in his back," said Kathy.

Sue said, "Maybe this ride will go by a little faster for the rest of us if you tell us some stories about what you guys have seen."

Sue was thinking of the newcomers more than herself and Charlie. They had already been around the Mud Island family long enough to have heard some pretty wild stories.

She turned toward Darren, Brett, Grady, and Caleb. "They found the President in a shelter in Ohio."

Mouths dropped open, and the four newcomers fixed disbelieving eyes on Kathy.

Kathy motioned toward Sim and said, "He was the navigator of the plane that flew the President out of Washington."

Grady said, "Now that's a story I want to hear."

"I'm afraid things didn't work out so well," said Sim.

That comment drew a general grunt from everyone, and Sim realized the story of the President and his attempt to stay alive was just another version of the same story they could each tell. It wasn't a good thing that it hadn't worked out well for the President, but in a way, it was a testament to their own survival. They were alive, and the President was not. Despite all of his power and safeguards, and despite their lack of those things, all of them had survived the destruction of most of the human race.

"I guess that goes without saying," said Sim, "but you have to admit that for a moment, each one of you was ready to ask where he is and if he's sending help. You didn't consider the possibility that he didn't make it until I said it hadn't worked out so well."

They felt the brakes being applied on the MRAP again, and the engine wound down for a second time.

"Not again," said Hampton. He reached up front and tapped Tom on the arm. "Is the road blocked again?"

Tom answered, "Everyone stay inside. We have people blocking the road this time...the living kind. It's best that they don't know our numbers until we have to show them."

"Weapons?" asked Kathy.

"Only one gun that I can see. The rest of them have ball bats, axes, and a variety of clubs. Cassandra could clear the road in seconds."

The Chief climbed out of the cab of the MRAP, and it was obvious by the way the people blocking the road shifted their feet that some of them felt like running. It was one thing to stare down the big armored vehicle, but it was totally unexpected to see someone of his size walking toward them.

"Good morning, folks. Just to clear the air, I would have stopped if you were standing on the side of the road waving. You send a different kind of message by blocking the road."

The Chief kept a smile on his face, but it wasn't the warm, friendly smile he gave people when he met them for the first time. It was the smile he used when he wanted people to know they had gotten off on the wrong foot.

There were six men blocking the road, spread out with the one holding a rifle at the front, but the Chief had no doubt someone was kept in reserve. He glanced left and right, moving his head as little as possible. His peripheral vision to the right picked up someone resting a rifle on top of a fallen tree. He was only about twenty yards off the road, and the Chief knew for certain that Cassandra would take him out first if it came to that. He saw someone on the left side of the road behind a snow-covered truck, but they were attempting to remain hidden. The Chief guessed they were the vulnerable members of the group, most likely women and children.

The man with the rifle appeared to be in his late forties, and judging by the way he held the rifle, he was used to aiming it and pulling the trigger. He gripped it with both hands without one even near the trigger guard. The Chief's assessment was that they were afraid but attempting to be bold.

"Good morning," said the man. "Where are you folks heading?"

It crossed the Chief's mind that the man had seen too many movies and that he was lucky to be alive. Highway robbery wasn't a skillset the man had cultivated.

"I think the obvious answer is that it's none of your concern. Unless of course, you want to keep us from getting there, but I have a better idea. Why don't you drop the bad guy act and have your sniper come out of hiding? While you're at it, have the people behind that truck get over here too."

The Chief could see the indecision written on the man's face, and the men spread out behind him were only one heartbeat away from leaving him standing in the middle of the road. The Chief dropped the smile, but he softened his expression just a bit as he took a couple of steps closer to the man. He could see the man's knuckles had turned white from gripping the rifle so hard.

"Relax, mister. Things must be pretty bad for you to get this desperate. If I was one of the bad guys, would I have stopped driving when you guys blocked the road? I could have just driven that thing right over you. Tell your people to come out of hiding."

There was only a moment of indecision before the man waved at everyone to come out, but he had most likely been questioning the wisdom of what they were doing the entire time. A large group of women and children came out from behind the truck, far more than he had expected. He was right about the sniper, though. There was only one, and his rifle was a small caliber Marlin. It was a decent rifle for hunting rabbits, but it would have been a tragedy if he had opened fire on the Cougar.

The Chief decided to hold off for a minute before waving at his own crew. The sight of them and their own weapons was likely to send the people scurrying for cover. He was surprised to find one of his people had come up to stand by his side. Iris met his disapproving gaze with a half smile.

She said, "This is what we talked about on the plane. Remember?

When we were flying over the mountains we talked about how we have to do more. We have to go out and find people who are desperate, not just people who are fighting to survive but people who have run out of hope. They've fought as hard as they can, but their hope is dying because it never ends. Maybe this snow is going to give us the edge we need."

Iris was tall, so the Chief didn't have to lower his head and eyes as much as he did when speaking with most people. He could see the drifts of snow behind her beyond the side of the road, and there was an infected dead frozen against a tree. He knew instantly what she meant by giving them an edge, but at the same time, the snow would force people to push harder to survive. It gave them an advantage over the infected dead, but now they would have to forage for food and fight the elements too. They would have to get desperate enough to confront a superior force such as theirs.

Iris walked toward the group of women and children before he could stop her, but one word was all he needed in order to get the answer to an unspoken warning.

"Iris."

She turned back toward him and said in a voice low enough for the others not to hear, "I know...watch for signs that someone has been bitten. I haven't forgotten."

Iris continued to walk toward the people, but the Chief saw her subtle gesture toward her lower back. She was wearing a one-piece flight suit just like the rest of them, but she had strapped a belt around her waist, and a 9mm pistol was tucked into it.

The Chief turned his attention to the leader of the group. The man with the Marlin 22 had joined him at the front of the men. From what he could tell, Iris was right. The desperation on their faces was easy to see. They were tired of fighting to stay alive, and the elements weren't as deadly as a bite from an infected, but the hardships that came along with the cold and the snow were overwhelming them. He checked the position of the sun and made a decision.

"You folks look like you could use a hot meal and a campfire. We weren't going to make it much farther today anyway. Care to join us for a bit?"

They had a moment of indecision, but it was a settled issue when they saw the rest of the Chief's crew emerging around the sides of the MRAP. They bristled with weapons, but the cautious way they spread out to set up a perimeter was a clear sign that they had not survived out of desperation. They were clearly fighting back.

Kathy and Colleen caught up with Iris. The Chief knew they would assess the threat of bites, and then they would enlist the help of the women to set up a campsite. A couple of the men hung back a bit, but the leader and the man with the Marlin stepped forward and extended their hands to shake. The relief on their faces and in the air was palpable. The Chief gripped their considerably smaller hands one at a time as introductions were done.

Sharing their food was never going to be an issue. They always felt like they could find more food, but some people didn't get better at surviving. For some reason, they could only manage to keep their heads above water. They were always living from day to day. This was one of those groups.

The leader was Juan De La Cruz, and he had been a high school principal when the apocalypse began. He was one of those men who had the qualities that made impressionable young people like him. It meant he never had serious problems, and he was automatically thrust into a leadership role when people started dying. As a matter of fact, some of the people in his group were former students.

When the Chief told them they had enough supplies to feed everyone, Juan couldn't believe they were seeing such generosity in light of the way they had confronted the armored vehicle. He confessed to the Chief they hadn't tried to be the bad guys before. It was their first time, and he swore it would be the last time. The Chief told him he would strongly suggest keeping that promise.

The snow was still coming down hard enough for visibility to be only a few yards at best, so they needed to set watches at four corners around the camp. They had enough people to rotate the watches before they would freeze to death, but it was still brutal. Normally the Chief would have been too cautious to allow people he didn't know to stand watch, but he didn't think they would risk the safety of their families. It also meant they could rotate the watches sooner.

The MRAP served as a wall to protect them from the weather on one side, and thanks to Charlie they were able to set up a large pavilion where everyone else could stay warm. Charlie had suggested to the Chief that they should bring along the large tarps they had used on the shrimp boat. Hampton had taken the idea one step further. It was his idea to remove one of the outriggers from the boat and roll the tarp around it. It was stowed along the top of the MRAP toward the driver's side, and when they needed to use it, all they had to do was unroll it like a patio cover on a recreational vehicle.

With a roof over their heads and walls made from the heavy tarp, they were able to build a fire to make the cold night almost comfortable. At least no one would freeze. Some of the women and all of the children were squeezed inside the MRAP. They couldn't spare the fuel to run the engine or generator, but it was still better than being outside. When the sun went down, the large group was ready for the cold night.

The Chief sat next to Juan and the two asked each other a hundred questions. Both wanted to know everything, and more often than not, their questions were the same. How had they survived? Where had they survived? Would it ever end? It was fair to say that the Chief's answers caused more jaws to drop than the other way around.

Juan shook his head at one point and said, "I feel like your lives would have made a good movie back in the days when it was fun to go to movies that scared us. You guys have had some adventures."

There were times when that comment would have drawn laughter from the members of the Mud Island family, but the onset of winter in June had dampened their spirits. They had never considered themselves to be on an adventure or that they were larger than life, but they had always felt like they were strong enough to overcome the obstacles in their way. They never lacked confidence, but none of them felt like they could actually beat the weather. They weren't even sure they could survive outside because they didn't know how bad it would get. It was possible that they would be forced to retreat to one of their shelters permanently, and even though they would still be alive, being banished from the outside would feel like a loss. Besides, the Chief had to finish something first.

14

King Midas

Kentucky - 2023

Silas was giving serious consideration to changing his title to King. It occurred to him that sharing the title of Brother with twelve other people made them feel like equals.

"King Silas the First," he said.

In the quiet corner of his tent, the heat didn't reach him well enough, and the cold was making him more miserable than usual. He had entertained visions of rolling into Fort Knox, sending men into the Depository, and then following them with a grand entry to survey his great wealth. The death toll for the first attempt did not bode well, especially with the added complication of toxic snow.

Silas had sent out his guards to see if any of his followers knew anything about why it was snowing. There were several who offered theories, including some who said the snow was most likely radioactive. That was why it had killed Demmings after he tasted it. The explanations fell short, though. No one had any idea why it had taken seven years to start, if or when it would stop, and most of all, why it was radioactive.

One man who said he had been studying meteorology when the apocalypse began offered the theory that the nuclear winter must have begun a long time ago. It has just taken time to reach them. He explained how winds from other continents traveled to great heights carrying all kinds of debris over the oceans, and that debris eventually descended to new places. He told Silas that radioactive debris would span the entire world if enough nuclear reactors went China Syndrome.

Silas had never heard of China Syndrome and took it literally. The former meteorology student attempted to explain to him that China didn't necessarily have anything to do with the term, but Silas had a habit of not listening to anything except his inner thoughts after a certain point. He wasn't listening when the man said it just meant a reactor core had melted through its containment and reached the ground below it.

Silas said, "I knew it was the Chinese. First, they sent us the zombies, and then they sent us radioactive snow."

Inside the man's own thoughts he was attempting to choose the best way to explain that it was quite probable that it was snowing in China and there was an infection there too, but he knew when to stop talking. He had seen Brother Silas snap out of his private reveries and lash out. He hoped Silas wouldn't even notice as he slipped silently out of the tent. Once outside, he made a hasty retreat into the depths of the camp where he might be harder to find if Brother Silas had more questions. He wasn't as cautious as he should have been, and he felt the slight burn of the acrid snow inside his nose.

For a panicky moment the man thought he had exposed himself to radioactive snow, and he waited for the onset of symptoms. He made it back to his own crowded tent and ignored anyone who spoke to him. When he found his corner, he rolled himself inside his dirty blanket and just tried to get warm. As the hours went by without signs of exposure, the man considered the possibility that something else must have made Demmings sick, but he didn't see the wisdom in telling Brother Silas. As a matter of fact, he didn't want to be anywhere near Silas when he found out.

When Silas finally ended his mental battle with the Chinese about the current state of the world, he vaguely wondered where the meteorologist had gone, but he let the thought go just as quickly as the man had left. It wasn't worth the time. His thoughts went back to the gold that was so close yet so far from his touch, and he wondered how he was going to take possession of it.

"The bulldozer," he said with excitement. "I'm going to push the whole front of the building down if I have to."

Silas wore an old wind-up watch that he set according to sunrise and sunset, and he adjusted it throughout the year. According to his own definition of time, there were at least six more hours to sunrise, and that would be the perfect time to make his next assault on the Depository. He told his guard to send a message to the bulldozer driver to be at the entrance of the tent at sunrise.

******

The rumble of the bulldozer outside the tent of Brother Silas was enough to rouse the rest of the camp, but he had been waiting as the second hand of his watch twitched toward his official moment of sunrise. The clouds and the swirling snow hid the light from the sun, but when he said to be there at sunrise, the driver knew it meant he should be there on time. Norman Boggs had waited in the cab of the bulldozer for half an hour ahead of schedule but didn't start the engine until it was time.

Before sunrise, the driver spent an hour erecting a canopy on the bulldozer. It had been easy for him to find the materials he needed on the Army base, especially the plexiglass and plastic he needed for windows. He couldn't do anything about windshield wipers, but he knew he could navigate the heavy piece of equipment straight to the entrance, and if he missed by a little, he would just run over any obstacles he couldn't see.

He found a large piece of curved plexiglass in a hangar near the airfield and was pleased with the way he fastened it over the cab. He would be able to keep Brother Silas safe from the toxic snow, and he knew their leader would be pleased with him.

Not far from the hangar, a large plane rolled into view with its four propellors turning. He could feel the vibration of the engines, but the sound was muted by the heavy snowfall. The bulldozer driver envied Brother Sparks for being the only pilot in their troupe. Sparks was young and arrogant because he had such importance to Brother Silas. He watched the plane rotate and come to a stop and wondered how hard it would be to learn to fly. Operating a bulldozer wasn't easy, and it would be fun to learn.

Norman was squat and muscular, and he seemed to fit in the seat of the bulldozer in the same way that people seemed to resemble their pet dogs. If he had a dog, that's what he would have…a bulldog, short, squat, and powerful like the bulldozer. Sparks seemed to fit his plane the same way, and Norman knew that he envied more than Sparks' ability to fly the plane. If he had a choice between being squat and powerful and tall and handsome, he knew which one he would choose.

Another thought crossed his mind when he saw the long, dark barrel of one of the weapons sticking out through the side. He had seen Sparks use the weapons at the Army base in Georgia. It was an awesome display of destruction. He had to wonder why they couldn't just circle the building where all the gold was kept and blast the doors off. As a matter of fact, they could blow the walls down.

He shook the thought off. The last thing he wanted to do was diminish his own importance by suggesting an easy way to get into Fort Knox. He went back to work on his project so he would be on time for Brother Silas, but he planned at some point to ask Sparks to teach him how to fly the plane. He hoped Sparks didn't see through his jealousy and realize that it would make Sparks replaceable.

Norman finished his project early and waited for sunrise, then he timed his arrival perfectly. He saw Brother Silas inspect his handiwork as he hurriedly ducked inside the protective cab of the bulldozer.

"Did you do this yourself?" asked Silas.

"Yessir. I worked on it all night," answered Norman.

He was insufferably pleased with himself, and he could tell by the smile that Brother Silas was pleased too. That didn't last long.

"You couldn't figure out a way to put windshield wipers on it? How're we supposed to see where we're going?"

Norman could figure out a lot of things for himself under the cover of the engine, but he wasn't a design engineer. If he had more time, he might have been able to take a windshield wiper motor out of a car and fasten it to the bulldozer cab, but he hadn't been given the time. He tried his best not to show how deflated he was by the criticism, but his attempt came out defensive, and he sounded like he was whining.

"If I had been given more time, I could have put on wipers and even run a vent from the engine for heat. I can see well enough to get us there, Brother Silas."

His defense backfired when he drew attention to the cold, and Brother Silas wasn't one to ever let a transgression go unrewarded. He glared at Norman and appeared to be assessing his appearance.

"Where did you find that foul weather coat?" he demanded.

Norman had felt like he had already gotten his share of the wealth in Fort Knox when he found the heavy field jacket in the maintenance building by the runway. It had sergeant stripes on it, and a name tag that said Walker, and he had slipped it on with gratitude. Not only was it warm, but he was glad the sergeant's name hadn't been Crawler.

He knew what would come next. Without being told, Norman pulled off the warm coat and handed it over. Brother Silas took it the same way a second-grade bully took lunch money from other kids. He put it on as if it had always been his.

Norman put the bulldozer in gear and lurched forward in the general direction of the road. It may have been sunrise, but he strained his eyes for the smallest amount of light in search of landmarks. The snow blew straight at the plexiglass windshield, and to make matters worse, it fogged up as the cabin temperature grew slightly warmer than the outside. He wiped furiously as he steered, and Brother Silas only made Norman nervous by constantly telling him to watch where he was going.

The bulldozer lumbered up to the front gates of the enclosure to the Depository, and it occurred to Norman that there was no one available to open the gates. His fear of the toxic snow made him make a last-second decision, and instead of stopping, he accelerated.

"What're you doing, you moron?" yelled Silas.

The bulldozer pushed down the fence as if it wasn't even there, but something didn't feel right. Norman felt the steering wheel pulling hard to the left, and Brother Silas grabbed at it to help pull it back to the right.

What Norman hadn't seen was that he had mistaken a section of fence to the left of the gate as the entrance. In the blinding snow, the pole in the middle of the section resembled the place where the chain and padlock were. Beyond the pole was an assortment of barriers designed to stop vehicles from entering the minefield. The right side treads of the bulldozer drove straight over one of the concrete barriers, and as it rose higher in the air, it turned the heavy vehicle to the left.

They fought the wheel to keep the bulldozer from turning, and Brother Silas was dumped from his spot to the right of Norman as soon as the angle became steep enough. He landed on Norman, and Norman's leg was forced down onto the gas pedal. He already had the pedal pushed most of the way to the floor, but the added weight of Brother Silas took care of the last few inches. The bulldozer gained speed and crashed to solid ground as the right tread cleared the concrete barrier.

The landing was hard enough to jar their teeth, but it wasn't half as bad as the explosion when the bulldozer hit the first landmine. The blast was strong enough to blow the tread off, and a large section of it slapped a second mine nearby. That was the blast that killed Norman as a piece of shrapnel cut through the windshield and hit him below the chin. It missed the artery, but he struggled to get air past his crushed windpipe.

If the bulldozer had been at an angle when the blasts happened, it might have rolled over. That would have been a small blessing for Norman because he would have died faster, crushed in his seat. The blast may have been strong enough to blow the tread from the right side, but it only bucked the vehicle a few feet upward before it slammed down to the ground. Brother Silas didn't feel any sympathy for Norman. If anything, the anger he felt toward the squat moron seethed from every pore. He didn't have to get out and inspect the bulldozer to know that it would be useless now.

Silas could see that Norman would be dead in a few minutes, and he didn't want to be around to see him turn into an infected dead. He also saw that the canopy over the cab was largely intact, with the notable exception of the hole in the windshield that signaled the end of Norman. Norman didn't have enough time to permanently bolt it in place, and Silas took advantage of the temporary nature of the structure. He pulled out a knife and cut a series of nylon tie straps Norman had used to keep the frame in place. He lifted the canopy free from the bulldozer and stood up. He was inside a bubble of plexiglass that kept out the toxic snow, and he jumped to the ground at the back of the bulldozer to avoid mines.

The closest he came to a eulogy for Norman as Silas walked back toward the camp was, "So long, moron."

******

Silas had plenty of time to think as he walked back to the camp under the protection of the plexiglass cab. For a moment he was Marvin Corn again…defeated and forlorn at the stupidity that surrounded him. Just like the day when he tried to entice other church members to join the fold at his place of worship, he felt alone and unappreciated. He trudged through shin-deep snow toward the camp and wondered where he had gone wrong.

The sun hardly made a difference through the clouds and the falling snow, but the lights on the tents gradually took shape. On the day when he sat with his binoculars watching the other camps, he was undetectable, and he was so invisible under his plexiglass dome that the people in the camp couldn't see him. He realized that they were at his mercy if he wanted to bring a rifle to this spot and just pick off a few. The thought made him feel powerful again, and with it came the understanding that he was always going to be Marvin Corn, but he was also a king, and a king could call himself anything he wanted.

Even though they had failed to get inside the Depository for the gold, there was never a moment since entering the fort when he didn't feel like it was already his gold. It would be pleasurable to finally touch the gold bars with his own fingers, but they were already his. He imagined them being arranged in stacks, row after row, in a great vault. He gave brief thought to changing his name to Brother Midas... no, King Midas was better.

Silas could keep out the falling snow, but he couldn't keep out the cold, and he lifted his canopy up to walk the rest of the way to the camp. A guard saw him approaching and hurried to him to see if he needed help with the plexiglass. Small groups of people who had watched the bulldozer drive toward the Depository were gathered under tarps with improvised stoves made from barrels. There had been more people, but when they heard the explosions in the distance, most of them had gone back inside to avoid the possibility that Silas would return angry. The ones who were still outside were waiting to see if he would return at all.

If Brother Silas had lost any control over his small army of followers, it wasn't obvious, but there were too many mouths to feed and too few ways to feed them. Gold wasn't going to feed them, and some followers quietly questioned whether or not he intended to share the gold. He couldn't hear what they said as they huddled around their stoves, but a few whispered derogatory disappointment that he had come back instead of Norman.

******

Brother Bernard and Specs were far enough from the camp and the Depository to miss the disaster with the bulldozer. They heard the explosions as a muted pair of thumps, but they couldn't see it. They had left before sunrise in search of the back entrance that Specs was sure existed.

They didn't have a map of the Army base, so they were only going on the best guess about where to search, but they did have an idea about the location of the train station. From there it was only a matter of finding the railroad tracks that would lead to the back door.

The train depot was nondescript. There was nothing about it that made it stand out as important. It was small, and it didn't have any security checkpoints around it. Both of them had expected to find gun emplacements, and the only thing they could figure was that the snow had buried useful landmarks. As they circled the plain little building, Specs had another idea.

"What if they stopped using the back door from the train station?" he asked.

"What's that supposed to mean? You think they stopped bringing gold here?"

"No, but it would make more sense for them to fly it in then drive it to the Depository in an armored vehicle. There's a whole garrison of soldiers to protect it, so that would be the robbery of the century if someone tried it."

Brother Bernard felt like he had enlisted the help of the right person when he dragged Specs with him. They had to sneak out while the tweaker was sleeping because he could be a distraction. He was likely to do something dumb like Demmings and Wilkes. Specs came up with some good theories, and if one of them panned out, they would find the back door to the gold. If they didn't find the back door, he could think of worse people to desert with.

"So, what do you suppose we're trying to find?" asked Bernard. "I hope it's not something buried under all this snow."

They couldn't see more than twenty feet ahead, and they were using the train station as a reference point. As long as they could see the building, they knew they were in the right neighborhood, but it was frustrating not knowing which side of the building was the best side to search.

Specs put a palm to his forehead and said, "I'm so stupid. We don't need to bother with anything behind the building, and the loading platform is the most logical place."

"Explain it to me, Specs. If you're stupid, what's that make me?"

"I didn't mean to insult you. I just wasn't thinking it through. It's simple math. You ever do any bowling?"

Bernard gave Specs a look that he reserved for moments when he wanted someone to spit out what they meant instead of dragging it out.

Specs took the hint and said, "I figure you for the kind of person who could handle a heavy bowling ball, maybe sixteen pounds. One bar of gold weighs twenty-seven pounds, and they didn't transport it one bar at a time. Anything more than three hundred bars would need a heavy-duty forklift, and the back door was probably constructed before forklifts were invented."

"Spit it out, Specs. It's too cold for me to listen to much more."

Specs talked faster and got to the point.

"We only need to find the ramp from the loading dock. They would have carried the gold straight down the ramp to a railroad handcar that sat on a pair of tracks parallel to the train tracks."

"A handcar…you mean those things where two people are pumping their brains out to get them to move?"

As Specs explained what they should be searching for, Bernard followed him around to the front of the building. He climbed a steep set of steps to the top of the loading dock and stood facing the side where trains used to unload. The tracks were either gone or buried in the snow, but the ramp was right where he thought it would be.

"I didn't bring a snow shovel," said Bernard.

Specs didn't understand the point at first, but when it sank in he laughed even though Bernard wasn't trying to be funny. He hadn't considered the possibility of needing to dig out the entrance.

Specs pointed at another building about fifty yards away.

"The tracks, if they're still there under the snow, probably curved away from the main tracks. There wouldn't have been any point in the entrance being right next to the main tracks. That building has a garage door on it, but I'll bet there used to be a barn door instead. It would've needed a big enough opening for the handcar to drive inside."

They walked side by side down the slick ramp into the snow, and even though their feet were wet and numb, they searched with each step for anything that might be a remnant of the side tracks that would have served as the transport system for gold when the place was built. About twenty-five yards from the train depot where the tracks would have curved the most, they came to a road that was only visible because of the street signs. Bernard felt something different.

"Of course," he said. "They pulled up the tracks above ground, but they left the ones that were on the paved road. This must be the road they used when they started bringing gold shipments from the airfield. It goes straight to that building."

It was surprisingly easy to open the big garage door, but there was nothing obvious to show them the entrance they were sure was somewhere inside. Two handcars sat side by side on railroad tracks. Judging by the rust and general discoloration of the cars, they hadn't moved since before the tracks outside were pulled up.

Bernard pulled the door down to block out the cold, but the room was plunged into total darkness. They fumbled for their flashlights, and he aimed his at Specs.

"No tunnel."

Specs didn't answer the unspoken question. Bernard watched the tall, younger man with glasses and messy hair as he seemed to be putting together some clues. Specs would aim his flashlight at the door, then at the handcars, and then at various points around the inside of the building. From the floor to the roof and back to the floor again, Specs wasn't just searching for the tunnel randomly.

"Are you going to tell me what you're thinking, or is it fun to keep me in suspense?"

"Sorry," said Specs. "I just like to be sure of myself sometimes. See those old pulleys up there?"

Bernard followed the beam of light where Specs aimed it. He saw there were four pulleys near the ceiling. Each one was eight or ten feet across.

"Yeah, I remember seeing something like that a long time ago inside a nice restaurant. I think it was in Charleston. It was one big pulley with a smaller one below, and it was like a big dumbwaiter or elevator. It went to a cellar where they kept wine cool."

Bernard aimed his own flashlight at one of the pulleys and said, "There aren't any ropes. Pulleys don't work without ropes."

"Yeah," said Specs, "but would you leave the ropes out where everyone could see them? They couldn't hide the wheels that power the elevator, but they could hide the ropes. We just have to figure out where."

"What makes you so sure there's even an elevator here?"

"People get lazy, Bernard. Back in the day, they probably used the elevator a lot. They didn't just use it for gold shipments. My guess is that they brought in supplies, ammunition, construction materials, and even foot traffic. If they used it a lot, they wouldn't want to move things away from the platform. Check out the floor. If they wanted to hide the elevator, they could have done a better job covering the gaps in the floor."

Bernard did as Specs suggested and aimed his flashlight at the floor. Directly below the four big pulleys and right where one of the handcars sat, the boards in the floor had a gap. They circled the handcar together, and the gap went all the way around.

"Well, I'll be..."

Bernard didn't finish the sentence because Specs disappeared from view. His flashlight beam reappeared over on the other handcar where he climbed up and gripped the handlebar on one side. He pushed down on the T-shaped bar, but it didn't budge.

"Give me a hand up here, Bernard. This thing has gotten rusty. It won't move without both of us pushing on it. You can get on the other side and lift while I push down over here."

Bernard was used to giving orders, but Specs was the one person who could get away with acting more like a partner than a subordinate. Besides, he felt like he had picked the right person to team up with. He jumped up onto the handcar and went to the handlebar across from Specs. With one lifting while the other pushed, they felt a small movement as the rust broke free. They gave one hard try together, and the grating sound of metal on metal changed to a squeal that meant the handles moved as far as they could go.

When they reversed directions with Bernard pushing down as Specs lifted, they heard the sound of something happening above them. Both of them stopped pushing and pulling and aimed their flashlights upward. Ropes extended outward from holes they hadn't noticed in the darkness, and all but invisible wires were fastened to the ropes. The men resumed pumping the handles of the handcars, but they kept their lights aimed at the ropes. They watched as each change of direction on the handles caused more rope to feed out to each pulley, circle around it, then disappear through holes lower down the walls.

"The corresponding pulleys must be behind that wall," said Specs excitedly.

Bernard was just as excited, but he hadn't quite figured it out yet.

"But what makes the elevator go down?"

Specs jumped down from the first handcar and climbed onto the other one that sat on the floor with the gap around it. Bernard took that as his answer and did the same thing. The handlebars gave them a fight, but once the rust gave in to their combined efforts, they felt the floor lurch downward. They didn't question if they should let the elevator go down with them on it because it was what they had wanted. They happily put their weight into pumping the handles, and the platform smoothly descended into darkness.

The infected dead that were standing on the platform directly below them were crushed by the combined weight of the elevator and the big handcar. The rest of them pushed and shoved each other as they attempted to climb the sides of the railroad vehicle.

Specs stopped pumping his handlebar just long enough to pull hard on a lever that stood almost to his height, and the elevator reversed directions. Neither of them spoke when it reached its former position flush with the floor, but they found it hard to take their eyes off of the number of hands that protruded from the gap around the edges. The fingers still moved on all of them. Three of them were forearms from the elbow up, and one had a grip on a wheel of the handcar. Both of the men played their flashlight beams around the edges below their feet. They were well enough above the fingers that appeared to be twitching as the light moved over them, but it still gave them the creeps.

Specs couldn't resist the obvious setup for the joke.

"Handcar...get it?"

Bernard wanted to laugh, but every part of his body was shaking from the adrenaline rush.

"How is it that you have a joke ready for everything, Specs?"

"I don't know. I guess it's just my way of dealing with things."

"Well, deal with this. We only have two flashlights. Did you bring spare batteries?"

Specs patted the pockets of his coat and said, "Four sets. They're old and die fast, but I've got it covered."

"Were you able to see anything before we had to haul ourselves out of there?"

Specs shook his head and said, "I was too busy. All I saw was hands and fingers waving in our faces."

This time it was Bernard who couldn't resist making the joke.

"They're still waving at you."

15

Betrayal

South Carolina - 2023

Just after midnight, the snow stopped falling, but it wasn't all good news. While the snow didn't fall, the temperature did. The Chief was ready to get some sleep, but he decided to check the people who were on watch before turning in, and it was a good idea that he did. One of them was gone, and fresh blood was spread over the snow.

The posts were designated as north, south, east, and west. When he found the east post deserted, the Chief called Kathy and told her to take one person with her to the north post and to send two people to the south and east posts. He was on his way to the west post, and he didn't want anyone to meet him there because he was moving fast. He would radio if he needed help.

One reason he was moving so fast was that one of his people, Colleen, was on the west post, and tracks in the snow went in that direction. The Chief also knew there was a strong chance that Hampton would figure out Colleen might be in trouble. If he did, there would be no force in the universe that could stop him from rushing blindly to her rescue. While Hampton would crash through the woods like an enraged bull, the Chief could move his incredible size as silently as the snowfall. His plan was to be there before Hampton arrived, but if he knew his friend as well as he thought, it would be a close race.

The Chief could be as gentle as a newborn kitten if he had to and if the situation was right, and he could be as lethal as TNT when he needed to be. This situation called for him to be at his best. Iris called it his hunter-killer mode. He was locked in...focused. His senses registered everything, and he heard the voices long before he saw movement. He changed course to get behind the men as they moved toward Colleen. She had her hands raised, which meant they had gotten close to her before she saw them, and one of them had her at gunpoint. He was the Chief's first target.

There were three of them spread out in a semicircle, and they were talking in soothing voices to Colleen like they didn't want to hurt her, but he knew that was just a ruse to get closer and to keep her from running. One had his left hand behind his back and was gripping a twelve-inch skinning knife with the blade pointed upward. He was in the middle, and the Chief gauged his chances of taking him first without getting shot by the guy on his left. He decided he could do it.

From Colleen's point of view, she saw the expression on the man's face change. It wasn't shock or pain she saw. It was more like a question. He didn't even fall to the ground before she saw the Chief cover the distance between the middle man and the one with the rifle. He turned his head toward the Chief but left the rifle pointed at her. He pulled the trigger, but Colleen expected it and had already dropped into the snow. The man tried to get his rifle aimed at the Chief before it was too late, but he wasn't even close to being on time. The Chief caught the man's rifle in both hands and brought the stock upward as he drove his weight through him. He was lifted off his feet and didn't feel anything before he died because the impact snapped his neck.

The Chief turned around to go after the third man, but he had run as soon as he saw what happened to the man with the knife. The Chief had thrown his left forearm around the man's neck and lifted him to make his back arch. With his own right hand, he pushed the man's knife hand upward. The blade had entered the man's back with enough force for the tip to exit at the top of his right shoulder. Before the man fell over and died, he stood for almost a full minute and stared with confusion at the tip.

The third man chose the wrong direction to escape. Only seconds after he disappeared, a single gunshot told the Chief that Hampton had intercepted him. Colleen let the Chief know she was okay, and together they ran toward the gunshot.

Hampton didn't know if it was Colleen or the Chief coming toward him, so he was happy to see it was both of them. He had the wounded man sitting against the base of a tree. There was a red stain spreading across the stranger's abdomen where he had both hands, trying to keep the blood in. In Hampton's experience, it was a good time to question people. Gunshot wounds to the stomach were painful and fatal without help, and the victims of those wounds were willing to negotiate for all the help they could get.

The man was already talking when the Chief loomed over him, and what he was saying made the Chief's blood run cold. If he wasn't enraged as he charged toward Colleen's guard post, now he was rapidly moving past the emotion.

"It wasn't my idea," whined the man. "The principal said if we could get half of you away from camp at the same time, we could take your armored vehicle away from you."

Hampton and Colleen had already gone a few yards in the direction of the camp when the Chief yelled at them to stop. He grabbed the man and pulled him to a standing position against the tree then punched him where his hands were crossed over his stomach wound. The man would have screamed if the Chief hadn't put his large hand over his face.

"What's your signal to De La Cruz that you were successful?"

The Chief didn't sound like he was asking as much as demanding an answer, and his victim obliged quickly.

Through clenched teeth, the man said, "Flare gun. Please, mister."

The Chief spun the man around and patted him down until he found the flare gun tucked in his belt. He yanked it free and then let the man drop to the ground.

"What do you want to do with him?" asked Hampton.

"Same thing he would have done to Colleen," answered the Chief. "Leave him where he is."

De La Cruz and his people had waited for Kathy to send out her own groups to the guard posts before making their move, but he hadn't counted on how well the Mud Island family reacted to surprises. They didn't just blindly rush out into the night to stop an attack, and his plan had never been for the Chief to be out checking the guard posts, but the last thing he expected was for Cassandra to button up the MRAP so no one else could get inside.

The Mud Island people were all armed and somewhere in the woods surrounding the camp, so his only bargaining chips were

Charlie and Sue. The couple had chosen to stay outside, thinking they were protecting the children. De La Cruz knew he had to move fast and get Cassandra to open the door before the others got back, so he had a gun pointed at Charlie's head.

The snow had almost strangely stopped, but the only light was from the big fire they had burning under the canopy. De La Cruz and his people pulled the canopy away from the MRAP so they could surround it, but under the thick clouds blocking out any moonlight, it was hard to tell which shadows were people and who they were. He wasn't used to the path he had chosen and was beginning to panic.

"If you make me do this, his death will be your fault, and you know the old lady is next."

He didn't know if Cassandra could even hear him, but he also didn't know what else he could do. He saw a red flare go up above the trees behind Charlie and knew he at least had reinforcements heading his way.

"I'm going to count to three. Don't make me do this," he yelled. "One, two…".

Sue had Charlie's hand in hers, and as brave as she wanted to be, she still couldn't hold back the sob that seemed to work its way out from her very soul. It burst through just as De La Cruz opened his mouth to say three. At the same moment, the Chief emerged from the darkness behind Charlie, and he was raising his rifle to take aim. De La Cruz turned the gun toward Sue and pulled the trigger.

Understanding comes slowly when a body is in shock. Charlie didn't understand. He couldn't process the magnitude of the sound so close to his head, and he would later say he never expected it to be that loud without feeling pain. Time slowed down, and he felt like he waited forever to feel something. He also didn't understand why he was blinded by so much blood and couldn't see what happened to Sue.

De La Cruz didn't have as much time to be confused as Charlie or Sue because the blow to his own head was so brutal. The Chief had seen that he could never reach him in time, so he had pulled up short and brought his M4 up in hopes of getting off a shot first. He was so focused on stopping De La Cruz from killing Charlie and Sue that he didn't see the barrel of the M240 moving in the darkness on top of the MRAP.

The 7.62mm bullets fired from an M240 are small, but at a muzzle velocity of over two thousand eight hundred feet per second and a firing rate of six hundred and fifty rounds per minute, the target will be shredded at point-blank range. Cassandra fired almost downward at De La Cruz, and one quick pull of the trigger sent an untold number of rounds through his head. The bullets removed half of his skull almost surgically from his nose to the nape of his neck, but it was the force of the impact that saved Sue. The bullets slammed into him a split second before the discharge of his own gun, and his shot went harmlessly wide into the ground.

Sue continued to sob and had her eyelids pressed tightly together. She was sure if she opened her eyes she would see Charlie had died. It took a few moments to sink in that he was still squeezing her hand. When she forced herself to see why he was able to hold her hand so tightly, she still thought he had been shot because he was covered with blood.

Colleen appeared out of nowhere and wrapped her arms around both of them. The Chief was there with Hampton, and there were other people who were running away. Women with children were crying and holding each other, and shots were ringing out from the trees.

Kathy's group came across several men who were coming back from the other guard posts, and she immediately recognized that the guards were with them. They had been waiting to ambush anyone coming to check on the guards, but they had seen the red flare and thought it was time to come back. Everyone scrambled for cover on both sides and opened fire. The men were no match for the skills of the Mud Island survivors, and after a short, one-sided firefight that left most of them dead, Kathy questioned one who was still breathing. When he told her what De La Cruz was doing, they hurried back toward the camp.

It was chaos in the surrounding trees as the "would-be" bandits scattered. Some ran into the group led by Kathy. Others ran into Captain Miller and Iris. In almost every direction some were either killed or captured. By the time it was all done, those who were still alive were kneeling in rows with their fingers laced behind their heads.

A headcount confirmed that none of their group had died, but the Chief in particular was still furious about what had happened to Charlie and Sue Sloan. He could see the mental trauma in every line of their faces, and he wished they could have stayed happily behind on their boat. They would have died sooner or later, but they wouldn't have been subjected to what De La Cruz had done to them.

Iris took the Chief by his big hand and led him away from everyone in a way that no one else could. They talked out of earshot for a few minutes until he was calm, and the others could see him nodding his head. When they rejoined the rest of their friends, the Chief seemed to gather his thoughts before he spoke.

"A long time ago, when this first started, we helped some people who were trapped in a house. Me and Kathy, Ed, and Jean…we planned on staying inside the shelter at Mud Island without ever coming out, but we realized that was never an option. We had to help survivors. Those people turned on us…tried to steal our car and leave us stranded. It wasn't so hard to leave them behind, and I would do the same to these people if not for the kids. I think the reason I'm so angry is that we were going to help these people, but they were willing to kill us and take what we have. Now, we still have to help them. We can't let ourselves act like De La Cruz. He felt like it was okay to do what he did because they were desperate."

Iris stepped closer and said, "What my husband is trying to say is that we can't ever let ourselves get that desperate. We can't justify what we do just because we need something. I also had to get it through his thick head that these people aren't the same as the ones we're going after who killed the soldiers. They weren't desperate people, and they need to be stopped before they can hurt anyone else. They proved they were motivated by something else when they attacked the village over Green Cavern. So, we need everyone to help decide what we're going to do with these people."

Iris gestured toward the rows of people being guarded near the MRAP. There were twelve men of different ages on their knees in two rows. Then there were six women and eight children who were sitting in a huddle together. They weren't being forced to keep their hands behind their heads, but Brett stood guard behind them with a rifle. Some of the women and children were crying, but the men mostly kept their eyes aimed at the ground.

The Chief clearly wasn't himself. He had genuinely liked Juan De La Cruz, so the man's betrayal hadn't been expected. It was easy to see that the Chief was taking it very personally.

"Let me talk with them," said Kathy.

The Chief was generally treated as being in charge of the group even though they had never established a chain of command. It was accepted that Kathy and the Chief had been a team since the beginning of the infection, and the Chief had the skills to be the leader. That made her his lieutenant, and she never abused the role. There were times when her steady presence was something the Chief needed to lean on, and this was one of them.

Standing in front of the male prisoners, Kathy spoke loud enough for the women to hear her.

"Who was second in command to De La Cruz?"

No one answered, but she didn't expect anyone to confess. She was watching for reactions, and she saw enough to get what she needed. One man glanced at the man kneeling directly in front of him. Another glanced to his right at the same man.

"Okay, so no one wants to be in charge. I guess I should just pick someone then."

She stepped over in front of the man identified by the other two.

"Are you afraid we're just going to execute you now? Is that what you would've done to us?"

The man kept his hands behind his head but lifted his face to look at Kathy. She was so relaxed that he wasn't sure what to think. It meant she was either cold-blooded or genuinely didn't feel threatened. He had seen the body of De La Cruz before being captured, and with the same gun that killed the principal aimed at their backs, he couldn't be nearly as relaxed as her.

"I don't know...I don't know what you plan to do, but we wouldn't have killed you," he said in a low voice.

"No? So you would've just eaten our food then taken our weapons and transportation then cut us loose, right?"

The man lowered his hands and shook his head. Kathy was good at reading people, and she didn't feel like it was a defiant gesture. He just seemed resigned to whatever fate she gave him. It was the way his shoulders slumped that made her feel like the fight had gone out of the man.

"Juan has always been our leader. No one else liked his idea, but he said it would be easy, and we could survive with your military vehicle and supplies."

"So you just went along with it? There was no consideration for what would happen to us or how many people might have died?"

"Lady, I heard your leader talking with Juan. You guys are going somewhere to do the same thing to someone else."

"Is that what you think? Mister, you have no idea what we're doing or why, and what Juan missed is that we were willing to give you the shirts off our backs. As a matter of fact, we're stupid enough to still do it."

The rest of the men slowly lowered their hands as they realized what was happening. All of them had expected to die, but at the very least they thought they would be cut loose without anything more than the clothes they wore.

"Listen closely, people. You have a long way to go to earn back our trust, so when we break camp a few hours from now, we're going north. Where you go is your business, but I'm going to give you directions to a place in Alabama. Go there, make camp, and someone will find you within a few days. If you decide not to go there, good luck to you."

"Can we go with you?"

It was one of the six men in the back row who spoke up.

"We can't take more people with us. There's not enough room in the Cougar."

"Juan didn't tell you everything," said the man. "We've been living in a high school not far from here, but we've been having to go further and further out to get supplies. Juan had access to the school district's warehouse, and it was full, but we knew there would come a day when we had to go somewhere else. When he saw you guys, he came up with a plan."

"You brought children to a hijacking?"

It was hard for Kathy to stay calm, but she was a bit angry at the rest of the people for being sheep that were so dependent on one man. They were so unlike her own friends. Any one of them could survive on their own if they had to, but they were even stronger together.

"Juan said it wouldn't work if the kids weren't with us."

"You're not helping your case, mister. What if we had been parasites who just take what they want? Wait a minute...don't answer that because I just described you."

The man saw that he was making things worse but there was one last thing he could offer to make up for what they had done.

"We have two school buses that run and lots of diesel. We could go with you and help. It would be better to die making amends than to just stay here and die of starvation or from the infection."

Kathy left them to think about it without giving the man an answer. When she glanced back at them, she saw they had returned their hands to the backs of their heads. If the apocalypse had taught her anything, it was that some people fought to stay alive, and some people fought just to survive. The two words were similar, but she knew how they made people different. People who fought to survive had no problem helping other people stay alive.

"How'd it go?" asked Iris.

"Interesting," said Kathy. "With a little work, I think we can get to Fort Knox with a small army."

After Kathy told her friends what was discussed, they came to a tentative decision to at least go to the high school and check out the buses. They could use the spare diesel fuel, and if the men were serious about helping, they could integrate them into their group. There was also the option to just provide them with an escort until they reached I-20 in Georgia. From there they could go west to Birmingham and then make a relatively easy trip north to Guntersville.

******

If there was any hope that the snow had stopped for good, it was gone before the sun could prove it still existed. At the time when they expected to break camp, the snow was heavier than before.

The Chief was wearing a pair of goggles because the wind propelled the cold flakes in all directions, and it constantly stung his eyes. He had a sack of them still wrapped in plastic and was handing them out to his own people first.

"I don't know which I prefer more," he grumbled, "the snow or the infected."

Captain Miller took a pair of the goggles from him and said, "I'm tired of stepping on the things. I don't care if they're frozen or not. It still makes you jump about four feet in the air when you realize what's under your feet."

"That reminds me," said Kathy. "Next time we make camp for the night, let's assign some of the new people to clear an area for a latrine. I keep expecting a hand to reach out of the snow while I'm taking care of business."

Despite his sour mood, the Chief had a hard time hiding his smile.

"How are the three new guys from the Marine base working out?" He directed the question at Hampton since he had brought them in.

"They're solid, smart. We can trust them, and they did well last night. When the attempted coup went down, they got the MRAP secure and then headed for cover. They didn't do any unnecessary shooting the way some people would."

"Good, let's make sure they know they're part of the team and not just tagging along."

When they gathered as a group around the fire, they agreed to keep the Cougar at the campsite while a patrol went to the high school. If the buses were drivable, and if other factors didn't cause a change of plans, the people who had been with De La Cruz would be allowed to follow them when they left. If they weren't, the Chief said they would take some of their diesel fuel to top off their own. It would be considered compensation for their attempt to hijack the MRAP.

Kathy, Tom, Captain Miller, Iris, Sim, and Brett were chosen for the patrol, and it was agreed they would be back in six hours, or it would be assumed they had run into trouble. The Chief told her to maintain radio silence until then and only check in by radio if they wouldn't be back by the deadline. Two of the men from the school were selected to be their guides.

Captain Miller took point and the rest formed a column behind him. It took less than a minute for the patrol to disappear from view in the driving snowstorm. The Chief and Hampton found themselves a quiet corner under a lean-to and got a fire going.

"You said you wanted to talk with me?" asked the Chief.

"Yeah, I think we have ourselves a big problem. Have you noticed anything unusual about our new friends?"

"I hope you're talking about the big group and not the four we picked up at the Marine base."

"Those guys are all fine. It's the group from the school. We probably could have spared ourselves the trouble and the time by leaving them behind."

Hampton had expected the Chief to be surprised by his suggestion, but he just nodded his head in agreement.

"Kathy noticed it last night," said the Chief. "That's why you and I are back here at the camp with the rest of the people. I was going to talk with you after they left, but you noticed it too."

"To be sure we're both talking about the same thing, I'll just come right out and say it. They're sick."

The Chief nodded again.

"Why did you send out the patrol?" asked Hampton.

"First things first, I want you to get together with the rest of our people one at a time without arousing any suspicion. Tell them to keep the people contained and to spread out on the perimeter of the camp. When we get to the time when we have to tell them the bad news, there might be a few who take it badly."

"Cassandra has been comfortable in the turret of the MRAP. Does she know?"

"I told her while you got the fire going. She's covering us right now," said the Chief.

Hampton stuck his head out from under the cover of the lean-to and saw Cassandra raise a hand in his direction.

"I sent the patrol because we could use another barrel or two of diesel. Brett's going to do what he can to get their buses running. If he can, Kathy will make sure they have enough to get them further inland. If they get far enough from here, maybe they can find a better food supply than seafood. We'll give them our extra MREs to help them along."

Hampton said, "I feel bad for the kids."

"I know. This isn't going to be easy. I sent Kathy for more than the fuel. She and Iris are going to use their judgment to see if there are any other options. Iris is a soft touch, so I know the decisions will be compassionate, but she was also the first one to figure it out. She feels guilty for not saying something sooner. De La Cruz might be alive if she had said something before they tried to hijack us."

"What made Iris notice?"

"It was when we passed out the food to them," said the Chief. "One of the children was eating so fast that Iris told her to slow down. The little girl told her she hated crab. Iris asked her when was the last time she had eaten crab, and the child said they couldn't catch crabs since the snow started, but that they had cooked some that day. They've been rationing it since."

Hampton shook his head and said, "In other words, they've been living on blue crab."

"You weren't with us yet when we came across those people on the Stono River who were using the infected to catch crabs. You know, I've always wondered why there weren't more children on those docks at the marina, but I've suspected they're the first ones to get sick from eating contaminated seafood. It could also explain why there were so many adults in this group and so few children. Frankly, I'm amazed there were so many children."

"I can't figure it out," said Hampton. "By now you would think people besides us would have figured it out, and judging by the ages of the children, they were all born around the time this all started. How did they last this long? They've probably been eating crab their whole lives."

"That's what Kathy and Iris hope to find out."

* * *

194

******

It took just over an hour for the patrol to reach the school. They had to circle it to reach a place where the snow drifts were lower. Fortunately, the infected dead that were around the outside of the tall fence that surrounded the bus parking area and the back entrance to the school were all frozen solid. One of their guides told Kathy that they used to have a big problem with them pushing on the fence, but back when all of the school buses were running, De La Cruz had them park the buses against the fences for support. They told Kathy he had been a good leader until he decided to hijack them.

It was cold inside the school even though they didn't have the wind biting at them. Brett took one of the men back outside with him to see if he could get the buses running, and Kathy asked the other man to show them where they had been living. He led them to the administrative offices and explained that most of them stayed in those rooms because De La Cruz could monitor their supplies more closely.

The school cafeteria was where most of the teachers stayed. Because the school had been fully stocked when the apocalypse started, there had been plenty of food for them to live off of at first. They rationed it and guarded it until it ran out, then they sent out resupply missions. The man said they were used to people not making it back, and their numbers decreased steadily over the years.

The man didn't know when he told them what they were waiting to hear. Kathy and Iris were with the man in the school kitchen while the others were out checking the school for clues about the history of the group. They were specifically interested in gravesites, where they dumped their trash, and what they did to improve the surroundings to make it a more defensible place. Those three things would tell them how the people had lived for over seven years. It was a lifetime of history.

In the kitchen, the man being escorted by Kathy and Iris opened a large Coleman cooler and pulled out a plastic container. He removed the top and sniffed the contents. Apparently satisfied that the contents hadn't gone past the expiration date, he dipped a handful of something white from the container and ate it.

"Still good," he muttered. "Want some?" He held the container out to them.

Even though they were already fairly sure what the container held, Iris asked, "What is it?"

"Crab meat. I don't think we could have survived without it."

16

Back Door

Kentucky - 2023

While Brother Bernard and Specs sat on the handcar laughing hysterically at the fingers that still twitched around the elevator platform, Brother Silas sat inside the safety of his tent and fumed at the loss of the bulldozer, not to mention his ignominious return to the camp.

Silas was supposed to ride in like a conquering hero. Instead, he walked in under a foggy plastic dome like the nerdy little kid whose mother had dressed him for school in an oversized adult raincoat. His mother had done that to him, and everyone had made fun of him, even the kids no one else talked to. That memory was dredged up because his feet were cold and wet. His mother had explained that the thrift store raincoat was something he would grow into, but the rubber boots wouldn't fit over his shoes.

As he walked past the gawkers peering from their tents, he saw the way they hid their amusement. He wasn't sensing the control he used to have over them, and he thought maybe it was time to get it back. Silas yelled at his guard and shouted an order to call for an immediate assembly of the Brotherhood.

Within thirty minutes, the Brothers filed into the tent and took their places around the meeting table. Sparks was in the chair to the right of Brother Silas, symbolically representative of his status. Noticeably absent was Brother Bernard. His empty chair next to Sparks seemed to be the focal point of the entire room.

"Where's Brother Bernard?" shouted Silas.

Everyone did their best to find somewhere else to look rather than at Brother Silas. Even Sparks didn't feel impervious to the anger that seethed out of Silas. He couldn't remember a single time that someone had to be summoned a second time for an assembly of the Brotherhood. Sparks stared at the empty chair next to him as if he expected Bernard to materialize at any moment.

The Brother in the chair on the other side of the vacant seat decided it was time for a bold move, and he slid to his left taking Brother Bernard's place next to Sparks. As he made his move, he discretely tapped with his hand on the thigh of the man to his right. The man didn't let him down and followed his move by sliding into his vacated seat. It caused a chain reaction around the table, and for a brief few seconds, it resembled a row of fans at a ball game doing a mini-wave. The last man to move was the man to the left of Brother Silas, and he was more than glad to put a little more distance between himself and their leader.

If Silas had been furious before, it was nothing compared to the tirade that followed. The screaming went on unabated for over ten minutes, during which time, Silas used every piece of profanity he had ever learned and even invented a few new ones. He ended with the observation that he would have preferred to see Brother Bernard's dead body in that seat before anyone else used it. The man sitting in the seat did his best to make eye contact across the table to get the line moving back in the other direction, but there was no way the last man in line was going to move closer to Silas.

It ended when Silas finally ran out of steam and sat down heavily in his own chair. Sparks was the only Brother at the table who hadn't moved, and he could fly the plane, so he felt like he was safe. The rest of the Brothers weren't so sure about their own futures.

The guard at the entrance to the tent had his eye on that vacant seat. During the time that Silas spent reducing the remaining Brothers to emotional puddles, the guard had run with his head covered from tent to tent asking for any information pertaining to the whereabouts of Brother Bernard. He had returned to report that someone had seen Bernard and Specs leaving the camp before dawn. They had gone in the general direction of the old railroad depot.

Silas could only think of one reason for the treachery. They must have deserted. He was torn between going after them and pursuing his original plan of getting into the Depository.

Sparks decided it was the right time to make a suggestion.

"Brother Silas, it seems that Bernard's failures were adding up, and it was only a matter of time before your generous patience would wear thin. The coward won't survive a week out there in the snow. We should focus on more important matters, and I think the efforts of your guard should not go unrewarded. If not for him, we would still need to be on the unsavory business of Bernard's absence."

It was a face-saving suggestion that served to vindicate Silas for being angry, but it also allowed him to move on. It was also a skillful redirection for him to give credit to the guard because it would give Silas an outlet for his emotions. While the remaining Brothers dared not to breathe, let alone speak, Silas digested the suggestion and visibly relaxed.

"Yes, Brother Sparks, it's time to get down to important business."

He gestured for the guard to take the empty seat but only wasted sixty seconds on an introduction. Once Brother Andrew was happily in his seat, Silas was ready to approach the real problem…how to breach the Depository and get to the gold.

******

Bernard and Specs stayed in their seats on top of the handcar and weighed their options. They could just leave and get away from the control of Brother Silas. They could also go back and report the good news that they had found what was likely to be the back entrance to the largest gold vault in the world.

They had no way of knowing that by now they were not exactly in good favor with the Brotherhood, and there were still some minor problems with their discovery. There was no real proof that the tunnel below the elevator went anywhere. It was just a reasonable assumption that it went to the Depository. Then there were the infected dead below the elevator. They had come back with a few fingers, hands, and arms, but they knew those were just inconveniences for the infected. They still had teeth.

Even if they knew the tunnel was the back entrance, and even if they could eliminate the infected dead, there was still one more thing to consider. Specs had brought it up in a way that suggested Bernard must have thought of the same thing.

"Do you have a plan for getting through the door at the end of the tunnel?" asked Specs.

Bernard didn't want Specs to think he hadn't thought that far ahead, so he just shook his head. Given a few moments of silence to think about it, it occurred to Bernard that it wasn't likely to be a security door like the one above ground. It was more likely to be a vault door.

"That's why I brought you with me. Didn't you say you could open any lock, or was that just bragging?"

Specs took off his glasses and pinched the bridge of his nose between his thumb and forefinger.

"Why does everyone leave off the last part of the sentence? I said I could open any lock with the right tools, and I don't see the right tools around here. Did you tell me to bring tools with us, Bernard?"

Brother Bernard wondered for a moment when he and Specs had gotten on a first-name basis with each other, then he remembered it was probably when he had told Specs they would just disappear if this idea didn't pan out.

"Let's just take this one problem at a time. We came too far to give up now, and look at us. Did anyone else figure this out? Let's work on what to do about all those deadheads below us."

"I have an idea," said Specs. "Now that we know they're down there. We could just lower the platform part way so we can reach them, but they can't reach us."

"Then what? Kill them with our charm?"

Specs actually laughed thinking Bernard was being funny instead of sarcastic. On the wall of the shed that housed the handcars, he saw a variety of tools. The rebar poles were promising for spiking the infected in the heads, but he saw another way to rid themselves of several at the same time.

"Remember what you said when Wilkes asked what they should do if they found ropes? You said to lasso the infected and bring one back to him. I thought me and the tweaker would die laughing. I was laughing so hard I thought I would cry."

"What's your point?" barked Bernard.

Specs was enjoying the memory of the exchange in front of the gold Depository, but he didn't miss Bernard's impatience.

"There's a bunch of rope in this place. We can lower the platform a few feet, drop ropes around their heads, and pull them tight. Some are so rotten that their heads will come off like we're popping shrimp heads, but for those that don't, their heads will get smashed when we raise the elevator."

Specs made it sound simple, and Bernard had to admit, it made sense from where he sat. If they didn't blow it by lowering the platform too far, they could get ten or twelve at a time.

"I like it. Let's get started."

It only took a few minutes to gather the coiled ropes and get them back to the handcar. They each sat and tied nooses on the ends of the ropes and then tied the loose ends to the wheels. When they had a dozen ropes in place, they each took up positions opposite from each other.

"Okay," said Bernard, "let's do this nice and slow."

Specs gave a nod of agreement, and they pumped the handlebars slowly. The platform dropped a couple of feet causing a commotion below. They didn't know which was worse, the growling or the smell. They stopped pumping and pulled out rags to tie over their mouths and noses, then they pumped again until the scrambling hands appeared over the edge of the platform.

"That's far enough," said Bernard. "Let's get this over with so I can get back up and take a normal breath again."

They moved to opposite sides of the platform to keep the infected spread out. In their panic to get back up the first time, they hadn't noticed that the platform swayed a little. Bernard looped a rope over his left hand and took aim with a noose in his right hand. He threw it at his first target but missed because the infected waved its arms enough to knock the rope away.

"I got one," yelled Specs. "This is just like that ring toss thing at the fair."

Specs pulled the rope tight and brought the squirming infected as close to the edge of the platform as he could, then he tied the slack rope in his hands tighter on the handcar.

"That's one," he cheered. "We can pull them tighter after we have all the ropes around on them."

Bernard wasn't too happy with the way things were going until he got lucky and snagged one.

"Whoa, I got one too."

After wrestling it closer, he was able to tie off that rope and move to another. The second one proved to be easier once he got the hang of it, and together they had a dozen of them tied to the lip of the platform in thirty minutes. They went around and helped each other pull the ropes tighter until the infected had their chins resting on the lip of the platform. Some of them managed to get their hands over the edge so far that Bernard and Specs were happy to retreat to their seats on the handcar.

"Ready?" asked Bernard.

Specs nodded, and they gripped the handlebars again. Bernard pushed down on his side as hard as he could, but the handles wouldn't move. They hadn't considered how much the infected weighed.

Bernard turned red from pushing too hard, and Specs began to laugh like it was the funniest thing he had ever seen. Bernard stopped pushing on his side of the handlebars and glared across at him.

"What's so funny, Specs? I'm going to push you over the side if you don't stop laughing."

"Sorry, Bernard, but I just thought of something. Do you know why they're so hard to lift? Because they're dead weight. Get it?"

Bernard felt like following through on his threat, but he needed Specs to open the door at the end of the tunnel if there was one.

"If I push you over the side, I'll lighten the load by what, a hundred and fifty pounds?"

Specs decided he had made Bernard mad enough for one day, so he said he was ready to lift as Bernard pushed down on his side. This time they strained, and Bernard swore the handlebars were about to bend, but the platform lurched upward. They quickly went into the next cycle of pushing down and pulling up, and the elevator platform picked up speed. Specs had explained to Bernard that there were probably counterweights on the elevator, and once they were in motion, they would make the elevator easier to move.

The results were nothing less than spectacular. When the platform reached the floor of the building, all twelve heads were caught in the gap that was barely two inches wide. The sound of a dozen heads being crushed at the same time was unexpected, and the fragments that flew across the platform made them jump up on their seats in front of the handlebars. They both cheered and couldn't wait to go back for a second load.

It took three trips to get all of them. By the time they were done, the platform was a mess, and there were over thirty headless bodies below the elevator. It smelled worse than it looked, but as far as they could tell, there wasn't anything between them and the end of the tunnel. Their flashlights were losing their battery power, so they decided to put fresh batteries in them before leaving the elevator.

The platform didn't reach all the way to the floor because there were bodies under it, and they had to step carefully to avoid sharp bones, but at least there weren't any heads with their teeth intact. They were impressed with the carnage they had created without any weapons.

Bernard said, "We're going to start carrying ropes with us when this is all over with. We might not always be able to hang them from an elevator platform, but I remember getting stuck in a tree once with one of them hanging around the bottom. If I'd had a rope with me then, I could've dropped the noose around its neck and then jumped out of the tree. Probably would've yanked its head right off."

"How did you manage to get out of the tree?" asked Specs.

The question didn't seem to set well with Bernard, but he grumbled the answer anyway.

"Limb broke...I fell on top of the dead guy's head."

Even without a flashlight aimed directly at his face, Bernard could tell Specs was about to have a stroke from holding back his amusement.

"Brother Bernard, I didn't know if I wanted to go on this exploration with you when you told me about it, but I'm starting to be glad I came along."

"Shut up, Specs."

******

The tunnel was much longer than the pair of explorers had expected. What they originally thought was the end of the tunnel was simply a gradual curve that they mistook for a wall. Their flashlights dimmed for a second time, and they put in their next set of batteries. They each had two more replacements, but they hoped they wouldn't have to use them.

"There's something ahead," said Specs.

"I see it. Well, how about that," said Bernard. "It's open. I guess I didn't need to bring you with me after all."

"Yeah Bernard, I'm sure you could have figured out how the elevator worked and how to solve the dead people problem all by yourself too."

For the second time, Bernard wondered when he had lost his authority and gotten on a first-name basis with Specs. He had to admit he had developed a better opinion of the man, but he was still supposed to be the boss, and that meant he was supposed to be

203

addressed as Brother Bernard. Specs either didn't see the piercing glare Bernard gave him, or he didn't care.

They approached a large door that was the same as any bank vault door they had ever seen. It stood halfway open, and there was debris scattered around the entrance. Closer inspection of the debris revealed it was human remains and clothing. Some of it was strewn over the threshold of the door.

Specs shone his flashlight back down the tunnel. The beam seemed to be absorbed by the darkness. He brought it back around to the debris.

"What is it? Did you hear something?"

"No," said Specs, "but I was wondering where all the dead people came from. I guess they came out of there. If this was a movie, do you know what the audience would be saying? They'd be saying don't go in there."

"I'm sure," said Bernard, "but two things come to mind. This ain't a movie, and I didn't come all this way to turn around and go back the other way."

"Why did you come all this way?" asked Specs.

"Same reason you did...to get the gold for Brother Silas."

"No, I came along because you told me I had to."

"Well, now I'm telling you to go through that door."

Specs knew he was stalling and didn't want to go inside, but now he knew Bernard was stalling too. He stepped closer to the opening and aimed his flashlight into the ink-black darkness. He couldn't make out the details of the room beyond, but something didn't seem right.

"I'm not going in there," said Specs.

"What if I tell you to?"

"Brother Silas couldn't make me go in there," answered Specs.

Bernard was shocked at the answer. It crossed the line from disrespect for authority to sacrilege, and he couldn't believe his ears. He was ready to shove Specs through the door, but something caught his eye.

"Was that there a minute ago?"

He played the beam of his flashlight back and forth across the human debris that was draped over the threshold of the door. Specs leaned closer, and he saw there was something different about it, but he wasn't sure what it was until he saw it move.

"It wasn't there before," said Specs, "and it's moving."

"That's the same stuff that was on Wilkes. Don't get any on you. It's made of spiders," said Bernard.

"A minute ago you were trying to make me go in there. Now you're saying don't get any on me. You understand if it's out here on the door, it's in there too, right?"

Bernard was frustrated with the whole thing. They had done a good job so far. They found the handcar shed, found the elevator, managed to kill a whole gang of the infected, and found the open back door. He figured there had to be a way to deal with bugs.

He felt around in the pockets of his coat and produced the one thing he never left behind.

"Here, see if they can burn."

Bernard held out a waterproof metal tube to Specs.

"What's that…matches? You want me to set fire to it? Why can't you do it?"

"When we get out of here, Brother Silas is going to find out everything, and…"

"And what? I've already made up my mind," said Specs. "We'll be lucky to get out of here without ending up like Wilkes, especially if we go in there. If you set fire to that stuff and it burns, it'll smoke us out, and I don't know if I wanna breathe that smoke."

"What's that mean, you've made up your mind?"

Specs said, "I'm leaving. If you want to go in, that's up to you, but if I were in your shoes, I'd leave too."

Bernard felt like he was so close to getting inside where it would only be a matter of time before he got to the gold, but he was also scared to death. He kept thinking about Wilkes, and the way that green mass of spiders made his body move. The way it moved on the ledge of the vault door gave him an idea.

"Specs, you're an expert on locks. Can that door shut without being locked?"

"Sure, it can be pushed shut, just don't turn that wheel and push that lever to the right. Why?"

"Give me a hand."

Bernard jogged back down the tunnel in the direction of the handcar elevator. Specs hesitated for a moment, but without the extra illumination from Bernard's flashlight, the darkness felt suffocating. He couldn't see what was happening around the door as well, and his mind made him think the spidery green moss was coming for him. It didn't take long for him to catch up with Bernard.

When they reached the bodies, Bernard told him to strip off the driest clothes. They made a pile of shirts and pants, being careful to pick the ones that had dried with age. It wasn't easy because of the way they had eliminated the infected. The ones that were dead for a long time were soiled with thicker body fluids than the ones that died later. From past experience, they knew that for some reason the thicker fluids burned better. That was fortunate because most of the infected they had smashed were dead for a long time.

They carried the clothing back to the vault door and then made a trip back for more. Bernard covered the decayed remains on the ledge of the vault door with the driest shirt he could find.

"Stand back," said Bernard. "I have a funny feeling that those green bugs aren't going to like this."

It turned out to be an understatement. When the spiders were together in a mossy-looking pile, they were slow-moving, but that was because they moved together. When Bernard held a match to the sleeve of the shirt where it hung down like a big fuse, the spiders poured out of the other side in a mass exodus to escape the flames and smoke.

Specs held up rags for Bernard to light them, and then he threw the flaming bundles through the open door. As the pile of clothes grew, the orange flames licked at the surrounding walls, and they saw the green clumps of moss dropping from the walls and ceilings adding fuel to the fire. It was spreading fast when the last piece of clothing was thrown, and the room resembled the inside of a furnace.

"We better close the door," yelled Specs.

It never occurred to either of them that the door wouldn't close, but when they both put their hands against the shiny steel door and pushed, their feet slid on the tunnel floor. With smoke billowing from the other side, their panicked expressions said it all. Close the door or die.

"On three," said Bernard.

When Bernard got to three, they put everything they had into it. It was like the handcar handlebars. First, there was a faint slip of metal resisting metal with rust in between. Then there was a feeling of success as the slipping increased. The vault door crushed the human remains that were in the way, and there was an audible click as the lock engaged. An odd sound began whirring inside the door. It was the strange rapid ticking sound that was made when someone started a kitchen cooking timer.

Bernard pointed an ear toward the door and motioned for Specs to be quiet.

"You hear that?" he asked.

"Yeah, sounds like it's working or something. For some reason I expect it to go ding when it's done working."

"I thought you said we could close the door without locking it."

"Maybe it didn't lock," said Specs. "Do you want to open it and find out?"

The whirring sound stopped, and they both stared at it expecting something to happen. In the dim light, he wasn't sure, but the shadows made the door appear to move slightly outward. It appeared to be opening again.

Bernard eyed the door and seemed to be giving it some thought, but his mind was already somewhere else.

"Where do you think we should go?" he asked. "I was thinking about someplace really cold where the infected are all frozen and spiders would never go."

"I think that's everywhere right now," said Specs.

"I don't care, but I'm going north just to be sure. We aren't that far from Ohio, and who knows, it may already be cold enough there. I just want to get as far from here as I can."

Even as they made it far enough from the door that they couldn't see it anymore, they felt the draft as the air was pulled past them going in the opposite direction, and they knew the door must have opened again.

They had become experts with the elevator by the time they made their escape, so they were out the front door of the handcar shack in only a matter of minutes. The cold, fresh air surprised both of them because it was so refreshing compared to what they had been breathing inside. They hadn't realized they had become accustomed to taking half-breaths to be able to tolerate it.

Bernard noticed that Specs didn't even try to cover his face to protect himself from the snow. As a matter of fact, Specs had his chin pointed upward, and his mouth was wide open. He was gulping in mouthfuls of fresh air and plenty of snow along with it.

"Are you trying to kill yourself? That stuff is poison, and that fool Demmings didn't last more than a few minutes after he ate it."

Specs regarded him with curiosity.

"You don't really believe that, do you? I thought Brother Silas was just making that up to keep everyone afraid."

"Why would he do that?" asked Bernard.

"That's what people in power do to make people dependent on them."

When Bernard had enlisted the man as a partner in this little expedition, he had felt like he was bringing along someone who needed to be protected, but Specs was turning into more of an asset than a liability.

"So, how do you feel? You having any stomach cramps, feel like throwing up?"

Specs said, "I'm fine. If anything, it's helping to clear my head after being down in that tunnel. You should try it."

Bernard was skeptical and said he was going to wait a bit to see if the snow killed Specs first. He figured it would be different for people just like when they were bitten. Some would get sick faster than others. In the back of his mind, though, he wondered about Demmings. He had noticed the limp, and part of him wondered why he hadn't told Demmings to show him his arms and legs, especially since he had obviously been rolling around in something bloody.

"I'm keeping an eye on you," said Bernard. "The first time you even have heartburn, I'm taking care of you."

He patted the pistol he had in his hip holster for emphasis.

"You should save your bullets for when the snow stops and the infected thaw out," said Specs. "I'm telling you the snow is...fine."

Something distracted Specs as he finished the sentence, and Bernard slipped the semiautomatic halfway out of the holster.

"I think we did something, Bernard."

Specs pointed toward a row of buildings in the distance. They both knew what was in that direction. On the other side of the buildings was the camp, and past that was the Depository. It was still dark, but the low-hanging gray clouds reflected back any light, and something was illuminating the night sky. There was also movement in the sky from the swirling smoke.

"We went that far in the tunnel?" asked Bernard.

Specs let out a short, unamused laugh.

"I'm glad it was that far now," he said, "and I know which direction I'm going."

Specs took a few steps in the opposite direction of the smoke before he realized Bernard was already ahead of him. Bernard's short legs were moving fast considering the depth of the snow and the slippery ground below it.

"Hey, slow down, Bernard. Why the rush?"

Bernard didn't turn around, but he yelled his answer loud enough for Specs to hear.

"If Brother Silas wasn't already asking everyone if they've seen me, he will be now, and I know how his mind works. If he can't find me, he's gonna put two and two together and figure I had something to do with that fire."

"But you did have something to do with that fire."

******

Brother Silas heard the shouting outside his tent, and his first thought was that they were under attack. He pulled on a hooded coat and a mask and went outside with his gun already in his hand. The crowd outside was facing the Depository, but no one else was getting ready for a fight. Just like in the days before the apocalypse, people would watch in amazement as the buildings made by men went up in smoke.

The thick cloud rising from the dark compound moved upward in drafts of super-heated air, and it curled to the sides as if it was bouncing off an invisible glass ceiling. It roiled in all directions and expanded outward toward the camp. For some reason, Silas didn't think it would be a good idea to inhale any of that smoke. He decided to duck back inside before the cloud arrived.

Within minutes after retreating to his tent, the smoke clouds reached the camp, and he could hear the exclamations of disgust even before he smelled it. It was coating the white snow drifts with a dark, greenish tint. Whatever it was that was burning so fiercely inside the Depository, it had the smell of wet paper. He imagined there was plenty of fuel inside the building that would burn, but he hoped the fire wasn't hot enough to melt his gold.

17

Bad Decisions

South Carolina - 2023

"I remember reading a sign," said Iris. "It said to stay back from the edge of the water because there were alligators nearby. Just past the sign, there were some people swimming in the water. I asked them if they had seen the sign, and they laughed. They said the sign was there just to keep people from swimming."

Kathy said, "Did you ask them why they were swimming in the water if there were alligators nearby?"

"Umm hmm. Sure did. And they said because the sign didn't say no swimming."

"Are you making this up?"

"No, it's a true story, and being as stubborn as I am, I tried again. I told them whoever put the sign up must have figured no one would be dumb enough to swim in the water. One of them asked me if I believed everything that was written on signs."

"Don't tell me an alligator made a believer out of them," said Kathy.

"No, I didn't have to watch someone die that day for making a bad decision, but my point is that by now, these people have seen the signs. They're choosing to ignore them. They could have a sign by the water that says crab meat is contaminated, but if the sign doesn't say don't eat crab meat, they'll ignore the fact that it's contaminated."

Kathy nodded. "They certainly noticed the crabs are bigger and meaner than they used to be. I guess you noticed the children are all about the same age. Kind of odd, isn't it?"

"Eating the contaminated meat took the youngest and the oldest first. The adults all seem to be around the same age too. The only one who was older was De La Cruz. Maybe he was finding other things to eat," said Iris.

"He controlled the supplies."

"So, did my husband tell you how to handle this?"

Kathy said, "Yeah, have Brett help the men get the buses running then drive them to our camp. All the extra fuel can be transported at the same time because there'll be plenty of room. When we get there, the Chief will pull a few of the adults aside and break the news to them. He'll give them general directions to Green Cavern, and they'll be told to stop eating crab meat. Any of them who make it that far will possibly survive. There's no way to know if giving up the crab meat will stop them from dying, but we know what will happen if they keep eating it."

"He expects them to take the news without a protest?" asked Iris.

"He said we'll be ready for it."

Iris seemed like she was about to say something else but stopped short. It was just obvious enough for Kathy to notice.

"You have something eating at you," said Kathy. It wasn't a question.

Iris rolled her eyes and said, "Great choice of words, but yes I do. We've already talked about this some, but I'm really worried about my husband. There was a time when he would've found a way to deal with this that guarantees everyone survives."

"Maybe we've been expecting too much from him."

"That wouldn't matter," said Iris. "It's how much he expects from himself. He's not happy with himself for missing clues that De La Cruz was playing us. He's not happy about being unable to get a plane in the air. He's not happy about the delays and the bad weather."

"He couldn't do anything about those things."

"Try telling him that."

Kathy thought about it and realized he must be saying things to Iris in their private moments. They were all close enough that neither of them felt like they were betraying his confidence by sharing what he had said, but Kathy didn't want it to get too personal. Iris was just as quick to pick up on the subtle shift of Kathy's eyes as Kathy had been when she detected Iris had something on her mind.

"Don't worry," said Iris, "I know where to draw the line. What I'm telling you isn't something he confided in me. It's something I've detected in his behavior. He's frustrated, and I think it's more than just the plane or the weather or even what De La Cruz tried to pull. It's the anger he's had simmering inside him since before we left for England. Face it, he was bent on doing something really special to the people who attacked the soldiers, but that was before Sparks stranded us up north and then devastated the town over Green Cavern. These delays are just causing the pressure cooker inside him to heat up even more."

"Is he okay?" asked Kathy.

"Honestly? I don't think so. Do you remember what he did to the guy who buried me? I think a side of the Chief that he doesn't want to set loose is dying to get out, and if it does, he won't be the same afterward. He's a good man, but he was trained to be a ruthless monster if the situation requires it. This is one of those times, I'm afraid."

"I want you to pay close attention to me, Iris."

Kathy took Iris by her upper arms and made her face her.

"This is also one of those times when he won't be the same afterward if he doesn't let that monster come out."

"So, we should just let this play out?"

Kathy nodded. "We can't stand in his way, and you can't protect him from himself. I think his final decision is going to depend upon the other guy."

"You mean whoever is in charge of the group in Atlanta?"

"Him and Sparks. I think the Chief will want to deal with each of them separately and in some special way. It was one thing to stab us in the back and strand us, but when Sparks decided to go after the Guntersville shelter, he earned a special place in hell. The Chief will want to be sure he gets there sooner rather than later. We just have to be there for him after he does whatever it is that has to be done."

"That's a given," said Iris. "He's a big boy, and he's also smart enough to know what he can live with."

"One thing he can't live with is letting Sparks live. As for the other guy, we don't know anything about him. I expect the Chief will weigh the situation when the time is right and then decide, but I don't imagine that guy will walk away from it."

The sound of a bus engine outside was disturbingly loud, but the freezing temperature had changed the need to be quiet. It still made them uncomfortable after spending seven years of making silence a habit, and they all scanned the perimeter around the parking lot for anything that was drawn to the sound.

Tom, Captain Miller, and Sim had been standing guard while Brett worked on the bus and while Kathy and Iris had gone inside the school. They found it difficult to tell if there was any movement in the trees that bordered the school property because the snow had swirled as it continued to bury everything under a white blanket.

"Are we ready to roll?" yelled Kathy as she stepped outside.

Brett gave her a thumbs up as he opened the door of the bus, but she didn't see it because she was too fixated on the two men from the school group. They were carrying a heavy cooler toward the bus, and she knew what was inside.

"Don't bother to bring that."

She knew one of the men heard her because he looked straight at her as he kept walking.

"Shut the door, Brett."

He didn't know what he had missed, but in the short time he had been around Kathy, he had become accustomed to her authority. Despite the fact she was one of the most attractive blondes he had ever known, she was all business when it came to survival, and if she said to do something, she didn't want to say it twice. He gave her another thumbs up and pulled the mechanical arm that closed the door.

The two men sat the cooler down next to the door. The man who had obviously ignored Kathy balled up his hand and banged the back of his fist on the door.

"Open the door, dude. That's our bus you're driving."

Brett reached over and gripped the handle that the driver used to open and close the door. The men thought he was going to listen to them, but Kathy knew he was just holding it in place in case the men tried to force the door open. The bus door didn't have a lock, or he would have used it. The man banged harder when he realized the same thing as Kathy.

The men turned around and faced Kathy, both openly dismissive. The one who hadn't spoken leaned his back up against the bus door and crossed one leg over the other. The grin on his face showed he mistakenly believed the situation was about to turn out badly for Kathy. The other man who had banged on the door took two steps toward Kathy with his arms hanging at his sides and both hands balled into fists.

"What is it, lady? You want the meat for yourself?"

Kathy laughed, but it wasn't her laugh that surprised him. It was the unexpected laughter that came from both the front and back ends of the bus where Tom and Captain Miller had appeared. Neither had a weapon drawn, but both would be able to draw and shoot before he could. There was a rap on the glass of the bus door, and the man leaning on it turned far enough to see inside. Sim had a semiautomatic handgun pressed against the glass. The man jumped away, falling over the cooler before scrambling to his feet. He wasn't sure where to go since they were surrounded.

"No, you can keep the meat," said Kathy, "but now that I can't trust you anymore, you and your partner can stay here. You're not riding back with us. Go on. Get your cooler and go back inside."

Iris had stepped up beside Kathy, but the two of them spread apart leaving a clear path to the door of the school. The man opened his mouth to speak again, but Kathy held up a hand, palm outward.

"I'm not saying it again."

There was something convincing in her tone. The men retrieved their cooler, and they hardly lifted their eyes from the ground as they passed between Kathy and Iris.

Iris regarded Kathy and asked, "Are you doing what I think you're doing?"

"You mean, am I making it easier for the Chief? Totally...these two would make him shoot them, so it's better not to even bring them back with us."

"The building is freezing. They won't last a day," said Iris.

Kathy called out to the men, "Catch."

She tossed a small metal container toward the men, but neither of them could catch it. They sat the cooler down and retrieved it from the snow.

"You're lucky that's waterproof," said Kathy. "Unscrew one end. There are about a dozen matches inside. Use them wisely."

Kathy and Iris backed away toward the bus. Behind them, they heard the door open, and Tom and Captain Miller climbed inside. The heater had been running inside the bus, so it was very comfortable compared to outside.

"They're going to need those matches," said Iris.

******

On the ride back to their camp, Kathy raised the Chief and brought

214

him up to speed about what had happened. She confirmed his suspicions about what the people had been eating, and he told her he was still going to wait until they got back before telling the others. They had the guns and the field experience, but he didn't want to be forced into a massacre. It was bad enough that they were about to do something that was likely to be a death sentence for most of the school group.

When the buses rolled into camp, the people were quick to notice that their men were missing. Questions were shouted, and when they went unanswered, the people became more aggressive. It was easy to see why the Chief had wanted to wait.

One man stepped forward and demanded to be heard. In the brief absence of De La Cruz, somehow he had become the new leader. His name was Frank Donovan, and the Chief had been watching him even before De La Cruz had died. He was the kind of person who skillfully played the part of a follower while being an instigator. The Chief had no doubt that Donovan had been part of the original plan to betray their rescuers, but when the plan failed, he was as shocked and outraged as the rest of his group.

"Someone needs to explain this now," said Donovan. He put extra emphasis on the last word as if the Chief or someone else would jump at the chance to do as he said. He even rested one hand on the butt of a gun tucked in his belt.

The Chief answered with a level of coldness in his voice that was a warning more lethal than the sound made by a startled rattlesnake.

"Take your hand off the butt of that gun before you say another word."

He didn't need to add what would happen if Donovan didn't listen. Everyone had a good idea already.

Donovan seemed uncertain, not speaking or moving his hand. He appeared to be thinking about what the Chief had said as if he had a choice.

Hampton said, "I don't think the Chief was giving you the option of staying silent with your hand on your gun, Donovan."

The Chief had been ready to deal with whatever happened, but if he could avoid killing anyone in front of the children, that would be his first choice. Colleen was the closest to Donovan, so she stepped quickly to his side and pulled the gun out from under his hand.

"Are you stupid?" she asked. "The Chief is like a hand grenade without a pin in it, and the big hand holding the lever in place is getting tired. You don't want to be the reason he explodes."

The Chief's friends all knew he was at the edge of a cliff, and it would only take a little push to make him go over. He had noticed the extra attention they gave him since the incident with De La Cruz. Until that happened, he had been accepting the delays and setbacks with as much calm as he could. He had even made a mental list of all the things that had still gone right. They may have been stranded by Sparks, but they accomplished their mission to get Henry back to his family, and they also returned in style on a submarine. They had failed in their hopes to get an Osprey, but they had gotten the MRAP. Then he pictured the gun pointed at Charlie and Sue, and something snapped.

The Chief crossed the distance between where he had been standing and Frank Donovan so fast that no one could have gotten out of his way. Donovan didn't even have a chance to raise his hands before the Chief hit him. Something in that split second told him it wasn't the same thing as shooting him in front of the children, but he also understood at the moment of impact that it was still frightening.

The onlookers, the friends of Frank Donovan, couldn't have been more afraid. Donovan's knees buckled under the vicious blow, and he collapsed into an unconscious heap. Women screamed, and children cried. The Chief heard them all, and he knew he had to get a grip on his anger toward Sparks and whoever the monster was that Sparks worked for. If he didn't, there was going to be damage along the way that he couldn't justify or live with.

"He's alive," said Hampton. He had rushed to the man on the ground to be sure. "Let's get him comfortable and get some ice on his head. I don't think his jaw is broken, but it's sure as hell going to hurt for him to chew for a long time."

Kathy told the Chief to take a break and let her talk with the people. He couldn't think of anything to say, so he just nodded and let Iris lead him away. Everyone knew that Iris would help him sort out his feelings.

Tom whispered to Kathy, "Maybe that was a good thing."

"Tell that to Donovan."

"I'm serious," he said. "The Chief has been way too mad. If he hadn't lost it tonight, he might have gotten careless against Sparks, and we don't know anything about the other people. All we know is that they killed some of Captain Miller's men, and whoever their leader is, he has enough power over Sparks that he had him attack Green

Cavern. The Chief will cool down now, and now that he has something out of his system, he'll keep from getting himself killed."

"I doubt that Donovan will agree with your assessment," said Kathy, "but you have a point. The Chief won't send him flowers, but I'll bet that he apologizes to Donovan tomorrow."

"If he isn't still unconscious," said Tom.

At sunrise, they were glad to find the Chief sitting with Donovan by the campfire. The man was holding a cold compress against his face, but both of them were visibly relaxed. Donovan even smiled painfully from time to time. He understood why the Chief had hit him, and maybe it had taught him something about survival. To survive it would be a good idea to form bonds instead of trying to take from others or assert his authority over them.

The part that was hard for him to swallow was the contaminated crab meat. The Chief told him he just didn't know the answers to his questions. He didn't know what would happen if they stopped eating the crabs. He didn't know if it was already too late. All he could tell him was that they couldn't risk taking them along on their trip to Kentucky. If they got sick on the way, it would just slow them down.

Despite everything, they would part as friends, and Donovan drew a map with the Chief's help. If they made it to Guntersville alive, the people at the shelter would find them.

******

After a much longer stay than they had anticipated, the Cougar was finally rolling toward the nearest interstate highway again. Everyone had mixed emotions about leaving the people, especially the children, but the decision had been made the day they began eating crab meat. There was nothing that could be done for them. They had also ignored the illness that had taken the lives of the youngest and oldest members of their group. Part of their reasoning was that they had to eat. Crabs had been plentiful, and the fact that they had grown in size meant more food.

It was obvious to everyone in the MRAP that no one else wanted to talk about the people. They needed to be forgotten, and if they somehow made it to Guntersville, their survival could be celebrated. If not, the burden of their deaths couldn't be carried on the shoulders of the Mud Island family.

To pass the time, small talk turned into a discussion about their history. The individual stories of the newest members of the small army that rode in the MRAP paled in comparison to what the Mud Island family had seen, but everyone took their turn, and there was plenty to tell.

There were six members of the group who had never seen the shelters, and they had a thousand questions. The Chief sat up front in the passenger seat staring out the windows at the snow, but he was listening. In his mind, he ticked off a checklist of the shelters he had seen, and when he thought about them, he wondered what else the government had done. Secret programs that protected national security had always been something Americans had accepted. Maybe they accepted the programs because they couldn't do anything about them, and maybe it was possible that people liked the idea of big secrets that would eventually be revealed. He didn't think they were accepted because people trusted the government. That was a certainty.

He remembered the reaction from the public when stealth fighters and bombers showed up. They were straight out of science fiction magazines, and there was a collective "ah ha moment" throughout the United States as people speculated that stealth fighters were the UFOs people had seen over the years. The Chief thought back to the first shelter he had seen at Mud Island. It was small compared to the rest of them, but Titus Rush had wanted it that way. It felt safer, and up until he had seen the shelter in England, he didn't think big shelters could survive.

When he was done listing the shelters, he felt like there was something he had forgotten. There was a nagging thought that tickled at the back of his mind. It was that feeling he got when he couldn't remember a name, but it was on the tip of his tongue. The thought became clearer but then became fuzzy again. He didn't realize it was obvious to Hampton over in the driver seat until Hampton asked him if he had something he needed to talk about.

"What? No, man. I'm good."

"That's not what I see from over here. Is it the people from the school? You know we couldn't really do anything more for them."

"No, that's not it," said the Chief.

Hampton waited because he knew that sometimes the best question was the first one. The Chief needed to talk about something, but guessing the topic for him wasn't going to be anything more than a game of twenty questions.

The Chief shut his eyes and let out a deep breath. In the back of the

MRAP, the discussion continued, but Hampton shifted his eyes between the road in front of him and the Chief's forehead where furrows came and went. He knew if he waited long enough, something was going to click in the Chief's busy mind, and he would tell him what was bothering him. He saw the forehead become smooth, and for a moment he thought the Chief had gone got sleep. Then he saw the Chief's eyes open wide and the eyebrows went higher.

"Why didn't I see it before?" said the Chief.

Hampton was dying to know what was causing the Chief to react as if he had just gotten an electric shock. But he knew it was coming.

The Chief swiveled in his seat and called into the overcrowded MRAP personnel compartment.

"Jim, squeeze up here where I can talk with you."

Captain Miller climbed over bodies that used up every inch of free space and elicited good-natured complaints about losing weight. He managed to fill the gap between the driver and passenger seats with his back to the crowd. It effectively made it quieter in the cab, so it was easier for them to talk.

"What's on your mind?"

"The shelters," said the Chief. "When you were out on the Navy ships, and they wanted to bring back people who were infected for research, they didn't know about the shelters."

"That's right. Why?"

"Why not? Why didn't the government bring in all of the military, especially when the shelters are all so close to military bases?"

"Where are you going with this, Chief?"

The Chief said, "We know some of the military was aware of the shelters and what they were for, but some military people thought they were something else. You know, research and development facilities or maybe something to do with our deterrent forces. Imagine how many missile silos are still in operation because they were airtight when the infection began. Dotted all over the open plains states there are probably crews of military personnel still waiting for orders."

"Would they have supplies to last this long?" asked Hampton.

"I doubt it," answered Captain Miller. "If I was in Strategic Command, I would've figured worst case scenario to be a year. So, all of those crews would've popped their hatches at least six years ago for supply runs. I still don't see your point."

"You just made it for me," said the Chief.

Hampton laughed, "I'm glad someone did because I'm lost."

The Chief went on, "The military believes in redundant systems the way I believe in having more than one plan. If there's a plan A, there has to be a plan B. If there are missile silos meant to last a year, then there are either support systems for them to extend those years or there are facilities intended to last longer to start with. Some may have been built right into a resupply center. If it was up to me, both of those options would have been in place."

"And that has what to do with us?" asked Hampton.

"Wait a minute," said Captain Miller. "I wasn't high enough in the chain of command to be told everything, but for a while, I felt like the ships were being resupplied from somewhere. The Navy had backup supplies at isolated places like Greenland, and they were able to tap those supplies for the first year, but they never thought they would need enough to last this much longer. They eventually ran out and had to start making stops in places like Boston. That's why we started losing ships."

Hampton asked, "So you're thinking we might be able to find resupply bunkers that were supposed to be there as backups for the other branches of the military? Wouldn't you need some solid evidence of where they might be? We're talking about a needle in a really big haystack."

The Chief got the grin on his face that was reserved for those times when he knew something everyone else didn't know. It was his way of teasing them by dangling it in front of them like it should be obvious to everyone.

"We have the two people at our disposal who have pieces to the puzzle. Our good friend Doctor Bus in Guntersville has a list of all known shelters...or at least the shelters Titus Rush was told about. I don't doubt when they built the shelters, the government built a few of their own and didn't tell Titus. They were already covering billions of dollars in costs. What would be a few million more?"

"Who's the other person?" asked Captain Miller.

"Gentry Campbell," said the Chief. "She's the only person we know who's been able to tap a wealth of data from the computers in the Huntsville shelter, and she's even managed to task a few satellites. Doc Bus is smart, and he was there at the time when the shelters were planned. He told me once that a General had commented about how much easier it would be to build all the shelters with their own internal power sources."

"We've already seen evidence of that in our shelters," said

Hampton. "We have external, internal, and hybrids."

The Chief nodded, "We do, so I expect to find out resupply centers were built the same way. One of the reasons given for external sources was that satellites could detect the heat signatures, and putting them in the same place would give away the exact locations. What if the military went ahead and gave their own resupply bases internal power sources?"

"Would Bus know anything about that?" asked Hampton.

The Chief nodded. "He might. Bus suspected that the military even powered the shelters from sources they could tap into without the power companies knowing. All we have to do is see if Gentry can use any satellites to search for heat blooms near any of the known shelters."

Captain Miller wasn't a pessimist, but he did feel the need to point out the obvious when he had to.

"A heat signature could be from another source, you know."

"I know," said the Chief, "but we can sort them out. I don't expect too many in one place."

"Where are we now?" asked Captain Miller.

Hampton searched the white landscape through the heavy, swirling snowfall for any signs that weren't buried yet.

"We're making good time on this stretch of interstate even with the buried vehicles I keep running into."

On cue, the big MRAP lurched a bit to the right as it pushed a rusted shell of a pickup truck out of the way.

"Like that," said Hampton. "Judging by the last mile marker I saw, we're somewhere close to the exit with I-26, about thirty miles northwest of Charleston."

"Home again," said the Chief. "Too bad we don't have time to stop. At this speed, it'll take a day to reach Georgia."

Hampton nodded, "We have to stick to the interstate highways. If we get off on two-lane roads, we're going to get stuck somewhere. At least we can go around the bigger pileups on the interstates. That means we have to use I-385 to cross into Georgia. We should be able to make radio contact with Gentry from the higher elevation though."

They settled into a comfortable silence while Hampton continued to navigate the vehicles he could see. Some caused large drifts where trucks had been abandoned, but there were long stretches of small cars that caused the MRAP to bounce and buck. It was snowing hard enough to fill in the road behind them, so there was some concern that they would collide with living people who were using the same road. There were no fresh tracks ahead, but something could have used the road the day before, and they wouldn't know.

Around midday, they stopped to let everyone out to stretch their legs and take care of personal business if they needed to. They stretched out their tarp into a makeshift awning on the side of the Cougar, and everyone huddled below it. Colleen and Iris passed out survival meals, and they all ate in silence as the large snowflakes fell around them.

Hampton said they were about a mile from Columbia, South Carolina, so they could expect the lanes to be blocked ahead. They might have to reduce speed and have scouts in front of the MRAP as they weaved their way through the debris left behind in the first days of the apocalypse. No one wanted to give up the warmth inside the vehicle, but it would be worse if it became entangled in the hidden wreckage. When they started out again, they knew it would be a long day, but in the short time they had parked for a break, all of them noticed the Chief was different. They knew he was approaching his goal, and he seemed almost happy.

18

Mutation

Kentucky - 2023

When the towers were added to the Depository, the idea was to add another layer of security to an already extremely secure facility, but the towers were more of a cosmetic feature. The upper floor that connected the towers to each other was the real security measure. The massive rooftop resembled the original upper floor, but it was the same design as the sarcophagus that had been built over the reactor at Chernobyl. It was a shell. The Army Corps of Engineers had done the work, but the architect who drew the plans had done some of the largest football stadiums in the country.

From a distance, the building just appeared to be bigger than it was in previous photographs. In reality, the catwalks that were suspended high above the original structure allowed the Mint Police to place more guards at strategic points. They also allowed the guards to walk from one tower to the next by going around or across to a platform at the center. From high above, they could prevent entry into the original building, and they could travel more quickly to head off threats. It was something that was known only to them, and they didn't talk about it outside work.

In the darkness of the Depository after years of death and decay, the humidity had taken its toll. As gases were released from decomposing tissue within, they mixed with the moisture trapped inside the vast roof, and every flat surface became a feeding ground for the smallest of predators. Mice and rats were drawn to the smell and burrowed inside. Insects of every variety were drawn to the tropical environment, and they found those tiny entry points that only they could see. As the bodies were consumed, the rodents flourished until they became food for the insects. The insects multiplied until they themselves became the prey of the spiders.

At the beginning of the apocalypse, there were over forty-six thousand species of spiders spread around the world, and in any given acre of green grass or trees, there were over fifty thousand of them. The death toll after the infection arrived had only served to multiply that number several times until the spiders had no food supply except for other species of spiders. The largest spiders were the weakest and the first to disappear inside the Depository.

Eventually, there was only one breed, a mutated breed of spiders that grew in colonies of lush moisture the way moss clings to a tree. They bred and fed on each other, but unlike other populations correcting themselves and numbers dwindling, the moss spread until it covered the walls and catwalks between the towers. The space above the Depository had become even more secure than before, and the spiders waited with patience for the next fortune hunters to arrive.

If the teams that had climbed into the towers of the Depository had waited another week or two, Ipolito and Wilkes might have at least lived a little longer. The upper levels cooled as the snow accumulated on the roof, and as the temperature inside dropped to freezing levels, the spiders moved deeper into the building. The creatures moved in mysterious colonies that made the walls and floors appear to be carpeted with a deep green coat of moss.

At first, the environment was acceptable to its new occupants, but as the inside of the building became as frigid as the outside, they moved even deeper. The smallest crease along a wall or gap under a door was all they needed to move from room to room. Stairwells drew the attention of the colonies because of the updrafts of warm air, and they multiplied as they descended. The lush green carpet became so thick on the stairs that large clumps fell over the edges below the rails and dropped quickly to the warmth on the bottom floor.

Millions of the tiny creatures died and were left behind to stain every surface, but the majority kept moving. The green migration of tiny predators found the vault door in the basement to be difficult, but they were persistent. They pressed into the groove around the door and found gaps around the locking mechanism that could be measured in micrometers, and they squeezed through. They found the air and temperature inside to be much more tolerable, and they spread in search of food, unaware and uncaring about what happened to their old environment.

Finding no prey to satisfy their needs, they went deeper, passing by the supplies that would have been valuable to men, searching for living prey. They searched but remained ever ready to feed if the opportunity arose.

******

Bernard and Specs didn't know how close they had come to another discovery. If not for the greenish moss that coated the human remains on the ledge of the vault door, they would have found the room where they had started the fire wasn't just the entrance to the Depository. They would have found a second door inside the dark chamber that strangely enough was a twin of the first one except for one notable difference...there didn't appear to be a lock. They would have assumed the gold was just beyond that door. In reality, the gold was only up one flight of stairs or a short ride in the freight elevator. It was only protected by a conventional bank vault door.

The back entrance was a typical feature of the shelters built long ago by the Titus Rush organization. This one had been incorporated into the back door of the Gold Depository for obvious reasons. First of all, it was incredibly convenient, and secondly, it had been ignored for so long that converting it into a hidden entrance had been easy. All Titus had to do was use some of his influence to have records altered until no one remembered there was a tunnel and a back entrance, and the finishing touches during construction were cosmetic. The casual observer wouldn't have noticed that one wall of the room outside the strange door was fake. Titus would have preferred that the back door connected directly to the shelter, but there had already been so many obstacles during the construction of the Fort Knox shelter that he had decided to accept it.

When he had made that decision years ago, he had no idea that it would play into the chain of events taking place after the apocalypse. The fire inside the Depository sucked in every bit of fuel it could find, and just like any good furnace with an air vent that would supply it from below, the draft through the tunnel caused the fire to burn hotter.

As Brother Bernard and Specs attempted to put some distance between themselves and the shed that hid the tunnel, they could hear a high-pitched whistle as the air was pulled through the gaps around the handcar elevator toward the fire. It energized both of them to move even faster. When their feet found solid footing, they knew they were at least on a road, and they didn't care where it went. For a long time, they could see the orange glow from the fire high against the clouds, but eventually, the snow and distance swallowed them in the silence of their surroundings.

"I can't tell where we are anymore," said Bernard.

"I can't either. We won't know until daylight, and that's if we're lucky enough to find road signs. I know one thing for sure. We're not on the Army base anymore."

"How can you know that?" asked Bernard.

"We followed the old railroad tracks. Remember when we went up a hill to higher ground? The tracks were elevated. That's why the snow was so deep on the sides. Anyway, the tracks went right out through a side entrance to the Army base. I saw the old sentry post."

"Is that what I've been tripping over...old railroad ties? I thought maybe it was frozen zombies."

"No," said Specs, "the frozen zombies are all down there buried in the drifts. They wouldn't have known to get to higher ground."

In the dark with the snow falling on them, Bernard couldn't really see Specs very well, but he had a growing appreciation for the man. Before the infected dead came along, he wasn't someone Bernard would have ever been friends with, and it made him wonder what Specs had done for a living. It was the first time in years that he had been curious about someone on a personal level.

"How'd you get so smart, Specs?"

"College, I guess."

It was an eye-opening moment for Bernard. He had always been condescending to Specs, maybe because Specs always hung around with the tweaker, but it never occurred to him the man had been educated.

"What college?"

"I got an engineering degree from Georgia Tech."

Specs kept walking forward, trudging through snow that was almost to his knees in spots. Bernard stared at his back and had a new respect for him. He wanted to ask how he wound up with their group of misfits following Brother Silas, but he knew the story was the same

226

with everyone. If it wasn't their group, it would be someone else's. People came and went, just as they were going now.

Specs turned around and asked him if he was coming, but he only made it halfway through the sentence. There were dark shadows on the elevated path they had been following. The shadows were moving with purpose against the deep snow, and they were getting closer. Spec's first thought was that they were the infected dead, but they didn't move that fast.

Bernard didn't have to be a college graduate to know Specs was reacting to something behind him, and when he checked for himself what it was, he got colder than he already was. His legs felt like they flash froze right where they were because there was no chance of escape.

The voice that cut through the cold night was a woman's.

"I would say freeze, but I'm not feeling funny at the moment. Who are you, and do you have any idea what's happening over there?"

They couldn't see her gesture, but they knew exactly what she was asking about. The glow from the burning Depository reflected brightly from the low-hanging clouds. From their vantage point on the elevated railroad tracks, they could almost see the building burn.

Four dark figures came up behind the woman, and as they came into view, the uniform patches on their heavy foul weather coats identified them as military. Bernard thought there was something vaguely familiar about the patch that was shaped like home plate in baseball. They were each holding rifles aimed loosely in their direction.

"We didn't have anything to do with that?" Bernard said defensively.

"I didn't say you did," answered the woman. "I asked if you knew what was happening."

One of the soldiers said, "He knows, or he wouldn't be acting like he was caught in the act."

The woman let out a low laugh.

"That much is obvious, so let me rephrase the question. Would you like for me to have you shot, or would you like to tell me everything you know about that fire?"

Specs stepped cautiously back to where Bernard was standing. He held both hands out palms up where they could see him better.

"It doesn't matter to us what we tell you, lady, as long as we don't have to go back there. Could we start with introductions, you know, like the kind that keep you from feeling like you have a reason to shoot us?"

The woman regarded the thin man for a moment, and something seemed to register with her. It was the way he spoke.

"I know you," she said. "Didn't you work for one of the spacecraft start-ups in Huntsville before the apocalypse?"

"I don't believe this," mumbled Bernard.

Specs ignored him and took a step closer to the woman so he could see her better.

"Well, I'll be...you're the lady at the Marshall Space Flight Center."

Gentry took a couple of steps closer. He was almost a foot taller than her, so she had to tilt her head backward to see him better in the low light. The soldiers stepped forward with her, obviously acting as bodyguards.

"Sergeant," she said over her shoulder. "Please break out some spare gear for these men along with something to warm up their stomachs."

The soldiers sat backpacks down and began pulling out supplies. There were lightweight but definitely helpful thermal sweaters that they could put under their coats, and each was given a pair of the warmest gloves they had ever worn. Wool watch caps were the icing on the cake. Bernard's ears actually hurt from the warmth as circulation returned. By the time they were in their new apparel, one of the other soldiers had a small fire burning hotly under a metal container, and a minute later he handed them each a tin of coffee.

"So, Doctor Johnny Burtram, what're you doing out here, and what's that over there?" asked Gentry.

"They call me Specs now. Not much use for titles anymore. How I got here is a very long story, but that over there is the Fort Knox Gold Depository, and it's really burning hot, isn't it?"

The way Specs said it made Gentry sure he was somehow connected to the distant fire, but she knew he would tell her now that he knew who she was. They had met when he first arrived at NASA straight from the school where he earned a doctoral degree. Unfortunately, there was a waiting list a mile long for his specialty, and he had to go to the private companies that had sprung up like weeds around the Space Flight Center.

"Yes, what did you use as a propellant?" asked Gentry.

Specs didn't see where it would matter if he told her the truth, so he shrugged at Bernard and said, "We lit the fire, but the propellant was something like you've never seen before. It was alive."

"Did you say alive?"

Specs made eye contact with Gentry for a moment before he went on. He wanted her to believe him, and she wanted to see the seriousness on his face.

"Spiders so small that you don't realize they're spiders at first. If it wasn't snowing out here and you saw a clump of them on the side of a tree, you'd think they were just moss. They're bright green, and there must be thousands of them in a handful of the stuff. Oh, and we watched them eat a guy. He even got back up after he was dead."

"The infected do that," said Gentry.

"No kidding, but can you imagine an infected grabbing you after it's covered in man-eating mutant spiders?"

"You used them as propellant?"

"We set them on fire, and apparently they burn hot. The place went up like tinder. We didn't know they would even burn, but they would've been on us fast if they hadn't."

Bernard had enjoyed his coffee and was grateful for the warm clothing, but he was still wary about the people who had shown up out of nowhere at night.

"What're you folks doing here?" he asked. He couldn't really hide the suspicious tone of his voice.

"We're not sure yet," said Gentry. "Why does it seem to me like you were leaving here as fast as you could? You're not really equipped for a long camping trip, are you."

One of the soldiers leaned forward and whispered something to Gentry, and she eyed Bernard with a gaze that made him uncomfortable.

The soldier held out one arm so the shoulder patch was more visible, and Bernard remembered where he had seen it before. It was down near Atlanta. He hadn't done any of the shooting, but he had been there when Brother Silas ordered his people to open fire on the squad of soldiers. The bodies had Army uniforms with the same patches on them.

"Remember this?" asked the soldier.

"It wasn't me," said Bernard defensively. "It was Silas. All we were doing was getting supplies from that Army base, and Silas said where there were a few of you, there had to be more."

Bernard expected to be shot as he became aware that the four soldiers had changed the way they held their weapons. They were still aimed his way, but not quite as loosely as before.

"Silas is the leader?" asked Gentry.

Specs said, "They call him Brother Silas. He's a short little tyrant who has that Jim Jones way of making people follow him. He kills people for no reason, but he's particularly hard on deserters. I've been waiting for my chance to get away practically since the first day I got sucked into it."

"I didn't take you for the cult follower type," said Gentry. "What about your friend here?"

Specs regarded Bernard as if he wasn't sure how much he should tell, but he decided everything would become known sooner or later.

"He's not as bad as Silas, but he's the cult follower type. He's one of the twelve Brothers, so we call him Brother Bernard. He's more of a follower who gives orders and then gets behind something for safety."

Bernard wasn't happy with the character assassination, but at least he wasn't being crucified.

Specs went on, "The one you have to watch out for is Brother Sparks. He's not just a follower. He's the kind of follower who likes being number two, and since he's the only man around who can fly their plane, he's indispensable."

"Did you say Sparks? Flies an AC-130?"

"That's him," said Specs.

"I know someone who wants to see Sparks again, and he plans to only meet this Brother Silas of yours once."

Bernard worked up enough nerve to ask, "Are you going to let us go?"

"You got somewhere else to be?" asked Gentry.

"I'm not trying to be smart, lady, but anywhere but here would be nice."

Gentry waited for Bernard to say why they were so desperate to leave, but he didn't add to what he had said. She turned back to Specs, and he nodded in agreement.

"Silas has been doing his best to get inside the Depository, and a lot of his people have died already. Then the snow started coming down in sheets, and he got it in his head that the snow is toxic. Then we set fire to the whole thing, and he's going to be really crazy when he finds out we did it. Silas comes up with some very creative ways to punish people."

Gentry had gotten a half-grin during the summary, and by the time Specs was done the grin had become a smile.

"Brother Silas thinks the snow is what?"

"Toxic," said Specs.

"Why?"

"One of his men caught some of it on his tongue, got sick, and died a few minutes later. I wasn't there but Bernard was."

Specs turned to Bernard for confirmation, but he was quick to tell Gentry he didn't think the snow was toxic. He didn't know what killed the man, but he doubted it was the snow.

"You're right," said Gentry. "We've been testing the snow since it started to fall. We had to make sure it wasn't carrying any radioactivity."

"Is it?" said Specs and Bernard at the same time.

Gentry didn't answer. Instead, she just stared at them both until Specs put his palm against his forehead.

"I'm sorry I asked. I've been around Bernard and Silas for too long. Of course it's not radioactive, or you wouldn't be out here in it."

Bernard was pretty sure he had been insulted, but he only cared about the immediate future and went back to his previous question.

"Are you going to let us go?"

"I thought we answered that," said Gentry. "The short answer is no. When we meet up with the Chief, I'll let him decide. Until then, you should do your best to get on my good side."

"Who's the Chief?" asked Specs.

One of the four soldiers said, "He's the guy bringing payback to Brother Silas. We all want to be there to see it, but we're not getting in between the Chief and the guy who ambushed our friends."

Bernard said, "Where's this Chief now?"

"On his way," said Gentry. "Everyone get ready to move out. We're circling around the base and heading south. Come on, Bernard. You're on point where we can keep an eye on you."

Bernard would have felt better without the soldiers behind him, but he imagined if they were going to kill him, they would've found it to be just as easy to do so while they were stopped on the railroad tracks. He went in the same direction that they had been traveling because it would gradually put them on the far side of the Depository. Then they could turn to the south. He wasn't looking forward to meeting the man they called the Chief, but he knew he had only been a witness to what Silas had done to those soldiers. All he had to do was convince the Chief it was Silas.

Gentry and Specs brought up the rear. Both of them had a thousand questions for each other, but Specs caught on quickly that Gentry had a far more interesting story. Gentry knew she was going to have plenty of projects for Specs inside the shelter, so she told him everything.

"That's how you were able to test the snow," he said. "You have resources most people don't have. Do you also know why it's snowing?"

"We have enough satellites working to be able to see that reactors are popping in Asia, and we've been tracking radioactive clouds, but so far it's localized to the Chinese mainland. The weather is another story. I don't think anyone would have predicted that nuclear winter would be contained in specific areas. We all thought it would be global."

"What's that mean?" asked Specs.

"Well, it's snowing here, but not in China. The radioactivity there appears to be causing a different weather pattern than here, and from what we can tell, as long as it keeps snowing, the radioactivity will stay there."

"And if it stops snowing here?"

Gentry shook her head. "We don't know. So far, you can throw out the book of theories about nuclear winter. It was supposed to be global because of the temperature drop worldwide."

After four hours of following the tracks to the east, they were able to begin their turn to the south. The glow of the fire in the Depository was visible on the horizon to their right, and even though they couldn't see the sun, they knew it was somewhere to their left because the black night had turned a deep gray.

Gentry called the group to a stop and asked the soldiers to help her set up a camp. Breakfast was the plan, and Bernard took the opportunity to do his part.

"I see you heard my suggestion about getting on my good side," said Gentry.

"Loud and clear, Ma'am."

"You can call me Gentry. If you call me Ma'am again, I'll have the Chief do unspeakable things to you."

Bernard knew Gentry was at least partly kidding, but the image he already had of the Chief made him nervous.

By the time the group broke camp, the color of the haze that surrounded them had taken on a yellowish tint, and even though the snow was white, the world felt dirty. It was the cloud from the fire, and it was nothing more than smoke and ash, but it was somehow evil. Bernard said it was the strange spiders, and Gentry wasn't in total disagreement. She had always been a fan of science fiction, and she had been fascinated by the theories surrounding cataclysmic nuclear events. Countless movies had portrayed genetically mutated monsters that preyed on human flesh, and it would be foolish to rule out mutations that had not been predicted. The thought made her grin sardonically.

They were trudging through snow that was knee-deep in places, and they were constantly changing directions when someone would find higher ground.

"What's so funny?" asked Specs.

Gentry didn't realize she had worn her thoughts on her sleeve, and for a moment she wondered how he had known she thinking about the irony that seemed to escape everyone but her.

"I was just thinking about how we've become so used to zombies, but we seem surprised when something else weird happens. Our ecosystem took a big hit when the virus showed up. The food chain was contaminated, groundwater became unsafe to drink, and viruses mutate all the time, so why are we so surprised when insects mutate?"

Specs was surprised at himself for not giving it more thought. He had been appalled by the voracious appetite of the tiny creatures, and he had been scientifically curious about the way they clung together like lumps of deep green moss, but for some reason, he had not taken it one step further.

"You mean, what next?"

"Not just that," said Gentry, "but why didn't we expect this? A year from now, what food item will be off the table because the virus has somehow managed to live inside it? What previously harmless creature will become a predator that eats human flesh?"

"Why'd it have to be spiders?" asked Specs.

"Would you have preferred something else?"

"Let me think about that for a second. Is there anything that makes my scalp itch when I think about it? I had a cat a long time ago that used to freak me out. He would sit in front of me and stare at a spot on the wall behind me above my head. I was always convinced if I looked, I would find a big spider hanging inches away from my hair."

"Were your suspicions ever confirmed?"

"No," he answered, "but that's not really important. It's what I thought would be there that counted."

"I think your cat just knew how to mess with you."

Specs knew Gentry was just doing the same thing as the cat, but he asked with less humor.

"Seriously, why spiders?"

"Why not? There are at least forty-three thousand species of them and only one living species of homo sapiens. They don't all mutate, adapt, or evolve, but all it takes is one."

"You're not making me feel better," said Specs. "As a matter of fact, you're making me wonder about something that should have been obvious to both of us by now. Assuming the virus that caused people to become zombies is what caused the spiders to mutate, wouldn't it be likely that the same mutation is occurring elsewhere?"

Gentry mulled it over for a moment, but she wanted Specs to understand that mutations sometimes depended on more than one cause, and that was why she had said mutate, adapt, and evolve. She remembered something she had read once in college.

"There was a grasshopper that was common in Southeast Asia, and during the Vietnam War, our military sprayed Agent Orange on the forests to kill the foliage. The idea was to reduce hiding places of enemy soldiers. The grasshoppers were exposed to Agent Orange, and a few years after the war, it was discovered that grasshoppers had developed a defense mechanism that allowed them to spray Agent Orange at predators. The mutation didn't spread to places where Agent Orange wasn't sprayed."

"So you're saying whatever it was that caused the mutation of the spiders inside the Depository isn't necessarily available outside?"

"Specifically," said Gentry, "the warm, moist atmosphere inside the building was conducive to the combination of the virus with something in the spider DNA. The lack of light may also have been a factor. They could even have been limited to portions of the building but not everywhere, so we may never know what vectors made them mutate."

Specs said, "I'm going to stay out of warm, dark places where the infected dead have been hanging out."

"That's pretty much what I already do," said Gentry.

Bernard raised a hand from up front, and one of the soldiers moved up to his position to see why he had signaled to stop.

"I can't tell where the railroad tracks are. I think we got off of them somewhere."

The soldier studied the terrain ahead but couldn't see more than twenty or thirty yards before everything was swallowed up in the swirling snow flurries. He pulled out a compass and then checked a map that he unfolded from a pocket. It was covered in some kind of laminate to keep the snow from ruining it. He was so professional that Bernard recognized the differences between the followers of Brother Silas and the well-trained soldiers they had ambushed. He already thought it had been a mistake, but he was beginning to sense just how big that mistake had been.

The uniformed man said, "We should be right here. The railroad tracks go off that way to the east, but we have to keep going south to meet up with the Chief and his people."

Hearing the Chief mentioned again made Bernard prefer not to be on point, but he knew it was useless to even ask if he could follow rather than lead.

"What's he like, this Chief fella?"

"Why? You worried about what he's going to do to you?"

The soldier had a serious expression, but he was enjoying seeing Bernard squirm.

"I wouldn't want him to get the wrong idea," said Bernard. "Not everyone who followed Brother Silas was in favor of the things he did. It's not like he puts things to a vote before he does them."

"Why didn't you stop him?"

"Are you kidding me? If I had even opened my mouth to disagree with him, I'd be dead too. You haven't met this guy. He's a stone-cold killer, and it's my guess he was that way before the zombies came along. Would you try to stop this Chief of yours?"

The soldier laughed, but he did it without smiling.

"Yes, I would, and maybe that's the difference between your Brother Silas and the Chief. The Chief has self-control. He's a killer when he has to be, and he doesn't do it for fun, but maybe he's going to enjoy himself this time. Now get going. We've got a lot of ground to cover."

19

Thaw

Fort Knox, Kentucky - 2023

Brother Silas had been on a rampage for hours, and sunrise hadn't helped. It was one thing to see the Depository in flames at night and another to see the smoldering ruins that still funneled dark plumes of smoke into the morning sky. No one had been able to find Brother Bernard, and he didn't know whether to be mad at him or consider the possibility his absence was because he was off on some mission that might be useful.

One thing that never crossed his mind was that he should be worried for Bernard. If some accident had claimed the man's life, Silas wasn't likely to mourn his passing. He would want to know the details, but only out of curiosity. If Bernard showed up unharmed, Silas was mad enough to kill him before he had a chance to explain where he had been.

Sparks stepped up next to Silas where he stood in the safety of the entrance to his tent, and he was just about to speak when Silas held up a hand. It was something Silas did when he wanted everyone to be silent.

"Is there less snow falling than before?" he asked without taking his eyes off the sky.

Sparks leaned forward and watched for a moment.

"It appears to be, Brother Silas. It's almost light enough for me to takeoff and land the plane. Do you still want me to see if I can spot Brother Bernard from the air?"

"No, forget about him, but it would be a good idea for you to check the surrounding area. We could be surrounded by scavengers and not even know it. I also want you to do a few passes over the Depository and see if there's anything happening we should know about."

"Like what?"

Silas didn't get mad at Sparks too often, but he wasn't in the mood for stupid questions.

"How should I know? Would I be telling you to fly over it if I knew what was happening? If you see someone with a book of matches in their hand, let me know."

It occurred to Sparks that he could really ruin the man's day by taking off and not coming back, but he had hung around and put up with the little man with the Napoleon complex this long, so he felt like he could put up with it long enough to find out what a few billion in gold looked like.

The snow stopped completely only a couple of minutes later, and Brother Silas felt elated as he stepped outside and breathed in the cold air. The sun actually peeked through a break in the clouds and reflected brightly off the blanket of white that covered everything. Brother Silas felt like it was odd, but he knew less about nuclear winter than he was willing to expose by asking questions of his subordinates. If anyone expressed a reasonable idea near him, he would simply steal it for his own.

Silas called to one of the soldiers standing guard and told him to find one of his officers. He wanted someone to examine the damage done to the Depository as soon as possible. It was his hope that the fire had done what his people couldn't, and they would find they could walk right through the front door.

The man disappeared, and Silas strolled at a leisurely pace through the snow toward the Depository. He was aware that there were other people out and about near him, but he was too engrossed in the sight of the charred building in the distance to notice people quietly slinking back inside their tents. Not that he would have cared, but his followers had spread the word throughout the population that Silas was in a foul mood.

"You wanted to see me, Brother Silas?"

The man had trotted up to Silas accompanied by four less-than-enthusiastic people. They had been recruited simply because they couldn't hide fast enough. They had been given handguns, and they clutched them as if they were ready to shoot something at any moment.

"Take your men inside the building and report back to me within the hour," said Silas.

The officer's eyes moved over his leader's shoulder to the building behind him. Its roof had collapsed, and the outside walls were black, but from where they stood, he could still see the door was just as it had been. Everyone already knew what had happened to most of the people who had tried to go inside. Even though he could see the door was still standing, and he had never heard of a fire unlocking a door, the officer knew better than to state the obvious to Brother Silas. The bulldozer may not be available for Silas to set another example, but the officer had no doubt the psychotic little man would find a creative way to dispose of him. He simply acknowledged the order and told the others to follow him.

They were hardly out of earshot when one of the nervous members of the quartet with the officer said in a low voice, "Someone remind me why we still do whatever he tells us."

None of them turned back the way they had come because they knew from experience that Brother Silas would be watching their progress. Getting caught looking back was a sure way to have him suspect that he was the topic of discussion.

One of the others said, "Because there's always someone else who's more afraid of him than they are of you."

The man who had asked the question wasn't ready to let it go just yet.

"But there are more of us than him. The five of us could turn around and shoot him right where he stands, and how many people would be happy to see us do it?"

"He keeps us safe, and he keeps our families fed," said one of the other men. "I'm not happy about going in there, but if it keeps me and my family alive, then I have to do it."

In front of the group, the officer could hear every word, and a big part of him wanted to do exactly what the disgruntled man suggested. In fact, he was leaning more in that direction when a single gunshot rang out behind him. It was deafeningly close, and the suddenness of the blast made him reel around and bring his own weapon up in the general direction of the shooter.

The body of the man who had been advocating for the removal of Brother Silas was crumpled over in a heap several feet from the road. The point-blank shot to his head had caused him to flip sideways into the deep snow. A red stain spread across the whiteness that surrounded him, almost hiding the faint greenish tint on the surface.

The officer knew why the shooter had done it. All it would take was for one of them to tell Brother Silas about the conspiracy, and the others would be killed for not stopping him. In a sick way, the officer knew the shooter had done what he was supposed to do, and all he could do was pretend he hadn't heard the conversation. He could see Brother Silas standing where they had left him outside the fence, and he wasn't too far away to miss the simple gesture from their insane leader. Silas simply lifted his chin as if he was giving silent approval for what the shooter had done. Something told the officer that Silas knew exactly what had happened.

"Get his gun."

He gave the order because it was tacit approval of the execution, and he directed it at the shooter as if it was a prize for what he had done. He also had forgotten why they had to stay on the road.

The eager recipient of a second weapon rushed into the snow toward the spot where the gun had landed, and he actually retrieved it before his foot discovered a landmine. The explosion threw his shattered body high into the air, and it landed almost exactly where he had been standing when he had shot the other man. Ironically, the gun landed next to him.

Silas watched with interest, but he felt like he had seen enough evidence that stupidity brought about its own rewards that were proportional to the level of stupidity. Whatever the first man had done to get himself shot in the head, it must have been stupid, but it didn't compare with going into the minefield. His chin rose a little higher, and when he saw the officer step forward and put a bullet into the head of the mangled body, he made a mental note to remind the officer that it was a wasted bullet.

Addressing the remaining two members of his squad, the officer asked if either of them had anything they wanted to say. Both shook their heads vigorously. He tucked one of the extra guns into his waistband and handed the other to one of the men.

"Let's just take a look at this place before we decide what we want to do."

Silas stayed where he was until the trio of men approached the blackened entrance to the Depository, and he could hardly contain his elation when he saw them walk inside. He was too far away to tell if the door opened or fell inward, but he didn't care. He bolted away from the gate in search of more people he could send to the aid of the three men who had made his day brighter. He didn't know if it was the brisk feeling of a clear, cold day or the fact that they had finally breached the impenetrable door, but he felt like things were finally going his way.

Inside the door that had stood as a symbolic protector of the country's wealth, the three men found it difficult to breathe. The fire had destroyed the frame around the door, and they didn't have to open it. They only needed to push aside the debris. The black cloud that hung around the door was an even greater barrier than the locks had been. Smoking ash still floated in the air, and the stench was overwhelming.

Fires inside buildings were by their very nature nauseating. When one considers the variety of plastics, carpeting, and other accessories that would either burn or melt, the combination of smells would eat into the moist passages of the nose and throat. The three men did their best to cover their faces, but they could do nothing about the acid that welled up from their stomachs and the chemicals that clung to the moisture in their eyes. Within seconds they were gasping for air and blind. Tear gas and pepper spray were not nearly as effective as the toxic mist inside the first room beyond the door.

It was by sheer luck that one of the men found his way back to the entrance and fell through the opening. The officer and the last of his men heard his shouts to them and turned in the direction of his voice. Both fell several times, often over each other, but they eventually landed on the concrete steps at the front door. Like everyone else, they thought the snow was toxic, but at the moment, it was cold and soothing to their eyes. The trio crawled down the steps and wallowed in the frigid relief they felt, and they eagerly stuffed handfuls into their mouths.

For less than a minute they sat back on their knees and savored the air and the freshness compared to the inside of the building. A minute was all the time needed to revive the millions of tiny creatures that had only survived the furnace because they drifted free in the updraft and were deposited outside. They had welcomed the coolness of the snow just as the men had, but they found the living tissue even more hospitable. They moved with greed to consume the larger creatures that only a minute before had consumed them.

When the new pain arrived, the men turned to each other, but there was no relief to be found in the faces around them. All they saw was an expression of the horror each of them felt as they were eaten from the inside out. They sat still at first, and then they tried to stand. It was only a small mercy that they had washed their eyes with the snow because the spiders entered their bodies as close to their brains as they could. The blindness enveloped them and brought darkness, and the pain only lasted a few seconds as the spiders flooded the soft gray matter inside their skulls. Their bodies fell over against each other and lay without moving as a silent predator consumed them.

Brother Silas arrived with a small army of reluctant volunteers several minutes after the men had fallen out of the entrance. From where they gathered at the fence surrounding the Depository, they could only see what appeared to be clothing, and it was as if someone had drawn a line across the place where the gate had once closed. No one ventured across that line even after he ordered them forward. He grabbed the man nearest to him with the intention of forcing him to go further, but like all tyrants, he imagined his own strength to be much greater than it actually was. The man not only resisted, he fought back until Brother Silas found himself sprawling on the ground.

All around him there was chaos as his followers scrambled away to safety. No one wanted to be the last one there to face his wrath, and someone stepped on his hand. Silas screamed for his guards and ordered them to shoot anyone who was running, but his guards were running as fast as the rest of the mob.

When the last of the people were gone and the silence was complete, Brother Silas picked himself up from the paved road at the entrance of the Depository perimeter and composed himself. He was surprised when he turned around and found that one man had the nerve to stay. Brother Sparks leaned against the side of a rusty vehicle as if he was totally relaxed, and he regarded Brother Silas in the same detached way someone gave attention to a movie actor with one line.

If Brother Sparks had ever been sure of anything, it was nothing compared to what he felt at the moment. His stock had just gone up in value again. He was likely to be the only person in the camp who Brother Silas wouldn't send into the evil building, and that gave him the chance to speak his mind.

"I'm sure you realize by now that the zombie apocalypse didn't make it easier to break into Fort Knox. If anything, it seems to have gotten harder."

Having just regained his composure, Silas was determined not to lose it again, but he was smart enough to realize Sparks had just suggested that he should give up.

"Stating the obvious has seldom been a solution. Do you have anything constructive to add?"

Brother Silas managed to deliver the question without letting his voice shake.

"It was my idea to raid the Army base in Atlanta. I said it would go a long way for us to be able to take over this base, but I don't recall ever telling you it would help us get to the gold."

His brazen tone almost pushed Silas over the edge, but he somehow held on.

"Go on," he prodded.

Sparks stood straighter and said, "You need to call the Brothers together and give them something to take back to the people. We need to get their support behind you again, or you won't have anyone to give orders to."

"Like what?"

Sparks put his hands in his pockets and sauntered closer to Brother Silas. He had the relaxed but confident air of a man holding a royal flush with no more cards to be dealt.

"There's one thing these people want more than gold. They want a safe place to live where they don't have to sleep with one eye open. Take a good look around you. The snow stopped, and the sky is clear. If this all melts, we're going to have our old problems back again. I don't know if freezing zombies will kill them, but if they thaw out, you won't be able to beat them to death with gold bricks. I think we need to talk about capturing one of those shelters."

Sparks made sense, but Silas wasn't ready to give up.

He said through gritted teeth, "I'm not leaving my gold."

Sparks made a sound that was close to the way teachers had clicked their tongues at Marvin Corn when he was a child in school. The last time he heard a teacher make that sound, the teacher had become seriously ill after he had slipped half a bottle of eye drops into her coffee. He was ready to boil before Sparks finished his suggestion.

"After we take the shelter, we can bring the prisoners back here and send them inside for the gold."

Neither of them knew exactly what they were dealing with or what was killing people inside the Depository, so the answer seemed so simple. They needed more people, and they had to be expendable.

Brother Silas had never been someone who handed out praise. He was more likely to take an idea for his own and then pat himself on the back.

"Gather the Brothers so we can discuss this further."

An hour later there were only six Brothers around the table besides Sparks. Brother Silas was furious when he was told there had been deserters. He especially wanted Bernard's head on a spike outside his tent because he had been his first disciple. He decided an edict was in order, and he declared it clearly to the remaining seven Brothers. They would capture a shelter, enslave the occupants, and use them as laborers to bring out the gold. All deserters from this day forward would be found, and they would be executed by dropping them into a pit with the infected.

"I'm sure everyone has noticed the snow is melting fast, but there were going to be infected people even if the snow had continued. It was only a matter of time before we would have had a death in the camp, and the dead would cause more deaths."

"Brother Silas, please tell us about these shelters. Where are they, and how can we capture one?"

It was one of the oldest Brothers in the group who had spoken. Silas had no doubt that the man's advanced years made him think he was the subject of the previous statement. He was frail and contributed little to the common good, but as long as people listened to his sage advice, Silas would keep him around. He would keep him around until he needed biters in that pit where he planned to dump deserters.

"Brother Sparks has been to one of the shelters, and he thinks we can find a way to breach their security."

He motioned for Sparks to take the floor. Sparks stood up, even though he didn't remember ever saying anything about how they would do it. When he surveyed the handful of Brothers seated in the conference section of the tent, he couldn't help but wonder what each of them contributed to the general good of their society. As a matter of fact, all any of them did was support Brother Silas and turn in the names of people who spoke out against him. He tried to remember if any of them had any actual skills, and all he could come up with was one. One of them had been a dentist, but he was so dependent on Silas that he wouldn't be able to survive on his own. Sparks doubted if he could even start a fire.

Another thing that stood out was the lack of equality with women.

The faces in front of him were all bearded, and he thought about the short time he had spent with the survivors led by the Chief. Sparks wondered if there was any way that a single man in the room would be left alive if they had to defend themselves from Kathy. Their self-important faces were pointed at him now, and they were waiting for him to tell them how they were going to capture a fortress. For at least the third time in the same day, he considered getting into his plane and flying as far from them as he could get, but there was still a side of him that even he couldn't explain. Something made him enjoy being the man behind the man.

Sparks cleared his throat the same way Brother Silas did before he spoke. Silas did it as a warning that he was about to speak, and anyone who spoke while he was talking ran the risk of having their tongue removed. Sparks did it for fun.

"The snow is melting. That means we'll soon know whether or not the infected will become mobile again. There are probably thousands of them between here and the nearest shelter, so we should move quickly. I propose that we should decide who our best fighters are. I'll fly them into the area closest to a shelter, and we'll attack on foot."

"How many men?" asked one of the Brothers.

"With the weapons we have, we should be able to carry seventy-five."

"And you say you can breach the defenses of the shelter? You're sure of it?" asked Silas.

Sparks wasn't sure of anything, but he knew when he decimated the town above the shelter at Green Cavern that the people had used escape tunnels that went into the mountain. They should be able to find at least one of them.

"So be it," said Silas.

The meeting was adjourned with the final order to the Brothers to each find twelve men with combat experience and to be sure they were armed, but before the leaders of the cult could even make their exit, the chaos outside caused Silas to push the others aside so he could get to the front of the line. His expectation was that he would rush into view, and there would be immediate silence out of fear. In the past, all he had to do was stand up. If he put his hands on his hips, people would shrink to the ground. If his eyes were fixed on a specific person, others around the target of his ire would open a buffer zone between themselves and the future victim.

This time was different. He stepped into the opening outside his tent, and someone collided with him, sending him spinning to the ground for the second time in a single day. The scream that escaped from his own lips was drowned out by the screaming from the crowd of people rushing past his tent. This time he didn't try to compose himself. As he rolled onto his back, his hand found the grip of his own semiautomatic pistol and pulled it free. He aimed and squeezed the trigger indiscriminately. Men and women fell away from him, and over the blasts of the gun, the screaming increased.

Sparks and the Brothers saw the faces in the crowd that belonged to the infected dead. They were mixed in with the others too well for them to shoot without hitting their own people, so Sparks waded into the melee and worked his way toward one. He had a knife held out in front of him and pushed it easily into the soft spot below the jaw. He pulled it free quickly and moved to the next one.

Some of the men who had panicked with the general population saw that Sparks was leading the attack on the infected while Brother Silas was shooting their families. The crowd spontaneously divided into three groups. Most continued to panic and make their escape, but the other two groups galvanized into attackers.

Sparks was aware that men and women were on both sides of him with knives drawn, and they soon outnumbered the infected. Where the dead had come from in such numbers was a mystery he could solve later, but the wide path of melted snow behind them was evidence that the infected could survive being frozen.

The other group of attackers went after Silas. The slide on his gun remained open after the last shell casing was ejected, but he continued to aim and pull the trigger until the gun was yanked from his hand by someone. The mob that had been frightened was now angry, and they directed their anger at their leader. For a moment, he thought they were helping him to his feet as he was lifted upward, but when his feet didn't touch the ground, he felt weightless as hands held him higher than the crowd. Sparks watched indifferently as Silas was body-surfed in the direction of the infected dead.

It was Brother Silas' good fortune that the infected were all eliminated before he was carried that far, but the screaming and shouts of alarm had changed to laughter and threats. Some were yelling to hang him, and some were yelling to cut off his head. None were yelling to put him down except Silas.

At the edge of the crowd where Silas had shot several people, family members were doing their best for the wounded, but some were beyond saving. It fell on them to complete the final mercy of eliminating loved ones, but they had to be restrained once the act was done. One by one they joined the crowd that was chanting for the execution of Brother Silas, and when they couldn't reach him, they were finding the Brothers who had stayed with Silas to the end. Sparks was the exception because he had fought the infected dead.

More Brothers felt hands pushing them upward into the air. Someone in the crowd pushed a knife upward instead of an empty hand. The knife went through the lower back and kidney of the unfortunate Brother who was being body-surfed to the front of the crowd where Silas still shouted orders. That single act of revenge met with the approval of the enraged crowd, and amid the cheers, there were high-pitched screams from the Brothers who met with the same fate. Knives came upward at every angle, most just inflicting painful cuts, but the Brothers became silent as their bodies went limp. They were finally dropped unceremoniously once they stopped squirming.

Sparks found himself facing the crowd as if they had collectively decided he was the new leader. Silas was held high in front of him as some gestured with knives toward the helpless little man's back and some still chanted to hang him. Sparks knew that the crowd was still in the mood for revenge, and all it would take was for one of them to point a knife at him, so he took his opportunity and held up his own knife. The crowd cheered in appreciation, although he wasn't entirely sure what it was they were cheering about. He didn't know if he was doing the right thing, but he knew that having Silas killed on the spot would remove a buffer between himself and the angry people.

"Take him to his tent and tie him up," yelled Sparks. "We'll decide what his punishment should be."

What Sparks didn't say was who else would be making that decision. Half of the Brothers deserted during the previous night, and the other half were all executed by the mob, and Sparks had always been content with being number two in the chain of command. He decided he needed a distraction of his own because flying to a remote part of the country was becoming a more attractive idea than before. A wild goose chase might be helpful.

"After you tie him up, someone go and find Brother Bernard."

For effect, Sparks pointed at a man holding a bloody knife.

"Take ten people with you, and if he resists, bring back his head."

It was a gamble, but it paid off. The man roared his approval and singled out ten equally frenzied people around him. They charged away in the direction of the main camp as if they knew exactly where to find Brother Bernard.

******

Almost ten miles south of Fort Knox, Bernard was still walking ahead of the lady from NASA and her four soldiers. Specs had caught up with Bernard and made an attempt to explain why it was a good thing that they were discovered by Gentry Campbell, but Bernard was trying to picture a world where it was a good thing to face the man they called the Chief. From what the soldiers had told him throughout the morning, the Chief was big enough and mad enough to rip out his arms before using them to beat him to death.

The snow was melting rapidly, and Bernard also wasn't sure if he had preferred lifting his feet and blindly putting them down or seeing what he was stepping on. Far too often he had changed directions at the last second when a frozen arm or leg appeared in his path. A few times they were moving. If the blue sky was any indication of what the weather would be like, then they could expect the snow to keep melting. The air was especially crisp, and the sky was a deep blue. If not for the prospect of meeting the Chief, Bernard would actually consider it to be a beautiful day.

An arm protruded from a snowdrift, and the index finger appeared to point directly at Bernard. He watched it nervously as he walked by and took his eyes off the path. He tripped over a bent metal pole and did an acrobatic flip over a railing. He fell hard onto a stretch of pavement where the snow had melted to reveal a wide, black highway. As the others came over the metal guardrail, Specs offered him a hand, but he brushed it aside and got up on his own. The road stretched out for miles ahead of them, and they could tell they were going to make better time now that they were on a main road.

Gentry called ahead for Bernard to take a break. The soldiers gathered around a piece of equipment that needed to be assembled, and they worked with Gentry until it stood on a tripod of legs and was connected to a solar power supply. Once it was powered up, she pulled a set of headphones over her ears and spoke into a microphone.

"This is GC the Science Lady calling the CPO, come in."

20

Silo

Tennessee - 2023

For every mile the MRAP rolled, the tension inside climbed higher. Sixteen people, most with formidable combat skills, fell silent and fed off the Chief's desire to meet his enemy face to face. They all wanted the Chief to have first rights to the unknown leader of the renegade group, but they knew the man wasn't alone. The information they had gotten months ago from the soldiers who had survived the attack near Atlanta was that he had an army. They had escaped with their lives, so they didn't have more information to offer, but what their attackers lacked in skill or training, they more than made up for in numbers. Their best guess was they were attacked by over a hundred people. The Mud Island family was outnumbered six to one, but they knew they could send the Chief and Kathy after half of them to even the odds a bit.

From time to time, one of the passengers would get restless and need to see outside. That meant stretching over the others and pressing their eyes against one of the small windows. They would squint at the brightness and blink furiously as they stumbled over people getting back to their seats. The sun reflecting off the snow would blind anyone who spent more than a few seconds at a window, but everyone wanted to know if things had changed.

The snow coming to a sudden stop had been a surprise, but even more surprising was the fact that there was no sign it would start again. When it had stopped before, the sky had remained gray and sullen. This time it was a crisp blue, and the sun was a welcome sight even if it made everyone dig through their gear to find enough sunglasses to go around. The rising temperature caused everything to shine where the snow melted, and the landscape was dotted with patches of ice and rivulets.

Captain Miller was taking another turn behind the wheel, but no one could pry the Chief from the passenger seat. It was as if he had to see his target in the distance while they were still hundreds of miles from their goal. Cassandra was the same way with her perch in the gun turret. She enjoyed the view even though it was considerably cooler bundled up behind the machine gun. When asked if she needed a break, she pointed out that the cold air eased the itching sensation she still felt where the crab pincers had torn open her skin. No one could argue with that, and they were happy to accommodate her.

The radio squawked to life, and they heard the familiar voice and callsign of Gentry Campbell.

"This is GC the Science Lady calling the CPO, come in."

Gentry knew that Joshua Barnes had been a Chief Petty Officer, and calling him the Chief on an open radio channel was too obvious.

The Chief grabbed a mic and held it to his mouth.

"CPO here. Good to hear your voice, Science Lady. Got anything new for me?"

"Expect no interference in your path. The target is stationary at this time. USGBD appears to be mostly destroyed, but I'm detecting an unidentified heat bloom near your twenty."

Of the four pieces of information provided in the brief message, the third and fourth caused the Chief and Captain Miller to sit up straighter in their seats.

"Did you say the USGBD was destroyed?" asked the Chief.

"That's affirmative."

The Chief had to take a moment to imagine what Gentry meant. He couldn't picture the facility as completely destroyed, and if Bus was correct that there could be a shelter under the main building somewhere, it would most likely be intact even if the building was nothing more than a pile of rubble.

He keyed the mic and asked, "Any idea what happened?"

"Too much to explain right now. Just call it a hot fire," replied Gentry.

"Okay, tell me about that heat bloom."

"It's more like someone turned on the power for a bit and then turned it back off. It was on long enough for me to get the GPS location. Sending it to you via email."

Both the Chief and Captain Miller frowned.

The Chief faced Captain Miller and said, "Any idea what she means by email?"

Kathy had been sitting in the narrow space between the cab of the MRAP and the passenger compartment. It was cramped, but she was able to see past the two men well enough for her to enjoy the view. It was far more interesting than watching the rest of the group catch up on their sleep.

She leaned forward and said, "Gentry and I talked about open transmissions once, and she said email was the hardest to intercept now because no one had a server that worked. Then she told me that it was only a matter of time before someone figured out how to get the internet up and running again, but in the meantime, our email would have to be coded over open radio. Maybe she's telling you she's going to give you the GPS coordinates in code. If she gave you the coordinates without coding them, they would give away our location."

"We just have to figure out her code," said Captain Miller.

"She'll give us a key," said Kathy

The Chief dug around in a backpack squeezed between his feet and came up with a pen and paper, then he spoke into the mic again.

"Ready for email, Science Lady."

"Sending now, and don't let Jasper write it down."

Gentry came back with a long stream of numbers, and the Chief wrote quickly because she also said she wouldn't repeat them. There were twelve numbers with no spaces, and when she finished, she signed off.

"Who's Jasper?" asked Captain Miller.

Kathy said, "That would be your key. After the Chief breaks the numbers into coordinates, we should be able to see how Jasper fits into the picture."

The Chief broke the numbers into two sets of six and then put a decimal point after the first two numbers in each set. He added an N for the north next to the first set and a W for the west next to the second set. Next, he spread out a map and folded it down to the section that showed the border of Georgia and Tennessee. GPS coordinates were next to major cities and landmarks. Being a former

Navy Chief, he wasn't surprised to see the numbers were way off from anything near them. He had to laugh when he understood what Gentry had given them.

"Those coordinates are familiar," said Captain Miller.

The Chief nodded, "They should look familiar to you. They're not that far from where the Navy was regrouping after the beginning of the infection. Maybe they were a little further south of there, but these coordinates as I've written them are somewhere in the North Atlantic."

Kathy said, "I'll bet if you reverse them, they would be right about here."

She reached across the Chief and put her finger on the map.

Jasper, Tennessee was too small for it to have its own set of coordinates written on the map, but it was easy to see the coordinates Gentry had given them were between Jasper and Chattanooga.

The Chief said, "Gentry couldn't have made it too hard to figure out because timing is important. We aren't far from there, and she didn't want us to pass it while we tried to break the code."

"How're we going to find whatever it was she detected at those coordinates?" asked Kathy. "I don't expect to see a road sign pointing to it or a big red X painted on top of it."

"She must figure we'll know," said the Chief. "She made it easy for us to figure out for a good reason."

The Chief pointed at something in the distance, and they saw an exit sign. They could go west to Jasper or east to Chattanooga. Since Jasper was close enough to see to their left, Captain Miller took the exit in the direction of Chattanooga.

Everyone in the back of the MRAP could feel the change in speed and turn to the right, and there was some good-natured complaining as people climbed over each other to see out through the small windows.

"We stopping?" yelled Sim. "I could use a restroom."

There was a chorus of shouts in agreement, and Captain Miller nodded at the Chief. He brought the heavy vehicle to a stop on a spot where the snow had melted enough for them to see the asphalt pavement. Cassandra shouted down from the gun turret that everything was clear, so Tom pushed open the rear door. The cold air rushed into the passenger compartment, and everyone breathed deeply as they climbed down onto the road. They spread out, stretching their backs in long arches and lacing fingers behind their heads to pull on stiff joints.

They all had various comments to make about the scenery, but it was the comment from Hampton that drew the Chief's attention.

"I grew up on a farm, and I don't think I've ever seen a grain silo that big."

The Chief walked over to where Hampton was standing, and he had to agree. The silo was a bright silver against the whiteness that covered the ground in every direction, and the Chief wondered out loud, "Why wouldn't someone just build more than one silo. That thing is huge."

"That's what I was thinking," said Hampton. "Farmers wouldn't need one that big in the first place, but if they had that much grain to store, they wouldn't risk losing all of it to a fire or contamination by putting it in one place. Two or three silos would be better."

Captain Miller and Kathy walked up beside the Chief.

"You think that's what Gentry detected?" asked Kathy.

"I would be willing to bet my next paycheck on it," said Captain Miller.

It was just loud enough for the others to hear, and most of them moved closer to see what had gotten their leader's attention.

"We're getting paid?" asked Colleen. "Does that include back pay?"

Her questions were like fuel on a fire, and there was a flurry of similar questions until the Chief said, "That's how far, about a mile from here? Everyone make sure to keep your socks dry. We have a short walk to take through the snow."

"Why can't we drive to it?" asked Caleb. He seemed so young standing in the group of adults, and everyone called him "the kid" but he felt free to speak his mind.

Iris put a hand on his shoulder as she spoke so it wouldn't make him feel dumb for asking the question.

"We don't know if it started snowing here at the same time as the coast, but since we're further inland, it may have snowed longer. We don't know what's buried under that snow."

He may have been young, but his next question showed he thought things through before he did anything risky.

"Right, so how is it safer to walk through that snow than it is to drive through it?"

Hampton said, "It's not safer, but it's an even longer walk to Kentucky if the MRAP gets stuck on something out there."

The landscape was flat from the highway to the silo, but that didn't mean it was flat under the snow. There could be steep drop-offs or even fences. The only way to find out for sure was to try to cross it.

Cassandra had climbed out of the turret and was sitting on top of the Cougar. She had also stretched some, but she didn't want to pull open any of the scars that itched every time she moved. From her high vantage point, she could see the crooked line that snaked from the east toward the silo. It began only about a hundred yards further down the road where they had stopped.

"Yo, Chief," she yelled.

When he looked up at her, she pointed.

"Is that maybe a road? I mean, if there's a reason why we're going over there, someone else had to have a way to get there before."

"You're not going," he answered, "but you have a point."

Everyone piled inside for the short ride to the spot where the snow had melted enough to see Cassandra had been right. The pavement didn't drop much, and if they were lucky, there weren't many old vehicles on the road from before the snow.

For a second time, everyone gathered outside the MRAP, and the Chief took the lead. He waved back at Cassandra, and she knew he meant it as a gesture, but he also wished she was on point. It was something she excelled at in the military.

The snow was only shin-deep in most places, but it didn't take long before they could see there was a rise in their path, and that meant one of two things. Either the ground rose higher, or a vehicle had been on the road. On a normal day, a derelict car or truck was something they would skirt carefully around, but a buried vehicle meant the possibility of getting snagged and cut on rusty metal. An infection would be bad timing since they had used most of their antibiotics on Cassandra.

The Chief pushed his machete into the hill of snow and felt the tip hit something solid. Judging by the slope on one side, he guessed that snow had been blown against it from his right, so he continued around the left side, poking holes as he went. On the fourth poke, the blade lodged into something and felt like it moved from side to side as he pulled it free. The blade came back with old blood and tissue hanging from it.

They had all expected to find the infected buried under the snow, but they had also expected them to be frozen. The Chief pushed his blade in for a second time, and the motion of the blade caused a cascade of snow to fall away from an SUV. At least a half dozen of the infected were buried along the passenger side of the car, and they were all coming to their feet toward the Chief.

Surprises were something the Chief handled well from his first day in SEAL training to this day on the road. Even when he had been faced with the crash landing of the executive helicopter outside the baseball park in Charleston, he had the presence of mind to hit the roof of a bus to make the helicopter slide instead of making an impact crater. This time was no different. He almost knew by instinct not to back away from the infected because there was no way to know what was behind him.

He lunged forward with his blade, pushing it further into the first of the dead, and he used his great strength to twist the creature around and give it a hard shove. The Chief hung on tightly to the hilt of his machete, and he only had a moment to realize that the infected dead he had thrown to the other side of the road had disappeared. As he would learn after disposing of the other dead, the left side of the hill dropped down a slope. It was a testament to how long and how hard it must have snowed because the terrain appeared to be so flat.

The rest of the group was strung out in a straight line behind him when the Chief reached the SUV. As soon as he hit metal, they paused and held their positions. Their instinct was to help him, but they had been surviving together long enough to know he would yell for help if he needed it. The nearest members of the group were Kathy, Hampton, and Tom, and they knew better than to get in his way. Kathy held up one hand to keep anyone behind her from running forward. The newest members, Darren, Brett, Grady, Caleb, Charlie, and Sue watched with fascination as the Chief attacked the infected with brutal force. One by one the infected were killed and thrown over the left side of the road where they disappeared into the snow.

When the road was clear, the Chief moved forward as if nothing had happened, but now his focus had shifted to places where the snow formed small hills. Not only were they likely to be buried vehicles, but they might harbor more infected dead.

Sim was toward the back of their long line walking on the road, and he had a nagging feeling that he was forgetting something. He watched the Chief cut with precision through the infected, and he had expected them to be there because he had seen it during the winter months in Ohio, but it felt like there should be something else. There should be more, but he couldn't put his finger on it.

Iris and Captain Miller moved forward on a signal from Kathy, and after she gave them some instructions, they nodded and went to the places where the infected had been deposited by the Chief. Using their machete tips, they cut a curving line along the road to mark the boundary of the pavement. One step over that line meant following the infected dead into a cold place deep enough to hide a body forever. Still, Sim felt like he was missing something.

The Chief reached the second place there appeared to be a buried vehicle, but he saw that Iris and Captain Miller had placed their line along the side of the road far enough away for him to go around this one. Iris caught his attention and pointed at a place close to the steep side. It was another hill of snow hiding another vehicle, and the gap between it and the next hill on the right side was narrow.

Even though the sun was high and they were the only people around for miles, they had kept to their rule of not talking when they weren't certain of what danger might be hiding nearby. Beyond the occasional snow hills, the fields appeared to be flat, and they all had a clear line of sight. Far behind them, they could see the MRAP parked on the main highway, and ahead the silver silo seemed even bigger than they had expected. The Chief made eye contact with Sim, and something on the man's face told him Sim was worried. This time the Chief held up a hand, and he signaled for everyone to come closer into a group.

His voice sounded loud in the stillness of the snowfield.

"What's bugging you, Sim?"

"I don't know. I think it's the same feeling I got more than once in Columbus. The snow always seemed to be hiding something, but once it showed up, I always felt like I should have seen it coming."

Sim scanned the rest of the road ahead of them, and it seemed to him that the feeling got stronger as they got closer to the silo. Under its shiny, almost new surface, there was something dark that was waiting for fresh victims to arrive. The white snow might as well have been painted black.

"I know what it is," said Sim. "The silo reminds me of the hotel in Columbus. It had so much stuff inside it that I needed, but it wanted to keep it for itself. For some reason, it also makes me think of the rats. Do rats eat grain?"

"Count on it," said Hampton, "but the rat population explosion self-corrected years ago. Besides, there's a strong chance there never was any grain in that silo."

The Chief said, "I'll take good intel over personal experience, but I can't count the number of times I've trusted my gut about something. Everyone sound off if you feel like the slightest detail doesn't feel right."

He was surprised when almost half of the group raised their hands. All of the new people waited with their hands in the air.

"Have I missed something?" asked the Chief.

Darren Blanchet said in his Louisiana accent, "If you look closely at the snow, it's kind of dirty, so I wouldn't be eatin' any of it."

Brett, Grady, Caleb, Charlie, and Sue all spoke at once confirming what Darren had said. This time it was the Chief who raised his hand, and they all went silent. The Chief scooped up a handful of the snow and studied it closely. He held it out for Kathy to see, and she did the same.

"It has pepper mixed in it," she said.

Sue said, "That's not pepper I would season my food with."

Kathy pinched off some of the snow and rolled the black specks around between her fingertips. The understanding moved across her face like a shadow. She had seen enough roach droppings in her lifetime to recognize them. She had chased people through roach-infested houses when she was a police officer, and the idea that people slept in beds covered in the little black grains had also made her shudder with revulsion. She wiped her hand across her pants in disgust.

Sim asked, "Haven't those things been around since before dinosaurs?"

"So I hear," said the Chief. "I don't guess I'm too surprised that they would take advantage of this much death and decay, but where are they?"

As if to answer his question, everyone faced the silo. Their eyes traveled from the base to its cone-shaped top.

No one bothered to speak or protest because they knew it was a foregone conclusion that they would still go inside the silo. They navigated through the remaining cars that were buried between them and their goal. The only ones that gave them any difficulty were the two that had a narrow gap between them. Since there were likely to be infected dead under the snow, they decided to leave them undisturbed. One by one, they slipped through the gap while the others stood ready to react if they were detected.

Kathy said to the Chief as they got the last one through, "This snow might have melted a bit by the time we come back this way. I hate leaving them to thaw out."

"Yeah, but we'll be able to see them better," he replied.

The door on the silo was easy enough to find, but the locking mechanism seemed to be missing. They took turns inspecting it, and they even sent scouts around the silo to the left and the right in search of another entrance. Brett suggested explosives, but once again Hampton reminded them that grain silos can be ignited easily just because of the dust in the air.

They spent almost a half hour searching for the lock when Tom pounded the back of his fist on the door. He discovered that it was like the door to a gas tank on a car. A simple push makes it pop open. With an audible click, the door went inward at first. Then a gap appeared along the right side as it traveled back toward him. He slipped both hands into the gap, got a good grip, and pulled the door open.

It was totally dark inside, and the light outside didn't reveal much. Captain Miller was the first to produce a flashlight, and he aimed the beam into the blackness. They saw a ladder on one side that just went straight up, a desk with a few office supplies on it, and an older model computer. Other than that, the silo was bare. Captain Miller played the light around on the floor and saw nothing but concrete. He tried the walls, and they were surprised to see a light switch at the end of a wire that snaked up from the floor. Old habits die hard, so he flipped the switch upward.

They didn't really expect the lights to turn on, but that was what they got. They also thought they were walking into a normal silo, so they were surprised that the ceiling above them was so low. There were several light fixtures around the curving walls that lit every square inch. The natural place to start was the computer, but there was no reaction when Tom pressed the power button.

"What is this place?" he asked.

"It feels odd," said Iris.

Colleen said, "Define odd."

"An empty silo in the middle of nowhere with working lights? I would call it unusual given the circumstances, but I guess it reminds me of the first time I went inside Ambassadors Island."

Captain Miller had walked over to the ladder and played the light from his flashlight around the top of it. The ceiling lights were bright enough to show there was a closed door in the ceiling, but he didn't see a latch or handle. It wasn't a far stretch to expect it to be like the front door, so he put his foot on the first rung to climb upward. That was when he saw he was standing on a square section of metal with a seam around it.

"Hey guys, I think this ladder goes up and down."

If there was any doubt in their minds that Captain Miller was right, that doubt was erased as the floor dropped away faster than he could have anticipated, and he disappeared from sight. It was an awkward fall because he had one foot raised to the first rung of the ladder, and he hit the sides of the hatch as he went by.

The reaction of everyone inside the silo was to rush to the aid of Captain Miller, but the trapdoor he had fallen through closed as quickly as it had opened. By the time they reached the ladder, the floor was flat again.

The Chief spread his arms to keep everyone from having the same thing happen to them.

"Everyone freeze right where you are," he shouted. "Check the floor near your feet for anything that could be a trapdoor. Whoever built this place knew someone would stand at the bottom of the ladder. Report what you see."

One by one they reported back that the floor appeared to be normal, and as they did, he moved closer to the ladder. He examined the bottom rung of the ladder and saw that it wasn't the weight of Captain Miller that opened the trapdoor. It was triggered when he started to climb the ladder. The first rung sat in slots on the railings, and the slightest amount of pressure made the rung travel downward. He examined the rungs above it and didn't see the same slots until he got to the last rung.

"You step on the bottom rung while holding the ladder, and the bottom trapdoor opens. I don't think it was actually a trap. Captain Miller just didn't realize it was going to open."

To prove his point, the Chief stepped onto the bottom rung with his right foot while holding the sides of the ladder. He lifted his left foot into the air and watched as the door beneath him opened. With his right foot still on the rung, he lowered his left foot down through the opening that Captain Miller had fallen through. Searching blindly with his leg, he found another rung below the floor, right where he thought it should be. He felt it give about an inch under his weight and guessed that it would be used by someone to open the door when they climbed out, or it was for the door to stay open if someone climbed downward.

"Jim, you okay?" he called down to Captain Miller. It was pitch black below the door, and he couldn't see anything.

His call was rewarded by a groan from somewhere below, and then he was blinded as the lights turned on brightly.

"I'm fine," said Captain Miller. "Just a little bruised. There's no way to fall ten feet gracefully, but I did the best I could."

The Chief saw that his friend was standing below him, and it had only been a fall from the height of a normal ceiling. It could have been much worse. He was leaning on the ladder and rubbing his right knee, but it was obvious that he wasn't seriously injured.

"What do you see down there?"

He saw Captain Miller lift his head and turn slowly from left to right.

"You need to come down here and see this for yourself."

The Chief felt like he also needed to find out where the ladder went above his head, but there was something in Captain Miller's voice that said he was surprised by whatever it was downstairs that he had found. He gestured with his free hand for Kathy to come closer.

"I'm going down the ladder to see what Jim found. If I'm right, the door will close once when I let go of the first rung of the ladder below this floor. Don't worry, it should open again for me when I want it to. I need you to keep an eye on the door above us. If it opens before I come back, be sure everyone is spread out to defend themselves."

Kathy nodded in understanding and stepped back from him. She used her own hand signals to spread everyone else around the room and had them cover the door at the top of the ladder with their guns.

The Chief stepped down through the door and climbed down to where Captain Miller had landed. As he expected, the door above him closed, but when he turned around and saw what was waiting for him below, he forgot all about the door. He could ask a thousand questions about who had made the silo and what had happened to them, but sometimes those things weren't important. What was important was the treasure trove that was spread out from left to right as far as he could see.

21

Rebellion

Fort Knox - 2023

Marvin Corn sat inside his tent with his arms tied behind him. If not for the gag in his mouth, he would have been shouting profanities at his captors and threatening them as if they were the ones tied to the chair. The three men standing guard over him didn't really know what they were waiting for. They had only been instructed to wait by Sparks, and he had left an hour earlier. They were getting nervous about the crowd that gathered outside and the occasional chants to turn Silas over to them. There were plenty of people in the crowd who wanted Silas to pay for getting so many of their men killed.

Just over a mile away, Sparks was wondering if the day could get better. At least that was the way he felt when he began doing his preflight check. He figured he would fly west until he found a good place to land far away from civilization. If he didn't have to waste ammunition clearing the area because of the frozen runways, he could take his time eliminating any infected dead that thawed out.

He was moving quickly until he was discovered by the same people who he had sent out to find Brother Bernard. Sparks wasn't sure someone was there until they were already boarding his plane, and he cursed at himself for not locking the door first. The big cargo door was closed, but the side door was still open.

"Maybe he's hiding in here," said one of the men as he excitedly climbed into the cargo area. "Whoa…check out the big guns."

Other voices chimed in when the men saw the heavy armament that made the plane so deadly. The loops of shiny ammunition chains caused more exclamations until someone yelled for everyone to keep their voices down. Sparks knew he had to say something first to keep them from figuring out what he was doing on the plane.

"What took you guys so long? Thank God I got here first, or Brother Bernard might have done something to damage the plane."

They were surprised by his sudden appearance from the cockpit, but before anyone could question his presence, he filled in the blanks.

"I didn't think of it until after you guys were already gone, but if I was him, I'd hide in the plane and then try to hijack it after takeoff. When I got here, he was trying to get the door open. He ran off toward the buildings when he saw me coming. If you hurry, you might be able to catch him."

It worked for the most part, but the leader of the posse stood his ground as the rest of the men jumped from the plane in pursuit of Bernard.

"What're you waiting for?" asked Sparks.

"I thought you might like to be there when we bring him in, Brother Sparks, and the people will want to hear from you about the future. You know, like what're we going to do with Silas and Bernard? Are we going to attack one of those shelters we've been hearing about? Are we still going to get the gold? Silas promised everyone a share."

Sparks was amazed by the man's lack of understanding and how Silas had been using them all. If Silas had gotten to the gold, he certainly wouldn't have shared it. As a matter of fact, he was more likely to kill anyone who would have dared to ask for their share. Despite being naive, Sparks could see that he wasn't going to budge, and his plan to escape would have to wait. He followed the man out the door, and just for show, he made sure it was locked.

The walk toward the buildings and back to the main camp was much different now that the snow was melting. Even though they had arrived at the fort before it had become freezing cold, there had been stragglers among the infected that had wandered in from the furthest reaches of the base. Some had made it to the airfield before they froze and were buried in the snow. There were random body parts appearing among the vehicles and along buildings where the sun didn't reach as fiercely, and anyone with a sharpened pole, machete, or ax would be a fool to pass up the opportunity to dispose of another infected dead before it thawed out completely.

All they had to do was follow the trail of spiked heads to know where the rest of the posse had gone. They caught up with the men as they were coming back out of a building, and the report was that they had killed a large number of the infected but had seen no sign of Bernard. The first part wasn't a surprise, but the second part made Sparks rethink his earlier plans to escape. Apparently, they had done a poor job of ensuring the base was clear of the infected when they first arrived. He didn't like the idea of sneaking back to the plane alone and running into a group of them, but he didn't have a choice. He realized he would have to come up with a reason for going to the plane during daylight and taking off that was acceptable to his new followers. He just wouldn't come back to the base as they expected.

"Let's go back to the main camp. If Brother Bernard wants to run around out here by himself, the next time we see him, he's going to be one of them."

He emphasized it by pointing at one of the infected that had already been spiked in the head, which drew a round of laughter from the posse. He laughed along with them as if he had meant it to be funny, but the truth was, Sparks wasn't too sure of how he should act to make the men still see him as a more benign leader than Silas or Bernard had been. He wanted to be less of a tyrant, but he didn't like being in charge. There were plenty of people who wanted to be number one and fewer people who were happy with number two.

The man he had appointed to be the leader of the posse seemed to think the temporary assignment had elevated him in status. He issued orders to the men to form two groups of five for the walk back to the main camp. He had them walk in two rows ahead of him and Sparks in order to be sure there were no newly thawed infected on either side along the way. They didn't seem to mind the orders and even attempted to stay somewhat organized as a marching squad.

Sparks thought to himself. "I guess there are plenty of people who don't mind not being number one or number two."

It took close to an hour to make the short walk back to camp because of the surprising number of infected along the way. If it hadn't begun to freeze outside, the large settlement of tents would only have been standing for another day before they would have been overrun. That gave Sparks another thing to think about. There must be a breach in the base security somewhere. Plenty of the infected still had tattered pieces of Army uniforms on their wasted bodies, but the vast majority were in civilian clothes.

It occurred to Sparks that he was such a bad leader that he never even asked the man who walked next to him for his name. That was when he realized he didn't know any of them, and it was ironic to him that he knew the names of the Chief, Kathy, and the rest of their crew. He knew the names of the people who most likely wanted to kill him.

"What's your name?" he said.

"Alex White, Brother Sparks."

"You can drop the Brother part. We have a new way of doing things now that the Brothers aren't running things. You're Captain White now."

The man beamed at the new title, and in much the same way that Silas had been named Brother Silas by Bernard, Sparks was suddenly General Sparks. If he could do it all over again, he wouldn't have painted himself into that corner.

"Listen up, everybody," yelled White. "General Sparks just made me a Captain, so I need myself a Lieutenant and a couple of Sergeants."

White didn't hear Sparks mumbling because he was busy picking his subordinates, but Sparks was telling himself to keep his mouth shut. The last thing he wanted to do was get saddled with an army and a caravan of followers, and his thoughts about the Chief reminded him of why he needed to put some distance between himself and these people.

When Sparks walked into the tent, Silas started ranting all over again. He dismissed the guards and his new Captain and leaned in close to Silas. Their noses were practically touching when he spoke, so he didn't have to say it louder.

"I'm going to keep you alive long enough for the Chief to get here. Then I'm hopping on my plane and flying so far from here that he'll never find me."

Silas became Marvin Corn in a split second. He was cruel as Brother Silas, but as Marvin Corn, he was callous and unafraid. If it was possible, he was more evil when he was Marvin Corn. There was no fear in his eyes, and Sparks backed away from him. At that moment, Sparks felt like his best option would be to cut his throat, but those eyes made him feel like even that was impossible. It would backfire, and he would be the one left bleeding on the floor. Then he had an idea.

Sparks called to the guards outside and told them to guard Silas, and under no circumstances should they take off the gag. For added security, he dug through his own backpack and produced a pair of aviator sunglasses. Silas turned his head left and right to prevent him from putting the glasses on his face, but Sparks eventually succeeded. He didn't want the guards to see what he had seen.

Next, Sparks found Captain White and gave him a new mission. There was something he needed, and he knew that every Army base had them somewhere. He described what he wanted and told Captain White to start with the Fort Knox Fire Department.

******

It was just after midnight when Captain White triumphantly returned from his mission. He proudly presented Sparks with four large canvas bags with rigid sides and something that resembled a generator. They were bright yellow, but the biohazard symbol stood out in red. Sparks unzipped the first one and lifted the flap out of the way. Four hazmat suits were neatly folded inside. The other cases carried breathing tanks that could be strapped on the back like SCUBA gear.

"I only needed one, Captain."

White shrugged his shoulders and said, "They were there, so I just thought you might want them all. What do you need them for, anyway?"

"Like I said, I only need one. Brother Silas is going in to get his gold, and he's going to need protection."

The Captain stood stock still for several seconds as if something wasn't quite registering in his mind. He understood what Sparks said, but so far there had been no success with the front door.

"Is there something you wanted to ask me, Captain?"

"Well, uh…did you find a way inside past those spiders, General?"

Captain White was missing the point that Sparks didn't care if the spiders got Silas or not.

Sparks cringed at the title, but it wasn't something the guards or Captain would have noticed. He saw that Silas noticed because the little tyrant leaned his head backward and laughed around the gag. It sounded more like he was choking, but Sparks knew what it was.

"Go ahead and laugh. You won't think it's so funny when we put you inside the Depository. The way I figure it is that the suit will keep those little green bugs out at first, but sooner or later they'll find a tiny little crack in your protection, and then it will be bye-bye Brother

Silas."

That stopped Silas from laughing, but Sparks didn't know if it was because he was afraid or if Silas had become Marvin Corn again. He guessed that he would know for sure if he looked into those eyes for a second time. It was something Marvin Corn would want to see if it was someone else inside the suit. He would want to watch as the green moss spread across the inside of the victim's visor and devoured their face. He would be fascinated by the flesh dissolving into nothing as the white bone beneath the skin was exposed, but most of all, he would watch their eyes to see if he could tell when the victim died.

Sparks turned back to Captain White and said, "I don't know what's on the other side of the front door, but people got inside through the towers. They just didn't make it back out again. The towers collapsed in the fire, but I'd be willing to bet that's the best way in. As a matter of fact, I guess it's a good thing you brought all of the hazmat suits. We might have to go partway with him to make sure he goes inside."

White had another silent moment. Sparks saw that the man had a habit of staring off into space whenever he had a revelation or intense thought. He wondered if the man could walk, talk, and chew gum at the same time, and it was possible that he had just understood it would have been better for him if he had only come back with one hazmat suit.

"Don't worry, Captain. The suit will protect you if you have to use it."

"But didn't you just tell Brother Silas it won't protect him forever?"

Sparks leaned closer to White and whispered, "That was just to scare him."

The gauge on the SCUBA tanks said they were rated for ninety minutes at surface pressure. Sparks had a little experience with tanks and opened the valves to empty them. The air they contained had gone stale after seven years. He checked the generator and saw that it wouldn't be a problem to start it up from a power outlet in one of their trucks. He turned it all over to White and told him to be sure the tanks were all charged. In the meantime, he was going to get some sleep.

"What should we do with him?" asked one of the guards. He hooked a finger in the direction of Brother Silas.

Sparks considered what it would be like knowing the man was staring at him all night and came to a decision.

"Take him outside and put him in the back of a truck. Just make sure he's tied up and can't get away."

* * *

******

Sparks was surprised that he slept as well as he did, but the second surprise was how much the snow had melted that night. When he stepped out of the tent, his eyes were drawn to what used to be the Gold Bullion Depository. It was a charred mass of twisted metal and collapsed walls, and he wasn't completely sure they would find a way inside, but he only planned to go so far. His main goal was to shove Brother Silas inside far enough that he would never come back out. The world would be a safer place without Marvin Corn in it, and maybe it would buy him an ounce of redemption if the Chief ever caught up with him.

The flattened area surrounding the building resembled a buffer zone between two warring armies. It was pitted with craters caused by exploding mines, and the only snow remaining inside the fence was inside those craters. The tall grass was limp and flattened, so Sparks could see the arms and legs of the infected dead protruding at irregular angles where they had become frozen. Far too many of them were acting as if the breeze was strong enough to move them, but considering the fact that they moved in different directions, it was likely that they would need to eliminate any infected that could walk before making their last assault on the main building. The number of infected was disturbing, and Sparks wondered how there could be so many of them in a minefield.

Captain White met Sparks only a few feet away from his tent and dutifully handed him a cup of coffee. He also provided answers to the questions Sparks had just been asking himself. White had gone with a team of men to the road that led to the front door of the Depository. From there they could see that most of the infected were attached to short chains that were staked to the ground.

"Are any of them loose?" asked Sparks.

"We won't know the answer to that until they start getting up or crawling. Right now they're just a tangled mess, but that explains why there were infected out there in the first place. I always wondered why they weren't constantly tripping mines. Some were loose, but they probably wandered in through the front gate over a period of time."

Sparks said, "Good job, Captain. We needed to know that before going to the Depository."

Captain White had become so accustomed to short, sarcastic

266

comments from Brother Silas and Brother Bernard, that he was somewhat surprised that he got a straightforward response from Sparks. He felt a rush of loyalty to the young pilot and was glad there had been a change in the leadership of their group.

"Let's get this over with," said Sparks. "I'm going to get some more coffee and breakfast. While I'm gone, get Silas into a hazmat suit and have the guards take him to the front door of the Depository. Tell them to be careful not to get too close to the sides of the road."

Sparks found a group of people who were serving up some kind of stew for breakfast, and they had pulled out a hidden stash of dark roasted coffee to celebrate the demise of the Brotherhood. He accepted a generous helping of each and savored the breakfast as well as the knowledge that he would be free of his relationship with Brother Silas soon. Captain White arrived thirty minutes later to let him know the guards were awaiting further instructions at the front door of the Depository.

He drained the last of his second cup of coffee, and the pair set off to say farewell to the little tyrant. Word had spread quickly through the survivors camped inside Fort Knox, and everyone had turned out to watch. There were family members who wanted to see justice for what Silas had done to the victims of his misguided power. They shouted their encouragement for Sparks to make sure he suffered a painful death. Sparks had no doubt that it would be painful if those little green spiders got inside the hazmat suit, but even if they didn't, Silas was at least going to have a terrifying adventure.

The crowd followed him and Captain White until they got to the gate. They spread out along both sides for a better view, but they became less vocal when they saw the large number of infected dead that was moving more and more as they thawed. It would only be a matter of time before they learned if some weren't tethered in place and could walk out of the mess, and no one wanted to be close by if one stepped on a mine.

Sparks and White covered the distance to the front door at a trot. Silas stood between the guards, his face hidden by the visor of the bulky suit. The suit had been made for a person of normal stature, and it illustrated just how short Silas was. He looked like a kid dressed up for Halloween.

One of the guards pointed upward, and they saw he had managed to get a rope around a collapsed beam about twenty feet above the door. The other end of the rope was tied around Brother Silas under his armpits. The guard pulled on the rope to demonstrate, and it made Silas stand up on his tiptoes.

There was a shriek inside the suit, and they heard Silas yell something. Sparks leaned closer to the visor and put his ear against it.

"What was that Marvin? Did you say something?"

"You can't do this to me," demanded Silas.

"That's what I thought you said. Just watch me."

Sparks turned back to the guard holding the rope and asked, "Is there a way inside up there?"

"Yes sir. When the roof collapsed, it tore holes in the ceiling beyond the door. You can't see them from down here because the weight of the roof pulled everything over with it. I climbed up there to take a look, and there's a dark hole right there." He pointed at a place above the door.

Sparks studied the beam and said, "I need someone to go up there and make sure he's over the hole when the rope is released."

The guard didn't hesitate, understanding that he was the best candidate for the job. He also wanted to be the one to see Brother Silas drop into the darkness on the other side of the door. The other guard and Captain White anchored the rope by holding Silas from behind while the guard shimmied up the rope. When he got to the top, he straddled the beam and signaled he was ready.

Sparks, Captain White, and the other guard got together and pulled. A cheer went up from the crowd when they saw the yellow hazmat suit containing Brother Silas lifted from the ground. He swung closer to the three men sending him to his death and Sparks gave him a big smile. He enjoyed the expression of terror on his face, but he saw the cold eyes of Marvin Corn glaring at him. Even in death, the man wouldn't change.

"You've got about forty minutes or so of air in that tank. Here's a flashlight that will last longer than your air. Maybe you can use it to find your gold, and you can be alone with it before you suffocate."

The three men pulled harder, and Silas rose smoothly to the top. The guard grabbed his shoulders and turned him to face toward the hole, then he shoved the lightweight man along the beam until he was directly above the black maw. He signaled to the men below, and they let the line go slack in their hands. The cheering outside the gate grew louder, but Marvin Corn couldn't hear it over the sound of his own heart pounding in his ears. The crowd and Sparks would have been disappointed to know that the terror was gone, and it had been replaced by the cold detachment that had made Marvin Corn a survivor. As the blackness wrapped itself around him, he simply turned on the flashlight and drank in his surroundings to decide what to do next.

******

Marvin Corn wasted no time freeing himself from the rope. He didn't want Sparks to change his mind and pull him back out. He had no way of guessing how much air he had left in his tank, and he knew survival meant making quick decisions. The first thing he had to do was assess the damage done by the fire. Specifically, he had to learn if it had burned hot enough to kill off those tiny green creatures. In the bright beam of his flashlight, he could see that the fire had warped metal, and practically every surface was black. The green flesh-eaters may have been vicious, but they also made excellent propellant for a fire.

His first few steps away from the sunshine that lit the area below the hole told him everything he needed to know about how to walk through the carnage. A black cloud rose around him with each movement. He knew he would have to avoid shuffling his feet, or he would stir up a cloud too thick for him to navigate.

Five minutes of air was all he wasted before deciding every corridor that led into the first floor of the building or above was blocked. His only option was to go down, and a pitch-black stairwell door was open to him. Once through the door, he was surprised to see that some of the surfaces were still shiny, and there was only a fine coating of the dark ash. Smoke had darkened the walls, but unlike the walls above there were no scorch marks he was sure were the traces of the green moss. Another door at the landing below was closed, but it wasn't blocked, so he walked carefully down the flight of stairs to it.

He guessed he had maybe thirty minutes of air left when he opened the door, but as soon as he shone his flashlight inside, he knew thirty minutes was enough. The fire and smoke hadn't penetrated the small room on the other side of the door, so he stepped inside and pulled the door shut behind him. A small cloud of soot followed him inside, and it clung to his hazmat suit like a static charge, but in the beam of his light, he saw that he probably didn't need the oxygen tank anymore. He hoped Sparks was right, and that the flashlight would last much longer than the air in his tank.

Marvin pulled off the hood of the hazmat suit and took in a short breath. The air tasted stale, but he preferred it to the air in the SCUBA tank. He closed the valve on the tank to save it for later if it was needed, but that was all just an afterthought. He had already noticed the shiny bank vault door along one wall, and the first thing that entered his mind was the gold.

"Could it be that simple?" he asked himself aloud. "Did I just find the gold before running out of air? Sparks, I wish there was a way to tell you about this before I kill you."

He didn't see a reason to keep the hazmat suit on, so he struggled to get out of it while keeping a curious eye on the door.

"Where's the combination lock and handle?" he said in a low voice.

Running a hand along the seam where the door met with the surrounding wall, he detected a difference. The door didn't seem to be seated into its recess as far as it could be, and the edge farthest from the hinges on the left felt slightly larger. He pressed his fingers along the narrow lip of the door and pried it open. It only moved a fraction of an inch, but once it moved there was more surface for him to grip, and he doubled his efforts. It was heavy, but it came outward to reveal the secrets hidden on the other side.

Marvin was convinced it would be row after row of storage shelves heavily laden with gold, but the room beyond was more like a waiting room in an office. There were chairs and tables, and across an aisle from them was a receptionist's desk with a sliding glass window.

"This looks more like my dentist's office than a gold storage area."

Beyond the reception area was a hallway, and when he aimed his flashlight in that direction, he saw a pair of elevator doors. Across from them was a door that had a sign above it. He wasn't surprised to see that the door opened into more stairs, but he wished the elevator buttons would be lit up. He pressed them just to be sure, but there was no response.

"Stairs will do," said Marvin.

The musty odor in the stairwell was not a surprise, but there was no way to know if it was from death or from lack of air circulating below. All he knew for sure was that he was still alive and that he was out of the reach of the people who had dumped him into the building. He almost told himself that he was alive and safe, but he knew safe was a relative term. After he found out what was below him on the next floor, he would decide if he was right.

The first door in the stairwell opened easily, and his only concern was the darkness inside. Once the batteries in his flashlight died, he would be feeling his way around in total darkness, and that would greatly hinder his ability to locate his next two priorities. He hadn't been given food or water since the night before. The guards had given him semi-privacy with a bucket once, but they had told him not to complain about being hungry or thirsty because he wasn't going to live long enough for that to matter.

There was a laminated poster in a frame across from the door, and he could tell it was a floor plan. It had yellowed slightly, but it was still clear enough for him to see some of the labels for various rooms. One was labeled in red as SUPPLIES and seemed like the best place to start. It appeared to be on his right side, three doors away from the spot where a red X marked the door he had come in through. The corridor to the right was as black as ink even when he aimed his flashlight that way, but he put one hand on the wall and walked. He counted doors as he passed them until he reached the third one, and he held his breath as he pushed it open.

The floor plan didn't really give him an idea of how large the room would be. He had expected a center aisle with shelves on the left and right, something like a walk-in closet, but this was enough to surprise even him. The beam from his flashlight was lost in the distance, not even reaching a wall on the opposite side of the room. He aimed the light to his left and right at shelves that reached toward a ceiling ten feet over his head, and he didn't know where to start.

With no time to waste, he read the labels on boxes and moved as quickly as he could. There were manufactured goods such as shoes, clothing, and bedding on his right. He switched to the other side and found boxes that contained toothpaste, soap, and shaving cream. There was enough of each to supply an army for a long time or a few people for a century, but nothing that would be useful once his flashlight batteries died.

The pattern of storage emerged after searching eight long rows. Medical supplies were grouped together. Sundries were grouped in one section that he deemed useful but not important to survival. What he was searching for was a hardware section. When he found it, the first shelf held an assortment of repair parts for everything from small appliances to machinery he didn't recognize. He moved on to the next row of shelves and found small hand tools.

His jackpot was discovered four rows later when he came to small appliances. Almost everything had an electrical cord for a power source, but he was hoping for something portable. The next section had battery-operated devices, but he was willing to bet the only working batteries in the place were the ones in his flashlight because they had been in a cold storage area at the Army base they had raided. The dark room he was searching through wasn't hot, but it wasn't nearly cold enough to preserve batteries.

A box had a label on it that caught his eye, and he eagerly tore the cardboard box open. Inside was a portable lantern that had a hand crank on the side. It was made back before plastic had begun to dominate every industry, so it felt heavier than what he expected, but all he cared about was whether or not it worked. He unfolded the hand crank from the side and turned it clockwise. The ratcheting sound of the gears was too loud in the surrounding darkness, but a red light on the top of the lantern slowly illuminated and then grew brighter. The amber light next to it glowed as the red light went out, but only seconds later the green light came on. He kept turning the crank until he felt the inner tension of the hand crank increase to its limit. When he folded the hand crank back into its inset position and pressed the power button, the lantern illuminated the room in white light.

There were signs at the ends of long rows, and the one that caught his eye first said ARMORY. The second one that said RATIONS made him smile, but the sign that made him feel like someone was watching over him said EMERGENCY EXIT.

"Now we're talking," he said.

He grabbed another lantern and headed for the armory.

22

General Services Administration

Tennessee - 2023

Captain Miller said, "Name me one federal agency that wasn't planning for Armageddon."

"Well, I think we can safely guess that the Congressman for this district was on a few committees that were included in the planning, but can you imagine the paperwork involved with getting anything out of this place? The GSA practically invented the government accounting system."

The two men stood side by side on a platform that sat above a warehouse. It was brightly lit and maps on the wall behind the ladder gave directions to each section. The Chief nudged Captain Miller and pointed at a sign that said WELCOME TO THE GSA DISTRIBUTION CENTER.

"I saw that, but it's making me a little nervous because I don't feel like it was meant for us. Why are the lights working?"

The Chief said, "That's what's been bothering me, among other things. I don't think those ladders were supposed to work. Whatever the power source is that's controlling the lights, it must also let the ladders operate. Otherwise, someone would have stumbled across this place a long time ago."

"So that bloom Gentry detected was when someone turned on the power?" asked Captain Miller.

"Yeah, someone must be here. Do you know what this place reminds me of? This is a lot like the entrance at Ambassadors Island. You can see almost everything from up here. Whoever built this facility must have been involved with that construction, and when I think about it, the GSA must have been working with the people who funded the shelters for Titus Rush. There's no way they could've gotten everything they needed and hidden the bookkeeping without help from the GSA."

"That's great," said Captain Miller, "but what now? If we go down there and start shopping, someone could be watching and have us in their crosshairs."

The Chief couldn't quite put his finger on what his good friend said that made him feel like he was missing something, but there was a moment when he felt like he was missing something obvious.

"What did you just say?" he asked.

"Huh? You mean you want me to repeat it or that someone might shoot us while we're helping ourselves to everything we can carry?"

The Chief said, "That's it. I get it now."

"You get what?"

"How much stuff can you carry up a ladder?"

Before Captain Miller could piece together his answer, the Chief told him what he had realized.

"This isn't the front door. It's one of the emergency exits. Titus Rush had stressed to the people building his shelters that they all needed several doors. Ambassadors Island didn't have as many doors as Mud Island, but Fort Sumter could've used more. The shelter in England had too many doors."

"That's why we had them permanently seal a few of them," added Captain Miller.

"Some of those big boxes of supplies down there had to be delivered by big trucks, so my guess is the main entrance is somewhere near the overpass we crossed before we turned off the interstate. A truck could pull off the road, wait for no traffic, then enter a hidden entrance, but we can figure that out later. First, we need to find out who turned the lights on."

The door at the top of the ladder snapped open, and Kathy's face appeared.

"We have company up here."

"Good or bad?" asked the Chief.

"Both."

It only took a minute for the two men to scale the ladder. They heard the thumping on the outside of the door before they saw the two young girls sitting on the floor against the wall. The thumping was random, so they knew that was bad company.

Kathy held up a small radio and said, "Cassandra gave us a heads-up a minute ago. Those big piles of snow collapsed when they melted far enough, and at least twelve infected dead followed the road right to the door of the silo. She said she can hit them from the MRAP, but there would be some stray rounds through the walls."

"Good to know," said the Chief. "I hope you told her to hold her fire for now. Who are our friends over there?"

Kathy grinned at the first part then pointed at the girls. They both stood and came forward when Kathy motioned with her hand.

"Gina and Bonnie Hart, meet the Chief and Captain Miller. They were in the silo at the top of the ladder. There's a manual way to open the upper door, and the power switch to everything else is up there. They cut the power to the computer just before we came in and figured if they killed the rest of the power once we got inside, it would give them away."

"You got all of that out of them while we were gone?" asked the Chief. "We weren't gone that long."

Iris said, "We didn't have to torture it out of them. They haven't seen living people go through here since before the snow started, and they could tell by watching them that they were better off not revealing themselves to that group. They looked like an army of scavengers."

Captain Miller said, "I'm just curious, but what do we look like."

Iris laughed, "We look friendlier."

"Why?"

"More women with guns," laughed Kathy. "They had their doubts about the big guy, but when Iris said he was her husband, they relaxed."

The Chief said, "I'll try to take that as a compliment," then to the girls, he said, "Hello. I don't expect you to remember all their names, but you've met Kathy and Iris. I assume they introduced you, but that's Tom, Sim, Colleen, Hampton, Charlie, Sue, Caleb, Darren, Brett, and Grady. Think of us as the good guys." As he named each of them, he noticed Caleb looked like he was ready to ask both of them to be his date at the prom.

"Teenagers," thought the Chief.

Gina and Bonnie were fraternal twins, so they were easy to tell apart, but they were eighteen years old and had grown up close before and after the apocalypse. They had many of the same mannerisms and finished each other's sentences so often that the Chief had to get them to slow down.

They had been living in one of the farmhouses a couple of miles away, but over the years they had lived in more than a few. It was always the same story. A place would be safe for a short time, but then things would get dangerous, and they would move again. Bonnie explained that they had always been able to see the silo in the distance, and they had always assumed it was just a silo until they were forced to retreat past it. That was when they discovered what it really was.

"Hold that thought," said the Chief. "Was the power on when you came in the first time?"

The girls shared a grin. They had remained hidden and watched people come and go from the silo several times. When people would get inside, they would attempt to pry open the hatches above and below the ladder, but they always failed and eventually moved on either to get away from the infected dead or to find food.

"That explains the rough edges around the doors. Someone used a crowbar, but I take it the doors held."

Gina nodded, "Those marks were there when we got here the first time. When we saw them, we knew the doors were made of something really strong because they were only scratched. We found the manual switches when we climbed the ladder together."

"There's more than one switch?" asked the Chief.

The girls both nodded this time, and Gina said, "After you pull down on the top rung, the switch is exposed on the backside of the ladder. The only reason we found it was because we both climbed up at the same time. Bonnie felt something different under her hand, and when she pushed on it the top door opened."

"We've been solving these puzzles for a long time," said the Chief. "Am I correct in assuming that the power switch isn't just sitting out in the open up there?"

They both laughed, and Gina said, "There's a bunch of switches with numbers on them up there, and there's a sign over them that says Main Power."

"And we were called nerds in school because we got good grades," said Bonnie.

Gina continued, "One of the switches had a decimal point on it, so we figured that it was a math problem, and when you're standing in the middle of a silo, what's the first math problem you would think of?"

Sim said, "The formula for the circumference of a circle."

Everyone including the sisters turned to face Sim.

"What? I'm a flight navigator. If we aren't math nerds, nobody is."

"He's right," said Gina. "We didn't have a tape measure handy, but anyone who knows their shoe size can measure a straight line."

"Especially when we already estimated the silo to be forty feet in diameter," said Bonnie.

Sim did the calculations in his head and said, "That would be 125.6, right? Most people would look at the numbered switches and assume it was a four-digit code, but you had to know where to put the decimal point. They also wouldn't have to write it down."

There was general agreement around the crowded room that everyone would have disregarded the decimal point, but even if they had noticed it, they wouldn't have known where to place it in the code.

"What's the code to turn the power off?" asked Captain Miller.

Gina smiled and said, "There are buttons that say POWER OFF for different things."

"Genius...Gentry Campbell is going to love you two," said Iris. "She's the biggest nerd I'd ever known, at least until now."

"What's downstairs?" asked Hampton.

"It might be one of those supply redoubts we've been speculating about," said the Chief. "As a matter of fact, let's change that to definitely a supply redoubt. These two knew a good thing when they found it, and they barely scratched the surface of what it contains."

The sound of infected dead bumping against the door became steadily louder, and everyone instinctively moved to one side of the silo. They could probably handle anything that came through the door, but they felt a little silly with nothing between them and the door except the desk and computer.

Kathy asked the girls, "What's the computer for anyway? You never said."

"Well," said Gina, "it took a long time to figure out the password, so we haven't had a chance to check everything, but we weren't surprised that one of the main files is an inventory of everything in the redoubt. There are other files that have lists of people and their jobs, but we haven't figured that out yet because there's no one else here."

Bonnie added, "There was that other stuff about a network."

"Oh, yeah," said Gina. "That list was map coordinates. That was easy enough to figure because you can drop the coordinates into a search field and it gives you a satellite view."

"Live or archived," asked Captain Miller.

"There's no snow in the pictures, so they had to be old pictures," said Gina.

Most of the group had just been listening, preferring to let the Chief and the other leaders in the group ask questions, but Brett wanted to ask a really obvious question.

"Will the search only show coordinates from the list, or will it show other locations?"

"We didn't try any," answered Gina.

Brett said, "The list might be preset locations of other redoubts, but if that's true, why wouldn't it just say they're redoubts? A search engine means this place is still tied to a network."

Bonnie said, "I think I just said that."

Colleen cleared her throat to get everyone's attention then said, "Why is the computer up here where someone could just...you know, wreck it?"

"That's easy," said Gina. "There's a whole row of them down in the storage levels. This one works, but we think this one was supposed to let someone else know this silo was occupied. I mean, once we got the power turned on, and when we booted up this computer, the camera light on the top of the monitor turned green."

"And if it gets wrecked," said Colleen, "someone would know that too. It makes me wonder if it has ever been replaced."

The Chief said, "If you're suggesting there's an army of nerds out there to support us, I'd love to make contact with them. Someone get that computer turned on, and if the camera light comes on, I don't care how you do it, but let the people on the other end of the camera know that we need to meet."

"We have another question," said Captain Miller. "Did you young ladies ever find another way in or out of here?"

They both nodded at the same time, and Gina said, "Yeah, but they've all been buried in snow. It was hard enough getting to the silo, but the other exits are in low places. Some of them are going to be underwater if all that snow melts fast enough."

"I saw some big hardware down there," said the Chief. "Once our mechanic checks it out, we'll want to go out the biggest exit you know of."

The radio chirped in Kathy's hand, and Cassandra's voice came through the tiny speaker.

"We have some company of the living variety, and I can't tell yet if they're friendly, but they're coming in fast. Please advise."

"What type of vehicle?" answered Kathy.

"That would be vehicles," said Cassandra. "Two extended cab pickup trucks. They must have snow tires because they're coming fast."

"Do they seem hostile to you?"

"Define hostile."

The Chief was about to order everyone outside to help Cassandra if she came under attack, but the next transmission was Cassandra laughing.

"I don't believe it," she said, "but one of the trucks is flying a flag. It's the flag used by Captain Miller's men with the baseball home plate design on it, and if I'm not mistaken, that's Gentry Campbell waving at me."

"Can you give us a head count of the infected outside the silo?"

"I can do better than that," said Cassandra. "I have a good angle on most of them if you want me to thin the crowd a bit. I'll give you a headcount afterward."

The sound of the heavy machine gun mounted on the MRAP was muted inside the silo, but its distinctive rapping sound was still loud enough to make everyone cringe. A stray round would pierce the shell of the silo easily.

"Everyone get down the ladder fast," said the Chief. "Kathy, tell her to wait a minute."

Kathy made the call while the Chief ushered everyone down the ladder, and he gave Kathy a thumbs-up signal when he was ready for her to open fire. Kathy joined him on the ladder as she called Cassandra, and this time she told her to shoot close to the silo if she wanted.

There must have been some infected dead against the door because there were loud thumps when they got hit. Then the machine gun stopped, and there was silence outside the door. Kathy and the Chief climbed back up the ladder and hurried outside to greet their friends.

The trucks had stopped just short of the Cougar, and they could see at least seven people waving at Cassandra and then toward the silo. With Gentry, there were four of Captain Miller's former soldiers and two men they didn't know. One of them was tall and skinny, and the other was a bit stocky. Both Kathy and the Chief were excellent at reading body language as well as group behavior, and they noticed the way the four soldiers were spread out around the stocky man, while Gentry and the skinny man walked comfortably ahead of them together.

"Why do I get the feeling this is going to be an interesting story?" said Kathy. "Are they guarding that guy?"

"We'll see in a moment, but considering that they just came from Kentucky, it wouldn't surprise me if they caught one of the people we're after."

Between the silo and the highway, there were far more bodies than they expected to see. Not only was the snow melting quickly, but the infected dead were also getting up fast. Kathy pointed at the open field to their left, and the Chief saw that several of the snow-covered infected were struggling to their feet like newborn calves. They wobbled as they moved cold joints, and a few fell down. Those that remained standing took tentative steps in their direction. They were still far enough away to be easily intercepted, but the sound of the machine gun had acted like an alarm clock.

When Gentry saw her friends come out of the silo, she broke into a run in their direction. The Chief did the same thing because he knew the snow on the side of the road was deeper than she could have suspected, and there was no way to know what was buried under it. Kathy jogged behind him with her semiautomatic in both hands pointed downward but ready to use if anything came out of the snow.

"I'm so glad to see you," yelled Gentry excitedly as she threw her arms around the Chief's neck. "You guys have been gone forever."

The boom of Kathy's gun ruined the moment, but it served as a wake-up call for everyone. The infected were also on the other side of the highway behind the MRAP. From the slight rise where they stood, they could estimate at least three dozen coming their way.

"How'd you get here so fast?" asked the Chief. "You were on foot before, and I didn't think there were many cars or trucks running that also had good tires. You found two of them."

"Thanks to an old friend of mine who can fix anything." She pointed at Specs who was following the path she had taken up the road. "They were up on lifts in a car dealership, and Doctor Burtram was able to get a compressor working. We put tires on them from the racks, and they still had batteries that held a charge. We got lucky, especially since I knew where to find you. You won't believe what's happening at

Fort Knox."

"You can tell me everything inside where it's safe. I hate to make anyone stay out here, but Cassandra might need a hand. Could we ask your squad to take up positions on top of the MRAP?"

Captain Miller had come out of the silo with Hampton and Tom, and he overheard the question.

"I'd be happy to stay out here with them," he said. "I know it'll be good for my morale, so I imagine they'll be glad to stand watch with their former old man."

He didn't wait for the Chief to agree and went ahead of them to where the soldiers were admiring the MRAP. They cheered when he joined them, and despite their military discipline, they exchanged hugs and back slaps. They climbed the side of the MRAP leaving Bernard standing on the side of the road. He turned in a circle, obviously unsure of where he was supposed to go.

The Chief saw Bernard's nervousness even from a distance and asked Gentry who he was. When she told him Bernard was a deserter from the Brotherhood, his first impulse was to send him out into the fields where the infected were growing in number. Kathy intervened and reminded him that it would be enough to get the leader. The Chief still felt like followers bore responsibility for what their leaders do because followers often do things to impress their leaders and vice versa. It was also how bad leaders kept easily impressed followers in line.

"You," bellowed the Chief in Bernard's direction.

Bernard actually turned in the opposite direction as if the Chief could have been yelling at someone behind him. In a strange way, it made the Chief feel sorry for the stocky man, but it didn't change his mind about dishing out some form of punishment. The Chief felt everyone's eyes on him as he strode purposely down the side road toward Bernard. He was keenly aware that the soldiers who watched from the MRAP with Captain Miller had lost good friends to the Brotherhood. They wanted to see justice done too.

Bernard appeared to be ready to run at any moment, but he was having the same reaction most people would have if escape was impossible and a bear was getting closer. He had his hands out in front of him, but he didn't know if he should put them over his face to protect himself or if he should ball them into fists. He went with a third option and brought them together as if he was praying. If the Chief was big at a distance, he was gigantic as he got closer, and

Bernard's knees wouldn't support his weight anymore. His legs buckled under him, and now he really was praying.

Gentry asked Kathy, "Is he going to hurt him?" She was surprised to hear her own voice shake.

"I don't know. We've been worried about the Chief and his need for revenge. It's been building up in him slowly, and he's had to delay it far longer than he wanted to. For what it's worth, I think he only wants to kill Sparks and the leader of that Brotherhood cult. Was this guy high up in their organization?"

"He wanted to be, but from what Doctor Burtram told me, he was more of the follower type. If the leader had ever ordered him to put a bullet in someone's head, he would more than likely have found a way out of it or had someone else do it for him."

"So he isn't totally innocent," said Kathy. "Let's see if he's any good at pleading his own case."

"Seems like begging is the direction he's going to go in."

The Chief towered over Bernard, and he would have preferred to see the man own up to his part in the ambush that took the lives of several soldiers. The Chief couldn't accept any excuses Bernard might offer, and begging for mercy wasn't an option given to the victims of the Brotherhood.

"Please, mister, I didn't have anything to do with whatever you think I did."

"Is that supposed to be some kind of blanket defense? Your people killed soldiers who were doing nothing but traveling from one place to another. They were people who would have saved your sorry hide if you had needed saving, but your Brotherhood chose to execute them. I've been waiting a long time to get even."

Bernard's eyes were wide, and tears were welling up in the corners.

"I didn't kill those soldiers," he cried. "I heard about them, but I wasn't even there."

"And I'm just supposed to take your word for that?"

Bernard opened his mouth to begin another plea for mercy, but the Chief held up a hand for him to stop. It had the desired effect because Bernard was sure he was about to get hit.

The Chief said, "I have to decide what to do with you, and I have to do something. I can shoot you, or I can stab you. I could hang you. I could tie you to the front of the MRAP and ram into something. Maybe I could just tie you to a tree and let the infected get to you."

The Chief repeatedly poked a finger toward Bernard as he ran through his options, and Bernard recoiled each time.

"Maybe I could let you go but then shoot you in the leg from a distance. Then we could watch you try to outrun the infected."

"I know you have to do something, mister, but do you have to kill me? Maybe I could do something to earn my keep. I've got valuable information I could give you."

"I don't need much intel to take out your leader or Sparks."

"I know where a tunnel is that goes into the place where they keep the gold."

Just like every other scavenger that had died trying to get to the gold, Bernard assumed that was what the Chief was after, but the existence of a tunnel was something that got his interest. If there was a shelter under Fort Knox, a back entrance would be part of the design. Bernard didn't need to know why it was of interest to him though.

"I'm listening."

Bernard knew he needed to cut a deal before the Chief found out that Specs knew where the tunnel was too, but he made the mistake of thinking he was in a position to negotiate, and he laid his cards on the table.

"Promise you'll let me go, and I'll tell you," he said hopefully.

The Chief moved with surprising speed that no one ever expected from someone his size. He closed the gap between them and caught Bernard by the back of his neck with one huge hand. He lifted him to his feet and spun him around to face the other way. Then he grabbed Bernard by the back of his pants and lifted him bodily over his head like he didn't weigh more than a pound. All Bernard could see was the sky above him, and the Chief lifted him so high he couldn't even turn his head far enough to see the ground. His arms and legs were flailing, and he screamed like a little girl.

"I'm going to break your back so you can't feel anything from the waist down. Then I'm going to hang you by your arms from a tree. While the infected are eating you, it won't hurt, but you'll get to watch."

Somewhere in all the screaming, Bernard said he was sorry and that he would tell the Chief where the tunnel was. The Chief didn't want to let him off that easy, so for the benefit and enjoyment of the soldiers, he kept walking until Bernard was wailing he was sorry over and over again. When he put Bernard on his feet again, they were at the front of the MRAP, and the Chief made a pretense of helping Bernard straighten his collar...right before he punched him in the jaw.

Everyone heard the sound of it, and there was a collective groan.

Cassandra said to the soldiers sitting around her gun turret, "Good thing the Chief pulled that punch, or he would be dead instead of just unconscious."

The Chief left Bernard where he was and walked toward the rest of the crew on the side road. He gave a small salute to the soldiers he went by, and they gave him nods to indicate the score was even with this guy. When he got to where Specs had joined Kathy and Gentry, he told them what Bernard had said.

Specs said, "It's just like Bernard to think you were after the gold. If we had found it, he would still be trying to score points with Brother Silas, or he would have tried to carry some bars in his pockets. I doubt that he has a clue how heavy gold is."

The Chief cocked his head to one side and studied the tall, thin man. "Why were you trying to find a tunnel? I get the feeling that Bernard was after the gold either for himself or for that guy Silas, but what was your game?"

Specs didn't appear to be at all concerned that the Chief was asking him a question that could make it appear that he was also blinded by the gold, and for that reason, the Chief believed him.

"Bernard thought he was dragging me along on the treasure hunt, but I was curious about some things. First of all, it was a challenge. I wanted to see if I could get inside. Second, I always wondered about Fort Knox. Why would the government make it the most secure place in the country and then just keep gold there? I have this theory that they would build some kind of secure bunker for the President in case of an emergency, and why not put it in the same place as the gold? If we ever get an economy going again, we'll need to bring back the gold standard."

The Chief had to laugh, "No, kid. The President's bunker is in Columbus, Ohio, and he didn't make it there safely, but that's some pretty good reasoning. You found the tunnel?"

Specs cocked his head to match the Chief's as if he understood it was a way the Chief had of getting the truth out of people. He wasn't so sure the Chief was telling him the truth about the President, but it would come out in due time.

"I'm not sure we can get into the back entrance the same way a second time. The fire we started under the Depository spread from where the tunnel entered the basement of the building. At least I think it was the basement. Those little green spiders burn like lighter fluid."

"That's good to know," said Kathy, "but what little green spiders? I'm tired of spiders. I don't think I want to go into any dark tunnels where spiders live."

Specs told them about the spiders that clumped together so tightly they resembled moss.

"Another mutation, but we can decide that when we get there," said the Chief. "Any chance Silas found a way inside after you left?"

"I doubt it unless the building burned down around the front door. I've seen stubborn doors before, but the front door of that place should be reassuring to the people who put the gold inside."

There was a groan from the direction of the MRAP, and they all turned expecting to see the infected had reached the road, but it was Bernard getting to his feet and holding one side of his head. The infected were there, too, but they were apparently quieter as they thawed out. The soldiers were watching the infected move toward Bernard, and there was some indecision about whether or not they should help him, but they had considered the score even after the Chief had knocked him out. They took aim at the infected and cleared them away long enough for one soldier to extend a hand down to Bernard and pull him to safety on the MRAP.

"It's nice to be with good people again," said Specs.

23

Assault

Tennessee - 2023

Even though there was a sense of urgency to reach Fort Knox, the silo had to be explored. When Kathy asked the Chief why they couldn't take a few days to explore the GSA warehouse, he said he had a gut feeling that he would only get one chance to catch up with Sparks. From what Specs had told them about the man, he wasn't sick like Silas, but he didn't care enough about other people. If he thought the Chief was getting closer to him, he would get into his plane and put some miles between them.

They took some time to sit with Bernard and Specs in a comfortable room located at the end of one row of supplies. It was apparently a reading room and somewhat of an office. There was a computer terminal that accessed the database of what the GSA had stored there.

They also learned a lot about the ragged army belonging to the man who called himself Brother Silas. Bernard admitted that he had been responsible in some ways for the man's rise to power. His real name was Marvin Corn, but Bernard told him he needed a name with some mystery surrounding it if he wanted to get followers. He had coined the name Brother Silas despite the fact that Marvin had settled on The Preacher. Bernard told him he needed mystery, not a scary movie character. It almost cost him his life, but followers took to it, and Bernard was given the honor of being second in command. That lasted until Sparks came along.

The Chief asked Bernard what did Sparks get out of the relationship. With the plane, he could go anywhere he wanted. Sim pointed out that he could fly north like his old friends from Executive One, and he could fly south for fuel and supplies because that plane could land on short runways. Bernard's answer made the Chief's blood run cold.

Bernard explained to the Chief that Marvin Corn only had one thing going for him. He knew how to make people afraid, and he did it mostly by killing people, but it was Sparks who had told Brother Silas that their biggest enemy in the new world wasn't the infected dead. It was the military. He said he remembered the day when Sparks told Brother Silas that the military would take everything from him. He would be plain old Marvin Corn again, so he should kill any soldiers they ran into. That was why they went to the base in Georgia in the first place. They had to get control of whatever weapons they could find.

"And did you find weapons?" asked the Chief.

"No, the place had been picked clean of weapons," said Bernard. "We found fuel for the plane, but no weapons. Silas was furious. Then Sparks started goin' on about the gold, and Brother Silas got all happy again. I swear Sparks could turn him on and off like hot and cold running water."

Iris had been listening to the discussion rather than to be exploring the supplies in the basement of the silo. Having lived underground in a shelter for years, she knew there would be treasures for everyone on the shelves, but her mind was on her husband and how he was going to be when the time came to face Silas and Sparks. She knew that time was soon.

"We got to see that manipulation firsthand," said Iris, "but what I don't understand is what Sparks really got out of it all. He could've survived on his own."

Bernard searched for the right words, and the closest he could think of was, "Sparks was the man behind the man. He disappeared for a while, and Silas was as mean as ever. He thought Sparks had left for good, but then he showed back up again with some story about losing his plane."

The picture had become more clear after hearing Bernard tell the story. After Sparks deserted them on that little island near Nova Scotia, he could have gone anywhere in the country, but he chose to come back to his life as the number two man working for a madman.

"Sparks was sick, and I never noticed," said the Chief.

Iris rubbed his big shoulders and said, "When did you start thinking it was all on you? We aren't stupid for being trusting people, but we learn from our mistakes."

The Chief straightened his back and seemed to reach a conclusion.

"You're right. It's not all on me, but it also isn't on everyone here."

"What does that mean?" asked Kathy.

Iris answered before he could. "I just triggered his commando button. From what Bernard has told us, this Brother Silas only has one thing going for him, and that's the plane. If we go storming up to Fort Knox with an army, we'll probably roll right over them, but Sparks might get away."

"Exactly," said the Chief. "We don't need everyone to go along because aren't going in there with guns blazing. It sounds like they would be inclined to scatter if we do this the right way, and some of the civilians might be people we want to save."

"Now that's the man I married," said Iris.

The Chief did something only Iris could make him do. He blushed and was at a loss for words for a few moments. He straightened again, which was his way of shaking off the moment, and said it was time to put together a plan.

******

Plan A was to reduce the size of their attack force so they could approach undetected. They would leave as soon as they assembled their gear into the pickup trucks. The MRAP was Plan B because the Chief always had a backup plan. It would give them a slight head start, and Gentry had said the interstate between the silo and Fort Knox was relatively clear compared to some of the highways they had traveled, so they wouldn't need the MRAP to clear a path. The Chief figured their best bet was to circle the base to the west and locate the AC-130 first. Once they secured the Brotherhood's main weapon, they could attack the camp from an unexpected direction.

In the meantime, the MRAP would approach the front gate to draw the attention of the bulk of their armed members. Bernard estimated there were over one hundred people when they arrived at Fort Knox, but they had lost some of their best people just trying to get into the Depository. They had limited weapons and not much ammunition.

"What about supplies from the base?" asked Captain Miller.

"Same as Atlanta," answered Bernard. They all noticed he rubbed his jaw every time he spoke. Getting punched by the Chief would be something he would remember long after his jaw quit hurting. "Picked clean. We found a lot of food that got missed over the years, but plenty of people went to Fort Knox after the gold, so they must've found the weapons first."

The Chief gave everyone their seat assignments in the vehicles. He would be driving the lead truck with Hampton, Tom, and Specs. Specs knew the layout of the base and would be their guide. Truck number two would have Kathy behind the wheel and Colleen, Iris, and Sim as her crew. The MRAP would be driven by Captain Miller, and Cassandra was still going to be in the machine gun turret. Their crew would be the four soldiers who had escorted Gentry to Fort Knox.

The Chief didn't expect anyone to complain about their assignments, but he was surprised when Darren Blanchet asked to go along. When the Chief asked him why he didn't want to just stay behind in the comfort of the silo, he simply said he didn't feel useful. He hadn't been given a real opportunity to show off any skills, but the Chief could understand the need to have a reason to live. Morale was a good enough reason for the Chief, so he assigned him to ride with the soldiers in the MRAP.

Gentry Campbell was placed in charge of the silo because it didn't appear that he would need her science expertise after all. He told her if he needed a nerd, he had Specs, and he also wanted her to track down the power source for the silo. She was the only person he had who knew her way around the computer systems well enough to get it done.

Caleb was quite satisfied with the assignment he got. Gentry told him to work with Gina and Bonnie to verify the inventory of the silo. She said the supplies could provide for more survivors, but they needed to be sure they were accounted for rather than relying on the database. Being a typical fourteen-year-old, he didn't have to be asked twice to work with two teenage girls.

Brett and Grady were put in charge of the security of the silo. Charlie and Sue said they would take over the duty of making sure everyone was kept comfortable and fed. That left Bernard, and he volunteered to stay behind and help at the silo.

When Bernard suggested that he would only be in the way with one of the combat teams, the Chief gave him his best "are you kidding me" look. Everyone within earshot of the conversation just waited because they all knew the Chief well enough to know something really sarcastic was about to come out of his mouth. The pause lasted longer than usual, but it was worth the wait.

"Bernard, Specs told me that you told one of the guys that if he found a rope hanging from a tower, he should use it to lasso a zombie and bring it back with him. Is that true?"

Bernard laughed at the memory of having said that.

"Yeah, it's true, but he asked me a stupid question, and I thought my answer was funny."

The Chief asked Hampton, "Seen any rope around here?"

"There's tons of it. Want me to get you some?" He had a feeling about what the Chief was going to do.

"Take Bernard with you, and give him about fifty feet of rope. I want him to lasso a zombie and bring it back. If he can do that, I'll consider his request to stay here."

Bernard opened his mouth to protest, but Hampton stopped him.

"Don't bother, Bernard. If you had known the Chief longer, you would have realized that was his way of telling you not to ask him stupid questions. You're going along, and the only vehicle with enough room in it is the MRAP. You get to ride with the soldiers."

The Chief announced they would leave within the hour. Kathy brought Cassandra in from the MRAP to stretch her legs and to check to see how her injuries were healing. There didn't appear to be any signs of infection, but she needed the chance to walk around just like everyone else. She told the Chief she would be ready in an hour.

"You could stay here and take it easy if you want to."

"I appreciate it, Chief, but I've become rather attached to that machine gun turret. It's a great view from up there, and sometimes I get to shoot things."

******

One of the true pleasures remaining in the world was the discovery of what had been left behind. When the GSA built the silo, they didn't hide their project the way the shelter builders had. As a matter of fact, it was quite the opposite. There were silos at rural and remote locations throughout the country, and the idea was that land bases could resupply from the silos in the event of a natural disaster. They weren't easily accessible, or they would have been cleaned out years ago, but according to the documentation they found in the computers, they were recovery supplies, and the GSA had worked with FEMA to decide what to stock. The first thing Gentry did was make several copies of the silo locations. If they ever lost power and couldn't use their computers, they would still know where they needed to go next. If they really wanted to help people recover from the infection, they had to show them where the silos were.

FEMA didn't think weapons would be necessary for recovery, but someone must have gotten them to make some concessions. There were several rows of ammunition crates even though there were only a few crates of M4 rifles and handguns. Still, they didn't need more than that. The Chief told everyone not to weigh themselves down with weapons or ammunition because they needed to make them last beyond their mission at Fort Knox.

An hour wasn't enough time to see everything, but the Chief joined Iris and Kathy for a quick tour of the treasures in the silo. It was hard to get excited about the tons of MRE boxes, but they knew there were still survivors out there who were wondering if they would ever taste peanut butter again. Everything that hadn't perished from old age was already found and consumed, and the processing plants weren't sending more. The packages had "best used by" dates stamped on them, but some things would keep forever no matter what the packages said.

"Check this out," said Kathy. "This aisle is like a corner drug store. Toothbrushes, toothpaste, floss, and vitamins. Name it, and it's here. Ah, first aid kits with real suture needles and thread in them, and here's something I hope we never need." She held up a bottle of iodine tablets. "I'll bet FEMA thought a nuclear disaster would be more likely than a zombie apocalypse."

Everyone who was staying behind at the silo seemed to be enjoying their discoveries, and it was almost a festive mood, but Kathy had noticed Charlie and Sue were somewhat reserved. The more she watched, the more convinced she became that the old couple had something eating at them. She asked Iris if she had noticed the same thing, and she said she had. They decided they needed to deal with whatever it was before they left for Fort Knox, so they intercepted them and took them to one of the reading rooms.

"What's with you two?" asked Iris.

Kathy added, "Don't even try to tell us it's nothing. We're too short on time, and it's written all over your faces, and you look like you're carrying the weight of the world on your shoulders."

Charlie and Sue shared a moment of resignation and nodded their understanding.

"We've been thinking," said Charlie. "Your friend, the science lady, said there are silos all over the country, and if you know where to look for them, you could save a lot of people. It occurred to us that there was probably one somewhere near where we left all those people not far from the Marine base, so we asked her. She checked her list and said there was one only about five or ten miles from that school."

"So, what are you saying?" asked Kathy.

Sue answered for them both, "We want to go back. There were so many children, and maybe it's not too late for them."

Iris said, "I've told the Chief we aren't doing enough to help people. I told him that when we were flying over the mountains going to the northeast coast, and he said once we got Henry home to his family in England, we'd find a way to focus on helping as many people as we can, but it seems like things keep pulling us away from it."

"Don't blame yourselves," said Charlie. "You and your little group have helped plenty of people, including us. Now it's time for us to pass some of that along. You know, we need to pay it forward."

Kathy immediately weighed the logistical impossibility that the old couple could travel all the way back to the coast of South Carolina without being killed, and she came to the quick conclusion that they would never make it, especially since the infected dead were thawing. She could tell that they were overcome with guilt about surviving, but she didn't see how to keep them alive long enough for them to reach the people they had left behind.

Iris had a puzzled expression that Kathy had seen before. As the Chief's wife, she took a backseat when it came to who was the leader of their group, but she had proven herself to be more than capable of carrying out that role. As the leader of the people inside the shelter of Ambassadors Island, she had held the population together very well for several years. Submarines didn't stay below water as long as they had stayed out of the sunlight.

"What if I told you that we can get you back to those people faster if you wait for us to come back from Fort Knox?" she said.

Kathy's eyebrows were raised as Charlie and Sue both asked at the same time how she could make that happen.

"I'll make you a deal. Just don't leave while we're gone. I have an idea, but I need to bounce it off my husband's thick head first. Don't worry, though. I think he'll go for it."

They left Charlie and Sue to go find the Chief, and Kathy said, "I can't wait to hear this."

"It's simple," said Iris. "What's the one thing the Chief wants more than anything right now?"

"That's easy...Brother Silas and Sparks both dead in some dramatic fashion."

"Right, but what if we get him to consider adjusting his priorities to include keeping the plane? With that plane, we could fly to every silo on the list, locate survivors in the vicinity and turn it over to them. We could make sure that the supplies fall into the hands of good people."

"Do you think you can do that? I mean, the Chief adores you, but if Sparks is ultimately flying away on that airplane because of some missed opportunity, I don't think the Chief would ever completely get over it."

Iris considered the possibility and said, "The Chief would spontaneously grow wings and fly after Sparks before he would let that happen. If I put the idea in his head before then, maybe he'll figure out a way to have his cake and eat it too."

They found the Chief outside the silo where they were loading gear into the trucks. Since ammunition was in large supply, the soldiers were wasting just a few bullets to eliminate the infected from a distance. They were also glad to get some practice. In a world where they were forced to dispose of the infected from close quarters, they had all become adept at stepping inside the arms of the infected and pushing their knives through skulls, but that had made them a little rusty with their rifles. They were good-naturedly teasing each other when they missed, but it gradually became a matter of pride, and their precision was approaching one hundred percent. The firing was less sporadic as they took careful aim, and they even began dropping the infected that were usually far enough away to ignore.

"Ready to roll?" asked the Chief.

"We're all set," said Iris, "but I wanted to run something by you."

He gave her a quizzical look with one eyebrow raised.

"Why do I have the impression that this is something I'll say no to, but then I'll give in because I can't say no to you?"

"I don't think you'll say no to this," said Iris. "What if I told you there was a way for us not to leave those people at the school behind? I know some of them deserved it, but the kids didn't."

Kathy saw the Chief's shoulders tighten. He hadn't said anything about it, but she knew he was the kind of person who hated leaving those people behind. It was like an open wound, and Iris had put her thumb on it and pressed. It was exactly what had to be said to get the Chief to hear her on the first try.

"I'm listening."

"I think we all know there's one main goal today. We need to kill Silas, or he's going to keep on doing whatever it is that people like him do. They're parasites, and the world is better off without them."

"And Sparks?" said the Chief. "Are you implying that he should get a reprieve?"

"No, not at all," said Iris. "If he dies, he dies. I'm trying to figure out a way to make sure you wind up flying that airplane when this is done, and if Sparks is alive to watch you do it, I imagine it would hurt him as much as dying."

If Kathy hadn't laughed, the Chief wouldn't have caught on.

"Are you manipulating me?"

Iris did her best to look innocent, which only made her look more guilty.

"Why didn't you just say we should kill Silas and Sparks and take the plane?"

"Because I wanted you to actually see it in your mind."

Iris smiled, and both she and Kathy could tell that was exactly what was happening. The Chief already had something enter his mind that would be fitting justice for Sparks, and he was seeing it from the pilot's seat of the plane.

"Now I know why I married you," he said.

"Oh? You mean you didn't already know?"

"Good grief," said Kathy. "You guys need to get a room before we go?"

They were interrupted by the rest of the crews emerging from the silo. Those who were staying came outside to see them off, but they knew the sun would be setting soon and they should go. If there were no major obstacles on the road to Fort Knox, they would arrive before midnight. The Chief gave some final instructions that included a brief stop about twenty miles from their target.

Captain Miller asked what the stop would be for, and the Chief said it was to explain the revisions to their plan that would allow them to capture the airplane back from Sparks.

"Why can't you explain it now?"

"Because it will take me until then to come up with something."

* * *
******

The thaw made for some unpleasant delays on the drive up the interstate. The infected dead were slower than they used to be, but what they lacked in speed, they made up for in numbers. When there were too many of them to drive through, the Mud Island survivors were forced to stop and waste time shooting enough of them to make a hole in the horde. The MRAP caught up with the pickup trucks and Cassandra swept the machine gun back and forth to cut them down faster. It didn't permanently dispose of the infected, but it cut them up enough to keep them from walking back into the road.

"We need to clear a path and get through it fast," yelled the Chief. "The sound of shooting will draw them to this spot from miles away."

Captain Miller suggested that they were losing too much time and wasting too much ammunition. Before the Chief could stop him, he jumped back into the driver's seat and put the MRAP in gear. The huge personnel carrier bounced from side to side as it rolled into the horde, but it did the job. The Chief pulled the pickup truck in as close to the Cougar as he could, and Kathy did the same thing behind him. It was like driving over a few hundred speed bumps, but the MRAP was so much wider than the pickup trucks that there was room to spare on both sides.

The personnel carrier broke through the horde into a clear stretch of highway, and they enjoyed the feeling of making real progress again. The Chief had counted on some delays, so he still felt like they were on schedule. Captain Miller slowed his speed and waved for them to pass him, and the two trucks sped past. After all the noise they had made, the infected would be likely to keep moving toward that same spot long enough for them to be well away from there.

About twenty miles from Fort Knox and almost exactly midnight, the pickup truck in the lead coasted to the side of the road. The Chief climbed out and went back to meet the others as they arrived. Hampton, Tom, and Specs spread out in the beams of the headlights with machetes and knives in their hands. Even though they were twenty miles away, they didn't want to take a chance that gunshots would be heard, and they didn't want to draw more infected dead than they had to. The three men who rode with the Chief had already heard his plan, so they could stand guard while he told the others. Some of it didn't make sense, but the Chief said they would understand when it happened.

"We have incoming infected dead," said Hampton. "Time to go."

They loaded back into their vehicles and drove through a small horde of the infected. At the next exit, they left the interstate and followed a narrow state road until they were almost to the base. The MRAP stopped and Captain Miller checked his watch. They would wait where they were for almost an hour.

"Why did we stop?" asked Bernard.

No one bothered to answer his question. The soldiers would have preferred not to ride with him, but they understood why he couldn't be trusted back at the silo, and he was less likely to try something if he was riding with them.

The two pickup trucks went around the base to the west until they came to the end of the runway. Like most bases, there were open fields and chainlink fences to deter trespassers, and if this had been before the infection, the trucks would have been detected from various guard posts that monitored the perimeter. It was slow progress without headlights, but the moon gave them enough light to make out the silhouette of the AC-130.

The trucks eased up to the fence with their engines barely above idle, and everyone but the drivers jumped out with wire cutters. With six people cutting the fence at the same time, it was only seconds before a large section fell away in front of them. They scurried back to their doors, and the trucks rolled over the fence toward the runway. If anyone was watching from the vicinity of the AC-130, they would have seen so much activity around the trucks and the fence that they would have missed the shadow that moved from the driver seat of the first truck and smoothly climbed into the bed behind the cab.

Now that they were committed to the plan, there was no need for stealth, but they used the darkness to hide the details of their attack. Their headlights stayed off until the exact moment when they would cause the greatest amount of distraction and blindness. The Chief rapped on the window, and Hampton turned the headlights on. The big man rolled over the side rail at a speed that would kill most people, but before the trucks had even passed the rear of the plane, he entered the shadow of the wing on the left side and dove under the protection of the fuselage.

When the Chief had explained the plan to everyone, he said he was willing to bet Sparks was living in the AC-130. He had lost possession of it once, and given the paranoid and psychotic behavior of the company he kept, he didn't want to lose it again. A frontal assault on the base would raise the biggest amount of alarm, but since the airfield was far enough from the front gate, he would have time to prepare the plane for takeoff. The Chief said Sparks would want to escape with the plane quickly, and the only way to do that was to make it his home. That's why they needed to be at the plane when Sparks began his preflight checks. The Chief also guessed Sparks would have the plane in a standby mode that would allow him to use an abbreviated takeoff list, so he had to move fast.

The only cause for concern was the part of the plan that would allow the Chief to get inside the plane because Sparks would undoubtedly keep the doors locked from the inside. There were multiple openings around the gun ports, but they would all be secured from the inside as well. The only other option was to get Sparks to leave the plane for at least a few seconds to correct any problems, and they had to appear to be problems that he had personally overlooked. The Chief could think of two that would both work, and if he had time, he would use both.

Sparks was asleep when something made him stir just enough to think he should wake up. He was too far away from the woods beyond the runways to hear any groans from the infected that were becoming mobile again. He was also insulated by the walls of the plane, so it was doubtful that he would have heard them even if they were walking past outside. This was something else, and it was causing a vibration that was just barely above a hum. It was familiar white noise that might have been ignored before the infected dead arrived in the world, but it was cause for alarm in the new world. It was the faint sound of engines.

He had been reading before drifting off to sleep, and Sparks cursed at himself for being so stupid to have left a white light on while he slept. Waking up to a white light caused his night vision to be wrecked, and it would take time for him to adjust. He switched off the light and made his way to the cockpit in the darkness while focusing on the darkest corners. By the time he reached the pilot's seat, he could see better, but there was just enough residual night blindness for him to be forced to strain to see. The distance was still a blurred-together blackness that lacked detail.

One stretch of fence appeared to be darker than the rest, and he wondered if it might be because there was something new on the other side of the fence. He didn't know that it was two large pickup trucks because they weren't moving, and he was still seeing white spots in front of his eyes. He cursed at himself for a second time because he hadn't thought to leave a pair of night vision goggles in the cockpit. He debated whether or not to go to the back of the plane and get them, and it was probably that delay that caused him to miss the rapid approach of the vehicles when they came through the fence.

The timing was perfect for the Chief's plan, and luck was on his side. Sparks arrived in the cockpit for a second time and stretched the straps of the night vision goggles over his head. The green illumination displayed the trucks for only a split second before Hampton turned on the headlights. The bright lights were virtually an explosion on the retinas of Sparks' eyes, and he recoiled away from the side window over the pilot's seat. He knew he was under attack, but the image that burned into his eyes was a confusing blur of vehicles and light.

Sparks fell in the cockpit twice before he regained enough of his sight to be able to function. His third fall was back into the pilot's seat where he began powering up systems from the generators to start the plane's engines. As he flipped switches, the white spots in front of his eyes made it hard to tell if the indicator lights were white, green, or red.

Under the plane, the Chief didn't know how much luck his plan had already acquired, but he found more luck right where he needed it. The two delays he planned to attempt were far enough apart that Sparks would need to leave the plane, and better yet, leave the door unlocked. The first delay was to connect the umbilical cord from the aircraft ground power unit, the GPU, to the connection on the fuselage just forward of the side passenger door. Planes were connected to the GPU for routine maintenance, and the Chief hoped Sparks would think he forgot to disconnect it. The umbilical was a heavy-duty extension cord that could be retracted to the GPU over a hundred feet away, and the Chief saw that Sparks had been too lazy to retract it. The plug end of the cord was on the ground right below the inlet port. The Chief lifted the heavy cord and easily connected it.

Inside the plane, Sparks was still trying to tell the colors on the indicators apart, and he didn't see the red light come on that indicated he was connected to external power. That gave the Chief the time to create his second delay. The chocks for the wheels had been removed because they were considered unnecessary at an airbase with no activity other than his one plane. They were only a short distance behind the plane and within easy reach for the Chief without being seen. He dragged one set to the front landing gear and shoved it under the wheel, and then laid the chocks for the rear wheels by the power cord, then he ran back to the rear wheels on the right side and waited.

Sparks applied a slight amount of power to the throttles and lifted the brakes, but the plane didn't move. His vision was improving, so he scanned the rows of lights and saw the GPU indicator was red, but he knew that wouldn't have caused the plane to stay where it was. The front landing gear of the AC-130 has its own power steering, so he tried to turn the wheel. It crossed his mind that he was either too tired or too lazy because he had forgotten to pull the GPU power cord from the side of the plane, and he had forgotten to remove the chocks from the wheels.

The moon gave off very little light, but Sparks didn't want to wear the night vision goggles again. He cautiously peered outside before pulling the door completely open, and he saw the rear wheel chocks lying next to the power cable of the GPU. He assumed he had only left the chocks on the front landing gear, so he only felt half as stupid. He dropped to the asphalt and disconnected the GPU power cable and then ran up under the nose of the plane and grabbed the rope attached to the chocks under the front wheel. He never saw the quiet shadow come out from behind the rear wheels.

Back inside the AC-130, all of the lights indicated the plane was ready for takeoff, and Sparks let it coast forward.

24

A Dish Served Cold

Fort Knox - 2023

The arrival of the armored vehicle at the front gate was well-timed with the sudden appearance of the two pickup trucks already inside the base, and the guards at the front gate wanted no part of the conflict. As soon as they saw Cassandra rotate the machine gun in their direction, they threw what weapons they had out into the road. Captain Miller and his men appeared from behind the vehicle and gathered the guns together.

The only casualty was Captain White. He had taken his new role as an officer appointed by the General too seriously, and he had expected his troops to at least give some resistance to the invaders. He took up a position behind a derelict vehicle and fired a few shots in the direction of the MRAP. Cassandra only meant to provide suppressing fire, but Captain White's lack of military training was apparent when he thought he could move from behind his cover to a different spot. He didn't move very far before he died.

The pickup trucks roared up behind the tents, and they were surprised that no one tried to flee in their direction. The camp was surrounded as they flooded the area with their headlights. The stillness that replaced the brief sounds of gunshots was so complete that the combat teams wondered if there were even people in the tents.

Kathy yelled for everyone to come outside, and if they had any weapons, they should hold them in the air by their barrels. She warned that anyone holding a gun in the wrong direction would be considered a threat. They waited and watched the flaps at the entrances of the tents and saw no movement at first. A child appeared from one, and she was carrying a white flag. Kathy motioned for her to walk toward her, and the little girl took a few hesitant steps forward. Behind her, a woman followed with her empty hands held out to her sides, and Kathy said in a low voice for her to follow the girl. Once they were to her, Colleen and Iris guided them out of the light to the back of the truck.

Behind them in the distance, they heard the roar of the engines on the AC-130 as it increased power. Moments later, they saw the plane's lights as it lifted into the air.

"I hope the Chief's plan worked," said Kathy.

"As long as he didn't have to use Plan B, I'm not worried," said Iris.

"I never heard him say what Plan B was."

Iris shook her head at Kathy, "I wish he hadn't told me. The idea of him hanging onto a rear wheel during takeoff is a visual I would prefer not to have."

Kathy decided it was something beyond her control so she simply hoped the Chief's plan to board the plane before takeoff had worked, and she returned to her efforts to subdue resistance at the camp.

Several minutes went by with no change until Iris told Kathy the woman had said there were mostly women and children in the tents, and they were afraid to come out. She said there had been a horde of the infected inside the camp the day before, and they had lost a lot of people. When Kathy asked where all the men had gone, she was surprised by the answer. Other than the men who had remained loyal to Captain White and stayed at guard posts, the rest of the men had decided to go into the Depository after the gold.

"Some people never learn," said Kathy.

With the help of the little girl who bravely came out of the first tent with a white flag, they were able to gradually coax the rest of them into the open. Under the headlights of the MRAP and the two pickup trucks, they found that the population of the camp had dwindled from over a hundred when they had arrived at Fort Knox down to forty-eight people. Twelve men had gone to the Depository figuring they could go inside the same way Brother Silas had entered the building instead of through the door like the last three had. According to the people who had wisely told them not to do it, they had been gone for at least four hours.

The Chief's plan for the camp had been vague because there was no way to tell what sort of resistance they would encounter. The expectation was that there would be a firefight, and there would be a few survivors. Since the firefight was so brief and so many men were missing, they set about the task of sorting through the people still in the camp. The first order of business was to triage everyone for injuries, especially bite wounds, so they set up the largest tent as a processing center. The survivors were escorted inside a few at a time while the others were kept under guard. After they were given medical inspections, they were interviewed by Captain Miller to see if there was any useful information that was being withheld.

It was during the interviews that Captain Miller sent a message to one of the soldiers to locate Darren Blanchet and bring him in to assist. He wasn't militarily trained and had felt like he was useless on the mission to Fort Knox, so he was glad when he got the message from Captain Miller. When he arrived at the tent, the soldier led him to a partitioned area where Captain Miller waited with four of the survivors.

Confusion immediately overcame him, not because he didn't recognize them at all, but because he knew them instantly. They had grown so much. The last time he had seen his children was when he had helped them onto the boat loaded with strangers, and their tear-streaked faces were the clearest memory he had of them in the years that followed. Whenever he tried to remember them, that was what he saw. Now he had a new memory because they recognized their father too. All three rushed toward him, and his legs didn't support him. They went down in a heap on the floor of the tent.

Darren didn't know the woman who stayed back from them... waiting, unsure of what to do. In the minutes that followed the excitement, Captain Miller introduced her as Angie Garner. She had been on the boat with the others, and she had a grip on his arm trying to pull him on board with his children when a man had hit him over the head. She said the man told everyone the boat was too full. She said people tried to help him, but he was soon out of reach. Angie said it was a long story, but they had stayed alive because they joined the group led by the Brotherhood.

When the interviews were all finished, there were no bite victims found among the remaining survivors. All of the weapons had been gathered, but the general opinion of the Mud Island family was that there was no threat in the camp. Everyone told the same story about the rebellion against Brother Silas and about how they had forced him to go inside the Depository. All that remained for them to do was decide what, if anything, needed to be done about Brother Silas, and to wait to find out what happened to the Chief.

******

Marvin Corn detested cockroaches, but in a moment of psychotic humor, he laughed out loud at the thought that he was harder to kill than a cockroach. He spent hours surveying the supplies he found in his dark sanctuary, and although he saw many indications that there were several floors below him, he decided that his best means of survival was not to press his good luck. He was well-fed, wearing fresh clothes, carrying a backpack full of supplies, and sporting an older model semiautomatic pistol on each hip. He went in the direction of the sign that advertised the emergency exit and laughed again about leaving without anyone knowing it.

The emergency exit turned out to be a tunnel, and Marvin cranked the handle on the lantern until it turned green again. He also checked his spare lantern to make sure it worked. Out of an abundance of caution, he wedged an empty food package in the door to keep it from locking behind him, and he took the first few steps of what would be a long walk.

At several turns in the tunnel, he considered going back, but by his estimate, he had been walking for more than an hour. The tunnel showed no signs of ever being used, and he detected no smells to indicate there was groundwater present. There was no smell of mildew and no dusty odor of anything dying and decaying in the tunnel, so he kept going.

He made a final turn, and the tunnel came to an abrupt end under a highway overpass. It was nighttime outside, so he turned off his lantern. He didn't want to make it so far and then draw the attention of something whether it was dead or alive…or in between.

The exit to the tunnel was hidden from clear view by being cut into the side of one of the large concrete pillars that supported the structure. The opening faced away from the road, and as soon as he stepped through it, he found himself on the slope that went down to the road. He slipped on the ice where it hadn't melted yet and fell on his side, sliding out of control to the bottom. His gear made plenty of noise, and he lay still for several minutes after he reached the bottom.

In the darkness, Marvin listened for anything that meant he had given himself away. A rustling sound nearby told him he had, and the sound was getting closer. Tentative steps, stirring of leaves, and at last, the sound of breathing reached his ears. He didn't know if he was being stalked by a wild animal or if an infected dead was trying to locate him. He eased one of the semiautomatic pistols from his right hip and waited.

"Are you okay?" asked a gravelly voice from somewhere nearby.

Marvin didn't hesitate. He pointed the gun in the direction of the voice and pulled the trigger twice. The sound felt like it tore his eardrums apart, but he aimed his lantern with his other hand and switched it on. An old man appeared in the beam, and he was clutching his hands to his chest. His lips moved, and Marvin moved closer to him.

He could barely hear it, but in the light, he could tell the man asked, "Why?"

"You shouldn't sneak up on people like that."

Marvin switched the beam around to see if the gunshots had drawn any attention. He saw that they hadn't and he also saw where he needed to go. The overpass was the beginning of a bridge over either a river or a large lake, and there were boats tied up at the docks on the other side of the road. Marvin decided one of the safest places to be was on a boat, and he left the old man dying where he was.

After years of sitting through bad weather at the docks, none of the engines would start. Marvin Corn had never learned how to sail, but he didn't figure it would be too hard. There were six boats at the docks, but only one of them was a sailboat. He considered the pontoon boat, but with no way to control it, he would be at the mercy of the current.

He climbed aboard and quietly descended into the cabins below. It smelled of decay, and roaches ran from the beam of his lantern, but it wasn't occupied.

"This will have to do," he said, and he untied it from the dock.

Drifting away from the shoreline, Marvin took the time to check the sails. He found there were some tears where the sun had worn through them, but they were still attached in the right places. The water was calm, and he had nothing to threaten him except maybe the insects in the cabins, so he decided to see if he could drop the anchor and stay in one place. He felt the anchor line become tight as it gripped the bottom, and the boat came to a comfortable stop.

Marvin stood on the stern of the sailboat and studied the stars. He spread his arms wide toward the sky as if he was daring God, and all he could say was, "Kill me if you can."

******

The hum of the engines was familiar to the Chief from his days when they flew in the AC-130 up to Nova Scotia. He could feel the steady vibrations and knew the plane had leveled off at a cruising altitude and speed. Sparks would be leaning back in the pilot's seat about now and feeling very satisfied with himself.

"What's our heading?" said the Chief in a voice very much like a commanding officer asking an officer of the deck. It wasn't as much a question as it was an order demanding an update.

Sparks recognized it for what it was and said, "270 degrees west," without turning around. He could see the Chief's large frame reflected on the glass in front of him, and he knew he wouldn't live sixty seconds longer if he tried anything.

"Smart man," said the Chief. "You know I can break your neck and drag you out of that seat without changing the course by one degree or the altitude by one foot. Nod your head."

Sparks nodded his understanding.

"Change course to zero degrees north. Maintain speed and altitude. When I tell you where to land, you'll land. If you don't, we'll both die. If you do, we'll both live. It's as simple as that. It's a short runway, and it hasn't been maintained in seven years, so it will definitely be a rough landing."

Sparks didn't know what the Chief had in mind, but he adjusted his course to zero degrees north. He could tell by the reflection that the Chief had gotten comfortable behind him, and he had to consider the possibility that it would be better to die now than to be on the ground with him. Being in the plane with the Chief was the same thing as being in a car with someone in your backseat with a gun except it was higher and faster. He could take him out either way, but it would also mean he would die. Sparks was painfully aware that the Chief knew it too.

The silence got to Sparks after thirty minutes, and he finally had to ask where they were going. He had seen light reflecting from the water below them, so he knew they were somewhere near Chicago. The

Chief didn't answer at first, and he was just about to ask again when the Chief answered with a question of his own.

"Why did you do it?"

"Do what?"

"Give me an answer like that again, and it will be the last thing you say."

Sparks saw by the reflection that the Chief was standing, and it crossed his mind that he had never seen the Chief angry except when he heard him talk about the soldiers being ambushed near Atlanta, and he remembered thinking he never wanted the Chief to find out he was associated with that group of people responsible for the ambush. For some reason, he had never felt like he was part of that group even though he had done everything Silas had asked him to do, including an attack on the village above the Guntersville shelter called Green Cavern. In Silas, the psychosis had run deep, but denial was Sparks' way of dealing with the world. To him, it had been Silas who had attacked the soldiers, and it was Silas who had attacked Green Cavern.

"I felt like you were a bigger threat than Silas."

The Chief was surprised by the answer. He had expected, "I don't know," or "I was just following orders." He even expected that Sparks was misguided enough to want the gold at Fort Knox, but he didn't expect what he heard.

"Why was I a threat to you? What did I do that made you feel like you couldn't trust me?"

Sparks actually laughed hard enough that he had trouble catching his breath, but the Chief waited. He didn't think he had said anything remotely funny.

"I'm waiting for you to tell me why you're laughing," said the Chief. The anger was close to a boiling point, and Sparks heard it in his voice.

"You took my plane like you thought it was yours to take. Then when I wanted it back, you drafted me into your little survivor army and made me fly you to Nova Scotia. Did it ever occur to you that you're the same as Brother Silas? You just take what you need because you think you need it more."

The Chief had a moment of self-doubt, and he wondered if he really was no different. He questioned whether or not he had given Sparks a choice. It lasted less than a minute.

"Sparks, let me explain it to you in a way that you'll understand. It wasn't your plane to start with, so I don't imagine you asked anybody if you could have it. You're so deep into denial you almost dragged me down that dark hole with you. Second, you were already part of the Brotherhood when we met. If I had known it then, you would have died before you saw this plane again. Third, you know I'm not like Silas because I didn't go after the gold at Fort Knox, and last but not least, you're right about one thing. When it comes to people like you, I'm not just a bigger threat than Silas. I'm the most dangerous thing you've ever met."

The Chief's voice was so cold when the last words came out that Sparks expected to feel his neck snap at any second, and he was sorry that he pushed him to the edge. The Chief moved closer as he spoke, and when he finished, Sparks could feel his breath on his neck. It gave him goosebumps, and he knew that the next thing he said might be the last thing.

"I'm sorry," was all that came out.

The Chief leaned in closer and simply gave him course, speed, and landing instructions. He told him to lower the landing gear and illuminate everything he could forward because there wouldn't be any runway lights. Sparks did everything he was told, and as the plane banked to the left and the nose lowered, he saw the plane was over water and approaching a small but heavily wooded island. The landing strip was literally diagonal across the entire island from the southeastern corner to the northwestern edge. He could also see they would need every inch of that runway to stop in time.

The wheels touched down only a few feet from the water, and the landing was every bit as bumpy as the Chief had said it would be. Sparks applied the brakes as hard as he could and practically used willpower to stop the plane. They could see the water ahead of them when the plane came to a stop, and the Chief told him to rotate to face the other way. It was like turning a bus around inside a garage, but he finally had the plane facing the other end of the landing strip. In the distance, they could see a single-engine Piper Cub sitting on the right side of the runway. It had been partially backed into the trees, or they would have hit it with a wingtip when they landed.

"Get out."

"What?"

"You heard me, and I didn't mean to just get out of the seat. Get out of the plane."

"Why'd you bring me all the way up here just to kill me?"

"Who said I'm going to kill you?"

Sparks got out of the seat, and it was beginning to dawn on him what the Chief was going to do.

"Are you just going to leave me here? I don't even know where I am," he whined.

The Chief grabbed Sparks by the back of his neck, and this time he really did think it would break because he held him so tightly. He felt like he was nothing more than a hand puppet as the Chief half-carried, half-walked him to the door. With one hand the Chief opened the door, and with the other hand at the back of Sparks' neck, he launched him from the plane.

Sparks landed flat on his stomach in sharp branches that scraped and cut his body through his clothing. There was nothing in front of him except the deep forest that had flourished on the island. He scrambled around to face the AC-130, his only lifeline.

From where he stood, there was nothing but blackness behind him because the woods were so dense. On the other side of the plane, he knew it was exactly the same. The only light came from the plane as a cloud covered the moon, and the temperature was much lower than it had been in Kentucky. There was still snow on the trees and the runway, and he could see his breath.

The Chief loomed above him in the door of the AC-130. He folded a chart and then drew a circle on it. He threw it at Sparks like a broken frisbee.

"There, now you know where you are. You're on the northern tip of Lake Michigan, and you're on Trout Island. Now you're about to feel what it felt like to us when you left us stranded on that island off the coast of Nova Scotia. Good thing for us we had friends we could call. Oh, and by the way, the infected dead can walk on the bottom of lakes from one island to the next. If you look closely at that map, you'll see there was a populated island east of here. You might say it's within walking distance from here, so you can't say I left you here alone."

The door closed, and what little bit of light there was around Sparks disappeared with it. He was desperate, but he knew he couldn't stop the Chief from leaving him behind. Something moved in the trees behind him, and Sparks recoiled away from the darkness. The AC-130 began to power up for takeoff, and Sparks knew his only chance would be to make it to the Piper Cub about a hundred yards away. He turned and ran as hard and fast as he could, but once the AC-130 roared by him, the light disappeared in front of his feet, and he stumbled and fell face-first into the scrub bushes on the side of the runway.

Behind Sparks, there was movement on both sides of the runway, and the familiar groan made him get up and run again. His eyes fixed on the white fuselage and wings of the Piper Cub as the lights from the AC-130 lit it brighter, but in a flash, all of his hope was gone, and he could only drop to his knees and watch.

The Chief was still gaining forward speed and had not begun to ascend when he passed the small, single-engine airplane, and from only a few feet away, he opened fire with one of the powerful side guns. The small plane disintegrated into thousands of tiny splinters as it exploded. The orange and black fireball was the same thing as ringing a dinner bell on the tiny island.

The Chief lifted off from the end of the runaway and banked hard to the right to head for Kentucky. It was time to find Silas.

******

Brother Silas lifted his anchor to the surface after getting some sleep and enjoying a very relaxing breakfast from the supplies he had packed. He would have been more content if he had been able to make a cup of coffee, but he was sure there would be time for that in the coming days.

In the light of day, he discovered that the sailboat was on a large lake, and that made it a bit easier for him to manage at first. A light breeze caught the remnants of his sails and pulled him forward, but it turned out to be much harder than it looked. At first, he picked up speed and make some progress, but he didn't know how to tack with the wind and was frustrated to find he was just going in a big circle. If he had to guess, he was still somewhere in the vicinity of the place where he had anchored for the night.

On his second attempt, the sails caught more wind than he expected, and he thought he was going to capsize. As soon as he recovered, Silas brought the mainsails back down onto the boat and then immediately lowered the anchor back into the water. His heart was pounding in his chest, and he had been frightened more than he would have admitted, but at least he was no worse off than he was when he started out.

He wondered if he could swim to shore, but he was not much better at swimming than he was at sailing. Besides, he had seen the infected dead in lakes often enough to know that they didn't drown. All he had to do was think about bumping into one of them in the water, and he decided there had to be another way.

He was searching for something to use as an oar when a familiar sound caught his attention, and he turned in the direction of the sun. He put one hand to his forehead and shaded his eyes until he was able to spot the sliver of light he expected to see. The sound grew in volume, and he knew it was going to pass directly over the lake.

"Sparks, I know we've had our differences, but maybe we could start over again."

He figured the worst that could happen was that Sparks would say no. He grabbed the backpack full of supplies and dumped the contents into a pile on the deck. He rummaged through the odd assortment of things he had collected, not knowing what would eventually be important, and what would be extra weight. There was one bulky device that he had found interesting because it resembled the lantern with the hand crank on it. He suspected it was a radio because it had a button on the side of it that could be depressed just like a microphone. There was also a dial that had numbers on it, and the label above it said CHANNELS. Now was as good of a time as any to find out if it worked.

Silas turned the hand crank furiously then held the bulky device close to his face. With one hand he pressed the microphone button, and with the other hand, he changed channels. In between changes he said, "Sparks, can you hear me."

The plane rapidly closed the gap between them with no response on the radio, and realizing Sparks might not even see him, Silas grabbed another oddity he had been unable to resist from the pile on the deck. He didn't know if he would ever need a mirror, but he had always liked seeing his own face reflected in them. He had been told once that he was a narcissist, but he figured his looks made up for his lack of height.

******

The Chief felt a measure of peace for the first time in months. The anger he had felt when he learned that the soldiers had been ambushed was a fire that burned inside him because no matter what Sparks said about him, he wasn't the same as them. Yes, he took things that were needed, but there wasn't a single time he could think of when he had taken something from someone else who needed it. He always took for the greater good, and he had become driven to save as many people as possible.

When the Chief thought back on the years that had passed since the beginning of the infection, he saw the faces of people they had saved, but he also saw the faces of evil that had crossed his path. His moments of peace came and went as he remembered the madman who had buried Iris in New Orleans. He remembered the people who had subverted the military in Huntsville and the rogue CIA people aboard the Yorktown. It seemed that there was no end to the evil that the living could do. The infected dead were driven by some unknown impulse to spread their disease, but he could blame them less than the living people who were driven by individual motives, and it seemed that so often those motives were personal greed.

Passing over the landscape below, the Chief was watching daylight approach from the east, and he thought about how easily the skipper of the Ambush had passed judgment and dispensed justice on the Wari, and he knew in his heart that he would have done the same thing. He told himself that he wasn't playing God, nor was he trying to do anything because it was the religious thing to do. He simply wanted to bring back as much good into the world as he could, and he felt like he had enough to do just fighting the infected dead. He shouldn't have to fight against living people too.

The AC-130 was in his possession now, and the Chief swore an oath to himself that it would be used to protect people. With it as his main transportation, he could help people reach the other silos spread throughout the country, and he could protect them while they harvested the supplies hidden within. He found his mood to be less dark just as the sky was becoming brighter, and he realized he was experiencing real hope.

The Chief brought the plane in from the east and banked hard to the right across a large lake. Light reflected from the surface of the water like a mirror, but one bright flash of light caught his eyes. Someone had just used a real mirror or something reflective to signal him. It was easy to see that it came from a sailboat that had its mainsails furled. He slowed his forward speed and put the plane into a gradually descending spiral over the lake. The plane tilted to the left as he leaned toward his window for a better view.

A choppy voice came over the radio, and the Chief realized the person in the sailboat must be changing channels on a handheld radio. The Chief keyed his own microphone and said, "Channel four." He said it repeatedly as he circled and figured that eventually, the person would hear his broadcast on channel four as he went by it, and he would stop on that channel. He could tell when it worked because the man started yelling excitedly.

"Sparks...Sparks, thank you for coming back for me. I knew I could count on you. You've always been my number one."

The Chief knew immediately that there was only one person who would think it was Sparks flying the plane, and only one person would call Sparks his number one. He keyed his microphone and said, "Brother Silas, is that you?"

"Yes, Sparks, it's me. I forgive you for what happened back at the Gold Depository. You did what you had to do to convince them you turned on me. I knew you didn't really. Find a place to land and then come help me get this boat to shore."

The Chief didn't answer the message immediately. Brother Silas undoubtedly thought he had understood the transmission because he was yelling, "Thank you," over and over. In reality, the Chief was establishing the optimal distance and altitude for a pylon pass.

"Sparks? Did you hear my last message?"

"I heard you, but I'm not Sparks. I think it's kind of ironic that the last time I saw Sparks, he was stuck in the middle of a big lake too. I couldn't have planned this better. It's almost poetic. I think he would've preferred a sailboat over an island, but I didn't give him a choice."

The voice over the radio that Silas held in his hands didn't sound familiar, but his confusion didn't stop him from understanding that Sparks wasn't flying the plane.

"Who is this?" demanded Silas. Even now he was still the same Marvin Corn he had always been.

"Sparks never told you about me?" asked the Chief.

"Think really hard Brother Silas. If I'm correct, he's been warning you about me for a long time. That's why he had you attack the village over one of my shelters. It took me a long time to get here, but I've been coming for you. Let me introduce myself. I'm called the Chief by my friends, but you aren't a friend. The soldiers you ambushed in Atlanta were my friends. For the next minute, you can just call me the guy who killed you."

For the first time in Marvin Corn's life, he felt like the person at the big end of the binoculars. All the power was circling above him, and he finally understood what it felt like to lose hope. A cockroach walked

312

across his foot as he sat down heavily in the stern of the sailboat and watched the plane appear to become almost still in the sky before little flashes of light erupted from its side.

As the Chief locked his weapons on the small target, he said, "Brother Silas? Can you hear me? There's a special place in Hell for you, and now I'm sending you there."

The high-caliber weapons on the AC-130 shredded the boat and Brother Silas in the first two-second burst, but the Chief continued to circle and fire at the spot until he had done a complete turn. The destruction was so thorough that most of the debris was already below the surface before the Chief stopped firing.

If he could have seen the debris up close, the Chief would have been satisfied to see a shoe floating on the surface with a cockroach clinging to it.

25

Epilogue

Kentucky - 2023

At dawn, following the night of the assault on Fort Knox, Captain Miller organized a rescue mission to at least try to bring back the men who had gone over the wall into the Depository. His men had the advantage of training in their favor, and they knew enough not to go further than they did. They were also equipped with lights and smartphones to use as cameras. They scaled the wall to the same beam used to drop Brother Silas inside and lowered two men into the darkness. Only three minutes later they were calling on the radio to get them out in a hurry.

The soldiers were extracted in time, but they were able to bring back evidence to show that the men hadn't made it too far and that the soldiers were dangerously close to meeting the same fate. It was impossible to tell if any of them were the remains of Brother Silas, but none of them were wearing hazmat suits.

The pictures showed a large mound of bodies covered in a thick layer of green moss. Limbs protruded from the moss at odd angles, and the corridor appeared to have carpeted walls and ceilings. The fire that had consumed the building had destroyed the malicious little spiders that had been near the surface, but apparently, it had not reached them in the lower depths.

Captain Miller considered the construction of a sign that would warn people not to enter the former Gold Depository, but Kathy suggested nothing would stop the foolish from scaling that wall, and treasure hunters might even believe the sign was fake. In the end, they decided to burn it again to at least slow the progress of the spiders. They used the MRAP to tow a fuel truck on flat tires from the airfield to the front door of the Depository. Once the fuel was pumped over the wall, it was ignited from a safe distance.

The orange fireball was still rising into the sky when the AC-130 came into view from the east, and as it passed overhead, the Chief's voice crackled over the radio.

"Finishing the job?"

"That depends on whether or not you have anything left to do," answered Kathy.

"Naw, I'm good," said the Chief. "As a matter of fact, I haven't felt this good in a long time."

Kathy knew it wasn't the right time to ask what had happened with Sparks, but she also knew it was a safe bet that Sparks was dead. The evidence wasn't just because the Chief was flying the plane. It wasn't even so much what he said as how he said it. She could tell by the sound of his voice that he was grinning.

"Hey, Chief...we're sorry, but we didn't get Silas. Before Sparks left, he had Silas dropped through a hole in the top of the Depository wearing a hazmat suit. We sent people in, and they got pictures of remains, but they could be anybody."

All the Chief said was, "Huh, must've been a good hazmat suit."

Kathy stared at her radio and wondered if the Chief had been drinking.

******

Iris couldn't have been happier. She had seen some hard times in the years since the beginning of the infection, but there had been the occasional triumphs. The assault on Fort Knox had been so one-sided that she and her comrades were almost embarrassed by their own actions. They were glad they threw on the brakes as early as they did, and they felt good about liberating the people who just needed to be out from under the thumbs of the Brotherhood. It would be even more gratifying once they were safely relocated to a shelter. She remembered how she had felt when she had led her own group of survivors to Ambassadors Island. It was so liberating to know she had gotten those people to safety, and now she was doing it again.

It seemed like everything that was left to be done, needed to be done immediately, and they were always racing against time. The next thing on her list was the promise she had made to Charlie and Sue, and it fell on her to ask her husband to delay the rest he needed as much as anyone. She knew him well enough to know that he never really rested. That was why she was waiting for him at the base airstrip when the plane landed.

The AC-130 coasted into the spot where it had been parked when the Chief had slipped aboard under the cover of darkness. It seemed like days ago instead of hours, probably because the last day had been fueled by adrenaline. When she considered how far they had traveled, and what they had done in the last twenty-four hours, Iris hoped there was just a little more adrenaline left in her husband's body. He could guess there was something else she wanted him to do, but it wasn't a surprise to him. Aside from the satisfaction he felt for ridding the world of Sparks and Silas in the same day, he had never been able to get the children near the Marine base out of his mind.

"Hey you," said the Chief when he popped the door open. His smile was so broad that she thought he looked ten years younger.

"Hey yourself...got any fuel left?"

"In me or the plane?"

Iris could see that he was one step ahead of her. He had that playful expression he liked to use on her when he would string her along and act like he didn't think of something himself.

"You can drop the act," she said. "When can we leave?"

"As soon as we add fuel to the plane. Seeing you is all the fuel I need to keep me going. I contacted Gentry to find out where the interstate is clear enough to land. We can pick up Charlie and Sue and be there in about an hour after that."

"You sure know how to sweet talk a woman. I brought my gear."

Iris settled into the co-pilot's seat, and it didn't take long for the Chief to take care of business before joining her. They shared a satisfied smile as he increased power, and the plane rolled forward.

"What's the plan for everyone else?" he asked.

"They have a lot of vehicles that still run well, and there doesn't seem to be a shortage of food. Of course, Silas was keeping the good stuff for himself. Kathy and Captain Miller are organizing a caravan now. They'll be on the road in a couple of hours, and if they don't have any major issues, they should reach Guntersville sometime tonight.

Did you want someone to check out the shelter under the Depository before they go?"

The Chief shook his head almost sadly.

"No, I don't think we can get to the supplies in that shelter safely. It's a shame to have that much inventory sitting in there going to waste, but we don't know what we're up against. Silas survived in there somehow, and he even managed to find one of the emergency exits, but I can't sacrifice lives based on dumb luck when we don't need the supplies yet."

Iris raised an eyebrow.

"We don't need the supplies yet? Is there something you haven't told me?"

"Well, I have more news for you from Gentry," said the Chief. "We assumed when we found out about the resupply redoubts that they would all be silos."

"They're not?"

"No, several of them are silos, but most of them aren't, and some of them are really much bigger than the silos. They would be too conspicuous in some parts of the country. They wanted the supplies to be easy to access, but not sitting out in the open. The redoubt in Beaufort was practically under our noses. There's a small executive airport a little over five miles from the school, and the entrance to that redoubt is in one of the hangars."

"A small executive airport? Is the runway long enough?"

The first thing to cross the Chief's mind was landing on Trout Island at night, and he had to smile.

"It's got enough room without a full load on the plane, so we should be okay. We'll pick up a few people at the Jasper silo, and the best news is that they used the back exit to bring out some new Humvees. We have plenty of room to take them along. If all of the people at the school survived, we should be able to pick up everyone and carry them back to the plane in a couple of hours. Then we'll get them to the Huntsville shelter where we can give them the best medical care. Gentry said they've really gotten the hospital up to nearly modern standards."

Iris thought again that she couldn't be happier. The people who used to be part of the Brotherhood were going to help rebuild the village over Green Cavern where they would live in safety. The people at the school near Beaufort wouldn't be left to die, and the children would have a chance to grow up without starving or eating contaminated food. She knew she would be relieved once they were sure it wasn't too late for them.

"Where would you like to go after we get everyone home?" asked Iris.

The Chief thought about it for a minute and said, "I never gave you a decent honeymoon. Why don't we take some time for ourselves?"

Now it was her turn to laugh. "Where would we go? I mean, reservations wouldn't be an issue, but there's this little problem with zombies."

"I'll let that one slide this time," he answered, "but only because we're talking about a honeymoon here. How about Hawaii?"

Iris studied her husband's profile for signs that he was either serious or kidding around, and she could tell by the half-grin that it was both.

"Under one condition," she said.

"Anything."

"We have to take along a few chaperones. I might know a few people with some time on their hands and who like to meet new people."

"Sounds like a plan," said the Chief.

ABOUT THE AUTHOR

Bob Howard (1951-) was born in New Jersey to an Army Sergeant from Ohio and a mother from Romania. He was moved from one Army base to the next, and before he began high school in Huntsville, Alabama he had lived most of his life overseas in Germany and Okinawa with brief stays in Maryland and North Carolina. He credits his imagination to his exposure to different cultures and environments at an early age. He began reading science fiction and fell in love with post apocalyptic novels. He still has an original copy of the first one he read in 1966, The

Furies by Keith Edwards. He joined the Navy after high school and continued to move from one base to another, including a submarine base at Holy Loch, Scotland. He eventually stayed in one place when he got stationed in Charleston, South Carolina. He graduated with a BS in Psychology from the College of Charleston. He married his wife in 1984 and together they raised a son and a daughter.

It takes a lot of work to get a book of fiction written and then edited. We want the book to flow, but we also want it to be grammatically correct whenever possible. If you see a spot where you think a comma was needed, it may be that I left it out because it interrupted the flow. The same isn't true for typos. If you see one of those nasty little things and would like to let me know, I would be pleased to correct it. I've learned that I've got some really bad habits when it comes to pet phrases, and I make mistakes. I hear from a gentleman in Japan regularly because he has such a keen eye for errors. I'm lucky to have him as an after-editor. That doesn't mean you won't see something that everyone else missed. Please make my books better by telling me.

I would love to hear from you, and I value your opinions and comments. The best way to help an author become better at his craft is to write a review, so please feel free to write one. If you would like to know more about me or get in touch with me, please visit my website at *realbobhoward.com*. You can also sign up for my newsletter and be notified when the next book is released.

With gratitude,

Bob Howard

www.ingramcontent.com/pod-product-compliance
Lightning Source LLC
Chambersburg PA
CBHW032243010726
47494CB00002B/611